When Eve was Naked

When Eve was Naked

A Journey through Life

JOSEF SKVORECKY

KEY PORTER BOOKS

Canadian Cataloguing in Publication Data

Skvorecky, Josef, 1924–
    When Eve was naked : a journey through life

Translated from Czech.
ISBN 1-55263-169-9

1. Skvorecky, Josef, 1924–   . Authors, Canadian (Czech)—20th century—Biography.*
I. Title.

PS8573.K86Z53 2000   C891.8'63   C00-931692-2
PR9199.3.S545Z478 2000

The Canada Council   Le Conseil des Arts
FOR THE ARTS   DU CANADA
SINCE 1957   DEPUIS 1957

The publisher gratefully acknowledges the support of the Canada Council for the Arts and
the Ontario Arts Council for its publishing program.

We acknowledge the financial support of the Government of Canada through the Book
Publishing Industry Development Program (BPIDP) for our publishing activities.

Key Porter Books Limited
70 The Esplanade
Toronto, Ontario
Canada M5E 1R2

www.keyporter.com

Design: Peter Maher
Electronic formatting: Heidy Lawrance Associates

Printed and bound in Canada

00 01 02 03 04   6 5 4 3 2 1

To my wife Zdena
who has shared forty-two years of my life
and many of the stories with me

Acknowledgments

M y thanks go to all who helped me with this book. To Julie Hansen and Rachel Harrell, who translated some of these stories out of sheer love for Czech language and literature; to my old and trusted friends and translators Peter Kussi, Káča Poláčková-Henley, Michal Schonberg, Paul Wilson, and the late George Theiner, who all personally experienced those evil empires of our century; to the editors at Key Porter Books; and to Honzlová.

TABLE

OF

CONTENTS

V. Another Interlude

VI. All's Well That Ends Well

TRANSLATORS

GT—George Theiner

JH—Julie Hansen

KPH—Káča Poláčková-Henley

MS—Michal Schonberg

PK—Peter Kussi

PW—Paul Wilson

RH—Rachel Harrell

Preface

When I approached the age of "three score and ten," some of my friends and readers began to tell me that I should write my memoirs. After all, like them, I had lived through nearly all the types of society that had ever existed—including modern forms of slavery and feudalism.

I gave some thought to it, but decided against it. We have now been told by historians and psychologists that even the most candid memoirs contain many a *reservatio mentale*—that to be absolutely true to what happened is not within human powers. Thinking about my *oeuvre*, I saw that there was very little worth telling that had not already been told in my stories and novels.

Naturally, things were not *exactly* as I described them. The title of Goethe's autobiography, *Dichtung und Warheit*, applies here, too. All I can say is that in my so-called "serious" fiction (i.e., stories and novels that are neither historical nor of the crime and fantasy genre), there is, perhaps, no character or event without a basis in what I actually knew and saw in real life.

In this, of course, I am no exception among authors who base their work on reality, not on experiments with texts which are comprehensible only to themselves. (And even they can't make soup out of clear water using no ingredients.) Even the most nonsensical crime stories and the wildest science fiction/fantasies are permeated with the germs of reality which were part of their authors' life.

Anyway, that is was I believe to be true.

—JOSEF SKVORECKY
Toronto, 2000

I

Introduction
to Life

Why I Lernt
How to Reed

*From the Diary of Josef Macháně, grade one pupil
at the elementary school for boys at K.*

Before I started going to school, Mother read to me every night at bedtime, to help me fall asleep. She would turn on the coloured glass lamp by my bed, put on her pince-nez, and read fairy tales. I really hated sleeping, but I liked listening to the stories: there was a wicked witch who ate children and a rotten stepmother who poked out her stepchildren's eyes, and then when the prince was betrothed to the prettiest of the children, she (the heroine) chopped off both her stepmother's arms and also one leg. Those fairy tales frightened me so much that I couldn't fall asleep, which was why Mother had to keep reading on and on, until *she* fell asleep.

But alas, those wonderful times were soon to be no more. I had to start grade one at the elementary school for boys. I didn't want to, but they made me. Our teacher, Mrs. Řeháková, taught us reading, and now, as Mother was turning on the lamp she would say to me, "Soon I won't have to read to you any longer, Joey, because in no time you'll learn how, and then you'll be able to read quietly to yourself." But I liked having Mother read to me, because she was pretty and had a scratchy voice that helped me to stay awake when she read me the story about Budulínek, the boy who gobbled up everything he could find in the pantry, but was still hungry and then became a cannibal. So I decided not to learn how to read, so that Mother would have to go on reading bedtime stories to me every night. I kept my resolution steadfastly, and at midterm I got a failing grade in reading from Mrs. Řeháková. My father got very mad.

"A failing grade in such an elementary subject!" His voice was so loud that it shook the chandelier, which was also made of coloured glass. "Even Voženil, the poor widow's son who comes to our house at least twice a week for lunch, managed a D minus, but look at this! My own son's report!" He stopped shouting and began removing his belt, then bent me over his knee and strapped me hard.

The pain soon faded, but unfortunately Father also had another punishment for me: in his righteous indignation he reduced my allowance by half, from one crown to a mere fifty hellers a week. This created a surplus in the family budget, which he immediately decided to pass on to my sister, Blanche, giving her the extra fifty hellers because during a visit to her gym class the superintendent of schools had praised her for beautifully vaulting over a vaulting-horse. But, even though the price I paid was very high, I did achieve my goal: Father did not forbid Mother to read stories to me, and I still didn't learn to read.

Soon spring arrived. A paunchy black gentleman appeared at the Julius Meinl Delicatessen, the same gentleman who at Christmas brewed various kinds of coffee on the premises and offered them to the customers in tiny cups. Father, Mother, and my brother Peter, who was sixteen, all tried the coffee. I wasn't allowed to because I was too young. They couldn't agree on which was the best brand of coffee and they sampled so many tiny cups that Mother suddenly began to experience heart palpitations. Father bought 100 grams of the house brand and took her home.

However, it was now spring, and the paunchy black gentleman wasn't brewing coffee this time. He was offering a new American beverage, and he could also be seen in an advertising poster hanging in front of Meinl's, in which he was holding a large cup of golden liquid full of silver bubbles. In the poster, the black man and his cup were encircled by a slogan printed in red-white-and-blue-striped letters, but I could only read the part that said "1 Kč." I had learned how to read numbers, because there weren't any numbers in the fairy tales, but of course I couldn't read anything else, so Mother had to continue reading to me. I figured the numbers meant the golden drink cost one crown, which I could have afforded if Father hadn't cut my allowance.

I spent the whole afternoon in front of Meinl's delicatessen glumly watching a parade of my schoolmates, boys and girls alike, entering the store and then coming out sipping the golden beverage and praising its quality. Of course, they had been cheated: the cups they had been given were made of waxed paper, and were so small that at least ten of them would have fitted easily inside the goblet pictured on the poster. I was dying to taste the golden drink, but naturally they all begrudged me a taste, as their cups were so very tiny. Nobody offered me a single drop.

At five o'clock the black gentleman closed the steel shutters over the shop window and the door. The last customer, who slithered out under the shutter just as it was coming down, was Irene, the councillor's daughter. "Gimme a sip, Irene!" I whimpered. She was my last chance. "You didn't get any?" asked Irene. She sounded surprised, but she let me have a sip. As soon as I had tasted the drink, I wanted it more than ever. "No, I didn't," I told her, "because I ran out of moo—" (I was going to say moolah, but Irene always spoke properly, so I changed the word halfway through) "—ney," and I added, "Let me have some more!" Irene's cup had only a drop left, though, and she gulped it down herself. Then, pointing to the poster, she said, "But it was free! Look—it was a giveaway!" She spelled out the slogan for me:

COME AND TASTE
THE NEW AMERICAN DRINK
GINGER ALE.
A CUP OF THIS DELICIOUS BEVERAGE
ON SALE FOR 1 Kč
BUT TODAY AND ONLY TODAY
IS OFFERED TO YOU BY
MR. POSITIVE WASSERMAN BROWN OF CHICAGO

ABSOLUTELY
FREE.

Then Irene handed me the empty cup and turned around, her long braids with red ribbons swinging against her back. I threw away the empty cup, realizing that there would be far greater advantages in learning to read than there were in having Mother continue to read to me. I soon mastered reading, and writing too, and eventually became an author.

1998

Eve Was Naked

We met in a sight-seeing bus, touring Prague. She wore her brown hair in braids with red bows at the ends. That much I remember. I have no idea what we talked about. In general, I have no idea what children talk about among themselves. Their world is foreign to me, and so I don't concern myself with it.

They say it's a happy world. Undoubtedly it is. It knows neither optimism nor despair. It passes by in a sort of permanent state of eager interest. I would like to know, though, just when it ends.

And perhaps I do. I know she was wearing a white linen summer dress, red sandals and white socks, that she was from Velim or some such small town and that she won a promotional contest by collecting the most toothpaste caps. Since I was eight at the time and she was much younger, she was probably about six. In any case, I think she was going to start first grade after summer vacation. It was her first time in Prague. The man with the megaphone pointed out the sights. Her red beret with the word THY-MOLIN created an almost coquettish contrast with her brown hair, parted in the middle.

On me it looked like the beret of a foreign legionnaire. But I had hardly caught sight of her before I lost interest in my beret. What was the beret next to her? Next to those braids with red bows? Next to those eyes the colour of chocolate? Next to those bare calves in white socks?

And so it was love at first sight, perhaps my first love ever.

Ahh!

I think it's futile to try to describe it in words. We were put into a third-class coach, together with a group of charity children from the Prague Paupers, piled in ten to a compartment, boys and girls together, and we were on our way. Two days and two nights on the train, then sunny Italy.

When Wilson Station disappeared from sight she began to cry. Small tears rolled down her red cheeks and the white front of her dress, devoid of breasts. The tears rolled down that delicate chest of a child's small body. At night boards were laid between the benches and on them blankets, and on the blankets they put us. Five heads in one direction, five heads in the other.

And during the night the cold beauty of the Alps appeared under the moon. The little girl sobbed at the wintry sight of those austere German giants covered with ice. With my feet I touched her legs, which were hot in the night car, in the dazzling light of the snow caps shining like the points of glass rooftops.

My neighbour Jiří Chrůma (her legs in tiny socks lay between us), wasn't from the group sponsored by Thymolin toothpaste. He was one of the children from Prague Paupers, and he made fun of her. Jiří had no understanding of the homesickness of a little girl. He was travelling for the sake of great adventures. For the sake of regular and substantial meals. He made fun of that midnight sobbing and flaunted his contempt for girls.

A girl?

No. She was something different.

On the second day I spoke to her about something. Only I can't remember what it was. I can't. She gave me a baba cake with chocolate filling, which I had never liked at home, but I ate it anyway. Naturally. Because it was *she* who gave it to me. Strange. I can't hear a single word. But I can see those brown, chocolate eyes clearly. They gazed wide-eyed at the North Italian lowlands, at the peasant women in the fields, at the Italian army's special units marching swiftly along with plumes in their caps, at the Fascist customs officers stuffed into riding breeches, who smelled of sweat and flirted with the teacher who was chaperoning us in the train.

Is it really such a happy age, that tearful childhood? Because she began blubbering again when we staggered out of the train and saw a column of black war prisoners being led around the train station, bound together with a rope. It was during the Abyssinian war. Perhaps she was afraid of them. Or perhaps it was the rope. Or perhaps she was still homesick.

Then came sunny days in Grada—days of ice cream, melons, crabs hiding in the little homes of conchs. A sailor from a minesweeper anchored in front of the villa serenaded the teacher on his guitar in the evenings. He was filthy and the teacher turned up her nose at him. A Hitlerjugend group was staying in the neighbouring villa. At sunset they lit a campfire and recited German poems in unison, which sounded uncompromising, menacing and slightly idiotic. One night Jiří Chrůma defecated in some newspaper and threw it through an open window into their kitchen. Since their kitchen faced the other direction, toward the villa of the girls from Ballila, the Hitler Youth leader hushed it up. The girls from Ballila sang sentimental, melodic songs in the moonlight about Santa Lucia and Duce Mussolini. Blond mops would appear in the windows of the Hitler Youth's villa, even though it was after curfew. The Hitler Youth observed the curfew. The girls from Ballila didn't.

We didn't either. After the lights were turned out Jiří Chrůma would launch a pillow fight by hitting Quidon Hirsch—the nephew of some gentleman from Thymolin, who got to travel with us thanks to his connections—with a pillow. Quidon, an obstinate, audacious fatty, attacked Jiří Chrůma back and Jiří Chrůma broke Quidon's nose.

Sometimes we killed centipedes. Another time Jiří Chrůma told about his Fruit Corporation, Ltd., an ingenious network of small fruit watchmen, secretly linked with little thieves who terrorized grocers in Žižkov, Karlín, and Holešovice.

I admired Jiří Chrůma and was a little afraid of him at the same time. Understandably. I was a well-behaved only child from a small town, and I knew that theft was a sin. Jiří Chrůma did not acknowledge sin. He wasn't a believer. I admired the devilish daring with which he opposed God, and it sent shivers up my spine a bit, too.

But when the pillow fights were over, I always thought about the girl. The girls slept in the neighbouring bedroom and also sang sometimes.

I collected sea stars and sea urchins for her. I made an African necklace out of them and she wore it one afternoon around her little wren-like neck, over her tiny red bathing suit, into which disappeared the groove of her tiny spine, elongated by the part in her brown hair.

Then she forgot the necklace on the beach.

It once happened at dinner that the cook chopped a flying cicada in two with a meat cutter and both halves fell into the girl's soup. The cook was a garrulous Italian who had contracted malaria in Abyssinia. He carried a torch for the teacher, and bisecting a cicada in flight happened to be his tour de force.

The body of the cicada floated in the girl's soup, flailing its legs about. The mandibles of the severed head bit at the beans. The girl cried in disgust. I gallantly traded bowls with her and then proceeded to eat both halves with interest. They tasted like bone marrow, or something of the sort. The girl got sick from watching me.

She had to leave the table. Suntanned feet in green sandals, white shorts, and a striped sailor suit. Inspired by this episode, Jiří Chrůma began catching cicadas and devouring them alive in front of the girls. The girls shrieked and ran away to the villa. But they weren't as sick as she was. As my girl.

Because she didn't shriek. She turned pale, then green, and had to leave the table.

The next day, from early morning on, a storm raged at sea. A steamship fought its way through the grey waves toward Trieste and the Hitler Youth marched out on their field exercises. The girls from Ballila, bare-legged and wearing funny, short, pink-and-white striped shirts, ran laughing in the rain to the church. Jiří Chrůma built a Tower of Babel out of polenta leftovers in the deserted cafeteria and told his circle of henchmen about how he was going to be a safe-cracker like his father. In reality it was only his uncle who was a safe-cracker. I spent the entire day on the glass-enclosed veranda, alternately playing ping-pong with the girl, managing just two returns on average, and sitting and chatting with her by the window. If only I knew what about.

My girl was the prettiest of all the girls and the teacher who chaperoned them favoured her. Several times she took her out in a sailboat, while we, waist high in water, hunted jellyfish and envied her.

After lunch I sat down to a game of Monopoly with Quidon Hirsch, the girl, and Jiří Chrůma. Quidon Hirsch lost his nerve early on and I acquired a hotel on Wenceslas Square, which I sold for far less than its value to the girl. Then I fell into financial hardship and the girl loaned me some money. It was a great game, albeit capitalist—its only flaw being that marriage between players was not provided for in the rules. I was very pained by this at the time, and had the rules allowed it, I know she would have married me. But as it was, we merely saved one another from bankruptcy, and in the end the game was won by the devilish capitalist Jiří Chrůma, whose uncle was a safe-cracker and whose real-life father a Prague Pauper. The favoured shareholder's nephew, Quidon Hirsch, was the first to go bankrupt and continued to grind his teeth until the end of the game.

He immediately proposed a rematch. But just as the dice were rolled for the first time, the sun suddenly came out. A rainbow appeared through the rain, the storm died down, the white buildings and villas further along the beach gleamed white, the brightly coloured tents shone in the sun. The Hitler Youth, soaked to the skin, were returning from their march singing a revolutionary song, and the girls from Ballila in short shirts snickered at them maliciously from the windows.

And then the teacher, in a polka-dotted dress, came along and called to the girl, Quidon Hirsch, Jiří Chrůma, and me to go for a walk on the beach with her.

We went. The girl went with a lovely tender smile, I went after her, Jiří Chrůma went because he interpreted all the teacher's wishes as commands that one had to obey, and Quidon Hirsch went because he had no one to play Monopoly with.

And so we found ourselves on the beach. The black clouds were retreating swiftly to the east and the teacher in her white dress with red polka dots stood on the sand with her dress flapping in the wind, and the girl in the short white dress stood beside her and her dress also fluttered against her in the wind.

Jiří Chrůma found a small turtle and stuck it in his pocket.

We gazed out at the sea. The wind turned warm. The sun became scorching hot once again.

The teacher turned to us and said:

"What do you say we take a swim, boys?"

"Yes, ma'am," answered Jiří Chrůma for us.

"You undress here while Eve and I go to the tent to change."

The green-and-white striped tent stood about five metres away. The girl blushed, turned bright red and whispered something to the teacher. The teacher bent down to her and listened. Her white teeth gleamed against her pretty brown face.

"But you don't need one yet, sweetie," she said, laughing, and bent down to the girl again, hugged and kissed her, and then led her by the hand to the tent. The girl was as red as a lobster.

We stripped down to our swim trunks, which we always had on under our clothes, sat down on the sand, and taught the turtle to walk on its hind legs.

Then the edges of the canvas over the entrance to the tent separated and the teacher appeared. She was wearing a bold two-piece bathing suit and her breasts overflowed a little from the top piece. But I wasn't looking at that.

Next to her stood the girl.

She was naked and red in the face.

She looked like a baby bird. Her tiny body was white except for her legs, shoulders and arms, which were the colour of light brown coffee.

We sat there and gawked at the girl with our mouths hanging open. The turtle escaped in the meantime. We didn't find it again.

The teacher broke into a run, her breasts bouncing, and pulled the girl along by the hand. "Quick! Into the water!" she shouted idiotically, or perhaps maliciously, or perhaps because she was excited too, without knowing why.

They ran off to the sea. I could see the teacher's turquoise two-piece bathing suit and the girl's white naked behind, above which bounced two bows in long braids.

I suddenly felt faint. Then strange. Then incredibly sad, so sad that words can't convey it.

Because I saw life's anguish, that anguish thanks to which man is not indifferent to death.

A green wave tossed the two swimming bodies up toward the sky. The big woman and the small woman.

"Hey, fellas, let's go get some ice cream!" I said. That much I remember. Because what else could I have done?

Really, what else *can* be done?

1961

Why Do People Have Soft Noses?

Czech language composition by Josef Macháně,
grade three student at the elementary school for boys in K.

I do not like brushing my teeth, although I know that dentally it is beneficial. I always dip the toothbrush in water, so that Mother, checking up, will not notice the deception. Then I squeeze the toothpaste down the drain.

On that morning, however, I forgot to dip my brush, and Mother inquired: "Joey, did you brush your teeth?" I nodded, but she retorted, "Let's see!" She touched my nose and finding it soft, she declared, "You're lying. Lying will get you nowhere, and besides, the liar sinneth." But noses are always soft. There is no hard-nosed person.

At breakfast Mother confided in Father, "Rudolph, I am out of sorts. Most probably it is nervous exhaustion brought on by the meeting of St. Martin's Charitable Association. Just imagine! The actuary, Mr. Kudláček, was elected chairman, even though he was recently seen in a cathouse." "In a cathouse?" I asked. "Mr. Kudláček has two dogs. He does not need a cat." Just then a bone stuck in my father's throat, which was strange because we weren't eating fish. Also, my brother Peter howled and my sister Blanche, blushing, berated me, "You don't understand things like that. You are too stupid." But she is the stupid one, because she is only a girl.

Mother said, "Be that as it may, today I cannot go to mass with you. Rudolph, you and the children will have to go alone."

And we went. However, while walking past Jonas Lewith's wine bar, Father said that he must make a quick business call inside, although he does not trade in wine, but rather in leather and textiles.

And we continued on with Peter and Blanche all the way to the church, where the Christian folk stood conversing. The simple folk at the main entrance, the fancy people at the entrance to the gallery. Peter said, "I will go to the choir loft. I intend to sing in the church choir today." Then he disappeared around the corner. Blanche poked me, and said, "Go and stand next to altar, so you can see the good father, shorty!" "I am not shorty," I said, "Mr. Pick, my teacher, says that I am very tall for my age." But Blanche had already disappeared in the side aisle of the church, and so I moved on toward the altar.

There, however, trouble found me: when the mass commenced and the altar boys entered, I recognized one of them, the carrot-head Milič Codr, the son of the district forester, who stole my pencil box with the picture of a pig. So I hid behind the statue of St. John the Baptist. Then I pried one of the tin stars off his halo and using my slingshot I launched it from the said hiding place at Milič Codr, just as the good Father Meloun, having ascended to the pulpit, began to preach about the profligate son. I always carry it on my person for that very reason. My well-aimed shot hit Milič's ear, but the sexton noticed the mischief and for my sins led me and Voženil out of the temple, not knowing which of us launched the star. Voženil stood next to me picking his nose. I denied my guilt by arrant lying, and the sexton took my word, Voženil being but a poor rascal.

Then I no longer wanted to dwell in the House of the Lord, as the weather was beautiful. So I walked carefully through the park and noticed Blanche, absent from the church, on a park bench, her knee in the possession of Aleš Neumann. I walked around them so as not be seen. Then, on my way past the wide windows of the Café Beránek, I spied Peter. Not intoning in the cathedral choir, he sat instead with the churlish youths, playing cards, although he is not allowed to. And yet there he sat.

I did not loiter very long. My journey took me past the wine bar, whose yard was attended by a noteworthy dog. He was remarkably small, but he possessed a giant head. I followed him into the yard, but the beast decided to enter the house. I followed him, but the dog crawled through an opening near the floor and disappeared. I too made my way in through the same opening, and with my head partly through, I could see the establishment. Father was there, flanked on the left by Mr. Lederer and on the right by Mr. Sommernitz. The two gentlemen took turns describing the adventures of another pair of gentlemen, named Kohn and Pick, as well as of a lady called Fraupick, while Father laughed at the stories all the time and very loudly. I do not know why he laughed, as the stories were rather boring; for example the one about Mr. Pick going on a business trip, but then, upon missing his train, returning home and finding in Fraupick's bed Mr. Kohn and so on, with no explanation of what Mr. Kohn was doing in Fraupick's bed, which I do not find at all laughable. But Father did laugh, possibly on account of the fact that Mr. Sommernitz buys skins from him and Mr. Lederer buys textiles, both in large quantities, and he wanted to endear himself to both the boring storytellers by his boundless laughter.

Time passed and after a while I ran back to the House of the Lord, where I mingled with the departing people. At the same time I noticed Peter mingling from one side and Blanche from the other, while Father stood in front of the church talking with Mr. Hejda, who is the choirmaster, as if he had been at mass all along. But he wasn't.

At home, Mother asked Blanche, "What did the good father preach about today?" and Blanche responded quickly, "About the virgins in the fiery furnace." To which I retorted, "No, he didn't, it was about the prodigal son." "Of course," said Blanche. "I couldn't hear too well. There was a hunchback woman sitting right in front of me who prayed very loudly."

Then Mother praised us and rewarded us for piously listening to the mass while visiting the House of the Lord. She gave me a coin, Blanche a lipstick, and Peter a sacred picture, which I later found on the floor in the lavatory. Also, she praised Father with the words, "Trade also prospers when the merchant's piety by his brethren is witnessed."

Then we sat down at the holiday table and partook of roasted goose. Good cheer spread throughout the realm. Which leads me to believe that lying is rewarded. All of us, me, Blanche, Peter, and Father, committed on that day a large number of sins and transgressions, but because we lied about it everything turned out well for us. From which I surmise that not only do cheaters prosper, but that they prosper very well. And that the commandment "Thou shalt not lie!" is itself a lie because if we observed it we apparently could not exist at all.

Also, since there are no people with hard noses, but rather everybody has only soft noses, I assume that everybody lies, ergo exists, and that our society, while lying its way towards the truth, will continue to flourish.

1965

A Remarkable
Chemical
Phenomenon

Czech language composition by Josef Macháně,
grade four student at the elementary school for boys in K.

"**A** sound mind in a sound body" the great Miroslav Tyrš taught our nation, and my father agrees with him. His body is very large and very healthy, measuring 197 centimetres and weighing 115 kilograms. At a tender age he was smitten with the idea of exercise and joined the Sokols' Gymnastics Association.

I too was taken by it, but I broke my leg performing a straddle vault over a vaulting-horse, and my body is no longer completely sound. My brother Peter, who is almost grown up, refused to remain a Sokol. The Sokols are compelled to perform in tight shorts with fringes, and Peter, who is a *zooter*, or as others might say, a *dude*, had to suffer too many insults from Jaroslava Cuceová, who is known to be his "squeeze." So he refused to wear the Sokols' colours, declaring, "I am a zooter. The Sokols' ideals and ours don't mix." "Your ideals consist of boozing," declared Father, already wearing his colours, ready to attend the county gymnastics assembly. "You have no other ideals. Whilst our Sokol festivities are veritable whirligigs of sound mind."

Then we went in procession to the county assembly, where I took part in the pie-eating races. I did not participate in the climb-for-sausages race, because my leg was not completely healed. In that race, the contestants had to climb and then try to tear off, using only their teeth, one of the large garland of sausages suspended on top. But when Voženil, the poor widow's son, reached the sausages, he started tearing them off with his hands despite the prohibition and devouring them. So Brother Sturdy, the exercise master, had to climb after him and pull him down. He had eaten seven sausages already. There also was a beer-drinking race, in which, owing to his considerable underagedness, Voženil was not allowed to participate. Here the garland of victory was carried off by Brother Rockabilly, the heaviest Sokol of the Foothills Regional Group, at 135 kilograms dressed weight (without clothes).

Father also took part in gymnastic exercises during which Sokols of the male persuasion showed their physical prowess by stretching their arms and legs mightily, towards the end chanting in unison the following poem:

Throughout the land of Czechs we hear
What to our sturdy hearts is very dear
With healthy bodies, sound minds we cheer
Hip hip hurray to Fatherland! Never fear!

At sunset the aforementioned pie-eating race took place, bringing the Sokol festivities to their conclusion. The Sokol ladies had baked for the occasion a blueberry pie that measured almost two metres in diameter. In the said pastry they concealed more than twenty one-crown coins, with one silver five-crown piece somewhere near the centre. The finale of the race was the silver coin, with the racers eating their way through the pie to reach it. Unfortunately, I had to drop out of the race early, because over the course of the day I had consumed a large quantity of Turkish delight, ice cream, sugar candy, candy floss, wieners, sausages and pickles. I was already much too full and could eat my way only twenty centimetres from the edge of the pie. Other athletes managed to go farther. For instance, Alois Wagner, the son of the blacksmith, ate sixty centimetres, swallowing three of the coins while doing so, and breaking one tooth. Pavel Bošek managed to eat even farther into the pie, but he began to choke on a coin that became lodged in his gullet and he had to be taken to the first aid station where repeated blows to his back forced the coin out.

One after another the athletes had to abandon the race, until only two remained. Eating their way from opposite ends, they found themselves very near the centre. These were Bertie Mintz, the son of the local wholesaler, and the aforementioned Voženil, the poor widow's son. When only a tiny blueberry-filled space separated the two foes from the silver fiver, Voženil began to show signs of fatigue. He was also mad because he hadn't come across a single solitary coin throughout his lengthy eating quest. On the other hand, Bertie Mintz had found seven coins, and seeing his foe beginning to falter, he began to eat even faster, spitting the coins out all around. At the very moment when it seemed that the merchant's son would carry off the palm of victory, Voženil in a final desperate effort thrust his fist under the pie into his opponent's stomach. Upon which Bertie Mintz turned green and began to vomit, and Voženil, perfidiously taking advantage of the delay, quickly ate his way through to the centre and swallowed the silver fiver.

But Brother Mintz, the father of the eliminated competitor, protested against the result, and in the end Bertie Mintz was declared the winner by virtue of a decision taken by the mayor, Brother Vejvoda. However, the fiver not being available to be awarded, Voženil was ordered to hand it over to its rightful owner as soon as it emerged.

The next day Bertie demanded the silver fiver, and Mr. Pick, the teacher, ordered Voženil to hand it over. But Voženil only handed over two metal singles and a copper. He said that even though he had swallowed the fiver, those three coins were all that came out.

The teacher assailed him repeatedly, even to the point of applying the switch, but Voženil stood his ground. If he spoke the truth, then this remarkable chemical phenomenon has no equal throughout the long history of the Sokols' pie-eating competitions.

1965

How My Literary
Career Began

One evening Ulrych showed up on the terrace of our *pension*, where my blonde sister was soaking up the rays of the setting sun, and asked me, "Have you heard who's staying at the Miramare?"

"No, I haven't."

"Jim McKinley!"

"You're kidding!" I said, but it turned out he was right.

Less than two days later, he brought him over in person. Jim McKinley, alias Jiří Rychtr, looked a little like Hercule Poirot: he was slight and bald, and the tip of his nose bloomed fire-red. He sat down in an armchair in my room and his watery eyes flicked back and forth over the hotel furnishings.

"Mr. Rychtr wants us to help him. He doesn't feel well and he has to spend all his days in treatment," declared Ulrych eagerly. "And he needs to have a new novel finished by next Wednesday."

My breath caught in my throat. "Oh—well—" was the best I could do.

McKinley's fleeting glance settled on the glass front of the china cabinet. "Hmm," he said, "might I have a drink? The mud baths have dehydrated my mucous membranes."

I leaped toward the cabinet, poured a glass of Dad's Bonekamp liqueur, disguised as mineral water, and placed it in front of Jim.

"Hmm," said Jim McKinley, having moistened his mucous membranes. "I think you could do it for me. They aren't all that particular, and Mr. Ulrych says that you write the best Czech papers in your school. You could do the descriptions of the countryside, the depictions of the characters, and, say, the lyrical dialogues. I'll give you the plot outline, and we'll split it fifty-fifty. I'll give it a quick look and put my name on it. Okay?"

I assured the Master that I would do just as he wished.

"The title is *The Rider from Sierra La Plata*. That's definite, because that's what they announced. The plot—" At that point, Jim fell silent. My blonde sister had walked into the room, and she directed a quizzical glance of her pale blue eyes at him. Just so you understand, my sister was a knockout. On account of her, and being jealous, our English prof attacked and beat up Dyntar, a senior who used to carry her leotard and toe shoes to ballet class for her. The Reverend Father Meloun stared at her on the street so hard he fell down an open manhole and busted his rib.

Jim McKinley was in a similar frame of mind.

As a rule, I used to take careful note of such goings-on, because it occasionally generated an incidental income for me, but this time I never really noticed that over the next few days Jim McKinley abandoned his treatment and instead started carrying my sister's tennis racquet. The reason I didn't notice was that Ulrych and I were devoting all our time to literary creation.

First I developed a scene depicting the appearance of the Rider from Sierra La Plata, Bob Hopalong, silhouetted against the blood-red horizon among the cactuses on the virgin prairie near Cantaras City. He had muttonchop sideburns—which I had too, incidentally—and he wore an elegant western outfit: a broad-brimmed black sombrero trimmed in white, a black silk shirt with white seams, a black vest with white embellishments, black chaps with white fringes, and high-heeled boots with spurs of Mexican silver. Of course, his two Colt six-shooters hung low in their black leather holsters trimmed with silver rivets.

Ulrych's specialty was the epic elements: he brought quick-on-the-draw Bob together with Jennifer, the rancher's daughter. The description of the raven-haired beauty was strikingly similar to that of Zorka Běhounková, national junior figure-skating champion, whose family had rooms in the neighbouring *pension*, and who occasionally tolerated my bragging in her presence about one or another of my accomplishments. Like Zorka, Jennifer also had black, widely spaced eyes and a mole on her left cheek, and like her, she peppered her conversation with the clever and delightful exclamation "Gee whillikers!"

When we had gotten to this point in our work, Jim McKinley paid us a surprise visit. He arrived cheery and freshly shaved in a white tennis outfit, carrying a bouquet of carnations in his hand. While he waited for my sister to finish changing, he asked us amiably how far along we were. He listened absentmindedly to our report, declared that he was prepared to give us an advance, and passed each of us a fifty-crown note. My sister sailed out of her room in a white tennis skirt, and Jim McKinley leaped up to take her racquet.

Burning with the fever of creativity, we opened the window. Downstairs, Zorka Běhounková was waiting. Beside her was an officer in red jodhpurs. I turned gloomy. When my sister came downstairs with Jim McKinley, the two couples introduced themselves and then set out toward the tennis courts.

Ulrych and I went back to work. Our first literary income had charged us up. The view from the window brought me a malevolent inspiration, and we proceeded to outdo ourselves. Big Bill Haywood, cattle thief, painted from life after the officer in the red jodhpurs, first spied on the rancher's daughter as she sunned herself on a rocky cliff in Horrible Canyon, in nothing but "the garb of Eve"; then he attacked her and finally carried her off. With true literary fervour, I dwelt for half a page on the charms of the girl's nude body. In the meantime, Ulrych had involved the Rider from Sierra La Plata in seventeen killings. Seven corpses bit the dust in the town saloon in Cantaras City, and ten more in the gorge behind Chichito Peak, where they made the mistake of attacking quick-on-the-draw Bob from behind.

Toward evening, as we were tying it all together, my sister burst into the room, her cheeks flaming. I had considerable experience with her in this state, so I glanced out the window.

The rays of the evening sun glinted off Jim McKinley's bald pate, but the red military jodhpurs glowed far more brightly. My sister reappeared in a chic turquoise cocktail dress, then vanished like the breeze. I looked out the window again. Receding into the darkening twilight was a blue cloud flanked by two red blossoms. The larger one represented the red jodhpurs, the smaller was Jim's tonsure, its tint indicating that the Master was extremely excited.

The fever of creativity was still upon us and we threw ourselves into our work without supper. This time we recounted the wild pursuit of Big Bill Haywood's gang in the night-time landscape of the Rocky Mountains. Heading the posse was the boastful Fred Blowstone, sheriff of Cantaras City, dressed in pearl-grey trousers and a brown leather vest with a gold star. Beside him galloped Bob Hopalong, all in black, barely visible in the dark of night.

Ulrych recorded the last seven of the Rider's killings. They culminated, in an isolated cabin overlooking a rocky gulch, with a wild fracas in which Big Bill Haywood knocked out the boastful Sheriff Blowstone and tied him up, only to be beaten to a pulp and tossed into the gulch by the Rider from Sierra La Plata.

The conclusion of the book was up to me.

The pale moonlight glistened on the raven hair of Jennifer Rodriguez, safe in the black-clad arms of the sideburned Bob of La Plata.

It was midnight by the time we had finished the novel and my father's Bonekamp. I heard rapid footsteps mounting the stairs, and then my sister dashed into the room. Her cheeks were more flushed than ever, and she disappeared into her room without a word.

I opened the door a crack and spoke into the darkness. "What's up, sis?"

"Leave me alone!" came her voice from the darkness.

I turned back to Ulrych and tapped my forehead eloquently. Ulrych grinned, turned the Bonekamp bottle upside down and held it over his open mouth. When he was sure that not another drop would come out of it, he gathered the papers from the table and got ready to leave.

"I'll give it to him tomorrow," he said. "He'll have plenty of time to look it over. I don't expect he'll change a lot of our work."

Early the next day, the dragoon officer showed up and took my sister down to the mineral springs. He had a bandage on his nose with blood caked on it. In reply to my question about what happened, he said that he got hit by a golf ball.

I spent the morning bragging in the presence of Zorka Běhounková. She didn't seem to be in very good spirits; all she wanted to know was if the dragoon lieutenant had been at our place that morning. So in addition to my usual boasts I mentioned that I had written a novel about her. That got her attention. "What sort of novel?" she pressed me. "Will you let me read it?" "Not till it's published," I said quickly, realizing that it might not be prudent to disclose the whole ghostwriting interlude before the book came out—especially to a woman. "I'll let you read it as soon as it's published. It's easier to read in print. You appear in it as a rancher's daughter," I said, and Zorka was flattered. She promised to go to the beach with me that afternoon.

Around noon, Ulrych called my room. "Come on down to the railway station—it's urgent!"

So I hurried down to the railway station. In the restaurant, Jim McKinley sat nursing a double shot of strong slivovitz and looking nervous. The knuckles of his right hand were bandaged. He got his hand caught in a door, he said, but the novel was fine. "You did a great job, fellows, fifty-fifty still stands."

Then he asked me to deliver a letter to my sister. He said he had to leave in a hurry and didn't have time to say goodbye in person.

Still drunk with the heady fumes of literary success, I hurried down to the beach. My sister was there too, with an extremely hairy young man with a flattened nose. I gave her the letter; she read it, gave a contemptuous sniff and tossed it into a trash can filled with crumpled paper bags. Later, on our way home, I realized that the hairy young man was in fact the dragoon officer. Without his jodhpurs he looked more like an ape man.

For the most part, it was a pleasant afternoon at the beach. Zorka, dressed in a white bathing suit, skipped around me and bounced a huge inflated rubber ball at me. I lay majestically on a towel, exulting in my literary prowess. I was still gloating that evening in the outdoor movie theatre; I even put my arm around Zorka's waist, and she left it there.

The outcome, however, was not so good. The novel was published within a week, but Jim McKinley had introduced several changes in the story that would have wiped me out in Zorka's eyes, so I had to pretend that the censors had banned the book. Naturally, she didn't believe me. She pursed her lips scornfully and said, "I knew right away that you were just bragging!" She turned her back and left for the mud baths, where I'd heard they'd hired a new masseur who looked just like Robert Taylor.

And so all I had left to console myself with was the novel, *The Rider from Sierra La Plata*, published as the 723rd volume of the weekly *Pocket Novel* Series. I knew Jim McKinley would make some changes with his masterly hand, but I didn't think they improved the story. He had transformed the raven-haired beauty, Jennifer, into a Nordic blonde with blue eyes and changed the mole on her left cheek to a coquettish dimple at the corner of her mouth. He seemed to have no objection to the exorbitant number of corpses—twenty-five, all killed by the Rider of Sierra La Plata—but he totally devastated my closing scene, of which I had been justifiably proud. In it, the fair Jennifer did not offer her raspberry lips to the Rider—McKinley had shaved off Bob's sideburns and given him a bald spot on the back of his head. Instead, she bent down to the dazed Sheriff Blowstone, the braggart, whose pearl-grey trousers McKinley had dyed blood red.

No wonder the disappointed Bob finally rides off alone, his silhouette joining those of the cactuses standing up against the blood-red evening sky, away from Cantaras City, away from the Circle M Ranch.

Jim McKinley sent one copy of the book, leather-bound, to my blonde sister. She was the wrong person to send it to, though. My sister never read *Pocket Novels*. She looked down her nose at trash. She subscribed only to *Popular Romances*.

1960

II

The
Thousand-Year
Empire

My Uncle Kohn

My uncle Kohn was a wealthy man and life had treated him well. He had a small Tatra car, and he came to visit us almost every week because he liked my father. Father and I would set out on foot in the direction from which he would come, and we usually met up with him just outside town, when it was already after dark, and he always recognized us easily in the headlights. First a light would appear on the horizon and move quickly across the sky, as the highway curved on the other side, below the ridge of the hill; then the light would catch us in a white cone and hold us there, as if in a fist. I was always completely blinded and couldn't even see my aunt as she kissed me with her soft, velvety lips and stuck a bag of candy into my hand. Her lips always smelled nice because she wore a lot of lipstick.

Not that she needed it, as she was very pretty to begin with. But this way she was even prettier. She was twenty years younger than Uncle Kohn, she was a happy person, and even crazier about soccer than he. Once they took me to an international match in Prague, and my aunt caused a scene when the referee called an unfair penalty against Sparta and she hit some foreigner over the head with an umbrella because he cheered. The police took us in that time, but they let us go right away, although it may have cost my uncle something.

My uncle was what they now call a headhunter—he dealt in soccer players. He owned a large snack bar in Prague, but he was so lazy that he leased it out and led a leisurely life. And so, to avoid boredom, he was a headhunter. In the afternoons he would sit in Café Paris, reading foreign newspapers, smoking cigarettes in a gold holder, and buying and selling players with the other headhunters. He liked Jewish anecdotes, as he was himself a Jew. And he loved to play practical jokes on people. For instance, he would offer fake rubber candy on which you could break a tooth, or cigarettes with sparklers inside that would start to crackle under your nose when the cigarette was half smoked. Or he would appear with a shiny pin on his lapel and when someone asked him what it was, he would put the lapel up to the person's face and spray him with water, because the pin had a rubber bubble underneath, so that water sprayed out of the pin when the bubble was pressed.

My aunt was sixteen when she met my uncle, and they dated for five years. Granddad wouldn't allow them to marry. Granddad was an anti-Semite. My aunt would meet my uncle secretly, out of town, and they would drive to Prague so that no one would see them together, and in the evening my uncle would drive her home from Prague. But one time the car stalled on the way back and my aunt arrived home late. Granddad had already long suspected what was going on, and he lit into her. My aunt confessed and Granddad whipped her with a belt, even though she was already of age. But she never would have married my uncle without Granddad's blessing; she was well brought up. Not so well brought up, though, as to stop seeing my uncle altogether.

The fact that Granddad finally did allow it was due to the efforts of my father. My aunt worked as a shorthand typist in Father's bank and always passed our house on her way home from work. Up in the attic we had a little room that no one lived in, and Father loaned it to them so that they would have somewhere to meet after Granddad had ordered her to be home by six every day, thus making it impossible to travel to Prague and back, even by car. So Uncle Kohn would leave his Tatra in the woods outside of town and walk the back way to our house—through the field, past the sunflowers, all the way to the back gate. My aunt would arrive first and I could always hear her scurry up the wooden steps.

Then they were quiet up there together. They met in that way for about a year, but Granddad still wouldn't let them marry.

Understandably, other young men were interested in my aunt; she was pretty, like all the girls on my mother's side of the family. But when word got around that she was seeing a wealthy Jew from Prague, everyone gradually left her alone—all but one, Albert Kudrna, who studied medicine and continued to court her in any way he could: first with flowers, and then, when flowers didn't work, he began threatening suicide. It always frightened my aunt, but he never actually went through with it. He finally sniffed out the fact that she was meeting Uncle Kohn at our house and wrote an anonymous letter to Granddad about it. Kudrna was a dirty rat, and whatever he couldn't have himself, he would at least spoil for someone else. During the war he joined the fascist party Vlajka and studied in the Reich. Then he met Dr. Teuner and supposedly wanted to organize some sort of Czech SS division, but that never came together, and so he was sent with an ordinary SS division to the Eastern front, and never came back.

Granddad lay in wait for Uncle Kohn among the sunflowers, and when my uncle was returning in the evening to the woods where he had hidden his car, Granddad pounced on him, grabbed him by the neck and began to bellow, "You stinking Jew, I'll strangle you!" He might actually have done it if it hadn't been for the fact that at that very moment Father had been shaving in the bathroom, and he could see out the bathroom window all the way to the sunflowers. When he heard them yelling, he ran out just as he was and pulled them apart.

I watched from the kitchen window and saw that Uncle Kohn was all red and sweaty and was rubbing his neck, and that Granddad, too, was all red and that his white whiskers glistened on his face like the cotton whiskers of St. Nick. Father was gesticulating, holding a lathered shaving brush in his hand, and then all three slowly walked away toward the woods on the path through the field of grain—Uncle Kohn in fashionable plumblue gabardine, Father in a striped collarless shirt and Granddad in his hunting cap with a feather. The sun shone against their backs, as it was already evening, and they disappeared from my sight at a bend in the path, far away amidst the fields.

Granddad still resisted for some time, and then suddenly there was a wedding. It took place in Prague at the Hotel Paris; I got sick from eating too much wedding cake, so I didn't enjoy the wedding much. My aunt wore a beige suit and looked very beautiful, for she was still very young. Uncle Kohn had a big gardenia in his lapel and looked very blasé.

My uncle was perhaps no big hero. Once I was with him and Father at a restaurant in Prague, and at the neighbouring table sat a group of people with Prussian crewcuts. They tossed back one drink after another and were drunk in no time. It was in the spring of 1936, about three months after the wedding. My uncle was nervous and it made Father uneasy as well—I noticed that much, even though I didn't understand it very well.

The rowdy Germans began singing "Fest steht und treu die Wacht am Rhein." I could see my uncle growing more and more nervous. One of the Germans noticed us, identified my uncle as a Jew, and when they had stopped singing for a moment he shouted: "*Es lebe Adolf Hitler!*" and shot us a furtive glance to see what we would say. I could see that Uncle Kohn was turning red and perspiring. I didn't understand why. The Germans started singing some song again, and when they had finished, the one who had noticed that my uncle was a Jew shouted, "*Die Juden 'raus!*" Uncle Kohn, bright red, stood up, approached him and said, "*Mein Herr—*" but he didn't get any further than that because the bully burst out laughing and gave my uncle a shove, which made him stagger and thud back into his chair. "*Die Juden 'raus!*" shouted the bully again, but Father pounced on him and socked him one. Something fell out of the bully's mouth—a denture, as we later saw—and he began to lisp furiously. The other Germans rose as one and rushed at Father. Uncle Kohn grabbed me by the hand and ran outside. Out on the sidewalk he began shouting, "Police!" An officer appeared from around the corner and my uncle sent him inside.

They took Father in to the police station with the Germans, but my uncle followed and they released him right away.

My uncle owned an apartment house in Prague, in which he had a large eight-room apartment. In two of the rooms lived his sister—a single woman fifteen years younger than he. She had short black hair in a boyish cut and usually wore men's trousers. My uncle called her the black sheep of the family. She was a Communist and the police often arrested her for causing disturbances at demonstrations. But they always let her go again.

Once, when I was visiting my uncle, she invited me into her room. A man was already there; he was wearing a white shirt and looked as if he had just come from a tennis match, had white teeth and was constantly laughing. Aunt Pavla smoked a purple cigarette in a holder half a yard long, called him Julínek[1] and poured me a glass of wine. Then he asked me, "What do you wanna be when you grow up, squirt?"

"A bank manager," I replied.

"Only there's gonna be a revolution," she said, "and you, little bourgeois pipsqueak, will be liquidated."

She fixed me with her black eyes, and I was frightened. I had no idea what it meant to be "liquidated," but I didn't ask—I was too scared.

At this point the man in the white shirt said, "Now, now, Pavla," and turned to me and said, "So, kid, you want to be a bank manager?"

"No," I replied, and looked at him, scared, then declared, "a deep-sea diver." The man in the white shirt burst out laughing and said, "Well, now that's another thing. That's a respectable profession." He smiled at me and slapped my aunt on the shoulder. Aunt Pavla also smiled a little, and after the man began laughing I was no longer afraid.

When Hitler came, Aunt Pavla fled across the border and we never heard of her again. She didn't return after the war.

Uncle Kohn had an old dachshund that had badly diseased eyes, but my uncle had him operated on at a dog sanitarium in Vienna and the dog recovered. He would walk from room to room, treading on the thick carpets with his crooked little legs, swinging his head and breathing audibly. He would go up to everyone and sniff at them, looking them in the eye as if wanting to ask for advice. Whoever gave him a piece of candy or salami won his heart; he wouldn't eat bread. He always slept on a pillow in front of the fireplace and no one ever heard him bark. I always thought he was mute.

Three years after the wedding, in early March, Uncle Kohn suddenly came down with pneumonia. He lay in the bedroom with my aunt at his bedside, while Father and I sat in the next room watching an oxygen tank being carried in. Yet before his death my aunt caught pneumonia, too. My uncle died, and three days later my aunt began to have difficulty breathing. Mother sat at her bedside, while I stood watching Father, who was standing behind Mother with tears running down his cheeks. My aunt was also crying and kept repeating, "Pavel! Pavel!" softly and sadly. That was my uncle's first name. An oxygen tank was brought in, and she died soon after. I cried, too, but Father cried most of all. I had never heard him cry as he did then.

During the night the dachshund began to howl. Father and I spent the night in the guest room, as my aunt died in the evening and Father wanted to arrange the funeral the next morning. The dachshund howled and it resounded eerily through the apartment. I sensed that Father was awake. Suddenly he got out of bed and began putting on his dressing gown.

"Where are you going, Dad?" I asked.

"Just stay there," Father said, but I climbed out of bed and we passed through the hallway, lit by the moon, into the room where my dead aunt lay. Moonlight shone on the carpet in front of the bed, where the dachshund lay, moaning. He moaned and moaned and I squatted down next to him and began stroking his head, but the dog still moaned and sobbed. I stroked the short smooth hair on his little head, and he moaned and then suddenly let out a single sob and lay there, still. I could feel him stiffening quickly under my hand. He had died.

I often recalled that sobbing dog in the years that followed. I'm not even sure why. The next day was March 15, 1939, and German troops arrived in Prague. Only a few people were present at my aunt and uncle's cremation. Aunt Pavla was abroad and the apartment had been confiscated by the Gestapo.

1957

1. "Julínek" is a nickname for Julius, which suggests that Pavla's friend was Julius Fučík, a well-known communist publicist and writer, later executed by the Nazis.

My Teacher,
Mr. Katz

When I was in the eighth grade, my parents sent me to German lessons, since German began in grade nine. They always did it that way. In the seventh grade they put me in Latin and in the ninth grade in French—only at that time I wanted to learn English, and so I didn't study French, but bought myself an English textbook and studied English in secret.

For German they entrusted me to Mr. Katz, who lived on Židovská Street in the building where the Jewish school had once been. He was a teacher of Jewish religion and the cantor in the synagogue. Mr. Katz was very small and bald, but he could sing beautifully and play the violin and harmonium. He charged eight crowns an hour, which was less than any other teacher.

I was very nervous when I went to my first lesson and rang the bell by the glass-paned wooden partition on the first floor of the Jewish school, where there had previously been a classroom; now there was a hallway leading to the prayer room on one side, and a hallway leading to the cantor's apartment on the other. I was nervous, but Mr. Katz was kind and friendly and showed me into the kitchen, where his plump wife sat on a stool by the stove in an old housecoat. Mr. Katz sat me down at the kitchen table and opened before me a new German textbook that crackled in its spine, and on the first page there was a black-and-white picture of something round and dirty, which was an egg.

Mr. Katz told me in a pleasant voice that egg is *Ei* in German, and so I began to study German from the very beginning, from an egg. "*Das ist ein Ei,*" said Mr. Katz, and I repeated after him.

"*Ist das ein Ei?*" asked Mr. Katz, and immediately answered him-self—"*Ja, das ist ein Ei*," and I repeated after him.

Mr. Katz taught not only German, but Jewish religion as well. Since that was taught in Hebrew, Jewish children had to go to Hebrew lessons first. Jews are required to wear a hat whenever they pray or do anything having to do with religion. So it hap-pened that once, when I had arrived early for my German lesson, Jonas Lewith and Itzik Kohn were sitting in front of Mr. Katz, reciting in very loud voices mysterious sentences of a language that was Hebrew, and on their heads they had Mr. Katz's hats—one for the weekdays and one for the Sabbath—which came down over their ears. Because it was summer and hot and they hadn't brought their caps to the religion lesson, Mr. Katz had to lend them his own hats, which were too big for them. They sat upright in their chairs and looked at me haughtily and scornfully because they were speaking a language I didn't understand, and they shouted out "*Loubalim selah shme ashboazim*," or something like that, but Mr. Katz constantly interrupted and corrected them, so per-haps they didn't really know that language so well—but I didn't know it at all, and so they could make fun of me.

The same thing with those hats happened again, when Mr. Katz's daughter Ruth was getting married. She was marrying Isidor Kafka from O., who owned a little notebook factory there and was an Orthodox Jew. The wedding, too, was Orthodox, performed by the famous rabbi from Kolin, and it was attended not only by Jews, but by many Christians as well, because Mr. Katz was well-known and spoken of as a nice Jew, just as the same was said of Dr. Strass, and as the opposite was said of Moše Čubkalöbl—that he was an evil Jew. Only it was summer, it was hot, they came without hats, and those in charge didn't want to let them into the synagogue. It was awkward because everyone wanted to see the wedding, but they weren't allowed in, so they stood in front of the synagogue and complained until Izak Eisner suddenly ran up with a pannier on his back and two baskets, all full of hats that had long ago gone out of style (and which he was unable to sell in his shop), all sorts of derbies and funny boaters; and he began renting them out for a crown each plus a ten-crown deposit; they were all snatched up in an instant, as the wedding was already beginning and everyone wanted to see it and quickly rushed inside. Since they weren't choosy but just thrust their deposits hastily into Mr. Eisner's hand, some ended up with hats that were too big and others with hats that were too small. My father, who had a large head and was very big and tall, had on his head a tiny grey derby, which he had to hold on to every second to keep it from falling off. I couldn't help but laugh, for which I got a whack from Father and was thrown out of the synagogue.

Mr. Katz always gave lessons in the kitchen, while his wife sat on a stool by the stove and listened. During the first years she said nothing; only later, when I spoke German well and we had begun reading fairy tales and books, the content of which I would recount—only at the very end, after the Germans came, and I continued going to Mr. Katz for one more year, during which we spoke of nothing but the political situation—only then did Mrs. Katz join in our discussion, and only to voice her agreement with Mr. Katz. But during those first years she remained silent.

Mr. Katz taught by his own method, slowly and systematically. He was constantly giving me German phrases to practise declensions—his favourite was *der gute alte Wein*. I would correctly decline *der gute alte Wein, des guten alten Weines, dem guten alten Weine, den guten alten Wein* and Mr. Katz would nod his head and I would get a terrible craving for good vintage wine, which Mr. Katz so gladly gave me to decline, although I don't think he ever drank any himself, at least not much, as he was poor. Later, when I knew German better, he would always say: "What you know, Daniel, nobody can take from you. Therefore learn, learn German." And he would tell how, during the First World War, there were hard times and how people couldn't get anything, not even for money, but that he went around to the farmers and gave German lessons, "*und dafür bekam ich Approvisation*," he would say, "*Mehl, Butter, sogar*

Fleisch," slowly and with emphasis, almost piously, and once again I would get a terrible craving for *Mehl, Butter, sogar Fleisch*, although I didn't eat much except sweets. "You can lose everything, Daniel, money, everything," he would say. "Only what you have here"—and he pointed with his finger at his own, bald head—"nobody can take from you. If ever a new war begins," he would say, "we won't go hungry." Because people will still want to study German and he could tell them that he didn't want money, but *Mehl, Butter und sogar Fleisch*. "*Auch Milch*," he said, when he remembered, smiling a contented smile.

Sometimes on Friday evenings he would end the lesson and send me home early because the evening star had come out and prayer was beginning. On Tuesday of the following week he would make up that short time. But I didn't go home. Instead I would hide in the dark stairwell and watch the Jews going through the classroom divided by a glass partition into the prayer room: Abraham Lewith (Jonas Lewith's father), Dr. Strass, Mr. Ohrenzug, who had a wholesale drapery business, and his son the high school junior Benno Ohrenzug, and others I didn't know. Singing would resound from the prayer room—it was Mr. Katz, who was the cantor, singing—and then there arose such an unruly medley of voices that it was hard to believe it was coming from Mr. Lewith, Mr. Ohrenzug, Dr. Strass, and Mr. Abeles, whose daughter Sara did the backstroke in swimming races for the sports club; the voices rose and rose and Mr. Katz suddenly had a voice that was strong and plaintive and beautiful at the same time—I listened and almost choked with a certain strange, unfamiliar and terrible longing, then made my way out of the dark stairwell and down the stairs to the front of the school.

Above the castle's tower on the hill, in the deep blue sky, the clear evening star shone like a tear, and as I walked home in a daze across the square of houses, an organ began to play in the church. I was blissful and melancholy and on the verge of tears.

I had always wondered why they lamented in that way, why

they pleaded and cried. Once when I was going to my lesson, the doors to the prayer room were ajar. I was afraid, but nevertheless I sneaked inside. I saw a dark velvet curtain with embroidery and, between the windows, a map of Palestine with a Hebrew legend. Only that map of Palestine stuck in my memory, because at that moment old Arno Kraus, the shammas, came into the prayer room and threw me out. Perhaps they were crying and pleading for Palestine, where their ancestors had come from; that school map was strange, as was the beautifully embroidered curtain beside it. I thought the curtain must be like the one that was once torn up in Jerusalem.

Before Mr. Katz's daughter Ruth got married, all sorts of rituals and traditions were observed. Mr. Katz gladly told me about Judaism and its customs. He showed me a small tubular case on the door frame, which the painter had painted brown to match the door itself, and he said that it contained a scroll with some sacred words, the meaning of which I have forgotten. Another time he sat unshaven and explained to me that it was the time of religious holidays and that it was forbidden to shave. Yet another time he didn't pick up pencil or pen, because manual work was forbidden.

He also explained that Jews have only the Old Testament, and in his presence I was suddenly filled with piety and said that we Catholics have the New Testament as well, and Mr. Katz said he knew, but that they didn't recognize Jesus as saviour, and I said that we Catholics recognized him, and contentment reigned between us and I was glad that things in this world are varied and interesting, each one different.

During other religious holidays Mr. Katz would give me matzos, which came in packages from some factory and which were then usually eaten up by my father, who ate everything. Mr. Katz said they were good for bad digestion, since they were made of nothing but flour and water.

On the eve of the wedding the bride withdrew with several

women to a separate room where, I was told, they bathed and washed her and rubbed her body with fragrant oils, although it's possible that I'm confusing it with something in the Catholic tradition. But the image of the naked, white Ruth Katz stepping out of a brass bath, naked and white and wet, and the Jewish women drying her and applying fragrant oils drove me out of my mind with desire, and to this day it excites me with its suggestion of something mysterious and beautiful and very chaste. She was undoubtedly a virgin, and Isidor Kafka, too, was most certainly a virgin; he wasn't at all handsome, he was well off but not all that rich, and he was an Orthodox Jew.

Mr. Katz liked to talk about matzos, about how healthy they are, because he was diabetic and not allowed to eat homemade sweets, cakes, and in general all those things that are forbidden to diabetics. This struck me as very strange and interesting and I almost envied him the fact that he was forbidden to eat anything, while I was allowed everything, although I liked virtually nothing but sweets. Once, later, when I was sick, and my urine was abnormal, Dr. Strass said something was wrong with my kidneys and ordered me to go on a special diet. The diet was the exact opposite of Mr. Katz's. "*Was?*" asked Mr. Katz, very concerned that I was not allowed to eat meat. "*Du darfst nicht Fleisch essen, Daniel? Und Fett auch nicht?*" he asked and I saw that he had suddenly become very worried and that he was thinking about something. I was proud that I, too, was on a diet, and had expected that we would discuss it, but Mr. Katz grew pale thinking of how hungry I must be. All of a sudden, with a quivering voice, he said, "*Sag nur, Daniel, was würde man essen, wenn man Zucker und Nierenkrankheit hatte? Dann musste man doch zum Tode verhungern!*" (Tell me, Daniel, what would a person eat if he had diabetes and kidney failure? One would starve to death!)

Nine months after the wedding, Mr. Katz's daughter gave birth to baby Hana. Mr. Katz was delighted and talked about her constantly. He said she was a beautiful baby with hair like an angel. "*Wie ein Engelchen,*" he would say. Once he was in especially good spirits because he had just returned from a visit with his son-in-law and daughter and out of a desk drawer he pulled a large book, bound backwards so that the beginning was at the end, and showed it to me. "*Das habe ich schon für Hannerle besorgt,*" he said. "*Eines Tages wird sie es brauchen.*" (I have bought this for Hannerle. One day she'll need it.)

It was a Hebrew primer for children, from which they learned the language in which their Bible was written. I don't think they even call it a Bible. It had pictures of eggs, kittens, little dogs, and boys in old-fashioned knickers, like our Czech primer, and I chimed in with my praise and said, "*Hana, das ist ein schöner Name,*" and Mr. Katz beamed still more.

Later Hitler came and instituted the anti-Jewish laws, but I continued to go to Mr. Katz, even though I now knew German and no longer really needed his help. We stopped reading fairy tales and books and recounting their content and spoke instead of nothing but politics. I railed against Hitler and the Germans and Mr. Katz complained and lamented. His elderly wife also complained from her place by the stove and I cursed Hitler, even though at that time I still didn't entirely know what exactly it was that Hitler stood for. "*Was wir Juden schon alles mitgemacht haben!*" Mr. Katz would say, and it seemed to me that he spoke not to me, but to someone above, on the ceiling or in the sky.

Afterwards, when I was heading home, I noticed on the religious council's bulletin board in the passageway lists of Jews who had left the Jewish faith.

Later someone wrote an anonymous article for the *Aryan Fight*, stating that a certain bank director in K. still sent his son to *German* (that was italicized) lessons with the Jew Adolf Katz, cantor of the synagogue in K. Father lost his temper. He soon calmed down, but I had to stop going to my lessons. That was the beginning of Father's ruin.

People began to regard him as a Jew-lover, and it was all downhill from there. He was constantly angry, constantly complaining, until one night at midnight there was a knock at the door and

Father was taken away. They didn't even give him time to dress properly. He disappeared into Belsen, Father did, and whenever I think of him I always picture him in that tiny grey derby, how he frowned and gave me a whack, or else how, all lathered up and wearing a striped shirt, he set out with Granddad in a hunting cap on the path through the field toward the setting sun. God only knows how he died, God only knows if he continued to complain. He probably did—it was in his nature. We never heard anything of him, not the tiniest piece of news.

Once, out of the blue, about three weeks after that article, Mr. Katz came to visit us. He came in a black overcoat with a greasy velvet collar; he rang, stood in the hall, entered, sat down at the table in his overcoat and smiled gently and politely. *"Was ist mit dir, Daniel?"* he asked me. *"Ich dachte, du warst krank!"* I blushed and said, "I'm not allowed ... *Ich—ich darf nicht mehr zu Ihnen kommen."*—*"Du darfst nicht?"* my teacher said with surprise. *"Warum?"*—*"Ich—"* I said, but at that moment I was interrupted by Father, who was as red as a lobster and told me to leave the room. Father and Mr. Katz talked for a long time and then Mr. Katz came out followed by Father. Mr. Katz had his bald head bowed and his fine Jewish nose stood out from his face.

He offered me his hand and said, *"Also, auf wiedersehen, Daniel."* *"Auf wiedersehen, Herr Lehrer,"* I said, and when the door was closed after him and his black overcoat, I began to cry. A tear ran down Father's face too, but he frowned, left the room, and scolded my younger sister Hanička for not practising the piano.

I didn't see Mr. Katz for a long time after that, and then all Jews were ordered to wear stars. One time, on the corner of the square, I ran into Mr. Vladyka, the head clerk at our bank who later manoeuvred his way into the director's position when Father was in the concentration camp, and who at that time had already taken over the management of Mr. Ohrenzug's apartment houses. He stopped and inquired about something or other. On the corner of the square there was a newsstand and at that moment Mr. Katz came out of it with a postcard in his hand and a yellow star on his black overcoat. When he caught sight of me, his face lit up with a friendly smile and possibly he forgot about the star and everything else, because he began cheerfully: "*Guten Tag, Daniel! Wie geht es dir? Ich hab dich schon lange nicht gesehen!*"

I answered somewhat awkwardly, but I too was glad to see him and to see that he was still the same. "*Guten Tag, Herr Lehrer. Und wie geht es Ihnen?*" I said and shook his hand. Just then I heard a rustling beside me, turned around, and saw Mr. Vladyka hurrying off across the square with only the tails of his trench coat fluttering behind him.

All of a sudden I was fuming mad and turned to Mr. Katz and asked him whether he was going home and if I could accompany him, and out of spite I walked across the entire square with him, and he forgot about everything and we spoke of Hitler and the war and diabetes and then about little Hannerle, who was three now and, I was told, was already talking quite well.

Many people saw us. It's possible that somewhere they gave Father a black mark for that. But I couldn't have cared less at that moment—because I liked Mr. Katz.

Later certain medications were restricted and the sale of them to Jews was forbidden. Insulin was among them. I happened to be in the pharmacy one day, talking with Vlád'a Nosál, who was studying to be a pharmacist, when Mr. Katz came in for insulin. He didn't know that it was not to be sold to Jews. I heard how he said hello and I saw him in his black overcoat with the velvet collar, between the bottles and retorts, behind which I stood with Vlád'a Nosál in the laboratory. I also saw Mr. Hesse, the pharmacist, stare at Mr. Katz and clear his throat and I heard him say, "Insulin?" "Yes," said Mr. Katz, "as always," and Mr. Hesse wanted to say something, something other than what he actually said, because he said that they hadn't received a shipment that week. "And when will you receive it?" asked Mr. Katz, alarmed, and then Mr. Hesse turned red, almost crimson, like my father at Mr. Katz's last visit, and said "Wait," and pulled a box out from under the counter and said that he had an emergency supply for hospitals and that he would give it to him for the meantime and would then keep his allotment from the shipment.

Mr. Katz thanked him and left. Mr. Hesse, still red, came over to us and instructed Vlád'a to write out an insulin card for a certain woman and to give it always to Mr. Katz, but cautiously, so that no one would know, in case there were others in the pharmacy.

And then all the Jews in the city were ordered to the transport. They went early in the morning. I got up and went to the station, because I had been thinking about Mr. Katz all night. It was a damp, cold, ugly autumn day. At the station there was a long line of Jews with suitcases and bundles. I hid behind the corner of the Hotel Star; I didn't want to be seen. A German soldier was keeping an eye on them. I searched for Mr. Katz in the line. I recognized the Löbl brothers, Dr. Strass, Sara Abeles with her small baby in her arms, Leo Feld, Mr. Lewith, Itzik Kohn and then I caught sight of Mr. Katz in his black overcoat and next to him plump Mrs. Katz, and Ruth in a green jacket. Alongside her stood lanky, homely Isidor Kafka—her husband, holding the hand of a little girl, with a brown face and dirty stockings on her legs. That was Hannerle. I was seeing her for the first time.

The soldier shouted something, the line began to move; I saw how Mr. Katz gathered up from the ground a bundle tied with string and went among the others to the station.

1957

Dr. Strass

Dr. Strass was always old—fifty, perhaps—small, frail and inconspicuous. He spoke so softy that I could scarcely understand him, and he had his office in a villa overlooking the river. It was called a villa, but it always seemed like a castle to me, and it did look rather like a castle.

Around the outside there was a fence made entirely of iron spears with pointed tips, with an artfully forged gate, and in each gate half was Dr. Strass's monogram: KS. A bar stuck up from each half of the gate, and two Aesculapian snakes coiled halfway up to the top of these bars, so that when the gate was closed, the snakes' heads bristled combatively, sticking out their gilded tongues at each other.

Beyond the gate was a wide gravel drive by which Dr. Strass went down to the street in his automobile, and whenever he drove down the small hill with the clutch out, the gravel would crackle under the tires. The drive gently curved to the left and up to the villa. The top of the villa had a tall tower with a wooden framework, in which heads, gargoyles and beasts were carved. Above them the pointed roof sloped steeply, with a flagstaff and iron weathervane at the top. The weathervane was engraved with the year of the villa's construction: 1900.

Stately weeping willows stood around the villa, and it was quiet. Steps led first onto an open veranda, then into a very dark waiting room panelled entirely with dark wood; a door, thickly upholstered in shiny, smooth, cold leather, led to the office. The leather was quilted with leather buttons, so that they made chilly bumps from the floor up to the ceiling. Above a carved bench opposite the entrance hung a large painting by Benes Knüpfer, depicting the green sea, very realistic and beautiful. Two or three patients sat silently in leather easy chairs—Dr. Strass never had more than that in his waiting room, and yet it was said that he was very wealthy. I could never understand how he could be wealthy when he had so few patients.

Dr. Strass drove to his house calls in a convertible Lancia that was at least six metres long, and he always sat in it alone with a wide black hat on his head. When he drove down the main avenue over the cobblestones the Lancia would creak and bounce, but Dr. Strass sat erect and steady, his expressionless face attentively fixed straight ahead. "Mama, Mama!" I would shout. "Here comes Dr. Strass!" "Yes," my mother would say. "That's a dear man."

Then the Lancia would stop in front of the glass windows of the café on the square, and when I pressed my nose to the thick glass, which had a frosted frame with flowers etched in the corners, I saw Dr. Strass sitting in a grey suit with a vest and watch chain, in a stiff white collar, behind a marble table, over black coffee, chatting quietly and inexpressively with Mr. Ohrenzug or with dapper old Mr. Löbl, or sometimes also with my father; on Dr. Strass's white hands, which had a big signet ring on one finger, fine red hairs shone golden in the dusk of the café.

It was thanks to Dr. Strass's help that I came into the world, and since that time I have often been a guest in the reticent waiting room of the villa that looked like a castle. I often crossed the threshold of that dark waiting room and entered the office—and it was as if I had suddenly stepped from dark night into bright day. The office shone like a freshly washed Sunday cupboard in a sun-filled kitchen. The chrome handles of the instrument cabinets gleamed coolly, and the enormous chrome sphere of the diathermy and the peculiar equipment of the examination table—covered with white leather, in the centre of the office— also shone icily. It looked like the stirrups of a horse's tack sticking up, and I didn't know what they were for, but I suspected that they were for something unpleasant and painful. The doctor, wearing a white coat, himself opened the upholstered door, behind which was yet another door, also upholstered on both sides with white leather. My mother would, in an anxious voice, inform him of my condition while the doctor listened, expressionless. Then he instructed me in a calm voice to undress to the waist, took out a chrome stethoscope, and proceeded to place it here and there on my tummy and back, chilling me terribly each time. As if he couldn't hear well with the stethoscope, he then took it out of his ears, pressed his cold hands to my back and tummy, and began putting his ear against my skin here and there. When he put his ears against my chest, I saw his white, slightly wrinkled bald pate. Sometimes the doctor would be unshaven because he was observing certain holidays, and his rough red whiskers would scratch my tender child's skin.

In the fourth grade I caught pneumonia, then jaundice, from which I barely recovered, eventually caught pneumonia again— as well as pleurisy, and in the meantime had an inflammation of the middle ear—twice, for good measure.

I lay in my room near the open window, even though it was winter, because that was what Dr. Strass ordered, and I knew that I might die. I prayed from morning to night that I wouldn't die— or at least during the intervals when I wasn't delirious with fever, dreams and reality mingling in my head. I promised God that if I didn't die, I would pray five Lord's Prayers and five Hail Marys every day as long as I lived, and as I grew worse and worse I raised the quota to ten, twenty, thirty, until I ended up somewhere around one hundred, but by then I was too weak to have any interest in promises. The following year I attempted to exact from myself that horrible daily load of devout gratitude, but it wasn't possible, and I substituted a promise that at the age of thirty I would join a monastery, but by the time I was thirty there weren't any monasteries, and so, unable to fulfil my promise, I simply broke it.

In those days, when dreams mingled with reality, the head of Dr. Strass, with the expressionless glance of his watery blue eyes, often appeared before me like a hallucination in my jumbled consciousness and semi-consciousness. Once a night lamp shone behind his bald pate, another time the unpleasant, prickly light of the winter sky shone through the window. Later they told me that Dr. Strass, regardless of whether it was day or night, came to see me every two hours for many days. His Lancia stood in front of our villa from one morning until the next, and once, when he didn't come all afternoon because the pharmacist's wife, Mrs. Holznerová, was giving birth, the rumour spread through the neighbourhood that I had died. Perhaps that was what saved me, my mother said, because if people say a person has died when he hasn't, it means he will live a long time.

But I know that it was Dr. Strass who saved me. In those moments when I was aware that he was with me, I felt his unshaven face scratching my chest and back like a friendly hedgehog. Afterwards he often appeared to me in that other world of dreams and fever as a hedgehog with a fine Jewish nose and fragrant apples stuck on his quills, who looked at me with human eyes. Those eyes watched me expressionlessly and thoughtfully, and I didn't know whether there was anxiety or concern or indifference in them—he never showed his feelings and never said very much. Behind him in the northern glow of the night lamp was the tear-stained face of my mother, with a necklace of teardrop pearls around her neck, and the tall figure of my father disappearing in the dark. On his face an eternal tear shone like glass; tear after tear flowed, tear after tear, like a water clock measuring out the minutes of my life.

Then Dr. Strass spoke, and I knew he was saying that I was very low, and requesting my parents' consent to use the latest, as yet untested, remedy, which, as I learned later, he had brought back from the International Medical Congress in London. Then I heard weeping, my mother's heartbroken weeping and my father's com-

forting drone and then, in a low voice, a curt command or acqui-
escence—I don't know which—and the rustle of our maid's skirt,
and then Dr. Strass's white hands with little red hairs, a hypoder-
mic needle, a sting, then sleep, and suddenly I felt well and the
morning sun shone over the garden and in through the window
at me and onto the bed, near which sat Dr. Strass with circles
under his eyes. In his eyes there was, for the first and perhaps last
time, something like concern or joy or sympathy, or possibly triumph—I couldn't tell.

Years later my mother said that what he had given me was an
injection of penicillin that he had brought back from London
where they had presented it at the medical congress as an
untested novelty, but I don't know. It was a few years before the
war, so perhaps it's possible, I don't know. I only know that Dr.
Strass saved my life through hours of his self-sacrificing presence.

When my father said once at dinner that Dr. Strass was going
to get married, I couldn't believe it, since to me he seemed too old
for that. But he got married and went with his bride to the French
Riviera. They had the wedding in Prague, and although my father
was there, I wasn't. Afterwards my father said that the doctor's wife
was beautiful and from the very wealthy Karpeles family, which
owned pharmaceutical and chemical plants somewhere in south-
ern Bohemia.

The doctor was away on his honeymoon for a very long time
and when he returned he no longer drove the old Lancia, but a
black Buick instead; otherwise he hadn't changed at all, and I continued to see him at his office and he continued to chill me with
the cold circle of the stethoscope on my back and chest, since
after the pneumonia I still had bronchitis, and was always sickly
in general.

I hardly ever saw his wife, but she was indeed very beautiful.
Once I was going to his office and from the drive to the villa I
caught sight of her on the riverbank in a white dress, with a baby
in white lace swaddling clothes.

Sometime after Hitler came we had to stop going to Dr. Strass. At that time my father had already been declared a Jew-lover in the newspaper *Aryan Fight* and Mr. Vladyka had replaced Mr. Pollak as director and watched him. We began going to Dr. Labský, who was also nice, but he had his office in an apartment house, with lots of people in the waiting room, and there was nothing beautiful or mysterious, no green sea or shiny black leather in the dark gloom. There was just an ordinary door, through which you could hear everything Dr. Labský said to his patients.

But I no longer needed to go to the doctor so much after that, because we organized an orchestra, and instead of ailments I became preoccupied with my unfortunate love for Irene, who was in the third year of secondary school, had braids, came from Subcarpathian Ruthenia, and haphazardly mixed Ruthenian words into her chatter; I especially fell in love with those words, along with those braids. Soon I squeezed a saxophone out of my father, and had no time at all to think about ailments. I started behaving like a bully toward my mother and did whatever I pleased.

Jews were dispossessed of their cars and forbidden to go into restaurants. Signs that read No Jews Allowed hung everywhere; only on a pub called Port Arthur at the very edge of town near the river did they hang a sign: Café for Jews.

One evening in late summer when the sun lay like honey glaze on everything, even one's soul, I walked past that café for Jews. I had just walked Irene home, she had winked her brown eyes at me, which at the time was enough to make me entirely happy, and it occurred to me to look inside the café through the window. The sun was shining on the pub's window, so I had to press my nose to the glass again as I had done at the café on the square when I was a boy.

Inside, at a table with a stained checkered tablecloth, sat Dr. Strass with Mr. Ohrenzug and the teacher Mr. Katz over three cups of beechnut coffee. All were unshaven and sat silently, without a word. They just sat, motionless, over that squalid coffee, looked straight ahead and didn't speak. They looked shabby, ragged, and very old.

I quickly moved my head away from the window, my joyfully enamoured mood suddenly vanished, and when I saw opposite me a squad of ruddy, healthy-looking German soldiers marching and singing some song about *Lebe wohl, Erika*, I chose to turn off into a side street so that I wouldn't have to look at them, because I was somehow ashamed, I don't even know why.

I saw Dr. Strass only once after that. I was running with my saxophone through a passage that led to Židovská street, and I ran into the doctor. I greeted him and stopped, in a quandary. The doctor smiled inexpressively, almost shyly, and said, "How are you doing?" "Fine," I said, ashamed that I had said *fine*, even though it was the truth, and I blushed when I realized that the doctor was addressing me formally, even though he had still used the familiar form when I last spoke with him. But it was true that I was only in the third grade of grammar school then. We both paused and I didn't know what to say. "What are you carrying?" the doctor asked and pointed at the long case with my tenor saxophone. "A saxophone," I said. The doctor looked at me, astonished. "A saxophone? But—" but he didn't finish. It seemed to me that he blushed, and at that moment I, too, blushed again because I understood why he didn't finish his sentence—he knew that he no longer had the right to ask about the state of my health, about how my bronchial tubes could support the saxophone, since he was a Jew, and it was my own Aryan business. And so somehow—I don't know how—he parted with me and walked away, and I knew what he wanted to say, that one day I would have to give up the saxophone because my bronchial tubes couldn't handle it.

That was, as a matter of fact, Dr. Strass's last diagnosis in our town.

Later I heard that they hanged him at Terezin. For no reason. Supposedly he didn't greet an SS officer. After all, he always had a weak voice; but I can still hear it, to this day, while those strong, healthy soldiers' voices have long ago been lost in the contempt of time.

1964

The Cuckoo

No one knows the story of the Cuckoo. Perhaps it never really happened and is, after all, only a legend, a myth. Seek realism in it and you will find only improbability. But realism is not the point in this story. For is not war more phantasm than reality? And if it is reality, are we then really human beings? And if war is possible, might not this story of the Cuckoo be possible as well?

Of course Sara Abeles, who lives in Israel (if she's still alive), knows the story. And old Mrs. Adele Rittenbach certainly knew it, as did Leo Feld, but both of them have gone the way of all flesh, Leo sometime between 1943 and 1945, though no one knows exactly where or how, and Mrs. Adele Rittenbach in 1945, in the municipal home for the aged and indigent in the town of K.

For years old Mrs. Rittenbach had been housekeeper to Mr. Husa, a shop manager in the firm of Arpad Ohrenzug, Textiles en Gros & en Détail. Mr. Husa had married a German, Tilda Schröder from B., and Mrs. Rittenbach was in fact part of Tilda's dowry. She had been taken on at the Schröders' a few months before Tilda was born, and, in addition to her domestic duties had doubled as the child's nurse. Mrs. Rittenbach's father had been a highland weaver, so she was used to hard work. But she was as German as the Kaiser, as they say, and in memory she lives on in her green dirndl, carrying a huge white shopping bag on her morning rounds of the milk shop, the butcher's, and the grocer's, braying aloud in that powerful Teutonic voice of hers, but speaking the kind of Czech that cabaret entertainers would use to rouse dead audiences to laughter: "I am a Cherman and never vill I learn Tschechisch before that I die."

Mr. Husa, on the other hand, came from a family that was twenty-four-karat Czech. He had a button nose, a round, carefully shaved Shweik-like face and curly hair. His father had been a gravedigger at the Jewish cemetery and ever since his youth Mr. Husa had been a very capable employee of Papa Ohrenzug's wholesale draper's firm, where he had advanced from apprentice to shop assistant, and from there to the post of shop manager. His pudgy hands manipulated the heavy bolts of cloth on the counter with the ease of a juggler and he was always willing to wrestle huge rolls of gabardine outside the shop so that a customer could judge the colour tones and quality of the cloth in daylight.

That is, until a certain time.

I had known Sara Abeles at school. She was a pretty girl with black hair and black eyes. She swam the backstroke and dived for the local sports club. By the time I was fifteen and she was seventeen, I found her more interesting than the other girls in K., but she had that two-year jump on me and moreover she was going with Leo Feld, who held the district record in the one-hundred-metre crawl. And she wasn't interested in jazz.

And finally—by the time I was fifteen, it was 1939.

Of all the remarkable changes brought to the town of K. by that year of destiny, one of the most striking was the metamorphosis of Mr. Husa. Suddenly the space between his upper lip and button nose sprouted a tiny black moustache, very like the one worn by the German Leader and Imperial Chancellor. For this leader had also become Mr. Husa's leader and transformed the former shop assistant into a revolutionary. Mr. Husa's curly locks fell before the barber's electric clippers, leaving in their place a head of Prussian stubble. The wrinkles around the once-obliging shop manager's eyes drew themselves into a stern, military glare, the slightly stooped shoulders straightened and a sharp and surly tone crept into the voice. Even the orthography of his name changed: two little marks appeared over the *u* and final *a* dissolved into an *e*, following a law that was scarcely linguistic. In short, Mr. Husa became Herr Hüsse, the shop manager became a *Treuhändler* and the former shop assistant's colleague became a sidekick of Herr Regierungskommissar Horst Hermann Kühl, Mr. Hüneke, and our school principal, Mr. Czermack.

Ruda Husa, a schoolmate of mine, refused to acquiesce in any of these transformations. In the school records his nationality was changed from "Czech" to "German" but he stubbornly maintained his ancestral name on his notebooks and schoolwork. In the end, he even refused to speak German during German lessons. Of course he was still under age and so he was sent against his will to the Reichsdeutsch Gymnasium in B. where, so the story goes, he insulted the Reichsmarschall during a lesson on National Socialist ideology. So they sent him away to school in Munich and ultimately he was handed over to the German Imperial Armed Forces for further education. I don't know what they did to him, but Ruda never returned to K. Strange things happen to people in wars.

It was because of Ruda that old Mrs. Rittenbach was, for all practical purposes, placed under house arrest. When the indignant Herr Hüsse sent his prodigal son off to Munich, she was heard to declare in the local dairy shop: "This Cherman of ours, he is no Cherman at all. I mean he is *ein ganz gemeiner Nazi*."

Mrs. Rittenbach had only one tone of voice—loud—and news of her pronunciamento soon penetrated to German circles in K. Ever after that, the Czech servant girl was sent out to do the shopping—the Treuhändler, naturally, could afford two servants—and Mrs. Rittenbach was assigned to tasks that kept her indoors.

And then in the spring of 1940, her duties were unexpectedly expanded to include nursing once again. That was at a time when the Leader had been calling for fresh supplies of male children and, ever obedient to the Leader's word, *Parteigenosse* Hüsse impregnated his wife again, after those many years. She gave birth to a son, who was christened with the Imperial German name Horst after his godfather, who was none other than the Regierungskommissar Kühl.

About that time Sara Abeles also—but it is here, perhaps, that the legend, the myth, begins. And before abandoning this objective account of actual events, it may be better to pick up the tale at another point.

I must tell you something about Tilda Hüsse, née Schröder. For all I know she may have been, in her own way, a *femme fatale*, and perhaps it was she, in fact, who was really behind Herr Hüsse's sudden Germanification. Naturally I don't remember their early years together; they were married in 1920, four years before I was born. I will always remember Tilda as a tall, robust blonde woman with a peculiarly German type of loud-mouthed irritability that was as disagreeable as paying the rent. Mrs. Rittenbach, of course, also spoke in a loud voice, but it was the voice of old Mutter Courage. Tilda Schröder had the arrogant and penetrating voice of those well-fed German women whose lives are untouched by any real problems, a voice that could command those five or six unhappy German girls who were members of the local branch of the German Girls' League. And Frau Tilda was not only the *Leiterin*, or perhaps even the *Führerin* of this local group, she was also the spirit behind all German social and political activity in K., which at first was pretty meagre because all told there were only eight families that adopted German nationality in the entire town, although their ranks were considerably swollen during the course of the war by the arrival of an infantry unit of the Hermann Göring SS Division, followed, like a swarm of bees after honey, by a caravan of German families who occupied the best Jewish flats and took over the most lucrative Czech sinecures.

But they say that earlier, before all that, Tilda wasn't that way at all. She used to be a rosy-cheeked German *Mädel*, bashful and well-behaved, who, right after marrying her Czech husband, eagerly began to learn his mother tongue.

But I never heard Frau Hüsse speak Czech. They say she stopped in 1933, when the Leader began to have an erotic and ideological influence on her, as he did on so many rosy-cheeked, blushing *Mädels*. And whatever she may have learned of that

Western Slavic language she concealed in the depths of her cold, Sudeten soul, and never admitted to the knowledge again.

"*Ach, die Tilde*," old Mrs. Rittenbach once confided to my mother before the war. "*Die ist schon ganz verrückt.* Do you know that every night before sleeping she kisses the portrait of that—*wie heisst der Kerl*—that Adolf Hüttler? *Na, was sagen Sie dazu?* Is that what you call normal?"

Dear old Mrs. Rittenbach! As a matter of fact she is the source of the only tangible key to the truth about the Cuckoo. At that time, Herr Hüsse was an AA gunner somewhere on the outskirts of Hamburg and so the old woman was able to show herself on the streets again. But loquacious as she had once been, braying her cabaret Czech in the shops of K., she was now very tight-lipped, wasting words on no one, walking through the streets of town in her threadbare green dirndl like a shadow of that gay old mother of the regiment, pushing a stroller with little Horst in it. Horst sat in his stroller gawking about at the world and shrieking incomprehensible German questions at his nurse, who replied in half whispers. Frau Hüsse, the boy's mother, no longer had any time for him. She was working herself to the bone for the victory of the Reich. She was leader of the *Arbeitsamt*, or perhaps she was already commander of the *Volkssturm*, because by this time the turning point of the war had come.

And so we met old Mrs. Rittenbach on the lower path behind the railway station, or rather we came across the stroller with Horst in it parked in front of the grocery store. Horst rolled his overripe blueberry eyes at us and stuck a finger in his nose.

"Look at that," said Lexa, who played clarinet in our Dixieland band. "Isn't that young Husa?"

"Horst Hüsse," I said. "Baby brother of Ruda Husa, may he rest in peace."

Lexa surveyed the black-haired child with interest. "Certainly doesn't look much like his brother," he said. "Look at those eyes, and that stuff on his head—man, he looks more like—"

Just then Mrs. Rittenbach came out of the shop. We greeted

her and, feeling a little embarrassed, I said, "We were just admiring Ruda's little brother, here."

The old woman's eyes turned somewhat glassy, or so it seemed to me. "*Ja ja,*" she said. "*Der arme Rudi.* I vunder vot becomes of him?"

"Do you have any news?" I asked.

The old lady shook her head. "He is on *der Ostfront.*" And then, with unmistakable irony in her voice, she added, "*Er kämpft für den Fuiah und Vaterland.*"

"Sure," I said. "So this is his brother."

"He doesn't look much like a German, Mrs. Rittenbach," said Lexa. "I mean like the pure race," he added, and glanced conspiratorially at the old lady. She stared at Lexa with damp, misty eyes and after a brief hesitation, she said, "Vy should he? After all, he's no Cherman," then she hesitated even longer, or so it seemed to me, and said quietly, "and he's no Tschech either."

"How do you figure that?" I asked, but just then some people appeared in the shop door and Mrs. Rittenbach said a hasty farewell and walked away.

"The old gal is taking things too seriously," Lexa declared. "I'm willing to bet that if Ruda comes back after the war, Horst will be as Czech as they come."

At the time I had no idea that this late afternoon encounter with Mrs. Rittenbach would one day put me on the trail of the Cuckoo.

But does it matter any more?

Ruda, as I've already said, never came back and God knows where the end of the war found little Horst. Mr. Hüsse, they say, was killed in the air raid on Dresden in the spring of '45, and Frau Tilda vanished from K. several days before the Red Army arrived. About a month before that, she had sent Horst to some distant relatives in Würtenberg, but no one knew who they were and no one really cared.

That's not entirely true. Someone did. Someone cared about the fate of the German family Hüsse. You'd never guess who. Sara Abeles.

Yes. It seems quite clear to me why. But perhaps I'm just imagining things. Mrs. Rittenbach, after all, was very fond of Sara, and they say that Sara's mother, who came from Vienna and spoke Czech only slightly better than Mrs. Rittenbach, used to be Tilda Husa's best friend when they were young. Which was quite natural, for in K. there were only about eight German families, and five of them lived in the poorer part of town. A young shop manager's wife could hardly have socialized with people like that. Quite naturally, therefore, she became friends with the young woman from Vienna who was still full of tales from Prater and the sweet shops around Am Graben. And so old Mrs. Rittenbach frequently found herself looking after not only Ruda, but Sara as well.

The lives of those young wives and mothers, however, were encroached upon by the higher interests of the socialist and national revolution, which Frau Tilda began to embrace. And so the friendship ended. I can never remember a time when Frau Tilda and Alice Abeles were on speaking terms and when Alice, fortunately, died in 1936, Tilda did not even go to her funeral.

But old Mrs. Rittenbach did, and her loud highland laments formed a counterpoint of grief at that sad event. Afterwards, she became a regular visitor in the Abeles kitchen right into the early years of the Reich's dominion over the town of K., but those visits ended when she was overheard at the dairy shop saying the fateful sentence: "This Cherman of ours, he is no Cherman at all."

Perhaps old Mrs. Rittenbach became, to a certain extent, a substitute for Sara's mother, or her aunt, or perhaps she merely reminded Sara of Alice, who had died young and in Sara's subconscious mind remained clearly linked with the good-natured face of the old domestic. So perhaps it was not so odd after all that the first thing Sara did when she got back to K. in 1945 was to visit that abandoned old lady.

Mrs. Rittenbach was lying in the municipal home for the aged and indigent, paralysed by a stroke, and some of the local ultra-radicals were asking pointed questions about what a German woman was doing in a Czech institution. Therefore the behaviour of Sara Abeles, who was the only one in her entire family to survive the camps, was not regarded approvingly by the local ladies. Especially not when word got out that Sara had spoken with the old woman entirely in German.

"Look at them, those Jews. After all Hitler did to them, and they won't stop speaking German," whispered those loyal ladies in righteous patriotic indignation. But a few days after Sara's visit old Mrs. Rittenbach died, thus providing her own solution to the burning political problem faced by the ultra-radicals. Naturally no one came to her funeral, if it could be called a funeral at all. Not even Sara, who had left for Prague right after her conversation in the home for the aged and indigent.

It was in Prague that I came across the next—and final—clue to the Cuckoo. Of course it was many years later, in that dark autumn of the year 1952, and at this point I have to bring Rebecca into the story.

Who was Rebecca? Do I say "was" because she is no longer? She was the kind of girl you find in large cities. She was alone. She had a room above a busy intersection in the middle of Prague, a room that was particularly beautiful when it rained, when we lay on the couch in the dark and the greenish face of a porcelain Buddha reflected the changing traffic lights below.

And in her mournful, gazelle-like eyes you could read all the sadness, fear and anxiety of life and death, could have, that is, if Rebecca had not looked as though she had stepped right out of the Song of Solomon. So you didn't really notice the sadness and anyway, it was glazed over by the glow of those eyes. In their moist reflections there sparkled an erotic light; her delights were exquisite, and her breasts, like two roes that are twins, had been seen by more painters, record-holding athletes, poets, musicians and n'er-do-wells like myself in metropolitan Prague than is good for the reputation of such a girl, and I was terribly jealous.

She was not even being unfaithful to me, not really, for polyandry was normal for her. But I could not accept that. I wanted her, that rose of Sharon, I wanted her all to myself, for six or seven months, as long as my love usually lasted in those days. But because I was stupid I did not know that she was terrified by the nearness of death, by the inexorable march of the clock. Quite simply, she had no time to devote six or seven precious months of her life exclusively to a bad tenor sax player with the character of a twenty-eight-year-old barfly.

And she was right, and I'm almost certain that she actually knew it, rather than merely sensing it, for that was how she was, Rebecca. It wasn't even her real name, she just called herself that. Jealously, I tried to sniff out the slightest evidence of infidelity, and naturally I turned up unannounced a great deal. And then I made scenes. Once I even tried to beat her, but she fought back like a cat and I failed ingloriously.

Perhaps, though, I did manage to be somewhat different from the others. Because with me she could be sad. And this happened sometime before Christmas of that dark year, 1952, the last year she ever saw to its conclusion. It was raining, the light from the street lamp shone into the room and Rebecca was in the bathroom. A book lay on the writing desk with the corner of a letter protruding from its pages. Spurred on by jealousy, I slipped the letter out of the book. It was written on airmail paper, and my doubts were put to rest at once, for in the bottom right-hand corner of the densely inscribed page were the words: Sara Abeles, Jerusalem, followed by a street number. Staring at me.

In my relief, combined with a rather masochistic sense of disappointment, I failed to understand the significance of those words, of that name. I was just about to slip the letter back into the book when a sudden association flashed in the vaults of my memory, long since buried under the indifference of years, and I saw her in a wet, black bathing costume at the top of a diving tower at the public swimming pool in K.—Sara Abeles—and then her brown, tanned body slicing through the blue-gold air, carving above the water an aesthetic, living image in the air.

I snatched the letter back and feverishly read a random sentence in the middle of the page, for I suddenly longed to devour everything in the letter in one concentrated gulp.

As fate would have it, I managed to read the one sentence that really mattered, or rather fragments of two sentences: "... thought that this death would give me the taste of revenge, and instead it was merely a double suffering. And so now I know that the blood cannot be on our children and that you can't hate an innocent ..." but just then the bathroom door opened and Rebecca came out.

"What are you reading? Don't touch that!" she shouted, pouncing on me, ferret-like and snatching the letter out of my hand. "I've told you a thousand times to keep your hands off my things."

"I'm sorry, all right? I'm sorry," I said. "It was sticking out of a book and I saw the signature."

"So much the worse. You saw it wasn't from a guy, so why didn't you leave it alone?" Angrily, Rebecca stuffed the letter into a little black lacquered Chinese box. She wore the key to it on a golden chain around her neck. Everyone thought she was just being eccentric, but God knows.

"Did you know Sara Abeles?" I asked.

"Did you?" she countered.

"She was from K., wasn't she?"

"Yes."

"Then how could I not know her? The local sex bomb," I said cynically.

"Never mind the wisecracks," said Rebecca in an oddly chilling voice, for she was not usually upset by words like that.

"I'm sorry," I said, "but I could hardly forget her. She was made for the movies. She and Leo Feld had a kid. Quite a rarity in K. back then—a Jewish kid in 1940. The child died in Terezin, didn't it?"

Rebecca lashed me with her beautiful eyes. It was almost as if she were mocking me.

"In Auschwitz," she said. "The only blond Jewish kid in the whole camp. Have you ever seen a blond Jewish kid?"

I didn't understand why she was asking. "Why not?" I said, "I mean if Arnost—"

"But you knew Sara and Feld, didn't you?" she interrupted.

It suddenly hit me. I whistled. Of course I was only twenty-eight and I had no idea what true love was, and what women were really capable of. I whistled.

"*I* see. You think Feld wasn't the father of Sara's child at all?"

"No," Rebecca frowned. "That's not—"

Just then the doorbell rang. Rebecca looked somewhat startled. "What day is it today, anyway?" she asked.

It struck me as an illogical question, and I realized, after the fact, how logical it was. Rebecca was very absent-minded, and she had so many friends that—but that wasn't till later, when I was getting drunk in the T-Club.

Because at the door, beaming seductively and carrying a bouquet of rare winter roses, stood the famous poet Jan Vrchcólab, who was supposed to be on tour, except that Rebecca always had a thousand and one things on her mind and got everything mixed up.

So instead of finishing that conversation about Sara Abeles there was an embarrassing scene between Vrchcólab, a blushing Rebecca, and myself, glowing like a boiled lobster. I settled the whole mess by going off to the T-Club in a fit of jealousy.

We never did finish our conversation about Sara because soon after that, Rebecca passed away.

So in fact, it wasn't the final fragment of evidence about the Cuckoo after all. I discovered another of those very few clues in a brochure that came into my hands not long ago, fifteen years after Sara Abeles came back from Auschwitz.

It was a list of Czechoslovak citizens deported to the Reich whom no one had yet managed to trace. Children from Lidice, victims of the *Totaleinsatz* system who vanished into the work camps, recruits of the Organization Todt, isolated unfortunates swallowed up on the periphery of the great war. As I was glancing over those human tragedies epitomized in names that meant nothing to me, suddenly one of them struck me as being out of place. And yet it was the only one of those many names whose tragedy, or perhaps only whose history, brought a flash of memory with it—of the town of K., old Mrs. Rittenbach, Tilda, and Mr. Husa-Hüsse. For among names like Boruvka and Sedlacek was the name Horst Hüsse, born 5.2.40 in K., last known to have been sent to live with relatives in Würtenberg in 1945.

And all at once everything became utterly clear. There was no point now in going to the appropriate ministry to determine whether the ministry agents had undertaken a search for Horst Hüsse at the request of Sara Abeles, born 1922 in K. Because I knew they did. Because that is the legend, the parable, whose truth goes far beyond the mystery story in my memories.

But perhaps one link in the chain of deduction is still missing. That link is contained in the topography of K. and a conversation old Mrs. Rittenbach had with my mother after midnight mass in the first year of the war, 1939.

For Mr. Husa, when he transformed himself into Herr Hüsse, instead of wearing those dark grey double-breasted suits that shop managers wear, began to strut about in black riding boots. He moved into the villa belonging to Mr. Abeles and shifted the original owner into an abandoned gardener's shack in the far corner of the huge garden that surrounded the house. Later Mr. Abeles and his family moved away to the old Jewish schoolhouse, and later still to the ghetto in the Terezin fortress.

And it was in that little gardener's shack that Sara Abeles gave birth to a son, Moses, in February 1940, an event that caused a certain sensation in the town. At that time young Jewish women did not usually have children, for by then it was a legally questionable matter, something about not perpetuating races designated for extermination—some kind of legal measure, I believe, did exist or at least was being talked about; in any case, the intervention of an angel-deliverer, as they called midwives who specialized in abortion, would scarcely have constituted a crime in a case like that. Yet Sara had her child, a son: Moses. Moses perhaps because that name was associated with a kind of desperate hope in a man who had led Israel out of captivity.

Do you understand?

And two months before that, walking home from midnight mass, through the frost and wind of a winter's night, I overheard fragments of a whispered conversation between my mother and old Mrs. Rittenbach. "Ve can't chust leave it at that, madame," the old lady was saying in her stage whisper. "I say there must come some punishment. *Gottesstrafe*. And each of us must personally help to bring about that punishment, otherwise ve cannot look Him into the eye ..."

So this is how it was, then. Horst Hüsse briefly saw the light of day on February 5, 1940, and Moses Abeles came into that same world at almost the same time. In those days women did not give birth in hospitals. Evening, and then night, and the garden was pitch black. Newborn babes are all the same; they have to put sticking plaster on their bottoms with a name or a number on it, and in those days women gave birth alone, at home, each by herself.

So it was a fairly easy thing to accomplish. Old Mrs. Rittenbach carried out her small duty, which she hoped would assist divine retribution. Thinking it up in the first place must have been more complicated, that, and working up the courage to do it. That is also the only part of the whole affair that I cannot imagine at all. I have no idea how Sara felt about it, how she imagined it would be, how she persuaded herself that she would feel better for it, that she would even derive some satisfaction from it, the delight of revenge when, somewhere in that as yet unknown landscape of smoke and stench, they would take that child and make it a tiny fragment of that grand plan with the horrifying official title, the Final Solution, *Endlösung*, Liquidation, Normalization, or whatever name they dreamed up for it. And that her own child would become another person altogether, but would at least survive, the Cuckoo's hatchling who would never know its own—

When all these incredible yet logical and therefore perhaps even truthful things began to come together to form a picture in my mind, I remembered those sentence fragments in Sarah's letter. From the forgotten depths of my library I pulled out the book of her ancestors and read: "Then Herod ... was exceeding wroth and sent forth and slew all the children that were in Bethlehem, and in all the coasts thereof. ..." And then: "... behold, an angel of the Lord appeareth in a dream to Joseph in Egypt, saying, Arise, and take the young child and his mother, and go into the land of Israel. ..." Here was yet another piece of evidence to round the story out: the source of the Cuckoo's inspiration.

I am not an authority on maternal love. Nor am I concerned here about maternal love, about the rush of tears to the eye, about psychological pain, about a chronicle of bare events. In fact, I'm not concerned about love at all, but about the meaning of this message, this legend that is never exhausted in the telling, about the meaning of the death of a second child, so utterly different from the death of millions of other children of Auschwitz.

Because there was another child here, who was to have been killed in sacrifice and in revenge. A single child among millions, whose death was intended to arouse in the maternal bosom at least a tremor of fiery delight that always rests at the bottom of every successful revenge.

I leafed through the book again and then I remembered Sara's words. And my eyes fell on this passage: "But who so shall offend one of these little ones ... it were better for him that a millstone were hanged about his neck, and that he were drowned in the depth of the sea."

I am no expert in the language of the Bible and I don't know exactly what meaning the verb "offend" had for its pious transla-tors. In that context I have always read it as "harm," which undoubtedly is linguistically incorrect. But then my reading of that entire book is obviously incorrect, for my childhood faith has long since become hardened and replaced by scepticism. Then again, Sara's inspiration was not religious, and of course the book itself was not written by God. It is a human work, the repository of human experience.

So in the end all that remained of Sara's revenge was human tears, perhaps the most human of any tears shed by any mother in Auschwitz. For they were not the tears of instinctive motherhood, but of human sympathy, which is, thank God, deeper than the Java Trench of our hatred.

How else are we to explain Sara's words "... thought that this death would give me a taste of revenge, but instead it was merely a double suffering ..."? How else can we interpret them but as—forgive me the rhetoric—an affirmation of humanity over atavism, of man over war, over bestiality, over the skeleton winter of that incomprehensible madness?

Anyway, that was the last clue to the Cuckoo's story. Who knows what really happened and whether it was not all just a legend from a lost time? Yet she was a human cuckoo, with human young. Perhaps somewhere—God knows where, for she never found him—he will become a person unwilling to embrace any Final Solution. That is, unless he perished in those spring days of 1945 when the last of the bombs were falling to earth. Or was seduced, later, by the banners flying and the fifes playing anew their fascinating Pied-Piper song of Solutions, of Answers, of Revolutions.

1964

Fragments about
Rebecca

Rebecca stood before the large door with polished brass fittings that May afternoon and she was just about to walk away, because she wasn't certain that the Růžičkas she was looking for lived there, when she noticed that the inside cover of the glass peep-hole in the door was slowly sliding back. A wary eye appeared in it, blinked, and stared. She tried to stifle a fit of coughing and the eye went on staring at her, motionless, from inside that goy flat until she became angry and stepped up to the door.

("The door opened," Rebecca told me, "and there stood an old woman like a pyramid and I knew at once that she must have the jewellery. 'Good afternoon,' I said. 'Good afternoon,' she replied, and stared at me blankly, coldly, as though I were a Jewish interloper.")

"Mrs. Růžičková?" said Rebecca.

"Yes," replied the matron.

"I'm Rebecca Ohrensteinová," said Rebecca.

The face did not move. "Yes?" said the matron.

"I've just come back from Terezin," said Rebecca uncertainly. "I understand my father ... left some things with you for safekeeping. ..."

"With us?" said the matron, raising her eyebrows.

"At least that's what he told me," Rebecca said. "At least I think he did. At the time I was still quite ... I don't recall the exact details. But I think that's what he said ..." and she felt herself blushing.

"I think you must be mistaken, young lady," said the woman. "But please do come in," and she stood back from the door.

Rebecca went in.

"I hope I'm not bothering you," said Rebecca, while she was still in the doorway. "I've just arrived today and I have nowhere to go."

"That's perfectly all right," said the woman. She led her into the living room.

"Please sit down," she said. "If you'll excuse me a moment I'll get Rose to make us some coffee. I'm sure you'd like some coffee, wouldn't you?"

"Certainly," Rebecca laughed. She felt very out of place. The matron left the room and Rebecca looked around. The living room was cold, polished, dark brown, spotless. Cut glass in the china cabinet, a crocheted cloth covering a table like an ice rink. A shiny tiled stove stood in the corner. There were landscapes on the walls. The room was cold, even with May outside the window.

The matron entered the room and sat down opposite Rebecca. "So you've come back."

"Yes," said Rebecca.

"Please accept my sincerest condolences," said the woman. At first, Rebecca was uncertain how she meant it. "I knew your father for years, and I even knew your mother. The poor thing didn't live to see it. And as it turned out, it was just as well she didn't."

"Yes," said Rebecca. "My brother too—he didn't come back. Neither did my stepmother."

"And what about your uncle, Dr. Ohrenstein?" asked the matron. Rebecca was still unaware that more than just conventional politeness lay behind the question.

"They didn't even let him stay in Terezin," she said. "He was transported immediately to Auschwitz. He was too old."

"Where did you say?"

"To Auschwitz," said Rebecca. "That's ... that was a kind of camp where they ... it was a death camp."

"And was it because he was old?"

"Perhaps. Some were sent straight to the gas chambers."

"God in heaven," sighed the lady, and Rebecca felt, with a sudden certainty, that it was a sigh of relief. She was convinced, now, that this woman had the jewellery. As if to confirm her impression, the matron asked, "So now you're alone. You have no living relatives, is that right?"

Rebecca looked straight into her eyes and the matron looked away. But Rebecca felt happy. For the first time since they had sewn the star over her heart, she felt that she was something more than the others. She could have tormented this woman now, kept her on edge with uncertainty, but she would not do it. She looked into her eyes and said, sardonically, "Yes, I'm completely alone."

"Oh, how terrible," said the matron. "But ... it will all pass, child. Look on the bright side. You've come back, you're young, your whole life is in front of you. And now everything will be all right again. I know that ... all this ... must have been awful for you, but the pain will go away."

The hell it will, thought Rebecca. What do you know about pain, you thieving goy, you sweet-talking gramophone.

The maid brought in coffee and cakes. Rebecca was hungry.

"Help yourself, girl," the matron urged her. "Those are still wartime cakes, but I'm sure you'll find them quite tasty."

"I'm sure I will" Rebecca smiled. She took a sip of the coffee and started in on the cakes. There was a whole plate of them. The old biddy was probably saving them for Sunday. She offered them just to be polite, thinking I would take one or two and that would be that. Rebecca was determined to devour them all. She started in with a vengeance.

"About those things you mentioned," the woman began. "Your father, you understand, originally wanted to leave them with us for safekeeping, but my husband gave it some thought and he and your father decided it would be dangerous. We lived in the same building and if the Germans had done a search, our flat would be the first place they'd look, since everyone knew my husband and your father were good friends. So they decided that, the safest place to hide them would be with Mr. Patrocha on Letna."

Rebecca looked up at her in surprise. Had she been wrong to

suspect the woman? She had been reaching for another cake, but now she let her hand drop to the table.

"Patrocha? And where does he live?"

The lady shook her head sadly. "It was a tragic business," she said.

Of course, said Rebecca to herself. She reached out again for a cake and stuffed it into her mouth. "Could I have another cup of coffee?" she asked.

"With pleasure," said the matron, and poured her another cup from the pot. "We managed to make it last the whole war. It's genuine Meinl coffee, just for special occasions like this."

"It's wonderful," said Rebecca. "And what actually happened to Mr. Patrocha? I suppose the Germans killed him."

"Not just him," said the lady, donning a tragic expression. "As you know, he was a great Czech patriot and supporter of the Sokol movement. He was unit head for all of Prague 7. When Heydrich was assassinated, he and his whole family were shot. It was in the papers," she added.

("She had the whole story down pat," Rebecca told me. "She probably spent the war working out the details, just in case. All for a stupid pearl necklace or whatever it was Dad gave her to hide. But I finished off all her cakes."

I laughed. "Rebecca," I said, "that wasn't much of a deal, was it? A pearl necklace for a plate of wartime pastry?"

Rebecca grinned. "It didn't do her any good anyway. She stopped wearing the necklace for fear she'd run into me some day. But her cakes were so terrible they gave me indigestion, and my stomach aches to this day when I think of them.")

"Would you like to go for a boat ride?" I asked.

"Mm-hmm," she nodded. In the half dusk that the fog had spread across the world, she had a pale, narrow Jewish face with a fringe of hair fluffed out over her forehead and the fog shone in her glassy eyes as it had in the large window of the Alfa Café on that rainy afternoon long ago. She walked in front of me along the path to the dock and she seemed somehow stooped. The chill, rippled lake reflected only the luminous grey of the sky. I fixed the oars in the oarlocks and we pushed off. It was quiet under the fog and soon we were alone on a small circle of cold water with the mist all around us. The oars splashed the water. We moved slowly through the fog. Rebecca sat facing me, her knees together, her hands stuck into the sleeves of her sweater and she looked about her at the water. A breeze moved the fog across the lake. Up close, it was not the thick, cottony fog we had seen from the hotel terrace; it looked more like thin white smoke scudding over the water. Several metres away, it became an impenetrable white wall stretching into the opaque distance.

A fish splashed in the fog. I looked around. Rings had formed on the water and were moving toward us. At their source lay something white.

"Did you see that?" said Rebecca.

"Yes," I said. "Why is it so close to the surface?"

"I don't know," said Rebecca. "Can you row us over there?"

I turned the boat around and began rowing against the regular advancing circles; soon the prow was cutting through them. A white object was lying motionless in the water. I stopped rowing and let the momentum carry the boat forward, the wavelets splashing gently against the bow. Rebecca turned around and looked at the thing as the boat moved slowly past it.

"What's that?" she said with disgust. "Look at it!"

I stopped the boat with the oars and looked over the side. It was just beneath the surface, a sleek grey fish, belly up. I looked more closely. The fish appeared to have two tails, one on each end. A freak of nature. Repulsion, verging on horror, passed through me. I leaned over and tried to pick it up. I felt it twitch, then it turned over and slowly, helplessly, weakly, it propelled itself down into the depths with one of its tails. A sick monstrosity. Soon it floated back to the surface once more, and as it did so turned belly up again.

Now I could see what it was. There were two catfish, almost the same size, and one had evidently tried to swallow the other in a fight and had choked on it. The smaller one's tail was sticking out of the larger one's mouth, still waving back and forth, weakly, but of its own accord. Both of them were dying.

"What is it?" asked Rebecca again, with horror in her voice.

"Two catfish," I replied. "One tried to eat the other, but it was too big to swallow. Now they've both had it."

"Let's get out of here," said Rebecca. "Go on, I can't bear to look at it."

I poked at the catfish with an oar. The fins fluttered feebly and the whole monstrosity submerged once again.

"Don't do that! Let's get out of here," cried Rebecca.

I took up the oars but looked around to see if the thing would come up again. It reappeared a couple of metres further on. The bellies flashed white in the cool lustre of the water.

"Come on," cried Rebecca, "let's get out of here, Danny. Don't look at it."

But I looked at it again. I caught sight of the wide stretched mouth with that slimy body of its own kind emerging from it, still moving. Then it disappeared beneath the sheen of the water. I pulled at the oars. In the fog, the slap of fins on the water could be heard once more. The catfish were still struggling. I rowed away with quick, regular strokes across the lake. In a while, all was silent again.

Only the rain was hissing, hissing, and Rebecca was silent. Now it was time to go. She got up, dressed and we went to a movie. It was a cinematic goulash about a marital triangle, served up with progressive sauce, and I was bored to death by it. But for two whole hours Rebecca's glassy eyes sailed through a world that was different from this one.

1964

Feminine Mystique

We were sitting in the warehouse waiting for Kadeřábek. From the church on the square came the sound of the organ and the wailing of the old women:

> *Joyously we greeet thee,*
> *Mother of Our Loooooord ...*

I tried to imagine Marie in her May dress, which was dark blue with a pattern of white flowers on it; and with a blue ribbon tied around her hair so that it cascaded down her back like a waterfall of gold. When she first showed up in school with her hair that way, Lexa told me a ponytail was a phallic symbol. According to him, it meant that my chances with Marie, which had up till then been practically non-existent, were about to improve. But I hadn't yet read *Introductory Lectures on Psychoanalysis* (I was in line for it after Lexa, who'd borrowed it from someone's library) so I asked, naïvely, what a phallic symbol was. Lexa guffawed out loud. The teacher interpreted this as a deliberate disruption of his maths class, and a chain reaction took place, the climax of which came when the teacher asked Lexa about integrals, which were as much a mystery to Lexa as they were to me. Both of them—teacher and student—maintained a three-minute silence, then Lexa received an F and an official reprimand, noted in the record book, for disturbing the class.

During break, Lexa explained phallic symbol.

I stared at the golden waterfall undulating and sparkling a few paces ahead of us as we promenaded through the halls. "But that's dumb," I told him. "It sure doesn't look like one."

"But it's called a ponytail, don't you see? 'Tail' is a homonym for 'cock.'"

"Synonym," said Berta, who as usual had done his homework.

"But it's just a word. It doesn't look a bit like the thing itself," I said.

"Words can be erotic symbols too," said Lexa. "Like, Freud says that when you dream about a room, it really means a vagina."

I thought about that for a moment, and then remembered a dream I'd had the night before, about how I was in church with Marie and—I quickly suppressed the rest of it and said, "Bullshit. If that were true almost all our dreams would be—" I stopped, and then said, "I'm always dreaming about being in some maths class with the teacher trying to prove I'm a mathematical idiot. Where's the vagina in that?"

"It's in the word," said Lexa. "In German, the word for woman is *Frauenzimmer*—in other words, a female chamber. And a chamber's a hollow space, like a vagina."

"Then it's a linguistic problem, gentlemen," said Harýk. "Only Germans can be surrounded by cunts in their dreams. And maybe inhabitants of the *Ostmark*."

"Why?" asked Benno. It was generally recognized that Benno was a little slow.

"What about 'boudoir,' maestro?" said Harýk, turning to him. "Could that be a synonym for woman?"

"Depends on what a synonym is," replied Benno.

"Or a homonym?" said Lexa.

"Boudoir and woman are not homonyms," said Berta firmly.

My conscience was assuaged. Dreams of Marie in church were not immoral after all. Not in Czech, anyway.

And Marie was certainly in church right now. Her superb contralto voice was somewhere in all that wailing. I tried to pick it out but the church was too far away.

You are a jeeewel in God's heavenly crown ...

sang the old women.

"Which one are you thinking about now, dreamer?" I heard Lexa say. Quickly I returned to the warehouse. Přema was standing in front of me, and he handed me a sheet of paper.

"Can you check my spelling, Danny?" he said. "Make sure I didn't make any mistakes."

I took the document. *Brothers!* it began. *We haven't forgoten the events that happened a year ago at the Charles Univercity, when the student Jan Oplétal got shot—*

I corrected the mistakes and then said, "You should add 'sisters.'"

"What?" Přema said.

"Trust Smiřický to think of the *Frauenzimmers,*" said Lexa.

"You mean I should start it off 'Brothers and Sisters'?" asked Přema. "I don't think that's such a hot idea. Resistance isn't for girls."

He took his fiery appeal, which amounted to an invitation to kill the Germans on sight, and went over to the corner where, in a box from the First Republic marked "Czechoslovak Tobacco Board," he had hidden a small stencilling machine.

"So how come we told Kadeřábek to go ahead?" Nosek asked.

"That's different," said Přema. "Gerta has got serious reasons."

Someone rapped out the prearranged signal on the warehouse door. Přema went to open it. Kadeřábek slipped into the room and sat down on the crate that Přema had just got up from. The murky light from a single bare lightbulb that hung on a wire from the ceiling made his features stand out. He looked like the mannequin in the window of the Paris Fashion House that Berta always dressed in a tux for the winter season, when there were a lot of formal dances in town. But Kadeřábek's masculine beauty was marred by a puffy lower lip, which he hadn't had when he went off into the woods on his assignment. My lewd imagination placed its own interpretation on the puffy lip, and I found myself silently agreeing with Přema: women had no place in a resistance movement.

"Well?" said Přema.

Kadeřábek coughed.

"Will she or won't she?"

"I—uh—" said Kadeřábek, "no."

"What do you mean—no?" asked Harýk.

"She—uh—" said Kadeřábek, and again he coughed uneasily, as if to clear his throat.

We had decided to rope Gerta Wotická into our resistance group because she'd had some trouble with Leopold Váňa, and Leopold Váňa didn't want anything to do with the resistance. Or perhaps he wanted to join but his father wouldn't let him, just as he wouldn't let him have anything to do with Gerta. That was what the trouble was all about.

Like everyone else, Váňa tried to make out with girls, but whereas my efforts along those lines came to nothing for reasons that were not clear to me (in the past year I had failed twenty-two times, each time with a different girl), the reasons why Váňa had the same rate of success were as clear as day. He was, as one girl put it, boredom in trousers. Precisely what she had in mind, or precisely what it was about him that bored her, she didn't say. Lexa professed to be morally outraged by her metaphor, if that's what it was.) But Irena told me that among the girls he'd tried to get anywhere with—and so far Váňa had tried it with only three, including Irena, so she spoke from personal experience—there was a general consensus that bordered on the telepathic. In addition, Váňa didn't look too great: he was as fat as Benno, but he didn't play an instrument, and he wore old-fashioned glasses with wire frames that hooked behind his ears.

But in the end he succeeded with Gerta, which wasn't really very surprising when you thought about it. Gerta was no Rachel, although both of them were avid swimmers. Gerta was good at high diving and Rachel was the district champion in the breast-stroke, both in and out of the water. But Rachel was a real beauty; she reminded me a little of Paulette Goddard in *Modern Times*. Gerta was skinny and as far as breasts went, Benno—as Lexa put it—was two sizes bigger. She had pretty black eyes, but they were separated by a caricature of a nose—like the ones in the cartoons Rélink, the painter, started publishing just after the Germans established the Protectorate of Bohemia and Moravia. Rélink called himself an anti-Jew, an expression he'd obviously made up: right after we were annexed to the Reich, Czech was widely purged of foreign words, and I guess Rélink thought the expression "anti-Semite" was too un-Czech. At the time, Lexa set up a club of pro-Jews, but it never got anywhere because Benno—who, as he said himself, was a half-Jew—refused to be president. Also, it soon became clear that anti-Jewishness wasn't going to be just a joke, the way the painter Rélink was a joke, so we quickly forgot about the club. Mainly, as a matter of fact, because of the trouble Gerta got into.

Anyway, Váňa finally made it with Gerta during the winter vacation in the Krkonoše Mountains in 1938, when Gerta saved his life. Váňa was a terrible skier. He couldn't go more than a few metres without falling and no one would ever go out on the slopes with him. One day while he was out alone, he fell and broke his leg, and of course he couldn't move. It happened in a ravine, right near a waterfall, so no one could hear his cries for help. A fog came down and the rest of us retreated to the chalet. No one missed Váňa until Gerta noticed he wasn't at supper because there were dumplings left over. Meanwhile the fog had dispersed and the hillsides were sparkling in the starlight. We lit some torches and set off to look for him. It was the first time we'd ever been on skis at night. Lucie applied her torch to the seat of Harýk's pants, making him yelp, then we all started fooling around and forgot about Váňa again. With a finger gloved in pink wool, Marie was pointing up in the sky at Venus with exaggerated interest, and I was just looking up at the planet of love when I caught sight of a flickering light quickly descending into the ravine by the waterfall. It was Gerta. Perhaps she and Váňa were destined for each other.

But they weren't, though it seemed that way at first, both socially and sexually. Mr. Váňa and Mr. Wotický owned the two biggest textile stores in Kostelec; one of them had an only son, the other an only daughter; the daughter was no Aphrodite and the son was no Adonis, more like Hephaestus (particularly after his skiing accident, which left him with a limp). It looked like a serious relationship—a little premature, perhaps, since Váňa was only in the sixth form and Gerta in the fifth, but that was hardly exceptional. That summer one of Gerta's classmates, Libuše Benešová, who was also no Aphrodite, got married a day after she turned sixteen. Not that she had to, but her father, Dr. Guth-Moravský, was pushing eighty and was afraid he wouldn't last till the plums ripened. It was an open secret in Kostelec that Mr. Beneš, the head waiter of the Beránek Café, wasn't Libuše's father, although he purported to be, just as he wasn't the father of her older sister Teta, who'd got married the year before, a day after she graduated from high school—nor of her eldest sister, Kazi, who had to wait a full year after graduation before Dr. Guth-Moravský finally managed to get her hitched. In her case, of course, he wasn't in any hurry; at the time he was only seventy-five and still took part in the Christmas polar-bear marathon swim in the Vltava River. And it was obvious to everyone in Kostelec that the head waiter hadn't built his villa below Černá Hora, designed by a famous Prague architect, from the money he made in tips. Even if there were people gullible enough to believe it, they might well have wondered why all three of the girls with pagan names were as ugly as night, when their father was an elegantly handsome man with a Clark Gable moustache and their mother, now in her early forties, looked like an eighteen-year-old model from Rosenbaum's fashion salon in Prague. The gullible, had they wondered, might have explained it as a freak of nature, but the rest of us knew why: the president's advisor, Dr. Guth-Moravský, looked like those paintings of troglodytes in anthropology textbooks. As well as being the author of a famous manual of social etiquette, Dr. Guth-Moravský had written a work called *The Mores and Customs of Czech Paganism*, which explained why he'd named his daughters after women from old Czech legends. It was also whispered that he had accumulated his fortune not as a famous man of letters or from his official salary, but as a marriage-broker for the old Austro-Bohemian aristocrats.

So a serious relationship between a girl from the fifth form and a boy from the sixth was more a rule than an exception at the Kostelec high school. We had some shining examples in the band. Benno had been going with Alena since the third form, but it was Harýk who had broken all the records of this odd tradition. In the spring of '38, after the municipal physician, Dr. Eichler, conducted his annual check-up of the students, he summoned the architect, Mr. Hartmann—who was Lucie's father—to his office. When Hartmann came home, Lucie's brother told us, he took a belt to her without a word of explanation and then put her under house arrest for three months, although it was too late, of course, to save her virginity. The reasons didn't remain a mystery for long because Dr. Eichler's son, who was studying Latin and was bored to tears, had heard Mr. Hartmann through his father's office door lamenting his daughter's fate, and of course he couldn't keep such sensational news to himself. At the time, Lucie was in the second form and Harýk in the fourth.

Gerta and Váňa had a serious relationship, but whether it was true love or not was another matter. It looked more to me like making a virtue of necessity. Although I wasn't really capable of understanding something like that—since of course all twenty-two of my attempts had been made when I was in love, at least while the attempt lasted—I knew such things existed, because people aren't all the same, except insofar as they're all after that one thing. So I supposed it wasn't passion that kept them together, but simply the fact that Váňa couldn't get anyone else, that and Gerta—

That was another one of the open secrets of the Kostelec high school: of all the girls who had fallen for the magic of Kadeřábek's model-like good looks, Gerta had fallen the hardest. And if all the victims were suffering from a form of night-blindness, Gerta was living in a permanent fog—or rather, in the heart of a Babylonian darkness. From the third form on, Kadeřábek had been fast friends with František Buřtoch, despite the fact that Buřtoch was ten years older. Buřtoch's father, a butcher, had disinherited his son when, upon completing his butcher's apprenticeship, František had set up a business in antiques and *objets d'art* using money left him by a bachelor friend. So the thing was obvious, but not to those night-blind girls who secretly, with hard-won money, bribed a photographer to sell them studio portraits of Kadeřábek. In short, love had blinded them, or perhaps they'd been raised so properly that the truth about Kadeřábek's preferences had simply eluded them, though I knew them too well to really believe that.

Kadeřábek was indeed a perverse Adonis. Instead of playing tennis, he was a shot-put ace for the Kostelec Sports Club, which was also why athletics suddenly became so popular with the girls that Kostelec had the largest club of young female hopefuls in the entire district, and also the best, because otherwise there wasn't much competition in women's athletics. The only girl who drove herself around the cinder track because she really liked doing it was Irena, but she was perverse about it too. Otherwise the girls would jog around the soccer field or leap into the long-jump pits for reasons that were clear, if not low and immoral. Marie, unfortunately, was not one of them, although I'd have loved to see her in shorts. Perhaps her boyfriend had emotionally neutralized her.

Gerta had done high diving since she'd been a little girl and now, having succumbed to the magic of Kadeřábek, she took up the high jump and eventually broke the junior women's record. But it didn't do her any good. The day when she made a name for herself came later: the heavy shot slipped out of Kadeřábek's hand and fell behind him, and Gerta rushed out of the crowd of admiring girls, picked the shot up, and ran to return it to the astonished athlete.

So it was as clear as day.

But whether this was passion or not, in the autumn of '39 Gerta didn't come to school for two days, and when she finally showed up her beauty carried another blemish: her large nose now glowed like a peony and there were big red circles around her pretty black eyes. Váňa stopped waiting for her after school, and on Saturday he came into the Beránek alone for the tea dance and tried to dance with Alena, but he stepped so hard on her shoes that she cried out, and he then sat by himself until the end of the dance, glowering into his lemonade.

Because we weren't very fond of him, and because Gerta looked so miserable, we went over to his table during the *Jauzepause* and Lexa spoke to him:

"What did you do to her, you murderer?"

"Nothing. I stepped on her corns. It could happen to anyone."

"I'm not talking about Alena. Don't tell me you don't know who I mean!"

Váňa said nothing.

"Well, sir, are you going to explain yourself?" said Harýk.

"It's not my fault," said Váňa.

"She dumped you, right?"

"No, she didn't."

"Then how come you ditched her? You were just stringing her along, weren't you?"

"No, I wasn't," said Váňa.

We looked at each other and shook our heads.

"OK, then. If she didn't come across, that's your fault. You had a year and a half to work on it. But that's still no reason for you to shit on her."

"I didn't shit on her."

"So how come you're not going out with her any more? Can't you see the poor girl's suffering?" said Lexa.

Váňa was silent again.

"What lies are you concocting now, sir?" asked Harýk.

Suddenly Váňa blurted out: "She's a Jew!"

We were floored. That was when we realized that all this anti-Semitic stuff wasn't a joke any more. But how could Váňa be such a jerk?

"You hardly seem a zealous enough Catholic, sir, to object to the religious affiliation of your bedmate," said Harýk.

"It's got nothing to do with religion," wailed Váňa. "You know what this is all about."

"Do we know what this is all about, gentlemen?" asked Harýk, looking around at us. We all shook our heads.

"It doesn't bother me a bit, seriously," said Váňa quickly. "But my old man—"

There are some fools in the world who obey the fourth commandment to the letter, that their days may be long on this earth. Their thoughts should be on heaven, but they're not. We couldn't get Váňa to budge. Probably he had nothing personal against Gerta. But he wanted his days to be long on this earth, just like his old man.

So Kadeřábek was queer, but otherwise he was ready for any mischief. The students of Moses' faith still went to the high school, but from the way things were going it was pretty clear that even the Jews in the eighth form wouldn't make it to matriculation. Soon after Váňa ditched her, Gerta had to sew a yellow star over her negligible breasts, but that was after her second, and worse, disaster. Then Mrs. Mánesová began wearing a star, and Rachel too, except that by the end of 1938, at least according to Father Meloun's records, she was married to Tonda Kratochvíl. For the longest time only Father Meloun knew about it, because it had been a secret wedding. Why it was secret when the parish records said it had taken place in '38, back during the First Republic, wasn't clear. The explanation came in '41 when we were rehearsing the school revue, but that's another story. Benno kept attending school even after the stars started appearing, and so did his sister Věra, because they were only half-Jews. I began to like Věra more and more, but I didn't try my luck with her a second time (although otherwise I had nothing against second and third and sometimes even fourth and fifth attempts, and, in the case of Marie and Irena, I'd lost track because there were no computers in those days). But not for the same reason that Váňa had dumped Gerta. Even people of mixed race were beginning to feel the heat now, because at any moment the Germans could up the "racial awareness" ante, though God knew when. And I didn't want Věra to think I was exploiting the situation or taking an interest in her as an act of mercy, or that I was trying to silence a bad Aryan conscience, since I was, well, an Aryan. I didn't know. I wasn't sure why I was so reluctant. I was just a jerk. But a different kind from Váňa.

I also can't remember who first got the idea. Whoever it was, he got it after Kadeřábek, of all people, came up with the notion of starting a resistance movement. It's hard to say which idea was more stupid. When I told Přema about it, he swore me to silence and then told me that they already had a resistance movement, of people in trades, and that he, Přema, was the leader. Přema had originally been a student at the business academy, but after 1939, out of pure patriotism, he'd refused to learn German. In fact, the teacher couldn't get a single word of German out of him, so the principal quickly expelled him from the academy. In his own interest, he went to explain it personally to Přema's father, Mr. Skočdopole. At first Mr. Skočdopole, as a former legionnaire, was somewhat crusty with him. But then, he pulled out a bottle of home-made slivovitz, a gift from his brother in Moravia, and they both got drunk under a portrait of President Masaryk, from which Mr. Skočdopole had removed, for the occasion, a picture of Božena Němcová with which he'd covered up Masaryk when the Protectorate was declared. Finally they both agreed that Přema had had it coming, and then they fell asleep. Now Přema decided that we should combine the groups so we'd have connections with the intellectuals as well as ordinary people, and one idea led to another until finally someone said we should also have connections with the Jews, who happened to have the best reasons for getting mixed up in a resistance movement, and as a final idea, someone said, "Gerta."

"We can rely on her," said Nosek. "In a way, she's already been hit by the German laws."

"But she's a girl," objected Přema.

"Well—" said Lexa, and he was going to continue, but then

stopped and said, "As a matter of fact, she is."

"Girls are timid," said Přema.

"Sure they are!" said Harýk. "Look, would you have the guts to dive off a thirty-foot tower?"

"I can't swim," said Přema.

"Lord!" said Harýk.

We were silent. Then Kadeřábek said, "In a democratic state girls are equal. And according to physiological research, they can stand more punishment than men, relatively speaking."

This sounded strange coming from him. The short sleeves on his elegant shirt barely covered his bulging biceps.

"But not emotionally," said Lexa.

"Bullshit. Look at Joan of Arc," said Nosek.

We were silent again. Then I said, "A girl who's not afraid to dive from a thirty-foot tower must have a pretty good set of nerves."

In the end we decided that Gerta, girl or not, must have nerves like Tarzan, and that furthermore, because of that jerk Váňa, she'd been the first in the school to suffer the consequences of Nazism, so she had better reasons for doing this than we did.

The next question was who would talk to her.

"Wee Daniel, of course," said Harýk, meaning me. "He's the champion talker."

"But he's not the champion persuader," said Lexa. "At least not of ladies."

By this time my embarrassing reputation had ceased to bother me.

Then came the final idea, the most brilliant of all, and I was the one who had it. "I have someone better in mind."

"Who? Berta?" asked Lexa. Berta involuntarily twitched and blushed.

"No," I said. "Květomil."

Květomil was Kadeřábek's first name. An appropriate name at that. Flower-lover.

"Gentlemen—" Kadeřábek was clearly taken aback. "I'm not—I mean, that kind of thing's not my—my cup of tea."

"This is politics, not erotics, sir," said Lexa.

"Besides that, you're the chairman," I said. "Or I mean the commander."

"And Gerta's always had a crush on you," said Harýk. "Remember the time she brought you back the shot-put?"

"Go ahead and have your fun," said Kadeřábek. "I don't mind. But it's not my cup of tea."

"I repeat: it's a matter of politics, not erotics," said Harýk.

"Or of politics through erotics," I said, "and the end justifies the means."

Because we were a democratic resistance movement, we put the matter to a vote, and decided that Květomil would be the one to establish contact with Gerta.

He tried next day during the lunch break. That morning an embarrassing situation had arisen during the first lesson, which was in German. Ilse Seligerová stood up and asked Miss Althammerová to make Gerta sit in the back row. Ilse had been sitting beside Gerta since the first form. She was German and preferred speaking German, even though the class was conducted largely in Czech. Miss Althammerová was a German too, but even so she asked Ilse, "*Warum den?*"

"*Sie wissen doch, Fräulein Doktor,*" replied Ilse icily.

Miss Althammerová turned red, took a deep breath, then exhaled and said, in a quiet voice, "*Na gut—wenn Gerta nichts dagegen hat.*"

Gerta burst into tears and ran to the back row where the overweight Petridesová sat. The classroom was as silent as a tomb. I saw Petridesová give Gerta her handkerchief.

Petridesová was walking through the halls beside Gerta during the lunch break when Květomil joined them, perspiring. Petridesová played fifth wheel for a while, then discreetly went off to the girls' washroom. With a shiny face, Květomil promenaded around the halls with Gerta, speaking to her while she raised her red-rimmed eyes to him. When the bell rang, I saw that the shot-put champion was smiling.

"So, what happened?" asked Harýk.

"Well—I established contact," said Květomil.

"And—is she for it?"

"We didn't get that far. I have to sound her out first, don't I?"

"Oh, Lord. And how did you 'sound her out'?"

"Well, we talked about movies and—"

"And what?"

"And so on," said Květomil.

"And then?"

"And then the bell rang."

So the first contact was just reconnoitring.

In the week that followed, Květomil must have discussed the entire history of the cinema with Gerta, because he couldn't think of anything else to talk about. Gerta's gaze became more and more amorous. He could have talked to her about bowel disease, or even about the resistance, and Gerta wouldn't have minded. The red circles around her beautiful eyes vanished, and her nose regained its accustomed whiteness. But they never got beyond what Květomil called "sounding out." Finally, at the end of the week, he said, "I can't do it in school. I'll have to invite her somewhere."

"You should have done that long ago, you jerk," said Lexa.

"Take her to the movies," said Harýk.

"That's even worse than school."

"Make a date to see her in the woods," I said. "No one will hear what you say there."

And so Květomil invited Gerta to meet him in the woods in a small meadow called By the Cottage—although the cottage, which had once belonged to a shepherd, was in ruins. The meadow was overgrown with an aromatic moss—not long before, I had tried to intoxicate Irena with its perfume. In vain, of course.

From the window of Mánes's villa we watched as Květomil—in corduroy trousers and one of his elegant shirts, beneath which his cultivated muscles rippled—strode into the forest. After ten minutes Gerta walked across the bridge to the brewery. She was wearing a Sunday dress.

Later we sat in the warehouse and waited for Květomil, and possibly for Gerta, if he'd managed to persuade her. Time dragged and this didn't augur well. Or perhaps it did. Finally Květomil himself showed up and said, "I—uh—no."

"Wait a minute," said Harýk. "What do you mean, no?"

"She—" said Květomil—and delicately, he touched his tellingly swollen lip, which I had misinterpreted.

So I don't know. I guess we made a mistake. We chose the wrong tactics. We were young and stupid. We held the glories of this world in contempt, but we had no a idea how to read its subtler signals. Three years later—where did Gerta end up? Back then, she could probably think things through more clearly than I could, than Lexa could. Everything. The resistance and love. Anyway, our resistance group faded away too, and for all I know it may have had something to do with Gerta. Only Přema stuck to it, probably because at the time he hadn't understood anything at all. Přema wasn't much for the girls, though his reasons weren't the same as Květomil's. He was naturally shy, he didn't understand girls and was even afraid of them. I wasn't afraid of them, but did I understand them? It had been my dumb idea to use her queer idol to persuade her to join us. So I didn't understand girls worth a damn either.

We could still hear the old women singing in the church.

The jewel of all the heaaavens thou aaaaart...

I no longer tried to make out Marie's sweet voice in that infernal, or perhaps heavenly, wailing.

"She what?" asked Harýk.

"Well," said Květomil, "I didn't want to come right out with it, so I began to—" He stopped.

"Don't tell me," said Lexa. "You talked about movies."

"No, about athletics. Then about swimming," said Květomil.

"Wonderful," said Harýk, looking at his watch. "God, how could swimming and the shot-put take up four hours of anyone's time! That must be a district record. Maybe even a world record!"

"We talked about literature too," said Květomil.

"Now that could only have taken you five minutes," I said. I knew that the only printed matter Květomil ever read was the illustrated sports weekly *Start*.

"And then about politics," said Květomil.

"And did you tell her what you were supposed to?" asked Harýk impatiently.

"I began slowly so I wouldn't frighten her, right?" said Květomil. "I said I'd been watching her for a long time, and that of all the girls at school she'd always seemed to me kind of—"

"Kind of what?" said Harýk.

"Kind of—the most mature. And—and the most interesting."

I could imagine them there in the tiny meadow, sitting on that aromatic moss that almost, but not quite, intoxicated Irena. I could see Gerta hanging on Květomil the Adonis with her beautiful Jewish eyes—and suddenly I realized what the mistake had been. Of course. Gerta hadn't paid any attention to his talk about the shot-put. She was in fifth heaven when they sat down on the moss, in sixth when she breathed in its aroma, and when he started babbling on about how she was the most mature and the most interesting of all the girls in the school, she arrived in seventh heaven. Then she was overwhelmed by that feeling they write about in novels, and she flew to him, as they say, on the wings of love, and cleaved to him in a long, passionate kiss until his lip swelled up, and he never managed to blurt out his more important message to her.

Thou art the jewel of hiiiiighest heaven ...

"Well, and then I said it," I heard Květomil say. "That we'd decided to invite her into our resistance group—"

And again, for the tenth time, he fell silent.

"And what did she say?" Harýk blurted out.

For a moment, Květomil looked as though he'd just tumbled out of the sky.

"She slapped my face," he said. "And then she ran away."

A silence fell over the warehouse. The only sound was the singing of the old women in the church on the square.

"You can't figure women out," said Květomil. "At least I sure can't."

1989

III

An Interlude

An Insoluble Problem of Genetics

From the secret diary of Vasil Machanin,
third form student at the Leonid Brezhnev High School in K.[1]

Our fatherland extends a generous hand to many nations, and a certain number of dark-skinned African students come to our town to take preparatory courses in the Czech language. Later they laud the good name of our nation far beyond our borders. But my brother Adolf lost his lifelong happiness because of their over-friendly attitude toward the population.

This is how it happened: for two long years Adolf was secretly in love with the movie star Jana Brejchová. He wrote her more than two hundred letters during this time. However, the film celebrity did not show a comparable interest in my brother, and so Adolf began to pursue Freddie Mourek, whose skinny figure and comely features resembled somewhat those of the aforementioned actress.

Our parents approved his choice because Freddie, as the illegitimate daughter of the secretary of the party cell at the Lentex linen factory in K., came from a family with an excellent class profile. Only a single flaw disturbed the very positive impression made by Adolf's girlfriend on our family, and that was her given name. One day at our house, Freddie sang a certain loud song in a foreign language, to the accompaniment of Adolf's bass guitar. To my father's uneasy inquiry concerning the origins of the song she answered that it was a black American song, whose lyrics protested against discrimination. Father applauded, then briefly extolled the black struggle for equality. After that he suddenly became very angry, and turning dark red, he began to curse the South African racists. Mother also became angry, and in the resulting friendly atmosphere Father asked Freddie why a thoroughly progressive girl like herself, an activist of the Young Communist League, would call herself by a name of English origin.

At that Freddie blushed and said that she could now reveal to them the secret of her name because she had just agreed to marry Adolf in a civil ceremony prior to the final matriculation examinations. Father was very heartened by the news as he happens to be in favour of early marriage for young people in their reproductive years, since these are called for by the appropriate authorities in an attempt to prevent population decrease. He then encouraged Freddie to reveal her secret without delay.

"I inherited my name from my father," she said. "He was a certain Frederick Positive Wasserman Brown, a migrant worker from South Carolina, who as a member of General George Patton's Third U.S. Army seduced my mummy in Pilsen, and then had himself transferred to the Far East." "An American?" Father recoiled and turned gloomy. Then he partially recovered: "A migrant worker?" and Freddie, attempting to aid the complete recovery of my father, who had earlier lauded so eagerly the heroic struggle of the coloured people, quickly added: "Yes. And besides, my father was black." Against all expectations Father's gloom became permanent.

In the following days he began to bring books by a certain Lysenko home from the People's Municipal Library; unable to find in them a satisfactory answer to what he was looking for, he borrowed a volume of the botanist friar Mendel with pictures of various types of peas, white, grey, and black ones. He studied those very diligently, and later when Freddie again sang at our house Negro songs in a foreign language, he asked: "Listen, girl, that father of yours, was he a very black black, or was he of a lighter hue?" "Very black," said Freddie, who is herself very white, but has very black, large, and beautiful eyes. "So black that during the war they used him in reconnaissance. In the darkest night, completely naked, he would penetrate through the German lines, since he was completely invisible." And Father turned once again gloomy and said no more.

However, that evening he advised Adolf to break off, without delay, his relationship with the black man's daughter. Adolf resisted. "I'm not a racist!" "Neither am I," replied Father. "If Freddie were a dark-skinned girl I would welcome her as a daughter-in-law, because your union with a girl who obviously belonged to a race that is persecuted elsewhere would doubtless even further enhance the class profile of our family. But she is white. There arises the danger, that on the basis of the reactionary biological laws determined by the friar Mendel, she will bear you a black child, and there will be a scandal!" "What scandal? Black or white, it's all the same," Adolf rejoined, and Father explained, "Nobody will believe that this black child is really yours. Everybody will think that it is the result of the efforts of our guests, the African students, and in that sense they will also slander your wife." And he concluded: "Which is why you will break off the relationship before it is too late."

Adolf turned crimson, and said ponderously, "It is already too late. It is impossible to break off the relationship." A deadly silence prevailed, interrupted only by Mother's moaning and Father's fidgeting. From that day on, Adolf devoted himself to a careful study of the writings of the friar Mendel.

No doubt it was too late; it was, I imagine, because Adolf loved Freddie much more than he had ever loved Jana Brejcová, although he almost never sent her any letters. Freddie's mother, the textile worker and Party secretary, was invited to our house, and I, hidden behind the large portrait of the Statesman, which conceals the hole where Grandfather's wall safe used to be, over-heard Mother emphasizing the terribly tender age of both the children and asking the esteemed secretary's consent to apply to some sort of a committee in the matter of an absorption (or something that sounded like that). I really could not understand why the Comrade Mother (Mrs. Mourek) got upset to the point of refusing to co-operate with the committee, slammed the door and left, when on other occasions, as a class-conscious woman, she had always shown full confidence in committees, councils, and organs of all kinds.

It did not end there: the comrade secretary of the Party cell at the Lentex linen factory in K. provided us with a further unexpected surprise. Soon after, when Father, Mother, my older sister Margaret, and even Adolf himself began spreading all around town that Freddie's father was the migrant black Frederick Positive Wasserman Brown, and at the same time introducing the people to the laws of heredity according to which a completely white person could give birth to a black child thanks to the genes of her progenitor (in order to pre-empt any criticism or damage to the reputation of Freddie in case of a child with other than Czech colouring), Comrade Mourek appeared again, and her squealing voice could be heard from the parlour, expressing herself to the effect that Father, Mother, Margaret, and Adolf were giving the girl (meaning Freddie) a bad name around town and causing trouble, of which she (Comrad Mourek) had had more than enough throughout her life, the result of some youthful transgression. And although Father immediately declared himself the enemy of bourgeois morality, and attempted to explain his intentions to her, he failed nonetheless.

Adolf deteriorated visibly, until finally he spoke about nothing else but the friar Mendel. This aroused the suspicion of the principal of the high school, Comrade Pavel Běhavka, who for several Sundays stationed himself at his usual table at the Café Beránek and carefully observed the entrance to the Catholic church in the town square (later on adding also the chapel of the Czech Protestants and that of the Czech Evangelical Brethren to his surveillance), to find out whether Adolf, as a result of being converted to the obscurantist faith of the friars, visited the services. He did not, but having been psychologically traumatized, he would acquaint everyone, on any occasion, even completely strange comrades, with the secret of the background of his fiancée Freddie, and lecture them on the laws of genetics. Finally, after a large number of arguments, fights, and confrontations, Freddie broke up with him. To the accompaniment of his bass guitar they sang together for the last time the protest song "Get Me a New Dolly, Molly!" and then she declared (I overheard it secretly, hidden behind the portrait of the Statesman): "Your indiscretion is getting on my nerves, and I don't intend to put up with it any longer. Also, I would like you to know that I haven't told you everything: for your information, the mother of my father Frederick Positive Wasserman Brown was Japanese, and his grandfather, who was brought over from Africa as a slave in chains, was a Pygmy, all of which, combined with the fact that my mother is one-third Jewish gypsy, leaves me with a very good chance of giving birth to a green dwarf. Your father could never explain *that* to the comrades, with or without his Mendel. So good-bye forever, my little imbecile!"

Having said that, she left forever; and so my brother, deprived of his lifelong happiness by the presence of the African students, did not become a father.

Some time later Freddie gave birth to twins: one is a boy and the other a girl, and both are completely pink. However, about that phenomenon Mendel says nothing at all.

1985

1. *Every week a group of writers assembled in Prague to read satirical, farcical stories. The texts shown to the censors differed, sometimes considerably, from the ones actually read aloud in the small theatre. "An Insoluble Problem of Genetics" was one of a series written by Josef Skvorecky; a popular form in the sixties, called "Text Appeals," it was one way of circumventing censorship.*

IV
The Evil Empire

Three Bachelors
in a
Fiery Furnace

On Saturday evenings in the spring the girls would appear in sensational short skirts and cinnamon coats, and the flawless whiteness of their petticoats shone in the rosy light of the setting sun. During the week the girls worked hard, but Saturday evening was a holiday.

In the mornings they usually hurried, skipping breakfast, because they all wanted to be slim, and I would see them in the early morning, flitting through the fog to the spinning mill. They came back in the afternoon, a parade of them thronging through town as soon as the sirens sounded. They would vanish behind the scratched gates of their decrepit houses, in the entrails of which they would devote themselves to some secret female activity.

But on Saturday evening they emerged, the Kočandrle girls, Mary and Magdelene, and they would set out on a pilgrimage along the town's promenade on a walk leading nowhere, just to swing those skirts on stiff petticoats and defiantly flash their lacy whiteness, in the twilight of our youth.

Meduna, Schultz, and I had been swaying up and down the street from six o'clock on, and the blush of spring, which didn't belong to us any more, was destroying us: Meduna, a stout locksmith with a not very active imagination, wearing an intensely elegant jacket of checked spring fabric, his good-natured face hidden by his Styl hat as he placidly lit an Orient cigarette; and Schultz, our thin old pal from the tobacconist's, with bright, beautiful eyes that nobody ever noticed and a Mongol face full of trust—an ageing hunter from the distant steppes of childhood.

A few people walked by, even some girls, and Meduna's eyes hunted among them. But I saw them coming on the opposite sidewalk, with their Moroccan collars, their cheeks like dog roses, their sky-blue skirts and stiletto heels tapping out tender periods after their hopes. The wall of sheer misunderstanding there can be between people is just awful; a mere difference of age and intelligence—such a misfortune. The very artful Molly, the prostitute from Holešovice, talked scornfully about such girls—just to talk. But I was bold. I obstinately believed that if I just had one more opportunity like the one during the winter, everything would be different, and Mary or Magdelene, it didn't matter which, would talk like Sappho, like our beautiful, sweet Božena Němcová.

"Let's go," said Schultz

"Wait," I said. The gold swan on the apothecary building glowed in the evening's rosy light. The incredibly pink, sticky, slowly flowing light was dripping, like watered-down blood, down the front of the building and onto the sidewalk over which they were approaching.

"Good evening, camellias," I said quietly. But they didn't answer. Their little heads like blackthorns drifted, sweet but haughty, through the pink lemonade. Perhaps they didn't know whether *camellias* was singular or plural. I didn't know either. And I didn't care. Plural, singular, dual, it's all the same.

"So, let's go!" I said to Meduna. And we went. Oh, hell. My heart was aching. That pink syrup on the pavement of the street. Ah, camellias! Ah, ladies, ah, my friends from the spinning mill, you had such hard hearts where I was concerned, you passed by so coldly, and never knew the damage you did, the wreckage you left behind.

When I looked back they were already far away, and only the white froth of their lace petticoats was still sending out luminous signals into the rosy dusk. But their signals weren't aimed at me; they didn't care about me, only about some young newcomers, know-nothings in Texas Levi's, who hadn't yet learned their Morse code. Nobody learns it, until it's too late. Until it's no use any more.

"Let's go somewhere where there's music," said Meduna.

"Let's go to the Graf," suggested Schultz.

So we headed for the Graf, but when we got there I didn't want to go in. Hadinec had just come from there.

"Ahoy, Hadinec," said Meduna.

"Ahoy," said Hadinec. And then, "Don't go in there, it's really dead."

"Are there any girls there?" asked Schultz.

"No."

"No girls at all?"

Hadinec shook his head.

"So let's go to the Sport," said Meduna. We went. The sky grew dark, but red streaks still flared through it like angels' swords banishing people from Paradise. This might be the last spring. Day after day was dropping from the calendar of our life, and those beautiful twins, Mary and Magdalene, would soon be married, maybe even within the year. In a year we might not even be on the earth any more. I was really sorry about it.

We reached the Sport Hotel and stopped; we looked at each other uncertainly, and Meduna nodded. Silhouettes behind the frosted glass door stirred, and then it opened. Inside we saw a little table with an empty saucer for money and a fresh pad of admission tickets, a man with a delightfully welcoming smile, and the deserted, bare corridor that led to the underground night club. We stood there as if paralysed, and stared in silence down the cool, endless corridor. The smile on the man's face lingered for a while, but then it faded away. He closed the milky glass door. Meduna turned around and looked up at the dark sky over the station, where cold, damp stars were beginning to appear through the rosy flames. Schultz swore. Meduna's eyes were full of a vast masculine weariness, I felt hideously sad, so sad I thought I might be dying. Meduna, looking somewhere in the direction of the spring stars, said in a tired voice, "Everywhere they are enticing, and everywhere ..."

1963

The End

of

Bull Mácha

*For Jan Hammer, Sr., in memoriam
and for Vlasta Průchová-Hammer, in fond memory*

*Das Spiel ist ganz und gar verloren,
Und dennoch wird es weitergehen.*
(The game is totally lost, and yet it will go on.)
—Erich Kästner

Bull Mácha was leaning against the pedestrian railing at the corner of Vodičková Street and Wenceslas Square. The thin mist of a dank afternoon was slowly falling into the streets, blurring the features of the people trudging past him. The streets were coming alive with the bustle of a Sunday evening in the big city. Through the silvery grey veil of a damp autumn dusk the lights in the store windows and cafés were coming on, and the faces of the girls Bull Mácha's impassive eyes were stalking in the crowd seemed to assume a new and mysterious charm under the misty, magic chiaroscuro of artificial lighting. Their hazy beauty touched him like a sudden pain, and in the depths of his heart he longed to draw close to them in a place where one could get closest of all: a café, one of the dance halls whose windows were already beginning to glow through the spidery mist that was slowly descending upon the city of Prague. It was the month of November in the year of our Lord 1953.

The figure leaning against the green railing, with his low, carefully combed coiffure turned to face the flaming entrance of the Soviet Book Shop, was in his own way a living human fossil. At the age of twenty-nine, František Mácha still referred to himself by his old nickname, Bull, in full "Gablik" Bull—Zoot-Suiter Bull—and he insisted that others do so too. And the vague notion of belonging to a grand conspiracy against something uncertain, a conspiracy he still felt a part of, was epitomized, even after all these years, by the nickname "Gablik," "Little Gable." It was an expression that had stuck to him long ago, during the vogue for a popular American Civil War movie and the actor who had played its raffish, devil-may-care hero.

Now Gablik Bull Mácha was standing on the corner of Vodičková Street and Wenceslas Square, his heart lacerated by those winsome, cosmetically improved young faces, and by a strange, miserable nostalgia. He was alone, his hands stuffed into enormous pockets, and from the overcoat, cut strictly according to fashion with the sloping shoulders of a wine bottle and a collar as wide as an acolyte's, a small head emerged, with a painstakingly fashioned coif in front and the sides slicked back into a ducktail. From that face two watery grey eyes stared: dull, bored, desperate. Bull had the heel of his left foot hooked over the bottom rung of the green railing, with his leg swung over as far as he could to the left, and he had pulled up his narrow trouser leg to avoid making a bulge at the knee, so that all might remark on his black-yellow-and-green-striped socks and gaze in wonder at the Gothic upturned toes of his Hungarian winklepickers. He was especially proud of those winklepickers with their snow-white soles flashing in the descending fog like crown jewels, cared for with boundless love and worn only on ceremonial occasions.

But Bull Mácha's soul was sad. He stood, erect and motionless above the crowds flowing from the square into Vodičková Street and back, like a solitary rock in the tide, alone, lonesome and rejected. And in the pain that gripped his heart, he remembered another age, and evenings like this, with the chiaroscuro lighting, the cold, the bright shop windows, when he wasn't alone, when crowds of people his own age, his cronies, would mill about together, and the strange, magic words of an exotic language no one had ever used before flew back and forth through the air, and from the Boulevard Café down below came the Dixieland sound of Graeme Bell, and up above in the Phoenix, Frankie Smith was singing and Leslie "Jiver" Hutchinson was blowing his horn and the sharp, bebop riffs of Dunca Brož drifting up from the underground wine bar tugged invitingly at his ears. Where had those times gone? Where was Kandahár, the tenor player with those tight black negro curls? Where was Harýk? Where was Lucie?

Gablik Bull Mácha was the only one left. He knew exactly where the rest were, and the question that had surfaced in his sad, nostalgic thoughts was only figurative, rhetorical. Kandahár the tenorman, whose real name was Nývlt, was now an architect with Stavoprojekt. He was married, and his wife went to chamber music concerts and was studying to be an opera singer. That had been the end of Gablik Kandahár. And Venca Štern, the trombonist with the magnificent, crackling, tailgating style? He was manager of some factory that made movie screens in the border district. Harýk was in the jug for an illegal attempt to cross the border and Lucie, determined to remain faithful to him, worked as a secretary at the Central Council of Revolutionary Trade Unions.

He was the only one left, unmarried, unchanged, just as he had been back in the nylon age. He was still willing to bloody his knuckles to get into a public recording session by Karel Vlach's swing band, which—like him—was all that was left of those wonderful things. He was alone, the last of his clan, and when he wanted to find a spirit that was even slightly kindred he had to hang out with seventeen-year-old punks who didn't even know what the word *gablik* meant.

And so now he stood at the corner of Vodičková Street and Wenceslas Square, a historic site that was part of a faded, bygone world, and as his eyes flitted from face to face, he said to himself, "Shit, there's no one here, no one in the whole damn city of Prague." He had nowhere to go. He was beat, utterly beat.

Just then a familiar face appeared in the river of people flowing by. "Mack! Hey, Mack!" Bull called out. The familiar face looked up, searching for a moment in the mist. Then it broke out in a friendly grin.

"Well, if it ain't Bullsie," said the wilted young man in an army coat with black threadbare epaulets and no regimental insignia. He was pushing a beat-up baby carriage, and at his side slouched a peroxide blonde. Once she'd been a real dish—a *luketa*—but now her face looked wilted and royally fed up.

"Hey, hand me some skin, man," said Bull, in the familiar accent of the nylon age, all his vowels tight and flat, the words drawn out. "How's it stackin' up?"

The soldier took the proffered hand and replied in the same fashion. "It's stackin' up shit, Bullsie, pure shit."

Bull glanced quickly at the soldier's woman, but Mack's crude language obviously didn't faze her.

"The wife," said the soldier.

"Pleasure." Bull held out his hand. She looked apathetically into his eyes.

"Like we've already met, right?"

Bull looked at the partially eroded features and suddenly, in the light of memory, they began to change. He felt a chill come over him. "Hey, right!" he said. "You must be—you're Maggie Vančuříková, aren't you?"

"Didn't recognize me, didja? Quite a shock, eh?" she said mechanically. Her voice was unpleasant, and Bull had the feeling that she was mad at him, that she almost hated him.

"Ah shit, Maggie, it's been a hell of a long time since I seen you last. You was still carrying on with Jackie Petráček, so I figured—"

"You figured I'd wait for him, right? Fat chance."

"Anyway, what'd he pull down that time?"

"Six," she said curtly.

"Right. Well, that explains it. But jeez, it's great to see you both. Hey, I should congratulate you!"

"What the hell for?" asked the soldier.

"Like you're married, ain'tcha? I never heard about it when it happened, so better late than never."

"Congratulate us for the brat too, while you're at it," Maggie said. Her voice reverberated with a deep anger.

"So this here's the family future?" Bull said as he bent over for a quick, obligatory admiring glance at the pale infant sleeping under a smudgy blanket in a carriage that had seen better days. This is Maggie? he was thinking, that blonde-haired chick from the White Swan? The one who won the 'bugathon in the House of Slavs back in '46? There's gotta be a mistake.

"Still in the army, Mack?" he asked quickly, so he wouldn't have to think about it.

"You got eyes, haven't you?"

"Yeah, but it's been a long time."

"Third f'kin year, man."

"Somebody slipped them a bum report, eh?"

"Believe it. But I got the bastard's number."

"Lemme know who the son-of-a-bitch is. We could have a heart-to-heart talk with him some night in a dark alley. I can get some people together—"

"Look after him myself," Mack interrupted.

"Suit yourself," said Bull. "But you're getting out soon, ain'tcha?"

"The word is, Easter. The word is they're gonna disband us," Mack said. "And how about you, Bull? Man, you're just the same as you always was. Nothing's changed, except you shit on everything."

"Bull always did that, didn't he?" said the wife. "Or maybe you're different now?"

Deep down, the couple's words made Bull feel good. Yes, he always shat on everything. Still did. Always would.

"You kidding?" he said. "Same as always. They ain't making me over."

"That's what you say," said the soldier. "You'd sing another tune if they shoved you in with the politicos."

"Hey, I did my stint, didn't I?"

"Not with the Black Barons you didn't. Real f'kin chain-gang stuff, I can tell you. And how long were you in, anyway, man?"

Bull Mácha laughed contentedly. "Three months, man. Pretended I wet the bed."

This made even the gloomy wife laugh. "Still a free man?" she asked.

"One hundred percent," said Bull.

"No plans to get hitched?"

Bull laughed again. "I ain't rushing it."

"Maybe you should," sneered the wife, "while there's still time."

The anger flashed in her eyes. Christ, said Bull to himself, it ain't my fault they went and made themselves a brat.

"Ever go dancing?" he asked, to change the subject. And also to find out—to reassure himself.

Mack looked surprised. "Dancing? We got other things to worry about, man. Take the brat, that costs something, doesn't it? And you make shit in the f'kin army."

The small flame that had flared up in Bull's heart when he saw his old pardner began to flicker and wane. "What I mean is, you still like jazz, dontcha?"

Mack shrugged his shoulders. "I got no time. Tell you, man, it's like licking shit from a liquorice stick."

"Mack, if we're gonna make that movie we got to move our bones," said the wife.

"Sure," said Mack. "Movie starts at five-thirty and we got to dump the brat at my mom's."

"If you gotta go, you gotta go," said Bull.

"Show up sometime," said Mack. "I'm usually home on Sundays. Made a deal with the brass."

"I'll do that," said Bull. "Take it easy."

"See you," said Mack, and shook his hand.

"So long, Bull," said the wilted girl who had once been Maggie Vančuříková.

"So long, Maggie," said Bull. "So long." The soldier gave the baby carriage a push and the couple blended into the crowd flowing down the street. Bull's impassive eyes followed them for a while. The wife was wearing an old coat. She'd lost weight, and it hung from her as if from a coat rack. Maggie! Shit, where had it all gone? Where? And Mack! In '46, '47, it was five nights a week, every week, in the Boulevard Café. Now he says he hasn't got time for it. Hasn't got time! What the hell else is your time supposed to be for?

Again Bull peered into the Sunday crowds parading through the thickening mist. Up there above the city it was night already, and the streetlamps were coming on. They hung like spheres of luminous honey dissolving in milk, with thin golden haloes forming around them in the mist. They've all given up, they've all just said to hell with it! It was like a betrayal. Maybe they're just scared shitless, who knows? They all used to be so wild about it, and now everyone's in such a goddamned hurry to drop it. All it took was closing down a few jazz gardens, slapping a ban on jazz in the cafés, and everybody says screw it. But they won't make me over. Never! Bull felt a wave of disgust and resistance rise within him. I can remember the beginnings. Back when I still wore the kind of moustache Gable wore. I can remember when the Nazi cops used to chase us down Wenceslas Square because we had our hair long in the back and wore our shoelaces for neckties. I wore oversized fedoras and flat-brimmed hats and strap belts low in the back, and in '44 the cops hauled me in and shaved my head and then got me tossed out of school on my ear, and then shoved me into the Technische Nothilfe. Can't forget stuff like that. I ain't gonna forget it, anyway. They won't make me over!

"Well, glory be to the Lord Jesus Christ! Bull Mácha!" The voice came from somewhere beside him, and he turned to see who it was.

There was a pale little hepcat in a double-breasted winter overcoat with narrow shoulders, a tie as loud as a fireworks display, and a brilliantined coif looping down over his forehead. He gave Bull a friendly smile.

"F'rever'n'ever, amen," said Bull.

"Hey Bullsie, why don't you tag along with me?" said the hepcat, still smiling.

"Where to?" Bull asked.

"National House up in Vinohrady. Jan Hammer's cookin' there tonight."

"No kidding?"

"Absolutely, man. They wangled the permish at the last minute. Never had a chance to poster."

"Seriously?"

"I kid you not. Come on, Bull! The joint'll be jumping."

Jan Hammer!

"Is he still hanging out with that bebop crowd?"

"'Course. Rhythm Fifty-three. Vlasta Průchová's singing."

Vlasta Průchová! The wave of rebellion building up in Bull's soul now took on a concrete shape. Even if everyone else said to hell with it, he wouldn't!

"So let's move," he said to the hepcat, and quickly unstuck himself from the railing. The hepcat trotted along beside him, trying to keep up. They walked up Wenceslas Square, hands in their pockets, shoulders slouched, the misty golden spheres of the streetlamps reflected in their slicked-back hair.

"Workin' these days, Bull?" asked the hepcat, partly to be polite, partly out of curiosity.

"Got a job in a junk depot."

"How's the bacon?"

"Sliced pretty thin."

They were silent for a while. Then the hepcat said, "Hey, man, have you heard? Prdlas put a group together. They cook at his place every Thursday."

"What's the line-up?"

"Prdlas horn, Šmejda liquorice stick, Rathauskej bull fiddle, Bimbo skins. You could bring your axe over sometime, Bull."

"I might." Bull was silent for a moment, then said, "They play hot?"

"They'll burn your ear off, Bull! Drag your ass over some night 'n you'll see."

"Sounds good."

They turned into the park around the museum. The dusk was thicker there, and people were hurrying to get through the park and back into the illuminated streets. They walked through the park and quickly up the side streets to St. Ludmilla's. The hepcat opened the conversation again.

"Líza said she was coming."

"Which one's she?" said Bull.

"Works in Pearl's, remember? She got really blasted last New Year's Eve at Tubby's."

"She the one they had to carry out?"

"That's her. She was screwing Hekáč."

"You goin' out with her?"

"Not me," said the hepcat. "She treats me like a piece of shit. But she's class, eh?"

"Yeah, she's OK, she's OK," said Bull. OK, he repeated to himself, but she's nothing compared to Lucie. Or to what Lucie used to be. He remembered a different evening in the National House in Vinohrady, when Terš was playing and Lucie wore a yellow dress with a wavy fringe on the hem of her skirt and they danced the boogie together and he rolled her right over his shoulders.

Why had it all dried up? When did it happen? And how? It just sort of happened by itself, and no one even noticed. But it happened, and in the end, he was the only one left, alone. And he missed Lucie. It had been a long time since he'd been with a decent girl like Lucie. All he knew were gangs of young teenies. He was too old for them. There was a whole generation between them. A painful longing pressed Bull's heart. Where had all those jitterdolls gone? Where, goddammit?

They began walking faster. The windows of the National House shone brightly across the square. They walked toward it, two figures, one tall, one short, a large coif and a smaller one, shoulders slouched like a wine bottle's. As they came closer to their goal, the smaller one said, "Jeez, man, you know, it's strange they let this dance go on at all."

"Finally got it through their skulls people are pissed off," said Bull.

The hepcat chuckled. "Like where I work," he said, "they're always after us to join some goddamned choir, can you believe it? Want us to sing some stupid Russian shit, stuff like that. I mean fuck that."

"You in the Youth League?"

"Yeah. Collective membership, like nobody even asked us if we wanted to join or not; they just signed us up. They expect us to play their little games, but like everybody's saying, fuck that."

"What else they expect?" said Bull, but he felt the touch of doubt. They won't make me over, he said to himself again. Not me. That'll be the day, when they get me to go to a bunch of meetings. Screw 'em; they'll never change me.

The windows on the second floor of the National House poured bright shafts of light down into the square, which by this time was quite dark. The walls of the church stretched blackly toward heaven, and they could hear the faint sounds of an organ. Dark figures stood around the entrance to the National House, and the puffs of breath that came from their mouths merged with the evening mist. They went through glass revolving doors into the lobby, and as the doors gently swept them into the building, their ears picked up the distant riffs of wild, delicious music.

"Hear that? They're already blowing a storm," said the hepcat excitedly. "Hammer's really belting it out!"

Bull stopped and listened. The crisp, metallic, halting tones of a vibraphone came tumbling down the stairs.

"Great!" said Bull, and both of them ran eagerly up the stairs. The music mingled with the hum in the crowded hall, that familiar, ancient backdrop to pleasure. They put their coats in the cloakroom and then, despite their hurry, stopped in front of the mirror. Beside it hung a poster displaying a caricature of an antediluvian zoot-suiter, and underneath this were the words Zoot-suiters Not Welcome!

"Hey, man," said the hepcat. "Get a load of these wise guys."

"Screw 'em," said Bull.

The diabolically beautiful music was drawing them inside, but the magnetism of the mirror was powerful. They appeared in its shiny, smudged surface, a big and a small coif, and they pulled out enormous combs and began grooming their hair. Bull's jacket, reflected in the mirror, was first-class English cloth, from which the tailor—who still had a private shop—had produced a loose-hanging garment with rows of buttons down the side and a collar that dipped down to a point midway between his shoulder blades. Bull Mácha put the finishing touches on his coif and pulled out his tie. In the past, he had worn his hair long at the back, and then in a crewcut; now it was coiffed in front, with long sides slicked back. Over the years, his tie had grown from a tiny knot that resembled a shoelace knot to a super-wide American windsor that he had to use the end of a fork to tie properly. It was this type of knot that now sat resplendent beneath his chin. He straightened the knot, jerked his arms forward to free his sleeves, then hooked his thumb under his collar and adjusted the slouchy jacket on his shoulders. Finally, he ran the palm of his hand over his coif, then turned around to look at himself from behind. He was ready to go. He was ready to enter a ceremony which—though he had never thought about it—he felt contained the meaning of life.

No longer paying any attention to the little hepcat still trotting along at his side, he entered the hall. He positioned himself in one corner, and the first thing he did was take a good look around. His eyes were no longer impassive, but bright and eager as he watched the band on the podium. The smile that flickered over his small face was almost happy. The vibraphone, Jan Hammer standing over it waving his sticks like a magician over a metal stove-top, bobbing his head to the rhythm, grinning like an ecstatic idiot as a wild foxtrot tumbled off the podium, Vlasta beside him in a blue dress, rotating her beautiful hips and clapping her hands to the rhythm, and Kyntych, his head bowed over his trumpet, the bell pointed toward the ceiling, Rocman with his glasses and clarinet, Tiny Vondráš with a tenor sax in his face. They played and played—man, how they played! Behind them, Poledňák pounded the drums furiously, then gently; then there was a sudden off-beat break, a roll of rim-shots, and he slipped back into the groove again and on they played, man, how they played! Bull felt a wonderful mood blossom inside him, and without thinking, he started stamping the parquet floor with his Gothic Hungarian winklepickers and staring intently, his eyes now alive with worshipful delight, at the sticks of the swaying vibraphonist. The desperate rebellion that had been building up inside him all afternoon, right until he had heard Hammer play, gave way to a victorious sensation of certainty that all this would last, that they wouldn't manage to suffocate it after all, that it was the same jazz it had always been, sounding just as sassy as it always had, with the same crowd of people dancing to it, and that no one in the world could wipe out this music, this world, the only one he had ever wanted to belong to.

Then, feeling the urge to dance, he started looking around at the girls. He wanted to have it all, the music and the women, because jittermolls belonged to this musical worship service too, girls who felt the dirty syncopated tone of the swinging tenor-sax player travelling through their nervous systems, just as it did through his.

It looked as though Lady Luck was with him. A luketa was just sidecarring past him, with some donkey pushing her back and forth. To those magnificent thundering riffs and swinging rhythms, these two were dancing, if that was the word for it, like a couple of hicks at a tea dance in the outer boondocks. He watched them for a while, a contemptuous smile on his small face. He saw the geek step on the luketa's foot, and the luketa looked fed up. What else? She wore a black, close-fitting skirt, a wide black nylon belt, and a blouse with big flowers on it. Her face was like a beautifully painted Easter egg. The geek's clothes were strictly John Farmer. Bull felt that fate had brought this woman across his path. She reminded him of Lucie in her best years. Class. You could see the kind of class in her that was missing in the women who went with the cats he hung around with now, for lack of anything better.

The band finished and the scarecrow led the luketa back to her table. He bowed, she thanked him coldly and sat down to her glass of lemonade. A fellow in a black suit and a nowhere tie sat down beside her.

The vibraphone started playing again. Bull kicked himself into gear, and in a flash he was standing in front of the luketa.

"Take your bones for a strut, miss?"

She looked up at him with blue eyes. "I suppose so."

She got up. Bull put the palm of his hand against her nylon belt and led her onto the floor. They began with an ordinary foxtrot, but he could feel right away that this girl was a marvellous dancer.

"They're really socking it out, eh?" he said.

She looked at him again with her blue eyes. He expected some warm, enthusiastic response, some affirmation of his statement of faith. But instead she said, "I beg your pardon?"

It sounded almost hostile. Almost unpleasant. At least he had that impression. Like some goody-goody defending her reputation. But he didn't believe that.

"You like the way they play?" he asked uncertainly.

"So so."

He tried a more complicated step. She responded immediately. Maybe she just didn't understand what I said, he thought. It's okay. He held her out at arm's length and tried something more daring.

"No. Stop it!" she said suddenly.

"Don't you want to jelly the goulash, darling?"

"I beg your pardon?"

"You know: kick loose, introduce a little juice, show 'em we're alive to the jive?"

"No. Just dance the way you did at first."

"Aw, go on," said Bull desperately. "You dance magnif. It's a pity to waste your talent tromping down sauerkraut."

"It suits me just fine."

"But it's got no jolt to it, my dear! Come on!" he said, and again he tried to execute a variation that required more imagination than the standard foxtrot shuffle. But she just stood there and left him hanging. It was embarrassing. He stopped.

"Don't do that!" she said threateningly. "If you want to cause a scandal here, find someone else to do it with."

"Scandal, miss?" He took her around the waist again. She relented, but he felt the muscles of her back go tense under her blouse. "Scandal?"

"You know very well what I mean. I don't dance any of that jitterbug stuff."

Bull's heart almost stopped. He couldn't believe his ears. Again, he felt that pain deep in his soul.

"Don't tell me that, miss," he said. "You're a champ! Okay, so what dances do you dance?"

Her reply sounded like an article in the Youth Union daily. "All kinds, but it has to be decent. If you don't like it, you can take me back to my seat."

"But it's such a drag, miss. It's for cripples!"

"It's good enough for me," she said.

Hammer hit the vibraphone, and Vlasta's voice was clear, bell-like. "Rhythm, that's my kind of thing," she sang. "Rhythm, that's what makes it swing!"

It really got to him. This chick can't be serious.

"All right, here's a surprise for you," he said resolutely, and grabbed her firmly by the hand, hit the floor with his left toe crossed over his right, then did a quick reverse repeat, and again and again, at the same time tapping the parquet with his heels and toes, step-dancing beautifully to the rhythm. There was a lot of art to it. And suddenly he felt her tugging on the arm he was holding and trying to struggle free.

"Let me go, let me go!" she hissed, pushing him away. He stood there helplessly, his arms hanging loose, staring at her in amazement. Her eyes flashed with hatred again.

"Find yourself some—some jittermoll for that, not me!" she shouted. Then she turned around and disappeared into the crowd.

Bull was thunderstruck. Then he realized that several couples dancing nearby were scowling at him. He felt himself beginning to blush, so he turned around and walked out of the hall, his heart pounding. At first, he was stunned by the realization that she had made him look like a fool. But in the foyer he came to his senses and once more felt that malignant, miserable afternoon pain in the depths of his soul. How could she have done a thing like that to him?

He stood leaning against the banister and began to hate her intensely. The whore! I'll bet she's in the goddamned Youth League. Dumb, just like the rest of them. But the sweet image of that face could not simply be driven off by the insults which, in his mind, he heaped on the girl's head. It was as though he were reviving other faces from the past, and it hurt.

"Hey, Bull!" said a fellow who was just coming up the stairs.

"Hi, René."

"How come you're not inside?" asked the fellow called René. He'd been a Gablik and zoot-suiter too. Then he got married and said to hell with it. So what was he doing here?

"Taking a breather?" said Bull. "Where's the old lady?"

"Went for a piss. Come on, let's check out the talent."

"Bugger all out there, I'll tell you that," said Bull. "Hammer's cooking, and that's about it."

"And he's not bad," said René, pricking up his ears. "Still tight as ever."

"Maybe. But Hammer and Vlasta's all that's left of the old Rhythm Forty-Eight. Rest are all new."

"They can still cut loose, though."

"That's a fact," said Bull. He felt a faint hope stir inside him. "So I see you haven't said to hell with jazz after all."

"Yeah," said René. "That's a fact. Always ready to listen to any-thing solid." He turned to Bull, half closed his eyes, and said didac-tically, "All the same, Bull, you know, the classics it ain't."

"No, you're right there," said Bull. He felt the hope dying still-born. "The classics it ain't," he said ironically, but René didn't seem to get his point.

"Any hookers around?" he asked casually.

"Take a look, why don't we," said Bull. But his hope was dead. He didn't want to spend time with René.

They took up positions at one of the doorways and scanned the dance hall. Bull tried to see his luketa. He found her. She was with the guy who had first sat down at her table. They were dancing a neat, nowhere foxtrot. Enough to make you puke.

"Know that woman over there?" he asked René. "The one with the black nylon belt over by the edge of the floor? The blonde?"

René looked in that direction. "Never seen her before. But she don't look completely useless."

"No, she don't," said Bull. "What do you suppose she does?"

"Who knows? Maybe one of the sexual proletariat. At least she looks like it."

Bull laughed bitterly. "I think you're way off," he said, and then he greeted René's wife, who had just joined him. "Evening."

"Evening." Her lips were thin, corpse-like, and her checks were painted with purple rouge. Her hair was done up in small tight curls, like a lambskin cap.

"Want to dance, Jarka?" asked René.

"Hmmm," she said coquettishly.

"You coming too, Bull?" René asked, out of politeness.

"Sure," said Bull. The couple drifted away. Bull looked around and saw a jittermoll type who had just come in. He knew her. She hung around with the beboppers. Called herself Evita.

"Greetings, Creamroll," he said.

"Hi, Apache."

"Want to polish the floorboards?"

"Why not?" she said. He led her onto the dance floor. Kyntych was just blowing a solo in the middle range, a diabolical, fast bebop solo. A deluge of short notes in foxtrot rhythm. Again, a desperate wave of defiance washed over Bull Mácha. If everyone else has shit on it, if they're all like that stupid broad, such a looker and yet so dumb, I ain't gonna change. They'll never make me over! And if the first one didn't want to, Evita certainly won't mind.

He took hold of Evita and started showing her everything he knew. Evita wasn't a bad dancer. They stayed in one corner of the hall and commandeered their own private dance floor, a space of several square metres where Bull really began to cut loose. Would zoot-suiters please refrain from dancing excessive dances? Just watch. He spun Evita around until her skirt was flying high above her knees. That's how it's done! Hammer laid down a groove on the vibraphone and everyone settled into it. They howled, they bleated, they wailed, the drums thrashed, the cymbals sizzled. Bull really cut loose now. He felt that this was something big, what he was doing, that it was everything you could possibly do here, everything you could possibly accomplish in this lifetime—

Suddenly someone was tugging his sleeve. He swung around irritably and saw a waiter.

"What do you want?" he blurted out, without waiting to see what he had to say.

"Sir," said the waiter. "You can't dance that kind of dance in here."

He felt a rush of anger. "What the hell are you talking about?"

"It's forbidden. Otherwise you'll have to leave the dance floor."

"Well now, ain't that nice," said Bull. "Why don't you just take a walk. I paid for my ticket. I can do what I damn well feel like."

"I'm telling you, you can't dance like that here. Wild dances are forbidden."

"Is that so? Well, you can kiss my ass," said Bull, turning back to Evita. They began dancing again.

But the waiter held on to him. "Watch your language, sir. I'm telling you to stop that kind of dancing."

"Look," said Bull, talking to him over his shoulder. "Why don't you just drop out of sight?"

"I'll have to call the police," said the waiter.

That was all they needed! Bull was outraged. "Get lost! You're in the way!" he roared at the waiter, and then he and Evita danced their way into the crowd. He saw the waiter stand there uncertainly for a few moments, then turn and leave the hall.

"Just let him try," he said to the girl called Evita.

"You shouldn't have been so rude to him, Bull," said Evita. "He'll rat on you for sure."

"I don't care if he takes it all the way to the goddamned ministry!"

said Bull. "I had the Germans on my back for dancing, and they couldn't stop me. Nothing to worry about, Evita."

He started dancing again, deliberately making wild figures on the floor, but he kept looking nervously over Evita's shoulders at the door. No one appeared. The number was over, Evita pressed close to him, and they followed the crowd off the floor.

The waiter was standing in the doorway, and beside him was a uniformed policeman with a revolver and a fur collar sewn to his tunic.

"That's him," said the waiter, pointing at Bull.

Bull tried to disappear, but the waiter caught him by the shoulder.

"Take your hands off me," said Bull.

"Come with me," said the cop gruffly.

"What's going on?" growled Bull.

"That's the one," said the waiter. "When I asked him politely to stop dancing that way, he started yelling at me and using very filthy language."

"Don't you know jitterbugging's not allowed?" asked the cop. "There's a ban on it."

"There ain't no such law," said Bull.

"But there's a ban," said the cop.

"Don't get your shorts in a knot!" said Bull. "I paid, I dance."

"You watch your language!" shouted the cop.

"I am," said Bull. "And what are you hanging on to me for, anyway?"

"Nobody's hanging on to you," declared the cop. "You were dancing forbidden dances and causing a public nuisance. I'm warning you to lay off. Otherwise I'm going to have to—"

"Introduce me to anyone who thought I was a nuisance," said Bull arrogantly.

"Shut up!" shouted the cop. "If you don't stop—"

"Well, this is just great, this is wonderful!" said Bull bitterly. "A guy forks over eight crowns and they don't even let him dance."

"You can dance all you want, but you can't make a public nuisance of yourself," repeated the cop.

"You're the public nuisance!" said Bull. All at once he didn't care what happened to him. He was only desperately angry. "You should be out chasing down some real public mischief. Leave people with regular jobs alone when they're trying to have some fun."

"That's it!" said the cop. "Leave the room at once!"

"You got no right! I ain't done nothing!" said Bull. He caught sight of Evita standing to one side, making herself small and watching him with wide eyes. A crowd of gawkers had gathered around them. A new wave of defiance washed over him. I'm not going to let these assholes trim me back, he said to himself.

"Don't tell me what I have a right to and what I don't," said the cop.

"You seem to think you got a right to everything," said Bull. "And just because somebody wants to have a little fun, you'd as soon lock him up as let him, right?"

"Shut up!"

"You'd like that, wouldn't you? You'd like us all just to shut our mouths!"

"You're coming with me," declared the cop.

"No I ain't. I ain't done nothing!"

"Let's go, then," said the cop, taking Bull under the arm. This guy has muscle, Bull realized.

"Take your hands off me!" he said, but the cop was already dragging him off toward the washrooms.

When they got there he said, "Show me your ID book!"

"You got no—" Bull began.

"Open your mouth once more and you're going with me," the cop interrupted him. His face had hardened, and Bull saw that the fun was over.

"This amounts to police brutality," he said, pulling out his ID book. And when the cop took out his notebook and began laboriously taking down Bull's name and address, he added more quietly, "This is curtailing my personal freedom."

Then he said nothing, and merely watched as the cop struggled with his notes.

A long time passed before he finished and returned the ID book to Bull. "And now clear out, fast!"

"You're trampling on human dignity," said Bull, quietly now, almost to himself.

"There's the cloakroom," said the cop.

Bull looked around for Evita, but she'd made herself scarce. There were only a few gawkers left, staring round-eyed at him.

"Well, are you going or aren't you?" said the cop.

"Yeah, sure, don't get your socks in a knot," said Bull. They've all dumped on me. He went to the cloakroom, got his coat, and walked slowly down the stairs. The cop watched him go. They've shit on me. And now I'm in it all alone, he said bitterly to himself. They've all shat on it.

The revolving door spat him out into the raw night. Light from the windows on the second floor was seeping into the fog, and he could hear the faint tones of Hammer's vibraphone. A trolley bus was going past the church. There was a pre-Christmas quiet in the air, as though nothing at all had happened. Bull stuck his hands into his pockets and started walking. But he had nowhere to go. He couldn't go back, and there was nothing ahead of him.

"The bastards!" he hissed between his teeth, without having anyone in particular in mind. But they were somewhere around. Someone must be responsible for all this. "The bastards," he repeated quietly. "But they won't make me over. They'll never make me over."

He walked down the square and soon was lost in the fog that seemed to be dissolving the streetlamps in misty golden globes of light.

1953

Spectator on a February Night

Life ... is really always a tragedy,
but gone through in detail,
it has the character of a comedy.
—Arthur Schopenhauer

For Marie

We were sitting in a booth at the Boulevard Café when we heard it. It came from down at street level, outside the window, desperate and determined and defiant. "Long live President Beneš!"[1] Freddy got up to look out the window. We saw him gape at what he saw. Then he absentmindedly raised a hand and waved down toward the people on the street.

"What's up?" asked Doddy.

"Students," said Freddy, still staring out the window. "Students or something. They have a flag and a picture of Masaryk."[2]

We stood up and looked out the window too. A modest crowd was moving up Wenceslas Square, two or three hundred young guys and girls, led by a pale, lanky fellow carrying a flag and looking dead serious. The ones behind him carried a big picture of President Masaryk that must have been stashed away since their party congress. Czech Socialists, obviously.

"Look! There's Tom," said Doddy.

"Where?" I asked.

"Over there. See the picture they're carrying? A little ways behind them."

I was looking, but I couldn't find him.

"See? Right beside him, that's Věra. See?"

Then I spied them. Tom, hatless with a multicoloured scarf around his neck, and Věra, smoking a cigarette. Clearly, she was agitated. I thought about how the papers tomorrow would write about it as a provocation by rich kids. Stupid. This wasn't the way to do it. They should have dressed down. Watching the demonstrators, I was sick at the thought of how they were fuelling the propaganda. Sure. Every other guy was wearing shoes with thick rubber soles. And the girls were smoking. Sure. Rich kids, golden youth, zoot-suiters, that's what they'd say, and leave it at that, because naturally, zoot-suiters couldn't possibly have patriotic feelings and stuff. Just plain stupid.

"How did they get involved there?" I asked.

"Why, sure, Tom was always an avid Czech Socialist."

"I never knew that."

"Oh, yeah. And Věra's even worse, I think."

"I thought they weren't political."

"No way." Freddy fell silent and stared out the window. I could tell he was rooting for them. Me, I took a rather cool view of the whole thing, but I knew how Freddy was probably feeling. A sense of solidarity, delight at not being alone, and a kind of defiant joy at showing no fear. I wasn't moved, though. I wasn't a hundred per cent on side. In the first place, I had my doubts about which side was right, and then, I viewed it all sort of like some great big drama. Theatre. What I felt was a perverse kind of pleasure. Pleasure that something was going on. That something was happening again, and that I was a part of it. Watching the streets fill up, people demonstrate, the tension escalate, newspapers publish special editions, the cops brandish their bayonets, that was for me. I hadn't felt so good, so excited, since the war ended. Yes, it was almost like during the war again. Inhumane or not, this was certainly better than their stupid, fusty, muffled peace.

"Damn," said Freddy. "Let's go. Come on, let's go march with them!"

"Don't be a dope," said Doddy. "Be glad you're not involved."

Freddy kept staring out the window, chewing on his lower lip. Then he said, "Nuts. Let's go. I'm going. Come on."

"Listen to me, don't be an idiot, man. When the shooting starts, then you'll—"

"So? Let 'em shoot. Just let 'em try it and they'll see!"

"The hell they'll see," said Doddy. "Sit down, man, and be glad we're up here, out of the way."

I was having fun watching them. Freddy got pretty worked up where politics were concerned. I'll never to my dying day forget how he punched some cop in the nose during the Czech Socialist Party congress. That's just what he was like. And as for Communists, he was always ready to kill them on the spot.

"You jerk," he said to Doddy, "what do you think will happen if everybody just sits on their duff?"

"Not a damn thing."

"Yeah. Because everything will be steamrolled by the Communists."

"You can't be any help to that dumb party of yours."

"Maybe not. But if everyone—"

"Then everyone will shit their pants in unison. Man, what can you do in the face of machine guns?"

"They'd never dare."

"They'd dare all right. You saw them, didn't you? Those faces of theirs?"

Doddy was right about that. That afternoon I had noticed them too, the cops strolling by twos up and down the square, submachine guns strapped across their chests. From the look on their faces, you could tell how they were getting off on sauntering among the crowd, and seeing how scared of them folks were.

Freddy set his jaw and bit his lip again. Outside the window, they were chanting, "No matter what they try to tell us, we're still Masaryk's girls and fellas!" As the chanting began to fade, I stood up and got a last glimpse of the flag swaying down at the foot of the square. People were standing around on the sidewalks, bewildered. Some, a very few, waved and shouted "Go for it!" but most of them just stared, stunned or blank, but clearly supportive. Supportive, but scared. I could tell they were scared, and that the only way it could end was badly. There was no movement in the crowd. In fact, it wasn't a crowd. They were still nothing but individuals, who would have liked to do something, but needed to protect themselves.

"Come on outside," I said.

Doddy gave me a look. "You want to get into it too?"

"Nope. I just want to go out in the streets and take a look."

"So, let's go," said Freddy quickly and got to his feet.

"Guys, let's not," said Doddy.

"Come on," I said. "It's not as if we're going to do anything."

"Leave him be if he's chicken, the jerk," said Freddy.

"You moron," said Doddy contemptuously, rising. "It's all the same to me, but I'm telling you right now, I'm not getting involved in anything. If you're hell bent on getting mixed up in it, fine, go ahead. It's your funeral."

"Let's go then," Freddy said. "Waiter!" he called out. The waiter scurried over as if nothing were happening and we paid. Doddy bought a pack of cigarettes from him, cool and calm. He certainly looked calmer than Freddy, and much older. As for me, I couldn't wait to be out there.

Downstairs, we emerged in the passageway. It was full of people, and freezing cold. Framed by the dark of the passage, Wenceslas Square looked bright with its snow and slush. Then we were outside.

"Down that way," said Freddy. I knew why. That was where the procession had gone. Of course. We turned down that way. The square was much more crowded than usual. It was a clear, crisp day, and people were moving in two thick streams, slowly and expectantly. A unit of cops burst out of the Bata passageway. We stopped to let them go by. I looked for the expressions on their faces. Most of them were older guys with beer bellies, obviously ill at ease. They were led by a loud-mouthed young cop who was moving so fast that most of them could hardly keep up. He carried a submachine gun under his arm, trying to look important and military. He was really getting off on his role as a cop. I wondered whether his feelings were any different from those of the Nazi Schutzpolizei in November of '39, when they were clearing the square here.[3] Probably not. The old guys in the police uniforms were sweating, struggling to maintain a foothold on the slippery pavement. They had no submachine guns, just ordinary rifles over their shoulders.

Freddy said what I was thinking. "So? You think these fellows would start something?"

"Those must be the unreliable ones. Besides, they're just being transferred someplace. Nobody would send them after you."

"Go on, most of them are like that."

"What are you, blind or something?"

"Well, the young ones would think better of it too."

"You really believe they think at all?" asked Doddy sarcastically. "Come on, they just follow orders. No different from the Krauts."

Freddy was silent.

"They're indoctrinated," Doddy continued. "Like the Nazis laid their propaganda even on little kids in youth clubs. As far as I'm concerned, those jerks are no different from the SS. Don't anybody tell me that only the Germans were swine. There are swine like them in every nation."

Doddy was on a roll. When he was on a roll, he was really good. All of a sudden he wasn't afraid of anything. That's him. Won't go yelling with a crowd, but on his own, he would say it all, and loud enough for everyone around to hear. He used to do that during the war too. Two days after Heydrich croaked, he started shooting off his mouth on Wenceslas Square about boss Frank[4] and about German brutalities, till all of us who were there with him got scared and split. But nothing ever happened to him. He was lucky.

"When is Beneš going to make his speech?" I asked, to shut him up.

"He's not," said Doddy tersely.

"How come?" Freddy goaded him.

"Come on. They'll never let him on the air. Like that Social Democrat minister, Majer."

"You're nuts. They have to let Beneš go on, of all people."

"Just wait and see."

"They've got to let him on, it'd be an international scandal if they didn't."

"What?"

"What, what?"

"What was that?" Doddy asked disagreeably.

"What?"

"What did you say? An international scandal?" he went on, sarcastically.

"Sure."

"You think the Commies give a shit about any international scandal? If you do, man, then you're pretty naive."

Freddy turned red. "I'm telling you they'll have to let Beneš go on the air, because he has the respect of the whole nation. Even the Communists."

"You poor sap," said Doddy in a condescending tone. "Is that what they taught you in those ideology classes of yours?"

"Well, so you imagine that they won't let Beneš go on the air?"

"And so you think they will? Man, when are you going to figure out that the Commies have their agenda and that they don't give a damn about how they get there, as long as they get there. Or do you believe them now when they make like patriots?"

Freddy did not reply.

"Do you think they care about any international scandal?" Doddy repeated, "or about any respect that Beneš has? Man, it's just a few guys making this happen, the ones on top, they say the word and the factory militia and the cops wave their bayonets and then the mob jumps up and down and yells whatever they're told. Just look around and see how well it's working for them."

"What's working for them?" demanded Freddy.

"Everything. Just look around. The radio dances to their tune, people demonstrate whenever they're told, factories send out letters of protest."

"Well, one of these days it'll stop working for them!"

"When? And why should it?" Doddy persisted. His piercing eyes narrowed into slits and he leaned over toward Freddy. His expression was downright diabolical. Damn, I don't know if I've ever seen anyone look quite that demonic. He was the embodiment of icy reason, and I knew what he was saying was true, but I didn't care about it as much as he did. And besides, I wouldn't want to rob Freddy of his illusions. That must be the main difference between Doddy and me. I didn't really care what happened or didn't happen for the Communists, whereas Doddy did. I knew how much he cared. But he was awfully hard on himself. Or else maybe he took some perverse pleasure in it. I don't know. Either way, he spoke coldly, clearly, and explicitly.

"It'll never stop working for them, man. Can't you see it's a lost cause?"

"Not yet it's not," Freddy broke in, but Doddy paid no attention and kept right on talking.

"A lost cause! The Commies have it all in their back pockets. This is just an episode in a tragedy for all of Eastern Europe. In that context, we, or some Czech socialist party, are completely irrelevant. There's only one thing that could conceivably get us out of this mess."

"What's that?"

With a cynical smile, Doddy leaned even closer to Freddy. I leaned over too, so I could hear. Sure, I knew what he was going to say, but I wanted to hear him say it. It felt good, hearing him say it.

"Nothing but war," said Doddy, straightening up. It was interesting to watch Freddy's reaction. He wanted to argue, but he suddenly realized that Doddy was right. And yet, war—Freddy had that fundamental aversion to war. That was what made what was happening different from what had happened in '39. Back then, that aversion didn't exist. Nobody had it. Now it was an underlying component to everyone's uneasiness. True, people talked like

Doddy, that it's all the same, the methods and the cops and all, but they could tell it wasn't the same. The thought of war terrified them. Because this probably wouldn't just be an ordinary war like against the Germans. Me, I didn't care, though. I knew how they felt, but I didn't care. For me, war was something else. I knew about the killing and stuff. But to me, it was different. That's why a passionate street crowd like that made me feel good.

All of a sudden I spied Petr rushing up the square. His overcoat was unbuttoned and he was in a hurry, "Hey, Pete!" I called.

He stopped and looked around with near-sighted eyes behind little spectacles.

"What's your rush?"

"Oh, hi!" He seemed pleased to see us.

"Hi. What's your hurry?"

He stepped over to us and said excitedly, "I'm on my way from the Party secretariat. The police are shaking it down."

"What?" asked Freddy.

"They're doing a shakedown at the secretariat. Three vanloads of cops and a heavy machine gun."

Freddy was visibly upset. "And isn't anybody doing anything about it?"

Petr shrugged his shoulders.

"Justice isn't bestowed, justice is taken," quoted Doddy stonily. "*Macht geht vor Recht.* Might before right."

"Yeah, that's how it is," nodded Petr sadly.

"Just like under the Germans."

"Well?" Doddy turned to Freddy. "Well? Are they going to let Beneš on the air?"

I felt sorry for Freddy. He stood there, red-faced and defensive. Then he said, "Let's go over there. Come on, guys."

"Yes, well, I'll say goodbye, I'm in a hurry," said Petr.

"Where to?" I asked.

"Home. My old lady worries about me."

"Well then, go ahead," I said, to be rid of him. I was grateful to him for the news, but now I wanted to be off myself. I wanted to see that heavy machine gun. God, how I wanted to see that gun. It's odd, but at that moment I really couldn't think of anything else.

"Okay, I'm off. So long," said Petr.

"So long," we said and started out across the square. At its foot an unarmed cop was directing traffic. It was weird. As we walked along Příkopy Avenue, I noticed that the crowd was getting denser. A yellow glow spilled out through the open door to Holy Cross. I glanced in as we walked past. I saw a priest, white and gold in the radiance before the altar, and I heard the murmur of prayer. It seemed serene, but I knew that the people in there were anything but serene. Except maybe the priest. I always thought that a priest has to maintain his serenity, no matter what. That's part of being a priest. I never believed in God, at least not in the Church's God, but somehow I was convinced that if I were a priest, I'd be serene all the time. That somehow I'd have nothing to lose, or I'd feel safe because I'd be sure of heaven. I'd just be serene. But now I wasn't. The excitement of the mob was gradually soaking in.

"Wow," I said, "it's getting crowded."

"Guys," said Doddy, "wait. Don't rush into anything."

"Well, you stay here if you're scared," said Freddy. "Let's go," he turned to me.

I knew Doddy wasn't scared. With him, it was more like an allergy. An allergy to the mob. Being in the middle of it and being dragged along with it, and crowded in a passageway with it and ultimately tossed into a paddy wagon with it.

I halted. "Aw, come on, Doddy. We'll be careful."

"No, guys, I'm not going there. It's dumb and besides, it's pointless."

"No, c'mon. I'm telling you, all we're going to do is take a look, and then we'll leave."

"And the cops will pounce and you'll just happen to get picked up and you'll be in all kinds of trouble. I know."

"Leave him be," said Freddy.

"Seriously, Doddy. We'll just take a look and see if there really is a big gun there and take right off." For me, it was really only a matter of the gun. Or mainly a matter of the gun. As for taking off right away, though, I wasn't entirely certain about that.

"Yeah, and as soon as you set eyes on the gun, you'll freeze. No, you guys, seriously, it's pointless."

"Leave him be," repeated Freddy impatiently and grabbed my arm. I could tell he was all fired up with the tension.

"You're serious, you're not coming?"

"No, I'm not." Doddy shook his head, and suddenly he wasn't the least bit cynical. Suddenly he seemed lonesome and withdrawn. "Don't hold it against me, guys, but I'm really not coming," he said.

"But listen," I said, "when will I see you?"

"Stop by at our place tomorrow. I'll be home all morning."

"All right. Well, so long."

"Bye."

"Bye," said Freddy, pulling me into the thickening crowd. I just caught a glimpse of Doddy turning and starting back. The belt on the back of his trench coat hung loose and a bit of yellow scarf was sticking out of his collar. All of a sudden, he was a sad and tragic figure. All of a sudden, the whole mob was tragic. From where we stood by the Živnobanka, the Communist Party secretariat building loomed tall and white, embellished with red flags and the red neon star on the roof. It was lit, even in broad daylight. The mob was silhouetted against the white of the snow and the red star shone brightly against the dark snow clouds in the sky. The loudspeakers were blaring some Russian march or other.

Freddy said, "Come on, we have to get over by our own secretariat," and he began to push his way through. I followed behind him through a relatively silent crowd, toward the sound of yelling from further up the square. As we approached, from time to time we could discern individual words, voices chanting "Down with totalitarianism!" and "Long live President Beneš!" and "Long live Mayor Zenkl!" But it was all pretty chaotic. We pushed through to the number 5 tram stop. At first all I could see was the grey front wall of St. Joseph's, because I couldn't turn around in the crush.

Through the door I saw St. Jude with his neon halo, and a bunch of people in front of him praying. It occurred to me that he was the patron saint of lost causes, and how apt it was, since this was truly a lost cause. The crowd resumed chanting "Down with totalitarianism!" Baloney, I said to myself, let's not get mystical. But I knew it was a lost cause. The round windows of St. Joseph's shone with a yellow light. Behind them I pictured pew upon pew of kneeling figures, dark in front of the radiant altar, repeating after the priest their eternal and monotonous "*Ora pro nobis*. Intercede for us." Some of the ritual phrases appealed to me. Father in Heaven, God the Redeemer, Son of God, Holy Trinity, One God. It was all kind of entrancing. Sort of a good spell. It filled a person with certainty and stuff, but that soon vanished and out here it was all too clear just what was what. I finally managed to turn around and face the front of the Czech Socialist Party secretariat. Four flags hung limp, and under the balcony were loudspeakers. The balcony was empty and the loudspeakers silent. The crowd stood there, facing the secretariat. Beneath the balcony, a heavy gun loomed over the hats and caps, beautiful, dangerous, with a matte gleam to it, the wheeled cart holding it out of sight, just the gun towering above the crowd, aiming straight into it, and behind it stood two cops dressed in camouflage-mottled sheepskin-lined overcoats, the ones Nazi paratroopers used to wear, booty from the war. It was an amazing sight. I felt a wave of utter bliss. This was it. Soldiers with submachine guns and an angry mob and excitement and everything out of the ordinary. Total bliss. Nobody was going to classes, out in the streets all day long, nothing commonplace. Everything abnormal. A strained situation. And exhilarating. Stinking of war. I loved it. I felt great.

"Shame!" yelled a fat man standing beside me. "Boo! Shame! Boo!"

"Boo!" echoed Freddy. His reedy voice sounded silly against the fat guy's bass.

"Fascists! Murderers!" the fat guy hollered. "Down with the totalitarians!"

"Long live Beneš!" Freddy chimed in.

"Long live Beneš! Long live Zenkl! Down with totalitarianism!" exclaimed the fat fellow. The cops by the gun sat silent and immobile. The sky over the secretariat was growing dark. Dusk was falling. In the twilight, the crowd was starting to look menacing.

Somewhere up ahead, a man emerged above the heads in the crowd. He must have been lifted onto somebody's shoulders. The crowd quieted down. "Brothers," sounded his muted voice—strangely muted, considering how near it was, "Brothers, take heart! We won't be terrorized! Long live President Beneš! Long live liberty!"

"Up and at 'em!" hollered the fat guy beside me. I was fascinated. I could tell something was about to happen. I couldn't wait. We were in the middle of it and it was great. I felt the mob move. The yelling rose in discontinuous waves of sound. I couldn't tell who was shouting. All I knew was that the crowd was in motion. I could picture myself inside the secretariat. And an entirely new situation. How the *New York Herald* would run a headline about it tomorrow. Mr. Seymour Friedin of the *Herald* was surely watching from somewhere. Maybe from nearby, right there by the secretariat. Violence in Prague. Shots Fired in Czech Capital. Czech Socialists Tangle with Police. Police Go Over to Mob. I could just picture it. I really got into it. Reds Grab for Power in Prague. I looked back to the cops over by the gun, still cold and unmoving as the crowd up front stopped short. From behind, though, the pressure didn't let up. There were shouts and exclamations. Then the shouting died down. More exclamations. All of a sudden, the crowd shifted backward. And then forward again. Then it seemed to move in several streams. Pushing and shoving. Someone stepped on my foot. A little space loosened up right ahead of me. I saw a man with arms outstretched to protect his body, furiously ploughing into others. Somewhere a woman screeched. One fellow fell and tried to get up, but then the space filled up with people again and I never saw whether he made it or not. I knew what was happening. Somewhere the police had charged into the crowd. An elbow rammed into my ribs. I spun around and felt my arm connect with somebody's jaw. It was fabulous. Then more of that awful, overwhelming, almost intolerable pressure as the mob behind me was halted against the wall of the church. I tried to take a deep breath, and then the pressure eased up. And then again. It pushed me up against a girl, pleasantly warm. I could feel her warmth through my overcoat. From behind, she looked pretty. I deliberately buried my face in her hair, and it smelled nice. I tried to get a look at her face. No way. And then the crowd swirled her out of sight. But that was all right. It was neat that I'd been pushed up against her, but all this was fine too. The crowd rolled back and forth on the square, the shouting and screaming sounding mostly female. I forced my way back to the church wall. Suddenly the crowd started to thin out. I stood with my back against the façade of St. Joseph's. The crowd had diminished from a crushing mass to a scattered throng. I watched as people retreated, ranting and protesting. Now and then someone would look around, shake a fist, stop, a few would step forward and then quickly back up again. And then I saw a line of cops in their camouflage-coloured SS overcoats moving in a wide arc across the square to the secretariat. The area behind them was deserted, only hats and caps scattered on the greyish slushy snow. They advanced slowly, step by step, leading with submachine guns and bayonets, and as they moved forward the crowd fell back, taunting and cursing them in the deepening dusk. The cops made slow, nervous headway, narrowing the gap between themselves and the mob. It was a spellbinding sight. I looked around, but of course, Freddy was nowhere in sight. I pressed my back against the wall. I felt splendid. I felt alive, and alive when it felt good to be alive. I knew what Mr. Friedin was going to write. Police with Bayonets Attack Crowds in Prague Streets. He'd write it splendidly. And I'd be part of it too. I was feeling something. Just like the last time, three years earlier, as the war was ending. Exactly the same. When the soldiers fanned out that day and advanced from the theatre, clutching hand grenades, with rifles at the ready, followed by their officers with handguns drawn, and the crowd backing down. The selfsame feeling. I pressed back against the wall. A splendid feeling. I pressed against the wall and waited. I watched the line move toward me. As they came nearer to the wall, they pulled closer together; two of them with submachine guns and one with a mounted bayonet were facing me. They came closer. I stared into their faces. They were tense and nervous. Only one of the two submachine gunners had a bit of a smile on his face. He was the one. He was the real beast. The kind Doddy talked about. He was actually smiling. In fact, I realized I was smiling too. But that was different. Entirely, totally different. But I was indeed smiling. And waiting. They kept coming, and the guy with the submachine gun spied me. He quit smiling. His face stiffened. I knew what he wanted to do. I was enjoying it. But for some reason, I didn't feel like getting out of the way, somehow. He looked like a storm trooper. Literally, like a member of the SS. "Get moving, now!" he barked at me, gesturing with his gun barrel. I could see his eyes, cruel and focused on mine. There was no hatred in them, no embarrassment. Just cruelty. He was enjoying it. I could tell. I didn't budge.

"Are you deaf?" he hollered. He was getting really close to me. Slowly, I pulled away from the wall, staring at him with as much contempt as I could muster.

"You! Make faces at me, will you!" he bellowed, leaping toward me. He tried to grab my collar with his left hand. I spun away from him, my arm jerked up and my elbow caught him in the face. Something crunched in his nose. The cop gave a roar. It felt exactly like under the Germans during the war. From the corner of my eye, I saw the other two lunge toward me, but by then I was rounding the corner, toward the entrance to St. Thaddeus. The saint's purple halo flashed past my eyes, I pushed a few people aside and slipped inside the sanctuary. I stopped, wondering if they would follow me inside. But they didn't. I just saw a few figures in those camouflage coats dash past the open doorway and then the square beyond looked pretty much deserted. Just those caps and hats strewn on the ground. Lights were on in the secretariat across the street. In the windows, I saw figures carrying stacks of papers. Only then did I notice the truck standing before the secretariat entrance. The cops were loading bundles of files tied up with string. They stood in a row, passing them from one to the next like bricks. Then there was a bright magnesium flash from one side of the square. I turned to catch sight of a man in a black overcoat with an upturned collar, holding a flash camera. It struck me that it had to be Mr. Friedin. I saw one of the higher police officers run over to him. The man pulled out an ID card or something, and moved to show it to the cop. The cop waved it away and reached for the camera. The man tried to hang on to it and kept waving the ID card. Another cop ran over from the other side and seized him by the upper arm. Then the two of them grabbed him and forcibly dragged him inside the secretariat. It was great. I knew it was going to be a sensation. I turned back inside the church, to the altar and the white-robed priest. "Well, isn't that something," said a voice inside me. "Oh, God! Oh, Lord! Oh my Lord! Thank you, God, for everything, for letting me live it, and please, God, let me live through a whole lot more!" I felt splendid, elated. Let the battle continue! Now they're chasing them out there and I was part of it. The only light in the dark and quiet church was the one shining from above the main altar. It was all amazing. Oh, God, oh, Lord, I said to myself. I stared around at those candlelit carved altars, and even though I had stopped believing, I called on God. I kept calling on God. Our Father Who art in heaven, I started praying, and I felt good. Just think if it all hadn't happened. We'd just rot. In all that peace. Good that things happen.

Everything. The whole world. Once more, I saw the war all over again. The liberator planes, guys in steel helmets behind bullet-proof glass, the sun reflecting off the helmets, the slow, majestic flight of long formations in the blue air. That was what I wanted. I felt great. "*Sursum corda*," called the priest, and my heart really lifted, almost to my throat. But then the euphoria began to fade, and I started thinking rationally again. It was stuffy and unpleasant inside the church. It dawned on me that I was losing precious time. Anything could still be happening out there. Whatever it was, I definitely wanted to be part of it. I touched my fingertips to the icy holy water in the font by the door, crossed myself piously, and split. There were a few people standing around in front of St. Jude Thaddeus. I glanced around the square. It was beginning to fill up with ordinary pedestrians. The lights were still on in the secretariat, but the truck was gone. The cart with the gun was still there on the sidewalk, though. The two cops were still up by the gun, but now they were chatting and laughing with some other cops down on the pavement. I started toward the Powder Tower, but I stopped. I thought maybe I should go over to the Institute. Yes. I turned around and headed toward Poříčí Avenue. Underfoot, the snow crunched with every step. It was almost dark, the lights were on in shop windows but the street lights hadn't come on yet. I turned the corner and soon I was within sight of the YMCA building. A cluster of guys stood huddled there, in front of the sign for the American Institute. I headed toward them.

"Hi," I said. They turned to me, glum and silent.

"Hey there," said Harýk. His hands were rammed in his coat pockets and his collar was turned up. The whole bunch of them looked gloomy and sombre.

"What's up?" I asked.

Harýk nodded toward the doorway. "Look."

I looked over where he was pointing. The American Institute's green glass sign was smashed. Somebody had hit it with a rock or something. There was a hole right in the middle of the glass, with cracks raying out from it. "Who did that?"

"Comrades," was Harýk's baleful reply.

"How come?"

"They wanted to get inside. A couple of loudmouths were egging them on, inciting them to ransack the place."

"Damn," I said.

"Yeah, we've had it," said Harýk. "And where were you?" he turned back to me.

"Over there, around the corner. On the square."

"What was going on there, man?" Mike asked with interest. The group converged around me. They were anxious to hear.

"The cops lit into the people there."

"We saw that. Some trucks drove by here across Poříčí. So, was there an incident there, or what?"

"Not really. People are too scared," I said. I was never much good at making reports. I preferred to be the one asking questions.

"Right. People are frightened. It's too bad," said Mike.

"We've had it all right," repeated Harýk.

"Wait!" Mike stiffened. We stopped talking. From somewhere came the sound of singing. We moved out of the entrance and stared in the direction of the sound. A fine snowfall had begun, the street lamps had come on, and a black procession appeared, moving through the cone of light under the lamp-post. The marchers were the ones who were singing, and the front ranks brandished a few red flags. We pulled back into the passageway. I thought of some of the films about the Revolution. That's what it felt like. Bunches of people with banners, in fur caps. Darkening night with white snow. Like something out of Aleksander Blok.[5] I took another, closer look. There it was, a splendid, turbulent parade in all its glory. Red banners flapping in the icy wind, men in overcoats with rifles slung over their shoulders. The straps on the rifles were yellow, with the shine of newness on them.

"Factory militia," Harýk said softly. "Guys, let's go upstairs. It's not a good idea to stare too hard."

"Right. Come on up. Maybe they'll know something up there," said Rudy. I didn't feel like it. I would rather have stayed and watched the procession troop toward Wenceslas Square. But the other fellows started away.

"What's up there?" I asked.

"The kids are hooked up to the Všehrd bunch at the law faculty."

"And?"

"They say some guys from the Catholic Students Club got pinched."

That fabulous feeling again! Something happening. Of course. It was entirely predictable. First they'd arrest the Catholic Students. And in a flash of clarity, I thought of the option we'd been considering the previous night. No, not an option, a probability. Of splitting across the border. We climbed the stairs. The YMCA porter was standing at the office entrance with a couple of other fellows in agitated conversation. When we appeared, they fell silent, glancing at us, resuming only after they recognized us. We climbed another flight of stairs to the Institute. Harýk opened the door and we stepped inside. Robby was there with Kitty and Lexa. Lexa was hunched over with his ear to the radio set, catching America. Kitty was sitting at the typewriter, smoking. She had rolled a piece of American Institute letterhead into the typewriter, but she wasn't typing. Robby was sitting at the phone, examining a Pan American Airlines brochure.

"Well?" said Harýk.

Robby gave him a frazzled look. He looked downright cinematic. He was wearing colourful socks and a blue-and-white striped tie. It struck me that before long, it was going to take guts to walk around Prague dressed like that. Certainly as long as packs with red armbands were walking the streets down there.

"Rand is at the faculty," said Robby.

"So they didn't get him."

"No, not yet. He took refuge on academic soil."

"Do you think they'll respect that?" I asked.

Robby shrugged. "We'll see," he said.

"Sit down," said Kitty.

We sat down wherever there was room. On the wall behind Kitty hung an American flag and photographs of Truman and Roosevelt. Harýk lit a cigarette.

"Have any of you been out there?" Kitty asked.

"I was. Down by the secretariat," I said.

"For God's sake, what went on down there?"

"The cops were breaking up the crowd. They brought a heavy machine gun along, just in case."

"Seriously?"

"Seriously. Mr. Friedin was taking pictures and they nabbed him."

"You saw Friedin?"

"Yup."

"And what did he say?"

"I never talked to him. I just saw him there, snapping pictures, and then when they picked him up."

"Did they really arrest him?"

"Well, I saw them drag him inside the secretariat."

"And the secretariat, did they ransack it?" asked Robby.

"Totally. They were loading whole boxfuls into a truck."

Just then the telephone rang. Robby grabbed it and said, "Hello?" Some static sounded through. Robby said, "Speaking." Then he listened, with an occasional "I see," and "That's awful," and such. We were all quiet. The room was dim, the only light came from the lamp beside the radio. Lexa had turned down the volume so Robby could hear. I looked around. The rest of them sat in silence, their faces solemn in the yellowish light.

"Right," said Robby. "I'll be there right away. I'll take it across the Old Town Square. So long for now."

We all looked at him. He hung up the receiver and said, "So— I've got to go down to the faculty. Rand wants me for something. One of you hold the fort here for me, okay?"

"I will," said Harýk, getting to his feet.

"All right, and I'll go part way with you," I said, "if that's all right."

"Sure," Robby replied in English, imitating an American movie star.

"Should any of us go along?" Kitty asked.

"No. You stay here. I'll be back in less than an hour. If I can't, I'll call."

"OK," said Kitty, also as cool and matter-of-fact as an actress in an American movie. I admired her. I knew she was finding it thrilling. Just like me. Yes, this was the life. Kitty sat back and took a long drag on her cigarette. Robby pulled a multicoloured scarf around his neck and looked over at me.

"Are you coming?" he asked.

"Of course."

"Well, so long, my friends," said Robby, switching to English again. The guys mumbled something. Robby opened the door and we stepped out into the hall. It was pleasantly dim there. A warm, hotel kind of dim.

Mr. Aplin, an American on the staff of the institute, came hurrying down the hall. When he saw Robby he slowed down and called out in English, "Hi, Robby! They've arrested Friedin."

"I know," Robby replied.

"I'm calling the embassy. I'll keep you posted."

"Thanks," said Robby.

"So long," Mr. Aplin called, disappearing around the corner.

"So it really was Friedin," I said, reverting to Czech.

"Apparently so."

"I hope there's a stink about it. After all, they had no right to nab him."

"Leave it to Aplin, he'll see to it."

We hurried down the stairs. Robby strode silently down the street. He was worried. Robby was probably in it up to his ears, I thought. Active in the Czech Socialist club, the university students association, and the Institute. But he was great. The picture of utter self-confidence, on the phone and out on the street, amid all the chaos. I was filled with a fierce feeling of fellowship with him.

"I'll only go as far as the Powder Tower with you. I still want to see what's up on Wenceslas Square," I said.

"OK, I have to go see Rand."

We went on in silence for a while. We came to the secretariat square, now filled with normal pedestrian traffic, and from there we could see the Powder Tower. We could also see the red star atop the Communist secretariat shining against the blackness of the night sky.

"Listen, Robby. Just between you and me. Are we really going to do it?"

He gave me a solemn look. And when he spoke, he spoke solemnly too, and I couldn't tell if he was being solemn like in a movie, the way it was all like in a movie, or whether he was being genuinely solemn. He looked at me and said, "My friend, we'll be packing our bags."

That was music to my ears. What a great life! "Robby," I said, "listen, call me about how things turn out with Rand. If need be, you can count on me. For anything, like we agreed."

By then we were at the Powder Tower. Robby reached out to shake my hand and said, "OK. Where should I call you?"

"At Harry's. That's where I'm going now."

"How about Harry?"

"I think he's a hundred per cent."

"Has he got the guts?"

"Absolutely."

"Well, then, look. This is how we've got things set up, Rand and me. The best way is to drive to Domažlice and go to Rudy's. He has a business on the town square. All you have to do is show him your ID. That's it."

"Just my ID?"

"Yes, Rudy knows who's coming. Anyone else shows up, he'll send him packing. Of course, it's all top secret."

"Of course."

We shook hands.

"And what about Kitty?" I asked.

Robby shrugged.

"She's staying behind?"

"Afraid so."

"Can't we do something for her?"

"No room."

"Maybe she could ride with us."

Robby stopped short. He probably didn't love her all that much if he could be so cavalier about leaving her behind, but he apparently wasn't entirely indifferent to her either. Or maybe it was just his vanity. Robby was thinking about how it would look. If Kitty left when he did, newspapers would write "Secretary of the Young Czech Socialists Robert Malý and His Girlfriend Defect to the West," and that sounds so much better than just plain "Secretary of the Young Czech Socialists Robert Malý." As for me, I kind of liked the idea of travelling the snow-covered roads with the warm, soft Kitty between me and Harry at the wheel. Kitty, with her blonde head on my shoulder. Somewhere in the West with Kitty and her exquisite little figure.

"Do you think you'd have room for her?"

"Sure. You mean she doesn't know?"

"No."

"Then she'll have to be told."

"I'll take care of that—look here—"

"What?"

"I'll call you at Harry's, and if it's all right with him, then I'll call Kitty, OK?"

"OK."

"Have Kitty meet you at Harry's—or no. She can wait for you by the Anděl Restaurant. How does that sound?"

"Fine."

"Because she lives near there, you know? To give her time to pack some things."

"Fine. But no big suitcases."

"Naturally. So that's—settled, right?"

"Settled," I echoed his English, and shook his hand again. "You can call any time after an hour."

His handshake was warm. "So long, my friend. Thank you."

"Don't mention it. I thank you too."

"So long," he repeated, still in English.

"So long," I echoed again, to please him. It was a little embarrassing, a little outré, but that was all right. Robby turned and strode off up Celetná Street and I turned back down Příkopy. Suddenly I felt adventurous. A crowd of people with red armbands was standing in front of the Communist Party secretariat, waiting and listening. Already I was feeling removed from it. And I was looking forward to the trip. A dangerous escapade. That's the life! Down with a stagnant, putrid peace with nothing going on! I was glad both for the ones with the red armbands and for naive, jittery kids like Freddy and Harýk and Doddy. All of them. This was a time when a fellow could truly feel alive! Maybe I was spoiled by the war, somehow. I knew that what I was thinking and feeling was warped, but that's just the way I was. There was no changing it, just like there was no changing the events of this whole week, and so a fellow might as well come to terms with it. Wring out of it everything he can. As I strode down Příkopy, in my head I was packing my bags. No thought of what would happen in the following week. Or that the adventure would come to an end, maybe in just a few hours, maybe a little way across the border, and then it wouldn't be an adventure any more, but a refugee camp in Bavaria. Right now there was just the adventure. Later it might turn into disease and Africa and heaven knows what. But it would be life. Life the way I needed it, life I wasn't prepared to give up. I suddenly recalled that I was supposed to drop in at Doddy's the next day. So what? I just wouldn't show up. It couldn't be helped. Not that I didn't like Doddy, but he was just a kid. A kid who wasn't in on anything. I'd send him a postcard from London. I knew that would get Doddy's goat, but it couldn't be helped. And besides, maybe Doddy would get away too. Sure. It was entirely possible. Then I might even be able to help him somehow. That's it, that's what I'd do.

I turned onto Wenceslas Square. I could see a sea of heads, all the way up to the museum, and the trams were squeezing through with difficulty. People were standing in front of the Koruna snack bar, staring up. A couple of men were arguing fiercely. A squad of men with red armbands was just passing the Koruna. I hurried up the square. That fabulous, ecstatic bliss was still with me. Alive! For once I was alive again! The crowd was denser and darker over by the Melantrich Publishers building.

The old neon flag on the roof wasn't lit. Instead, there was nothing but blackness up there. Up there nothing but blackness and down at sidewalk level, the lights from individual shop windows. I could hear shouting, but I couldn't see anything. People were pressing forward toward the Melantrich building. I stepped off the sidewalk and hurried to the edge of the crowd.

A rumple-haired man bumped into me. "What's happening?" I asked.

"They've taken the Melantrich. The police have," he said, and he was gone.

Around me, people were moving here and there. I blended with the crowd, and made my way to the raised streetcar stop in the middle of the thoroughfare. There, I stood on my toes and looked at the Melantrich building. A heavy iron portcullis had been dropped to bar the doorway. Through the grating, I could see lights, and two cops with automatic rifles pacing back and forth. Just then a hatless, coatless figure leaped out of the crowd ahead of me, grabbed the bars and started to rattle them violently. A chorus of wild voices arose. A red banner appeared, out of nowhere. "Let me at 'em!" screeched a woman's voice. They were Communists. The People. And in a hanging mood. They were out to hang the journalists at *Svobodné slovo* in there. Typical. I grinned to myself at the thought of Rand safe and sound at the faculty, and how Zenkl was probably packing his bags. Zenkl was surely not inside the Melantrich building. But the People rattled the gate. "Let us at 'em!" they hollered. And "Long live Gottwald!" Not far from me, I saw a bunch of crones in red bandannas. The crowd was rocking them back and forth, but passionately and excitedly. I glanced at my watch. I had to get going. I made my way out of the crowd and hurried on. Better to walk than to get stuck in a streetcar. There was a whole line of them, from Můstek at the foot of the square to Vodičková Street in the middle, blocked by the crowd at the Melantrich building. I walked fast. The lights from Lucerna Hall shone out onto the square, and the neon sign for Krohn Brothers Whisky flicked on and off down at the Můstek end. A procession started down from the museum at the head of the square, waving red flags and placards. It was made up mostly of women. The placards read *Down with the reactionaries* and *We're behind Gottwald*, and it struck me that the latter slogan was apt. Behind Gottwald. They would go behind him no matter where. The People. But it was really all the same to me. I had no opinion on the matter. Maybe they were right, but maybe nobody was entirely right. The main thing, as far as I was concerned, was that it was happening. All of it. The crowds and the cops and the night and the excitement. This was living. I hurried past the museum and up, past the park behind it. It was darker there, and not as crowded. Soon I was at my destination. Inside Harry's building I dropped a half-crown piece in the elevator slot. The halls were silent and deserted. The lighting was dim. The elevator arrived and I stepped inside. I pulled all the gates shut and pushed the button for the fifth floor. Slowly and noiselessly, the elevator started up. I watched the steps outside dropping away, flight by flight, and row upon row of pale yellow doors appearing and disappearing. There was nobody in the halls. Harry lived in a great building. The elevator stopped and I stepped out. The brass plate on Harry's flat read "Harry Rosenblum." That was all. I rang the doorbell. For a while there was no sound, then I heard the shuffle of footsteps. Harry was probably in his slippers. Another moment of silence as he peered out the spyhole, and then he opened the door.

"Hi," I said.

"Hi," said Harry. "Come in."

I stepped inside. "Has Robby called?"

"No," said Harry.

"Good," I said, taking off my overcoat. Then I turned gravely to Harry. "Harry, we're packing."

"So it's definite?"

"Definite."

"And when?"

"Probably today."

"Did you speak with Rand?"

"No. With Robby."

"Where's Rand?"

"At the faculty. He took refuge on academic soil," I said sarcastically.

"Oh," said Harry. "Come on inside."

He opened the door to his room. A lamp on the end table was lit, and so was the green eye on the radio. I dropped into an armchair. Harry sat down across from me.

"So the time has come," said he.

"Right. Robby should be calling within the hour. You probably ought to go pack up what you want to take along."

"There's plenty of time."

"And listen," I hesitated. "I promised Robby that we'd take Kitty along. There's no room for her in Rand's car."

"All right."

"You don't mind?"

"No, why should I?"

"I just thought, since we hadn't talked it over first—"

Harry waved a hand. Then he offered me a cigarette. "When is Robby going to call?"

I looked at my watch. "Any time now."

"And then you'll go home and pack?" he asked.

"Yes. He'll check with us to make sure it's OK about Kitty, and then he'll tell her. And then we'll rendezvous with her at the Anděl."

Just then the phone rang. "May I?" I asked.

"Feel free," said Harry.

I picked up the receiver. "Hello, Robby?"

Robby's voice came through, a little distorted. "Yes. So you're at Harry's?"

"I am."

"So listen. It's all set for two hours from now. How about Kitty?"

"It's fine."

"Good. So you be waiting at the Anděl two hours from now, OK?"

"Fine."

"Anything else?"

"Nothing else."

"OK." Robby paused. "Like I said. It's Rudy, and he has a sign on the square. Understood?"

"Sure."

Another pause. I get a malicious kick out of making people a little uncomfortable. I never have any trouble hanging up when I need to, but some people don't know how. So sometimes I let them dangle there in silence, feeling ill at ease. After a while, Robby said, "Well—good luck. So long. I'll be seeing you. Give my regards to Harry."

"I will."

"Well—so long."

"See you," I said, and deliberately waited to see if he'd hang up. He didn't, not right away. He was waiting for me to say something else. I didn't. Then I heard the click as he hung up, so I did too.

"Well?" asked Harry.

"We're all set," I said.

"Right now?"

"Now. In two hours, we're picking up Kitty at the Anděl." Harry was silent. He sat there, holding his pipe in his hand and staring straight ahead. I stood up. "I'd better go pack. I'll be back in about an hour."

Harry shook himself out of his reflections. "Oh, gosh," he said. "All right. In an hour. I'll throw some stuff in a valise too. But don't pack too much."

"Don't worry."

Harry rose. "Do you want a drink?"

"What have you got?"

"What would you like?"

"Whisky?"

Harry opened the liquor cabinet and poured two glasses. I didn't particularly feel like drinking, but since he was offering .... Besides, it went with the situation. This was living too. This was the way a fellow ought to live. Maybe it was just a game a fellow plays for himself, but even if it was, it beat the hell out of the fusty muzziness at the faculty, for instance. But I wouldn't be going back to the faculty, I thought. Never again, probably. I picked up the glass and downed the whisky. At first I didn't feel anything, but then my stomach began to warm me.

"Well, so long for now," I said, my voice cracking.

The whisky was strong. I wasn't used to drinking any more.

"Goodbye," said Harry, opening the door for me. "Here? In an hour?"

"Yeah," I said. "Bye." I started down the stairs at a run. When I heard Harry shut the door behind me, I slowed down. The steps were low, carpeted in rubber, their edges covered with some sort of sandpaper to prevent slipping. The hallways were still dimly lit and deserted. On the third floor, I could hear a radio blaring. Someone was making a speech. I stopped, wondering if it could be Beneš. But it wasn't. Probably Gottwald or somebody. I heard a few words about reactionaries and that was enough. No, it wasn't Beneš. No way. They wouldn't let Beneš on the air. I kept on going. The next floor down, I passed Colonel Lamprecht. He didn't notice me. He had the classic look of a man in distress. A former colonel in the wartime army attached to the Western forces, here, during a Communist coup. He was married to a Janet from London. They surely wouldn't be sticking around for long. I slipped out the front door. Outside, it was dark and chill. I walked fast. Across Fruit Market Square, then down to the right, onto Sokolská Street. My street looked hellish. Narrow, gloomy, silent as death. Two rows of buildings facing each other, so black that even the night sky beyond them appeared lighter. I got out the key and unlocked the front door. There was no elevator; I had to walk up. The hall was lit by dusty little lamps, and the carved heads of Medusa over every apartment doorway wore identical silly, insipid scowls. This used to be a modern building too. Back under the Habsburgs, I suppose. Maybe then it was worth a fellow's while to marry into this building. Times change. Maybe even for the better, in their own way. But especially now, I thought. I clambered up the four flights and unlocked the door. The old woman I sublet from was in the kitchen with the light on. I slipped into my room and locked the door, carefully, so she wouldn't hear me. Then I switched on the lamp on my night stand and pulled the curtains shut. I looked around the room. Everything was clean and orderly, the old woman insisted on it. My glance fell on the snapshot of Marta on the desk. I decided to take it along. Not that it mattered particularly, I wasn't actually thinking of Marta at all, and wouldn't be, but I'd take it along. It wouldn't take up much room. Later on, I might even write to her. In her own way, Marta was a swell girl. But, still, she was a girl. Only a girl. And this was a man's world. Yes. That's what I said to myself. In this man's world, girls were only there to pleasure a man. Like Kitty, who would be sitting between me and Harry later on, her thighs warming mine. I could have taken Marta along. But actually, it was better to take Kitty. At least, when we got there, I'd be free, while Robby would be stuck with Kitty. I could see myself with American girls. I knew my idea was straight out of the movies—again—but there would surely be some American girls there. Some WAF or ARC or something. I took the photo out from behind the glass and put it down on the table. Then I pulled the smaller valise out from under my bed, picked up the picture, placed the case on the table and stuck the picture inside it. I walked over to the wardrobe. It dawned on me that I hadn't asked the guys what they were going to wear. Should I put on my skiing outfit and pack some dressy clothes? But what would I do there all the time, dressed in ski clothes? No. I decided I was going to do it in all elegance. I undressed and changed into a suit tailored from the fabric of American army officers' uniforms, dyed a dark brown. In front of the mirror, I put on a necktie, the same kind Robby had on but with brown and white stripes, and combed my hair. I folded two shirts into the valise, two pairs of shorts, a few handkerchiefs, four pairs of socks, my black oxfords, a tube of toothpaste, a bar of soap and four cans of food distributed by UNRRA. That almost filled the case. When I took my best suit out of the wardrobe and carefully folded it on top, the lid still closed. I looked around the room.

What else? I didn't have any jewellery, and my nine dollars were in my wallet. My gaze rested on the bookshelf. A book? But which one? It suddenly seemed to me that there wasn't anything I liked enough to take along. An English Bible lay on top of the bookshelf. A pocket edition, from the Bible Society. There was room for it in the corner of the case. The Bible was good. Some of the Psalms and such. I'll take it, I thought, picking it up and tucking it inside. I stopped to think. No, that was all. I closed the lid and locked it. Then I set it down on the floor and took one more look around. Neckties! Of course. I have to take them. I lifted the case back up on the table, unlocked it, took my neckties out of the wardrobe and folded them into it. They fit just fine. Now, that was everything. By then, my landlady's light was out. She went to sleep early, the old woman. That was good. I picked up the valise, and took one more look around the room. I was leaving everything else behind. Suits, books, clothes, and linens. Those used to matter most to my mother. But Mother was dead. Actually, that was good too. Otherwise I probably couldn't do it. But Mother was dead. I turned out the light and tiptoed to the apartment door. Not a sound from the kitchen. I opened the door and moved the suitcase out into the hallway, careful not to bump it against anything. Then I locked the door. That was very important to the old woman too. Somehow, I didn't want to upset her. After I locked up, I grabbed my suitcase and started back down the stairs. The Medusas were just as silly and insipid as ever. The radio in the landlord's flat was on. The same voice was still talking. The landlord was probably worried. I opened the front door and then I was out on the street. I closed it and set out with my valise towards Fruit Market Square. The air was colder and the sky was darker. It had turned cloudy. That was good for us. There were fewer pedestrians on the streets. People had obviously retired to home and hearth. The bourgeoisie had retired. I thought I heard voices singing from Wenceslas Square. But maybe I just imagined it. Workers and plant militia won't get much sleep tonight, I thought. They had taken to the streets. And the bourgeoisie had retired to their flats. Karlín, Žižkov, Košíře, all the working-class districts had emptied out onto Wenceslas Square. And in the middle-class districts like Vinohrady and Střešovice, people were huddled in the dark around their radios, listening to it all. I thought maybe we'd run into trouble on our way. After all, Harry's little Packard was pretty conspicuous. That would be good. Maybe we'd even get shot at. But I had no doubt that we could pull it off. I went inside Harry's building, rode up in the elevator and rang his doorbell. He let me in right away. There was an open suitcase in the vestibule, half full of clothes. I put mine down and looked at my watch. It was half past nine. We still had almost an hour.

"What are you packing?" I asked Harry.

"You know. Stuff," he said. He took a tuxedo out of the closet and folded it into the suitcase. "What are you wearing?" he asked me.

"This."

"Wouldn't something less dressy be better?"

"No way. What would I do with it there?"

"We'll be walking some. And in the snow."

"I can manage."

Harry hesitated. "I don't know, man. I think it's a good idea to bundle up for it."

"But what to wear once we get there?"

"Don't worry. Something will turn up," said Harry. That was when I realized that Harry wasn't going to be travelling on the cheap like me, with just nine dollars to his name. Of course. That was for sure.

"Whatever you say."

"I say it's better that way."

"Whatever."

Harry hesitated again. Then he took a pale grey skiing outfit out of his closet, tight pants and all.

"Are you sure you don't want something too?" he turned to me. "I have two."

"Well—" I faltered.

"Feel free, really."

"I don't know—"

"Take it, man. You'll see. It's going to be cold out there."

Actually, he was right. And one thing warmed my heart. Harry had money and I could apparently depend on him. Harry had always been a swell guy.

"Well, then, thanks." I said, and he handed me his other skiing outfit, light brown with yellow trim on the collar. Harry opened the door and we stepped into his room. I took off my brown suit and laid it across the back of an armchair. All of a sudden I felt bad. It was the best suit I owned, and the best made. I hated leaving it behind. It was better than the black one I had packed. It wouldn't be out of place in the Savoy or the Ritz. I pulled on Harry's ski pants and his Norwegian sweater. It was a good fit, Harry and I were built the same. But I still didn't feel right about leaving the suit.

"Damn," I said, "it's too bad about the suit."

"Which suit?"

"This one. It's the best one I've got."

Harry looked at it. "Hmm. It is a good-looking suit," he said.

"I don't know, Harry. Maybe I'll bring it instead of the black one I packed. What do you think?"

"Better not, man. You're going to need a black suit. Why don't you put it in my bag?"

"What?"

"Pack it in my suitcase."

"But what about your stuff?"

"I'm not bringing much of anything."

"No, Harry, that's no good."

"Sure it is. Don't worry. I have other things I'm bringing," smiled Harry. It was his first smile that day. He gave me a look. I understood what kind of other things he meant.

"You know," said Harry.

"Well, then, thanks. Really. Thanks," I said.

"Put it in my bag out in the vestibule," said Harry. I picked up the suit. Harry added, "And don't worry, man. Don't think we're going to be hard up when we get there. You don't know my uncle in London."

I chuckled. "OK," I said. "If that uncle of yours is half as generous as you are, then it's in the bag."

Harry waved a hand. "And besides. I told you I wasn't going empty-handed."

"OK," I said, walking out into the vestibule. Harry was really a swell guy. Without a doubt the best kind of guy for a venture like this. For that matter, everything was swell. I folded my brown suit carefully on top of Harry's tuxedo and closed the suitcase. It was just full. Harry's suitcase was a bit bigger than mine. I returned to his room. Harry was standing beside an open wall safe.

He turned to me as I walked in. "Look here. Just so you'd know what we're bringing along."

I stepped over beside him. He showed it to me. It was a chest, fair-sized, full of gold and gems. "It's what's left of all my relatives," said Harry. Almost his entire family had perished in the concentration camps. But obviously, they had known where to stash their valuables.

"Besides," Harry reached in his pocket and came up with a roll of banknotes. Dollars. "Ten thousand, man," he said. "That ought to be enough for the trip, don't you think?"

"Certainly," I said reverently. Damn, this leaving the country was turning into something much more grandiose than I expected. But that didn't bother me. On the contrary. That's right, very much the contrary.

Harry reached way inside the safe, feeling around for something. He brought out two British army revolvers and a box of cartridges. "Here," he said, handing one to me.

"Damn. Where'd you get all that?"

"Souvenirs from England. Do you know how to handle one?"

"Well—"

"Look," Harry proceeded to show me how the revolver worked. "You load it here, see, and this is the safety, all right?"

It was easy. With the feel of the cool, dark steel in my hand, the intensely blissful sensation returned.

"But just in case of utmost urgency, understand?"

"Sure," I said. "Don't worry."

"Here," said Harry, passing me a pale leather holster on a strap. I tried to buckle it around my waist. "No," he said, "it goes over your shoulder. Like this," and he fastened it so the holster rested on my chest. "That's for speedy access."

It was a good feeling. The weight of the gun on my chest felt good.

"This is swell. Now we're all set," I said. Harry laughed.

"But like I said, only in case of utmost urgency."

I put on Harry's ski jacket with the yellow facings. There was a bit of a bulge in front where the holster sat. It wouldn't show under my overcoat though. I looked at my watch. Ten o'clock.

"Shouldn't we get going?"

"Right away," said Harry, placing the jewel chest inside a small briefcase. Then he put on his jacket and looked around. "I guess that's all of it," he said.

I said nothing. I was wondering what they would do with such a posh apartment when they found out that Harry was gone. They'd probably assign it, with all its luxury trappings, to some deserving party comrade. That made perfect sense. And it struck me that I would have a lot more trouble giving up a place like Harry's. Leaving my little sublet room was easy, but a place like this would be much harder.

"Yes, well," Harry paused. "Adieu, au revoir," he said finally, switching off the light. The lamp from the vestibule lit our way. We went out and put on our overcoats. Harry opened the door to the corridor and stuck the key in the lock from the outside. I moved our two suitcases out into the hall and Harry locked up. Then he picked up his valise and we walked silently down the stairs. In his other hand, Harry carried the briefcase with the valuables. We didn't meet anyone. Everyone had retired. The muffled sound of radios came from behind several apartment doors. We went down to the underground garage, and Harry turned on the light. There were five cars in the garage, two big American limousines, two little Skodas and Harry's Packard two-seater. The modern shine of the cars mirrored the dim overhead light. Harry opened the trunk and put his bags inside.

"In here," he said. I lifted my own bag into the trunk, and there was still room.

"Just enough for Kitty's," said Harry, closing the trunk. Harry was swell. Sitting three in a two-seat Packard would be crowded, but Harry took it all in his stride. Matter of fact, maybe it wouldn't be too uncomfortable after all, when the third one was Kitty. And Harry was no angel. I knew he wasn't. And neither was Kitty. I was rather looking forward to it.

"Could you open up?" said Harry, handing me the key. I walked up to the garage door, unlocked it and slid it open. It went smoothly, letting in a blast of freezing air. I looked outside and saw that the street was deserted. Harry was in the car already and he started the engine. Its loud roar echoed inside the garage and reverberated down the empty street. Then the headlights went on, shining on the second-floor façade of the building opposite. The car drove out of the garage, up the steep ramp to street level. Harry stopped while I locked the door and walked around the car. He opened the door for me. I handed him the key and climbed inside. There was plenty of room for two. It was dark in the car, except for the glow of the red light by the starter.

"So," said Harry in English. "Goodbye, sweet Piccadilly."

"Bye-bye," said I, as Harry shifted gears and stepped on the gas. Outside, the engine didn't roar at all. The car moved silently and turned onto Ječná Street. We drove on down, quickly and softly, and we were silent too. The streets were practically deserted. As we drove past Štěpánská Street, I turned to look. The steeple of St. Stephen's towered in the dark. I always liked churches. I don't know why. But I knew every church in Prague. Then we drove past the Church of St. Ignatius, and glancing back through the rear window, I saw the faint gleam of the statue's halo. Against the black background of the clouds, it shone like an almost extinct, cooling sun. I often used to come and pray in this church. There was a painting over the side altar depicting sinners roasting in Hell, gazing up at the crucified Christ in supplication. They had those neat medieval faces. Beards and all. Yes, that was a great church.

A pack of plant militia were marching back and forth by the engineering school but they were silent. You could tell they were freezing. My stomach got a bit of an anxious feeling, but they didn't stop us. Then we drove past the Russian Orthodox church, where during the war the parachutists who assassinated Heydrich took refuge. I caught a glimpse of the brass plaque. Right across from the church was the building where Marta lived. Damn, I thought, I should have brought her instead of Kitty. But no. Better not. Better this way. I had her picture. That was better. Harry turned onto the embankment. In the dim light, the back of the National Theatre looked the same as ever, not all that impressive. On the Slavonic Island, the lights were off. They were on at the Mánes Tower, but it looked empty. We drove along the frozen Vltava River. It shone white against the dark of the sky, its frosty surface marked with tracks left by people and motorcycles. We turned onto the bridge and made for the Smíchov district. Both ends of the bridge were deserted. Way up on our right were the two red lights of the broadcasting tower on Petřín Hill, and further on, Hradčany Castle. There, all the lights were on. I wondered what Beneš might be doing. I couldn't imagine how Beneš felt just then. Me, I felt pretty good. In fact, I really felt wonderful. We drove onto the street across from the bridge.

"Do you know just where Kitty's waiting?" asked Harry.

"Right on the corner by the Anděl Restaurant."

"Beside Girgal's bookstore?"

"Right." I thought of that bad-tempered old man. Well, I thought, they probably wouldn't be publishing his *History of Surrealism*. Not any more they wouldn't. I didn't know just what was going to happen, but my sense was that it would be all progress. Onward and upward. I was glad. This was something a person just had to rebel against. Something that gave him cause for rebellion. And that was what I needed. Cause. Incentive. Opportunity. And now I was rebelling. Now I felt good again. Harry slowed down as we approached the Anděl. I had a moment of uneasiness, maybe Kitty wouldn't be there yet. But she was. We spied her silhouette standing on the sidewalk right at the corner. She had her hands in her pockets and beside her was a small suitcase. A really small suitcase. Good old Kitty. Harry pulled up beside her. When she registered us, she just picked up her suitcase and stepped off the curb. She didn't wave or signal at all. Good old Kitty. I felt a wave of affection for her. I opened the door and Harry pulled up. I jumped out. Kitty walked around the car.

"Hi!" she said.

"Hi!" I said. "Hop in."

"Put her case in the back," Harry called from the driver's seat.

"Sure," I said. Kitty stooped over and got inside. I caught a glimpse of a leg in a nylon stocking. She wore elegant high boots trimmed with sealskin. I felt a wave of eager anticipation. Looking forward to sitting beside her, to our being crammed close together. I grabbed her suitcase, it was very light, probably nothing in it but silk lingerie and stockings and stuff, I thought, dropping it in the trunk with the rest of the luggage. Then I got back in the car. It was a bit of a squeeze. I shut the door with some difficulty, and locked it. We were packed tight and I could feel Kitty's hot body against me. My left shoulder was pressed against her right. That wasn't going to work.

"Wait a minute, Kitty," I said, raising my left arm and placing it behind her on the back of the seat. Sort of as if I wanted to put my arm around her. "Now lean back," I said, and Kitty tittered.

"Thanks," she said. I looked at her. In the red light by the starter, her skin looked white and smooth. She was looking straight ahead. Beyond her I saw Harry's profile, with his classical Jewish nose and a cigarette in his mouth. The car started forward. The headlights caught the windows of the Ringhoffer plant as Harry pulled into the right lane. On our left, a synagogue slipped past. They were using it for a warehouse or something now. We were pressed right up against each other and through the thin fabric of Harry's ski pants, Kitty's leg felt nice and warm against mine. This is just how I imagined it. This is it. Me and Kitty and Harry, and behind us Prague in the red fever of revolution. We were fleeing like the aristocrats fled St. Petersburg in 1917. Or like Harry and his uncle in '39. We were fleeing the way fleeing should be. This was the life. Finally, this was living. This was finally living. It was dark inside the car, every so often it would sway and tip Kitty even closer to me till I could feel the muscles in her leg tighten. We drove through Smíchov and the streets were empty, just here and there clusters of people carrying red flags drifting home from the demonstrations in the cold. They hadn't hanged anyone. That was life.

"Say, guys, how come you made up your minds in such a hurry?" Kitty asked. Harry didn't answer. The way Kitty said it, you could tell it was bothering her. Actually, it must've blown her away. Sure. When Robby phoned her out of the blue to pack her bags. I recognized something like apprehension or suspicion in Kitty's voice. Like it was OK now, but it wouldn't have had to be OK, and the fact that it was actually OK just happened, accidentally or coincidentally. Oh, Kitty was no fool, Kitty probably knew exactly what was what. That was fine. She likely knew how much Robby loved her. Not all that much. That was fine. Kitty was a pretty girl and now Robby had let her down a little. More than a little. He had hurt her.

"You only just decided today?" she persisted.

"No. We arranged it already yesterday." I said.

"Who is we?"

"Well, Rand, me, Robby and Harry."

"And why didn't you tell me then?"

"Didn't Robby tell you?" I asked, deliberately, to make sure she got it. It was mean of me, but Robby didn't really love her anyway. So there. And besides, she appealed to me.

"No, he didn't."

"Well, he probably didn't want to worry you unnecessarily."

"Oh, really?" she said with a touch of sarcasm.

"Really."

"Am I that delicate? Have I ever let anyone down?"

"No, but—"

"But Robby didn't want to worry me, is that it?"

"Really. Probably."

"Unnecessarily."

"Huh?"

"He didn't want to worry me unnecessarily."

"Right."

"So yesterday, you still didn't know how things would turn out, is that it?"

"No, yesterday it was still—"

"So how come it occurred to you, all of a sudden like that?"

"Well—it was more or less—it was sort of predictable, right? And when that Catholic newsman, Tigrid, split—"

"Tigrid is gone?"

"Right."

"And it still wasn't clear to you guys?"

"Why should—"

"Tigrid took off and you still didn't see it coming?"

"No, that's not it, we just didn't know exactly how we were going to pull it off."

"But you didn't want to worry me unnecessarily."

"Robby didn't."

"So you discussed it."

"Discussed what?"

"That you weren't going to worry me. Unnecessarily."

"No. That was Robby."

"So he told you that, did he?"

"No, it's just what I think. Otherwise, why wouldn't he have told you, right?"

"Oh, come now."

"Well, can you think of any other reason? Like, that he forgot, or—"

"No, I'll tell you why."

"Quit squabbling, you two," interjected Harry. We were still in Smíchov, or maybe we'd crossed into Košíře district already.

"We're not squabbling. I'm just trying to find out why Robby didn't tell me yesterday."

"He didn't want to worry you, that's all."

I felt a mild shiver pass through Kitty's body. Or maybe I just imagined it. But now she knew for sure that Robby hadn't been counting on her, and that it wasn't till the last minute, like an afterthought, that she got taken along.

"All right," said Kitty, "let's drop it." And she leaned her head back. Right on my arm. I gave her shoulder a little squeeze.

"Right," I said. "Robby didn't want to worry you, but the main thing is that you weren't worried."

She turned to face me. She smiled and said, "I wasn't the least bit worried."

"Well, then," I said, and squeezed her shoulder again. Then I definitely felt her press her leg against mine in the ski pants. She wanted to play. This Kitty girl, she was swell. I pressed back.

"When do we get to Domažlice?" she asked.

"Harry, when do we get to Domažlice?" I said.

"About five in the morning, if we don't have car trouble."

"Five in the morning," said Kitty. "So I'll catch me some sleep."

"If you can," said Harry.

"Sure I can, comfortably," said Kitty. "Joe has such soft arms. No muscles."

"I beg your pardon," I said, and felt good. It was a great beginning. "You hurt my feelings."

"You really don't have any. Muscles, I mean."

"Have I got muscles? Have I?" I said, and tensed my biceps. They were well developed from my fencing. Biceps were something I really had.

"Oh, yes, I see. I take it all back," said Kitty.

"You'd better."

We drove out onto the square at Zámečnice. On our left, high on the hillside, the terribly slender tower of the modern Košíře church pointed up at the sky. The church was unfinished. I thought of Ota, how he'd slaved for two months over the painting for the altar there. It was supposed to be the Last Judgment. Ota based his on the one by Leonardo and the archbishop didn't care for it. He said it wasn't modern enough. That pissed Ota off. In the end, Zrzavý got the commission with something symmetrical that looked like an ad for Radion laundry soap. That was more to the archbishop's liking. The archbishop was actually quite a modern fellow. He used to go to soccer matches, too. And now there probably wouldn't be any altar painting after all. God only knows what would happen to the archbishop. It occurred to me that maybe they'd lock him up like the Nazis had, but it wasn't a serious thought. Besides, it really didn't matter. The buildings kept getting sparser, until finally we were driving through nothing but hills and farmland. Up on the hill glowed two little lights from the farm at Kotlářka. Straight ahead of us in the west, the sky was black and cloudy. Only down close to the horizon did a little moonlight show through. The road was straight, and climbing. I could feel Kitty's leg warm against mine. She was breathing softly. Maybe she was asleep. I turned around and glanced out the rear window. Down behind us lay the puddle of night-lit Prague. Strings of streetlights swayed gently along the suburban streets, and downtown gave off the glow of red and blue neon. I turned back. Harry was driving in silence, his face lit red by the starter light. Kitty's eyes were shut, her lips were closed too. In this light, her lips looked black. In front of us, the road rose straight ahead and up toward the black sky. I settled back comfortably in my seat. I could feel the car moving.

I realized abruptly that some of the excitement and bliss had petered out. But I had no regrets. None at all. Besides, regrets are stupid. Everything a person does in his life is done and over with and can't be changed. So regretting anything is stupid. Absolutely. Really stupid. Real stupid. Absolutely. Absolutely for sure.

1948

1. *President Edvard Beneš headed one of post-war Europe's more or less democratic regimes, but the Communist coup of February 1948 (events described in this story) put an end to his government and ushered in forty years of totalitarianism in Czechoslovakia.*

2. *Tomáš Garrigue Masaryk (1850–1937), philosopher, educator, first president of Czechoslovakia (1918–1935), considered "father of the country."*

3. *Refers to November 1939 and the student anti-Nazi demonstrations on Wenceslas Square, violently suppressed, followed by the closing of the university and the deportation of several thousand students to concentration camps.*

4. *Reinhard Heydrich (1904–1942), Reichsprotector in Nazi-occupied Czechoslovakia. His assassination by Czech underground fighters led to extreme tension and reprisals. Karl Herrmann Frank (1898–1946), the Nazi official responsible for brutal reprisals after Heydrich was assassinated.*

5. *Aleksander Blok (1880–1921), Russian mystical revolutionary poet and dramatist.*

L a w s
o f   t h e
J u n g l e

For that which befalleth the sons of men
befalleth beasts; even one thing befalleth them ...
so that a man hath no preeminence above a beast
—Ecclesiastes 3:19

I stopped in front of the monastery and looked up. Its towers seemed to float lazily westward against the grey-white clouds, above a gilded weathervane that glowed like a sun with a nibbled border. My gaze slid down the musty tower walls, their peeling façades revealing glimpses of weathered red bricks. It was not an unfriendly place. Its consummate bleakness warmed me. I sensed in it the same decay that was in all the buildings in Broumov, in their sombre, dank, smelly staircases, except that here the decay was deliberate, derisive, poetic, and there was plenty to decay. The windows of the monastery chapel mirrored the snowy white landscape and a strip of blue western sky with the winter sun, the refectory walls perched above the railway tracks in the valley. Far beyond them scurried wisps of fog, alternately hiding and revealing Broumov's snow-capped sandstone bluffs.

I still felt like a visitor in my own body, standing there ready to abandon it, far from Prague and Kobylisy and Líza. The same body that last night rode the Broumov express, dressed in a striped shirt and colourful socks, still stunned at the realization that there wasn't a hope in hell of returning to Líza, to the life of gilt-edged days, of jealousy-racked expectation and enough material well-being to bear all that anguish. This was the end of it. Off to the remoteness

of the frontier land, full speed ahead toward socialism and desolate days that sounded good in your dreams, and in prospect had
even been able to mobilize Líza's waning sympathy. Ultimately,
though, those days would consist of nothing but interminable
sixty-minute hours. I'd been full of wonder, then, that my grief
wasn't proportional to Líza's tears. Now I realized why. With Líza, I
had never looked ahead: during those jealous and doleful afternoons when her eyes were red and her nose like a stoplight, when
she was like a fox in a trap (as I would be, come the lonely night),
trying in vain to resolve the rationally unresolvable, the problem
of fidelity and love, fidelity to Robert and love for me. I would sit
in her room on a low canvas-webbed footstool, in rapture,
warmed by my bliss, with eyes so dry that in the end, Líza got
ticked off and threw me out in the cold. She thought I didn't love
her any more, but the truth was that it was just my love for her
that allowed me to be so happy. She didn't, couldn't get it. How
could our love be anything but unhappy when it wasn't leading
anywhere? Not to Líza's bed, or to the bed in the Hájeks' villa in
Kostelec (where we'd spent a week the summer before), or any
other bed, and so, unfulfilled, it had to be an unhappy love.
Naturally, I was miserable over it too, but it was an ecstatic
anguish, occasionally so strong that it even supplanted the ecstasy.
Often so strong that Líza—a female after all, who came to tears
naturally—hadn't the remotest idea what I was feeling. But when I
looked at that sweet little mug of hers, the green eyes rimmed
with red, and everything else about her, the breasts and the butt
and the erotic legs, all of it sitting there being miserable on my
account, well, I was endlessly and helplessly happy. Of course, the
sum total of my happiness was then and there. At night, I would
writhe with jealousy, amazed at how much pain one's stupid soul
can endure, and how the human soul resides in one's gonads. But
the next day, I would without fail board the number 3 tram to
Kobylisy and make Líza's favourite face at her, noble and mourn-
fully wise, instead of—I don't know, say, beating her up. Or raping
her. No, I probably couldn't have done that, she was too strong. So

I chose noble-mindedness, but only for want of anything else to do. Though I'd like to know if anybody was ever noble for any other reason. Probably not. Probably certainly. The function of noble-mindedness in life is the same as that of evil-mindedness, and smart people are only noble when ignobility doesn't work. So, nobly, I ended up boarding the train for Broumov. I stood by the window of the moving train, watching Líza slip away, ever so sad in her blue coat with its fashionable collar, insubstantial under the dirty glass roof that arched over the platform, motionless, slipping back ever so slowly into the proverbial sunset. Never to return to me. It was stupid even to hope for anything else. So much for dreams. And yet at that moment, I was happy again, because—what future? There is no future. All there is is the present, with a sad, terribly sad little Líza, loved and loving me, and my awareness of the pain gripping her wise little soul on my account.

That was over, though. Just as I couldn't be sad about the future when the present was happy, I also didn't know how to bask in the warmth of the past when I was in trouble. Trouble was what I was in now, and in order to keep from going mad with sorrow, I had to find some warmth somewhere. I had decided on the mouldering monastery, because its decay could be cloaked in the poetry of extinct Latin and forgotten orthodoxy. I approached the baroque steps, my shoes crunching the snow, the cold penetrating their soles. On the wall facing the entrance was a stucco-work sculpture of the Crucifixion, a skinny Christ hanging woodenly from the cross, with snow in his belly button. Behind him a gilt sun with a human face smiled fatuously at the tiny figures turning St. Peter head downward on an X-shaped cross. Emerging from a cliff beneath the cross was an apocalyptic dragon with a gilt dorsal fin and gilt eyes, and some wretched souls swimming among calligraphic waves alongside a scaly whale vomiting up Jonah. He was still up to his waist in the whale but his hand was already raised in blessing. The whale was throwing him up right at the feet of the Virgin Mary in the habit of a Franciscan nun, seated in front of a knight in chain mail who was poking a spear into Christ's side.

The spear was bent, the artist must have realized just in time that if he were to continue straight in the direction of the stave, it would stab Christ in the ear. The thought made me giggle, but I thought better of it. Laughter was inappropriate for me, now. Líza never laughed when we were together. She only smiled in front of people and in photographs, to show the pretty teeth in her sexy mouth. Here, I was falling apart, and in my disintegration it seemed wrong to laugh. At best, I could smile sadly. To show Líza I was suffering. So she wouldn't for a moment think that I was taking it all lightly. And so I could be happy about it.

I turned away from the Calvary and walked toward the monastery. In the embrasure of the broad flaking archway was a tall wrought iron gate with tin strips nailed across it. I opened the door in the gate, the freezing handle chilling my hand through my leather glove, and stepped through. In the courtyard, two fellows were shovelling snow. Otherwise, the courtyard was deserted. Around its perimeter was the covered cloister, bordered with columns, and each of the four façades rose to an oriel that seemed suspended above the snow-covered ground. Slow-moving clouds looked as if they were pushing the cornices westward.

"Good afternoon," I said to the nearer of the two, dressed like a skier. "Could I speak with Father Roger?"

"That's him," said the fellow, pointing to the other one. I started toward him across the immaculate snow of the courtyard. He stopped shovelling and looked at me, but I was still too far away to speak to him. He watched me from behind his glasses and I didn't know if I should smile or not, and I couldn't walk any faster, so I was ill at ease. Father Roger stood there in a green sweatshirt with a zip up the front, just like the one Líza had. I felt a shiver of sorrow. Where was Líza now? I faced Father Roger. He was about thirty, and looked like a baseball player on some varsity team. Maybe he was a baseball player. He leaned on his shovel and before I could invoke God in a greeting, he said with a soft accent, "Good day."

That set me back. I had expected something a little more pious. I had originally considered greeting him with "Praise be to the

Lord Jesus Christ," but thought better of it, recalling the time I tried to say that to old Papa Nedochodil, where it was *de rigueur*. Back then my voice had caught, and the phrase had just hung in the air, and everyone in the dining room had fallen silent and stared at me. After that I took to just saying "Good day," even to the godly Papa Nedochodil. But this time I had intended to come up with a truly Christian greeting, so the American Benedictine[1] caught me by surprise.

"Good day," I said. "God willing."

"What would you like?" he asked.

"My name is Smiřický," I said, and waited. Father Roger just looked at me from behind that American face of his. I continued, "My uncle is a chaplain in Plzeň. Father Smiřický."

The Benedictine kept staring impassively. Apparently he wasn't the Dr. Cherf who knew my uncle.

"I've been assigned to teach in Broumov[2] and I don't have a place to live. So I thought I'd come to you—" I paused. This place was sure to have more rooms than a grand hotel.

"Oh," said Roger in English, "I see." He looked me straight in the eye. Czech priests didn't usually make eye contact like that, because anybody observant could see right through them. But Father Roger was an American. There, faith was a foregone conclusion. Maybe because American adversity could inspire a person to believe. Not so the adversity we faced here. And I was in it up to my ears. I was beyond help, and all I wanted was a place to live.

"Best you go talk to the prior," he said in his drawled Czech, and then called to the other young man. "Pitshen, would you take the gentleman to the prior?"

"Thank you," I said.

"Happy to oblige," said Father Roger, and returned to his shovelling. His college-boy face lingered in my mind. So that's what Elmer Gantry's buddies looked like. Well, they didn't bother me any.

The young Pitshen ran up to me and said, "Follow me, please."

We headed straight for some baroque steps, flanked by banisters with two rows of saints. Sporting little caps of snow, the statues looked old and lonely and they struck a chord in me. They were like me. Once long ago the Benedictine monks who walked here with psalters and rosaries used to tend them, but now no one tended them and the gold leaf on their haloes and robes was dimming, dimming proudly and poetically. They knew they were in possession of the Truth. All is vanity, but somehow they transformed it into a captivating vanity. On the other hand, secular vanity was devoid of poetry, bleak, coated with a veneer of optimism.

We went on. The young man unlocked a heavy door and led me down a corridor with paintings on its high ceiling, to a wooden staircase spiralling upward around a massive column. It was cool and gloomy, just gloomy enough. We climbed the scrubbed wooden steps, and from niches in the wall, the wooden eyes of all sorts of Christs and Thaddeuses and Marys with burning or burnt-out altar lights gazed out at me. At the top of the stairs was a sign that read "Cloister," with something else written in red beneath it. When I came closer, I could read it: "Women Strictly Forbidden." Líza should see this. She'd probably blush, embarrassed and annoyed at being a girl. Sometimes she saw her femaleness as a burden, or so she said. She did like off-colour stuff and we used to spend long afternoons talking about sex and about how stupid girls are. And they really are. With their petticoats and their costume jewellery and their hair in curlers, and their narrowness of mind. There's only one exception in the whole world. Líza. But she's married and besides, she has a number of idiosyncrasies, one of which is marital fidelity. There's no talking her out of it. And so we would go out together, sneaking around in secret, and later even with the knowledge of her husband, who knew her very well, including those idiosyncrasies of hers. We told each other how much in love we were and how great it was to be in love with each other, and Be a little happy, and Are you happy? And Líza told me how she sometimes felt like a guy, with her sexy girlish mouth she said it, and how odd it is that she's a girl, and that when she stands up in the bathtub and looks in the mirror, she can't believe it, and it was hell for me because when she said that, I could see her in my mind's eye, standing naked in the tub, her breasts with tawny nipples and the dark triangle below, and merciful God, that was the worst kind of hell there is. And I wasn't even allowed to touch her, I had to listen to her reflecting on her problematic femaleness, and make like, yeah, that's interesting. God! Damn! I shook it out of my head and followed Pitshen through the door.

We entered a low, wide corridor with windows on one side and a row of doors on the other. Pitshen's ski boots clacked on the stone floor as he strode past a number of doors until he stopped at one and turned to me.

"Will you knock for yourself?"

"Yes, certainly, thank you," I said.

"Excuse me, I have still lots of work downstairs."

"Yes, of course, thank you."

"Goodbye," said Pitshen.

"Goodbye," I said.

He turned, clacked back down the corridor and vanished through the entrance. On the door in front of me hung a leaflet written in Latin, with the picture of a fat bishop on it. I couldn't understand the text, but under the picture was a name: Guillelmus, Archepiscopus Chicagensis, Episcopus Bahamarum Insularum or something like that. I felt a breath of America waft over me. I wanted to see the man behind this door, the one who knew my uncle, this Dr. Cherf, Prior of the Benedictine Monastery in Broumov, formerly professor of biblical history and Hebrew at Loyola University in Chicago, Illinois, and now here, in this godforsaken hole. From Dr. Cherf's point of view, though, it wasn't that bad. He had his faith and, here in this awful place, he had his calling and his belief in what he was doing: by his good deeds building himself a treasure in Heaven. He loved God above all, and anything else he loved came after God, if he still loved anything else at all. Me, I loved Líza and nothing else. Except I had this odd feeling about God and all of His demands, confession, Sunday mass, that stuff. God was here, they had built a baroque tabernacle to him, but Líza wasn't. Nor did I have a calling. Nor any faith in what I was supposed to be doing here. Dr. Cherf was much less an exile from Chicago than I was from Prague, from Kobylisy and the hillsides of Libeň, from Líza.

I pushed down on the handle and entered a long narrow room. At the end was a window set into a very thick wall; outside it wispy fog rolled past the Broumov cliffs. The prior was seated at an old-fashioned desk, with a black skullcap on his head. He was slight, dry, enveloped in the black robe that draped over the carved arm-rests of his chair. On the wall behind him hung a large crucifix, at its foot a kneeling desk with a breviary. The prior didn't look up from his work and continued writing. The only sound in the room was the ticking of an unseen clock and the scraping of his ballpoint pen across the paper. I stopped where I was, silent, looking around. Beside the secretary stood a harmonium, with some sheet music open on its rack, and beside the harmonium a spinet. On the wall opposite was a pair of bookshelves, separated by another crucifix. I tried to see what books he had there, but I had only time to register *Folk Sayings* and *Kingsblood Royal* when the prior sat up, put down his pen and pushed himself away from the desk, chair and all.

He looked at me with clever eyes and asked, "What would you like?" His Czech was grammatical if a bit stiff, but pronounced with American softness.

"Good day," I said, "my name is Smiřický."

The prior nodded. "Yes, I know Smiřický."

"My uncle is chaplain in Plzeň."

"Yes, I remember him well—he is Josef?" He fixed me with his eyes. I never saw a more obviously questioning look. The prior was testing me. Smart as a Jesuit, he was, even if he was a Benedictine.

"No, your reverence, he is Karel," I said. "Josef is my father, his brother."

"Ah yes, now I remember. How are things in Pilsen?"

The test continued. The prior didn't take his eyes off me. But I knew what he was looking for, to see if we understood one another.

"Well, their numbers are down, now."

"Why is that?"

"Father Doležal disappeared."

"Oh?"

"Hadn't you heard, your reverence? It was a couple of months back."

"Dolezhal, I remember him," said the prior in his clumsy Czech. "The long one. Skinny."

"Yes. The jolly one," I said. Gone was the cool, penetrating tension in the prior's eyes. He smiled, displaying snow-white teeth.

"Funny fellow, yes. I remember when we arrived in Pilsen with the Third Army."

The test was over. I felt that we had connected, if I could ever connect with a priest. All the same, he couldn't see deep inside me, *ubi habitat veritas*, where truth resides. If he could, he would probably have cooled off considerably. Or else started battling for my soul. But those gonads of mine were beyond even his priestly grasp.

"Yes," I said. "Funny fellow—" I paused.

"And what can I do for you?" he asked. From there it was easy. I jumped right in, *in medias res*. Funny how being in a monastery recalled vestiges of my schoolboy Latin.

"Reverence, I have no place to live."

He nodded.

"I've been assigned here. I teach English, and when they relocated me and I couldn't find a flat, I thought of you, from what Uncle Karel always used to tell—"

"Are you teaching at the high school?"[3] he interrupted me.

"Oh no, they assigned *me* to the basic school. For *people like us*,"[4] I said, so sycophantically that I thought maybe I was overdoing it, "there aren't many jobs."

"There is someone teaching English here at the academic high school, but his English is not good," said the prior. "They wanted me to teach too, but I did not want to. If I did, they could accuse me of being a spy and I would not want anything like that."

"Of course. Better safe than sorry," I interjected quickly.

"They keep watching us," the prior continued. Clearly he considered me to be OK. "We have to get permits for everything. It is terrible. I cannot believe it. We do not have anything like that back home."

I smiled agreement. "Of course."

"But here is such a bureaucracy."

"Of course," I said. "I experienced it personally."

"But I want to help people here. And I do, where I can," said the prior, reaching a skinny hand across the desktop. He slid a card file, crammed full, to the edge of the desk. "Look at these," he said, "these are all requests for medicines." He started flipping through the cards, pulling one and another out at random. "Here: streptomycin. And here: liver extract injections—prednisone—more streptomycin."

The cards flipped through his fingers, scraping against his gold ring. Across the top of each card was a name and address, in the centre the medication and the diagnosis. So many hopes were shut up in that little box: images flashed by my mind's eye, yellowish faces, needle-marked thighs and butts, swollen ankles, all the pains and ailments I remembered from four years earlier when I helped Nurse Udeline at the hospital in Kostelec. They couldn't be happy in this country; precisely in this country they couldn't. Nothing could help them. Nothing except maybe Father Cherf and America's Catholic Action. Here in this country, nothing but that. The prior's monotonous voice recited drug after drug, like a litany: "Streptomycin—viteolan—penicillin—more streptomycin."

What compelled all these people to let their hopes be shut up in this silly little box? I would never do that, I decided. Why on earth are they so awfully anxious to stay alive, when they have the opportunity to die without exerting any effort of their own? As if they truly believed that it's better to be than not to be, when you aren't, really. You're aware of a lot of stuff, including the fact that you're going to die. That colours everything. Let someone lock up your hopes in a little box? No way! The disadvantage of death is that it never comes when you want it to. All a fellow can do is bring it down on himself, but then, who can muster the guts to do it? It's a funny dichotomy, between the yearning for death and the courage to choose it. In my mind it springs from a belief in Hell, where suicides wind up. Otherwise, though, being able to die, good God, I'd lock up all my hope and solace in Líza and not in some little box. Whatever there was when I wasn't with Líza, it wasn't living. It wasn't for me. I'd rather live a year or even half a year with Líza, and give up all the rest of time. Even if I were to go to the devil. If I could take all the days I was ever going to be able to spend with Líza, all the Easter and Christmas vacations that the school board and her husband would grant me, if I could collect them all in advance, back to back, I'd do it in a flash, even if all together they only added up to a month. And then I'd die, my sole regret being that there weren't any more of them.

I yanked myself out of the flow of my thoughts and back to Father Cherf. I saw that he had pulled one card out of the card file and was contemplating it. "Here," he said scornfully, "radioisotopes. For leukemia. An awful sickness. And the only place to get them is from the States. And the Czechoslovak ministry of health has put a ban on importing them. They say it is espionage."

"How?"

He looked at me sarcastically. "Why, because radioactivity has to do with the production of the atom bomb."

"Oh."

"That fellow is going to die. There is no other treatment."

The priest shuffled through the cards some more.

"How many requests do you have there?"

"About fifteen hundred. This is only part of them."

"And how many of them can you fill?"

The prior gave a wave of his hand. "Oh, we could fill them all. American Catholics are good people. And they have money. But the ministry will only give permits for a few."

Fifteen hundred. One thousand, five hundred people who are guaranteed a letdown. Who are sad even in the cheery glow of the five-year plan. But then, what's fifteen hundred people? A little more than the population of Lidice.[5] Czechoslovakia has eleven or so million. What do fifteen hundred matter? And besides, most of them would never really get well, anyhow. I wondered about the prior. And I wondered about them. Why hang on to life so absurdly, such a handful of people?

"Ah yes," said the prior. "And now abideth faith, hope, charity, these three; but the greatest of these is charity. Charity. That is what is lacking most."

"Yes. It certainly is," I said.

The prior rose from his chair. I was glad he was dropping the subject, it was beginning to bore me. He was a small man, but he looked strong and healthy for his age. He probably played football when he was young, before he became a missionary. To Broumov.

"So you need a place to live," he said pensively.

"I do, your reverence."

"Hmm. I do not know if you would like it here."

"I'm sure I would, your reverence."

"We have plenty of room, but—it is cold, you know. We do not get much coal and it takes a lot. It is large here."

"Don't concern yourself, your reverence, I'll get the coal I need," I said impetuously. "Let me worry about that."

"And no comforts. This is a monastery, you know."

I laughed. "I'm not accustomed to luxury. And here, it is—" I started to say "splendid," but my hyperbole was starting to get on my nerves, and "swell" was too common, so I corrected myself. "I really like it here."

"Good, I am glad. But it is not comfortable. So come with me," said the prior, moving toward the door. I opened it for him and stepped aside. The prior walked out into the hallway, and I followed.

"This is my cell," he waved a hand, "and here is Father Roger's. Two brothers over there, and a reverend father in the back. Now we go this way."

I glanced at the row of doors and then I turned to follow the prior. We walked quickly down the empty hallway to the click of our shoes. Then we turned right and found ourselves at the head of a spiral staircase, but not the one I had come up by. We descended to another hallway with another row of doors. There were paintings with holy scenes all along the walls. I would have liked to stop and have a look, I liked those images of aristocratic Italian faces and monks, fat and skinny, and torture, and flocks of cherubs on clouds, and sunbeams raying down from the heavens. Lots of them. But the prior was striding away like a tourist, and I had to keep up, so I could only glance at them in passing.

"This is the library," he said, indicating a row of doors, "and upstairs too. The library is on two floors."

I wanted to indicate that I was impressed, but again, I didn't know how to do it credibly without sounding phony. So I just gave an appreciative mumble. We took another sharp right down a narrow hall, and the ceiling suddenly rose extremely high, with windows along both sides near the top, and bright beams of light spilling down through them.

"That is the church," said the prior. At the end of the hall he opened a wrought iron door and we started up another spiral staircase, narrow and dim. I lost count of how many times we went around the centre column, but it was quite a few, and then the stairs turned us out into another corridor, and I had lost track of which direction we were taking. More pale faces and haloes stared out at me from rows of paintings on the walls. Then the hall turned sharply to the left, and the prior halted and indicated a partition made of boards.

"In there is the clergyman from that other denomination—the Czechoslovak Church, you know?"

"Yes, I know," I said.

"His wife is principal of the high school. A rabid Communist."

"Well—" I didn't quite know how I was expected to respond. His eyes were on me, and this time they seemed to take on a mischievous twinkle.

"Their son comes to our residence and in the evenings he prays with us," he grinned.

I forced a laugh. "Really?"

"Really. They try to turn their youth against priests. But kids come here and see how things truly are and play ping-pong, and we win them over."

"Naturally," I said. Clearly youngsters were more likely to buy into ping-pong than compulsory hop-picking brigades and Marx-Leninism.

"Here," he said, indicating the partition, "is the Broumov Youth Union. They have their club room here. But they come to us and play with our boys. They see how good it is here, and so when they hear bad things about priests, they do not believe it."

"Naturally," I said, ill at ease about constantly repeating the same unconvincing affirmatives, but the father seemed not to notice.

"Over there," he pointed. We moved on, through a small door to another hallway. "That is the way to the dorms. But we go this way." Through another doorway to a narrow staircase. The corner of the landing would have been dark if it weren't for a little light under a painting of St. Veronica's veil. I had lost all sense of direction. At the top of the stairs, the prior opened another door. We found ourselves in another long, tall clerestory corridor with the slender windows high up in the wall. On one side was a row of doors, and with the names of saints over them in faded gold. There were no paintings here.

"This is the other side of the church," said the prior, "and here are what used to be monks' cells." We walked past the doors and I read the Latin names above them: St. Valerianus, St. Bernardus, St. Crispinus, St. Dominicus, St. Hieronymus. The prior tried the handles on each of the doors until one opened. St. Ambrosius. We went inside and I looked around. The cold cell warmed my heart. The quintessential monk's chamber. I needed that, yes, it was just what I needed. Now, far from Líza, in this Broumov exile. It was a long skinny room, with a little round coal stove in the corner, at the far end a barred window deep in the thick wall, a bed, a large crucifix with a kneeler, a writing table, one chair, and a washbasin in the corner.

"Not very cosy," said the prior.

"No, no, I like it. Really. It's wonderful," I said, and this time I sounded sincere, because I genuinely did like it. This was where I could spend the rest of my life, if I couldn't have Líza and I couldn't die. It occurred to me that I might actually enter a monastic order. Then maybe they'd release me from my teaching assignment. Yes, go to a monastery and—but stay in a monastery, only there, forever? There would be too little happening. If I couldn't be with Líza, the only thing that held me together was things happening, like this moving from place to place and looking for lodgings. But if there were to be a war, then I would leave the monastery, because in a war, a lot would be happening and I could go back to Líza for a few days. Go back to Líza. God, I didn't believe it could happen any more, it would be like a miracle. Still, I wished for it with all my heart, yearned for it, although I knew my yearning was futile. I knew it would never change. My sorrow would always and forever have its clear and palpable source, prohibited by law. I pictured interminable days on the teacher's podium, with the endless jokes and patter and moralizing and grading, and ranks of stupid snot-nosed kids. And then, all of a sudden, I experienced an intense visual and physical image of Líza, naked in bed in an embrace, but not my embrace. I felt my soul down there clench in pain. I shut my eyes and jaws tight. Excruciatingly slowly, the pain faded.

Father Cherf was saying, "We would have to bring you some coal here. And a bucket."

"No, thanks, this'll be just fine," I said. I wanted to be alone already.

"You mean to sleep here tonight?" asked the prior.

"Yes."

"But you will be cold."

"That's fine, I'm used to it."

"Well, all right," said the Prior. "I will get you some coal."

"No, thanks, that's fine, your reverence. Really. I'll get hold of some for myself," I was quick to assure him, if only to get rid of him.

"Whatever you think," he said, looking around again. "Otherwise you have everything you need here, no?"

"Certainly, your reverence. I truly thank you."

"The monastery closes at seven o'clock. You will not mind?"

"Not in the slightest."

"Well, if you come home later, you can ring the bell at the gate."

"No. I'll be home. I have—I still have studying to do."

We stood there. I needed to get him to leave. To say goodbye. I'd had enough of him. I wanted to be alone so I could concentrate on my jealousy. I knew how rotten it would make me feel, but I was drawn to it like a fly to a candle.

"Reverence, will you show me the way to get here from the street entrance?"

"If you please," he said, and moved.

"It's a bit of a labyrinth," I joked.

"A historic building," said the prior, "but you are right, there is an easier way to go from here."

We emerged from the cell and strode on down the corridor. I gave up reading the names above the doors, there were too many of them. We turned a corner, the ceiling dropped lower again and I saw more paintings. Different ones, though. We walked through the other wing of the monastery. Down a wide wooden staircase to the ground floor, where I saw a door very much like the one I had entered by. We went outside and the prior stopped on the steps. His black figure was silhouetted against the snow. I stopped beside him and saw that Father Roger and Pitshen were still shovelling snow.

In American English, the prior called out to Pitshen, "Still at it?"

"Yeah, father," the young man replied. "Another five minutes or so."

Father Roger stopped shovelling and straightened up. He puckered his lips and started whistling the pop hit song, "*Give me five minutes more—*" He chuckled, and so did Pitshen.

"Well, thank you, your reverence, and God bless," I said.

"Goodbye," said the prior.

It seemed somehow too abrupt, to take leave of him like that. "May I come see you some time, your reverence?"

"Feel free. I would be pleased to see you."

"Well, then, God bless."

"Goodbye."

I turned away from him and went down the steps.

"God bless!" I shouted to Father Roger.

"Goodbye," he called back, and then, in English to Pitshen, "Open the door, Pitshen!"

Pitshen chuckled, dropped his shovel and loped over and opened the gate wide for me and, when I walked up, bowed cheerily.

"So long," he said.

"Thanks, so long," I said with a smile and hurried outside.

It was cold, and the sun was just setting. The strip of sky below the scudding clouds glowed orange. I stopped smiling. It was freezing. I was alone. I turned and walked toward town. The narrow street seemed to close over my head, confining me in its bleak fustiness. Blind windows with nobody living behind them, flaking paint on doors leading into musty darkness, shop windows bereft of merchandise, not a single living thing in sight. I trudged through the deep snow, and reality weighed heavily on my soul. In all my eighteen months with Líza, I hadn't ever admitted it to myself, the reality that was inevitable in this country, this state. My doubts multiplied. I walked under a faded old sign in an indistinct German script, announcing to the entire lifeless street that this was once Franz Schneiders Gasthaus u. Weinstube "Zum grünen Baum," with a primitive image of a green tree, its crown like a round lantern, and it came to me that this was all just a little chapter in my life's curse, and a bit later it came to me, further, that it wasn't a curse, that there is no such thing as a curse, that all there is is life's course, the inevitable scheme of life, proceeding according to ironclad natural laws dating back to the time of prehistoric seas or even further, back to the red-hot matter of primordial mists, the initial swirling of primordial particles; back to that uncomplicated primordial relative movement of two insignificant grains of primordial matter. But it seemed odd to me. I wasn't sure about those ironclad laws of nature. They would have had to exist even before those twitching little bodies of matter, of course, they must have enclosed, embodied them? No. The course of life, concocted in some remote past as a blind, mechanical, neutral and factual ongoing existence, devoid of good and evil, was contrived by some God for His own amusement. All I knew about the course of life was that it takes the path it has to take, that it must be the way it is, that even if Robert were to die, Líza would never move to this frozen hell with me, not Líza who was accustomed to Prague, to Berger's pastry shop, to the neon lights and the movies and the Kobylisy hillsides, and at worst to the mild discomfort that comes with the adventure of a vacation pleasure trip. That was the substance, finally, of my doubts and my fear: that she would never move here, and that with me here, and him beside her all the time, she'd forget me. That, and the naked embrace I couldn't be part of. And the desolate, snow-covered town square seemed to jeer at me with the rusty clang of its tower clock. It was half past four. They had just turned on the lights in the Ultraphon record shop, and the loudspeaker over the door was blowing strains of New Orleans jazz across the virgin snow. Amazing, here, on this shoal of civilization. Whoever would buy Kid Ory, here? Or any record, for that matter? An old woman in a babushka and sweatpants was plodding up from the hotel lugging two shopping bags. Lights went on in two or three other windows. I turned down the street toward the basic school, and by the time I got there, dusk had fallen. My skin was crawling with the awful cold. I entered and stamped the snow off my shoes onto the mat. By the staircase I vaguely registered two white posters with the faces of Gottwald[6] and Stalin, both of them grinning, under a banner that said, in heavy black letters, Helping to Build a Happy Land and under it, A Socialist Land!

I wished them every success. As for me, I wouldn't be much help to them; I didn't know how. A ray of light shone through the keyhole in the door to the faculty room. I opened the door and said, "Good evening."

Three teachers looked up at me. The principal said hello, but the others ignored me. I was a professor, and they were plain, ordinary teachers.[7] And to make room for me, one of their number had been sent away to teach in the elementary school. One much older than me, with a family. And seniority. But I was a professor, and professors didn't have to teach elementary. I picked up my suitcase with the feather quilt and pillow, and the one with my clothes and records.

"Say, colleague," the principal said to me. He was seated at the conference table, filling in some kind of questionnaire. The whites of his eyes were yellow, and his teeth were broken off from the wartime concentration camp. As compensation, he had been named principal in Broumov.

"Yes?" said I.

"You're a philosopher. We need a bulletin board about Engels."

"Bulletin board?"

"Yes, for 3B."

"How—is it done?" I was still holding the two suitcases. It was starting already. Bulletin boards, questionnaires, bringing cultural enlightenment to rural youth. I was in a hurry to get away.

"Well," said the principal, "we've got some pictures, you'll take those and then you'll write something about his life, and some quotations."

"I see. By when?"

"Well—could you do it tomorrow?"

"All right," I said. "So—"

The principal interrupted me. "Come to my office in the morning for the materials."

"All right. So—"

"Have you got a place to live yet?"

"Yes."

"Where?"

Idiot. He had apparently decided to take an interest in me. Of course, I was no threat to his position here. I replied coolly, "In the monastery."

They all turned to me and blurted, in unison, "The monastery?"
"That's right."

There was a long silence. Then the principal asked, "Do you like it there?"

I knew what was bothering them. I understood at least that much about conditions here. They were thinking of the entry that would go in my personnel file: *Resides in a monastery with American Benedictine monks.* And they didn't even know about the preceding notations: *Member of American Institute and Union of Friends of the USA. Father, former functionary of the National Democratic Party, expelled from the Sokol Club; resided in Prague with Dr. J. Nedochodil (former People's Party deputy, expelled by Action Committee from People's Party); receives letters from England and from refugee camps in West Germany.* If they had known all that, the monastery might not have come as such a shock. How far would I get with a personnel file like that? Given my scant enthusiasm for this line of work? In this happy land? But that too was the course of my life.

"I like it." I grinned. "It's perfectly swell there."

Another silence. Then the principal said, "Well—so you'll come pick up those materials tomorrow?"

"Yes. So, I'm off," I said. I tucked the valise with my clothes and records under my arm and picked up the phonograph case off the floor "So, good night," I said, kicking open the door.

I heard a grumbled "Good night" as I slipped out. The principal shut the door behind me. I stumbled down the stairs and squeezed out through the main door. I could sense the dark mass of the boarded-up church across the street, and as I started toward the square, the cold began to numb my hands on the handles of my luggage. I moved quickly, but the sidewalk was slippery with snow. The sweat on my back felt icy. Around the square, five stores were lit up, as were the windows of the hotel-cum-tavern and the round clock atop the town hall. It could have been rather like Christmas, had I been in the mood for Christmas. Burdened with my suitcases, I slipped and slid straight across the square to the monastery street, misery flooding my soul. In Kobylisy, Líza would just be switching on the lamp on the end table by the chesterfield, the one with the parchment shade and the tiny Trnka figurine with the silly benevolent face, the one I had given her. She called him Kolmaník, because she'd lent him to me to take along for luck at my first orals in philosophy under Professor Kolman. And now this tiny red-nosed mannikin is tucked into the shade of Líza's lamp and gets to watch her lounging on the chesterfield with a book, with her breasts under a green sweatshirt like the one Father Roger had on this morning, in a brown checked skirt, nylons, and tiny brown slippers on her feet, my very own love Líza, who wasn't destined to be part of the ultimate course of my life. And her husband Robert is sitting at his desk across the room from her, writing something for radio, something dumb, because that's the only kind of thing Robert ever writes. Or maybe he's coming over to lie on the chesterfield beside Líza, and she's leaning back against him, and they're talking. Maybe about me. And Robert is analysing me with cool logic, dissecting me, what I say and how I act and how I am, and doing it so cleverly that there doesn't seem to be a trace of hostility or calumny or malice or jealousy in it, it's just clear and logical and when he's finished there's nothing left of me except a doubt in Líza's little head as to why she—maybe—is in love with me. In fact, it's just possible that right now, at this moment as I stand on the square in Broumov, she doesn't love me at all. I never even noticed myself slipping back into my old doubts. Of course she doesn't love me when she's with him. Or at least she doesn't think of me. My fingers were numb and a cough started creeping up from my lungs. The sweat on my back chilled me. And I was so alone. Líza, what does she know of me? And what does she think of me? Right now, what is she thinking about me? In the comfort of Kobylisy? Nothing at all. Maybe they're just now kissing. The cold, the wind, my sweaty back and the misery all flowed together inside me and turned into a single huge anguish. I was thinking like a primitive beast. Once I was a happy, careless young buck, but now I was hungry, I was cold, I was tired, and I was alone. I was lonely, defeated and standing outside in the night.

There was no other way I could think. That's why it seemed perfectly all right, all the more so since everything in my vision of the flat in Kobylisy and my misery was real. Líza couldn't understand it or feel it. And I couldn't even hold it against her. If I were in her place and she in mine, I wouldn't feel it either. A fellow can't actually feel anything that doesn't pinch him personally, in his body and his soul. That too is part of life's course.

I plunged into the darkness of the street and stumbled toward the monastery steps. A lantern burned faintly on the wall, its light making strange shapes of the carved figures on the Calvary; and the moon shone through the clouds over the monastery. The sheer walls of the presbytery, only a shade lighter than the darkness behind them, hung there in the frosty night. I made it to the iron gate and carefully set down the phonograph and the suitcases. Right away I felt better. I began stamping my feet, first one, then the other. I suddenly realized that I hadn't settled things with the prior. But what was there to settle? He had given me a room, shown me the way to get there, told me what time they locked the gate. That was all I needed. Yes. I was alone and there was nothing more I required. I grasped the handle on the door in the gate, opened it, picked up my cases and the phonograph, and stepped inside the courtyard. There, I put everything down again and shut the door behind me. I stood there in the silence and the dark. I wasn't breathing. I began to register my surroundings. Overhead, a bank of moon-silvered clouds was sweeping past the stationary square baroque walls. Here, I wasn't in Broumov any more. Here I was simply in hell. The hell of loneliness. It was a new, unfamiliar hell, though, and so it still held my interest. I picked up my luggage and walked over to the steps. Gradually the snow grew discernible against the black mass of the buildings. I scrambled up the steps and repeated the opening and closing procedure at the door. Inside, there wasn't even a trace of light. Only darkness: dense, cold, black. I put one suitcase down and fished a flashlight out of my pocket. Its light pierced the dark and lit on a painting. It was Veronica's veil and the tortured face of Christ. I ran the finger of light across the row of paintings, but only the closest ones were visible in its weak glow; farther away its tip vanished in the darkness. A dense, absolute silence lay over everything. From somewhere far away among the twists and turns, the archways, the stairwells, the niches, came what might have been the sound of time ticking past, although how time could pass here I didn't know, when there was nothing to measure it by, in this immutable stone world of insensate paintings and statues. I picked up my baggage and, with the flashlight in my right hand and the phonograph under my arm, set out through the darkness, led by a wavering cone of pale light and accompanied by the huge flickering shadow of myself. Despite the exertion and the pain in both my hands, I was noticing the paintings. By the light of the flashlight, they looked ghostly, as if they had always hung in the dark of night. The armour of orderly knights gleamed against sombre backgrounds, the purple of their mantles burning with the long-lost lustre of battle, the grandeur of religious rituals and the salons of Christian countesses. They followed my progress with dull, expressionless eyes. The half-naked bodies of martyrs against strange, extinct landscapes emerged from the jagged shadows behind them. All of it moved past me, appearing out of the darkness and slipping back into it in silence. The only sound was my footsteps and the wheezing of my exhausted bronchial tubes. Sluggishly I climbed the steps, their creaks echoing their own echoes, and, tired as I was, I kept bumping my suitcases against them. The hollow sounds made me think of the fellow I'd met on the train coming here and his tales of mysterious dungeons under the Broumov monastery, with torture chambers and barrels containing the pickled remains of victims of historical Benedictines. The fellow was probably some Party member of the folksy persuasion. His story was fun to contemplate, it titillated the nerves a little, it just wasn't very credible. People on trains were always full of such tales. With perfectly straight faces, they would come up with, say, the story of a powder sprinkled on Greek guerrillas that had made them emerge from the woods with their hands up, or unfold a theory about how the Vatican rules the world, with a convoluted rationale to explain why the Pope sanctioned the rise of Communism in Russia, a rationale so arcane that it truly seemed like God's Providence. I used to think they were kidding, but they weren't. People are always glad to have something to believe in. Anything to believe in. For instance, that one can cultivate one's will, as the parapsychologist Kafka recommended, with incantations. Ten times a day: *I can do it*, or *I shall succeed*, three times before starting a task, and it never occurs to them to wonder what would happen once they succeed, and achieve their will. What good would it do them? But they were content, and the word "futility" was about as useful to them as the word "amphibole" or "demotic." That's why they could function like ants in an anthill, in any situation, no matter where the shoe pinched. All they needed was a few broad outlines for comparison and then a few generalized disbeliefs in biology, history, etc. to arrive at their conclusions. I never possessed a faith like that, firm and crass. In fact, I had only one belief: that things would stay this way forever, the socialism and the five-year plans and the deployment of labour, and that right or wrong, I was stuck in it, no matter how pointless it all seemed to me. Yes, sometimes I did think that the Communists were right: revolution and the dictatorship of the proletariat and the escalation of the class struggle, but while I could appreciate all the accomplishments of industry and the visions of a just future, I was moved much more by my own misery and the troubled lives of a few guys I knew and of the girls who, irrespective of socialism, were forever—unhappily—in love. That was my dilemma. There were too many troubles in my life to let me be content working for a cause, even one I could have believed in. Winning the cause couldn't change anything about my troubles. Líza would never marry me and the bureaucrats at the employment office would never recognize that I am simply not made for working at a job, for a lifelong, day-to-day civil occupation, that the thought of it makes me ill, that without Líza I was dying here in this hole called Broumov. No five-year plan could ever change that. I believed in the happy future that their cause might bring to a statistically significant majority of the people, but I couldn't believe it would benefit me, bring me happiness. Their cause was simply outside my context. That was my belief, and my disbelief. And I wasn't the sort to relinquish my share of well-being for the good of that statistical ninety percent. Particularly when what constituted my well-being was so specific. Particularly when my well-being was so achievable. All I needed was some pull at the Ministry of Education, or a war that would abolish this regime. But I didn't believe in any such war, and so I was willing to go along with this regime, if only it would leave me be. I had been all for it until it drove me away from Líza. And I'd be all for it again if I could go back to her. As long as it pinched somebody else, it was all the same to me, because maybe it was right. And everyone was like that: active in their cosy jobs, reactive only when unseated. Or at least, a mathematically significant majority was. They muscled their way ruthlessly to the top, treading on the political corpses of old friends, turning in their own children if they did things that were politically embarrassing. The predatory law of the jungle ruled here as much as in the wild.

I turned a corner and the flashlight beam spilled out into the corridor that bordered the church. The row of doors emerged black from the half-lit dimness, and the gilded saints' names gave off a faint gleam. I found St. Ambrose and turned the handle. The door opened. The cone of my light flashed into the room and fell on a lamp standing on the table. That hadn't been there before. The prior must have brought it. I set down the suitcases and picked up the lamp. There was a new stearin candle in its metal holder. I fished some matches out of my pocket and lit it. The dim light cast a black shadow across the crucifix and my breath formed a little white cloud of steam. It was terribly cold. I switched off the flashlight. I put the lamp back on the table and placed the phonograph beside it. The narrow cot had a white sheet on it. That must be the work of the prior too. His solicitude warmed me a little, but then again, it goes with his vocation. I opened one suitcase and put my comforter and pillow on the bed. Then I took off my overcoat. Right away, I began to shake with the cold. Fingers trembling, I took the flannel pyjamas out of the other valise—the red striped ones that had been a gift from Líza, the hockey sweater that Přema had left at my place before he fled across the border, and the sweatsuit I'd had since high school, bought by my mom when I was supposed to go to Onkel Otto's summer camp to learn German. Each of those things called up a flood of memories. Of Líza and my grief at not being able to wear the pyjamas to bed with her; of Přema, my buddy from wartime spring evenings in Kostelec, strolling the monotonous loop of the town's promenade, night after night, making dirty cracks about girls we didn't dare approach; memories of my mom, dead now from the agony of Bright's disease; of the Jew Otto Felix who wound up gassed in Auschwitz and fat Quidon Hirsch likewise. I took a deep breath to brace myself and pulled off my jacket. There was no controlling the cold that assaulted my body. I yanked the sweater and shirt over my head. I could hear my teeth chattering. The touch of the flannel pyjama top on my skin felt like the touch of death, only much more tangible. I buttoned it hurriedly and pulled the hockey sweater and the sweatshirt over it. Little clouds of my congealed breath floated in the light of the lamp. I stood there, half dressed for bed, and bent down to take off my trousers. I was still shivering. Standing there naked from the waist down, I abandoned my usual fastidiousness and left everything where it dropped. I yanked up the pyjama pants and the sweatpants and a pair of ski socks on my feet. Then I started jumping up and down, waving my arms furiously. There was no warming up, though, it was as if all the cold issued to the Broumov monastery was concentrated in that tiny cell. I shoved the table with the phonograph and the lamp over by the bed, snatched a roll and a chunk of salami out of my suitcase and jumped into bed. My boudoir. Líza called her bed her "boudoir." I wrapped myself in the comforter as tightly as possible, and sank my teeth into the salami. It was the temperature of ice cream. I gobbled it down without chewing to allay the hunger that fused with the chill to form one single integral discomfort. The only sound was that of my lips smacking and my teeth grinding the roll. With my stomach somewhat satisfied, the freezing tension subsided a little. I lay there in bed, my body just beginning to warm the inside of the sweatsuit and comforter. As soon as my thoughts could move from my stomach, they slipped into their old rut. All ruts led to Kobylisy. On the ceiling, my lamp cast the flickering shadow of a square quartered by a cross, and on the crucifix, Christ bowed his tortured head. It's Líza, only Líza, Líza is everything. Overwhelmed with loneliness, I gnawed on the salami. Then my eye fell on the phonograph. One piece of my world that went with me the way my thoughts did. I finished eating and opened the lid of the phonograph. I bent over and picked up my sweater and muffled the speaker with it. I reached into the compartment in the lid where I had the records I'd intended to give Líza as a going-away present. I pulled out the top one and looked at it. The label was hard to read in the dim light. "Dark Blue World." Yes. Suddenly I longed to hear that voice, its sarcasm touched with futility.[8] I took the record out of its paper sleeve and placed it on the turntable. Then I turned the handle to wind it up and placed the needle on the rim of the revolving record. For a long moment, the only sound was a gentle hiss and then, muted by the sweater, the sound of a piano. The old-fashioned piano style reminded me of poor old Ježek.[9] I felt awfully close to him. Why wasn't I born sooner, so I could have known him? But it's better this way. There would have been nothing to say. He would have known all about futility and bliss and justice and stuff, just like me. We wouldn't have had anything left to tell each other. He must have been like Líza and me. And Líza was the only person that I could talk with who knew it all. Because Líza was a girl and because I loved her. Then Werich's old voice sounded. Him too. He sang, and I listened, in the depths of a monastery far from Prague and from Líza. I devoured that voice. Every semitone, every caesura said so much to me, embodied life, embodied all of my stupid miserable life, muted and ironically uttered into the monastery night.

So what if I'm not hungry,
Food ain't bad,
So what if I'm not hungry,
my soul's still sad.

Yes. Now, everything was better. Everything in the world. Except for my silly soul, still sad, still sadder. My eyes started burning with tears and a huge sob worked its way up from my gut. The record was over. I stopped the phonograph and a tear fell from my eye onto the record. I wiped it off with my elbow. I pulled out another record and looked at it under the lamp. "Joe Turner Blues." I knew it would make me cry, but I put it on anyway. Or just because it would. Muffled by my sweater, the saxes started syncopating. Where was Líza? Why wasn't she here? Why did it have to be this way, why couldn't a fellow revolt, for heaven's sake, why couldn't something be done about it? A mocking, melancholy voice started singing. Líza. Líza. Líza. Little Líza. My sweetheart, my sunshine, my soul, my universe, why wouldn't she sleep with me, why couldn't she marry me. I thought about Líza and those thoughts brought her image to my mind's eye, her remote green eyes, her adorable lips, irretrievably lost, forever, infinitely unattainable, those adored lips of hers, all of it, her life, her past, her present, her presence, her absence, and the pain gradually spilled out, grating on my brain, and along the nerves to my hands and feet, an awful biting pain, clenching with the strength of a grizzly bear somewhere down below my belly, somewhere in the wellspring of life, and the madness of the pain started to wrench itself into words that dripped one by one from my brain. Líza. Fidelity. Nobody has the right to it. Not to practise it, not to demand it. Nobody, not even Líza. And nobody who ever suffered this agony could practise or demand it. This awful suffering. This awful agony. This awful, ghastly loneliness in a freezing body. *Some day, when you and I must part,* sang Joe Turner in his mocking, terribly sad voice. It gave voice to everything, everything inside me. *And every time you hear the whistle blow,* even the saxophones wailed my pain, *hear old steamboat whistle blow,* wailed the saxes, *you'll hate the day you lost your Joe.* Desperately, finally, I burst into tears. I stopped the phonograph, put out the candle and collapsed onto the cot. Never, never, *nevermore,* I whimpered through clenched teeth, and great gobs of pain pulled loose and poured out. Damn, damn, oh damn! Nevermore. Líza. Oh, Líza. Oh, oh, Líza. God, oh, God. Oh, Líza. Líza. Líza darling. Darling, oh, God, my darling. After a while all my tears had spilled out and I lay there unthinking, becalmed, desolately becalmed. I wanted to die. That calm, that's always the worst of all. The worst is that you never die of it. That it tortures you insidiously, tortures you and tortures you. And lets you think it's over, and then tortures you some more. Every time, so many times. I remembered Líza's discourse, her stories about him, how they had met, how attractive she had found him, how he spoke to her, how they were together, how his parents were out of town and she told her folks she was going camping with Bibi, and she stayed with him in his flat the whole four days, then about the first time they went on a vacation together, and he waited for her at the railway station, how she told him she was going to have a baby and watched him sitting on the park bench all worried, but he wanted to marry her, and then how she had admitted it wasn't true. How they maintained chastity on account of Father Paul and in the end how they couldn't help themselves. How they broke up and how finally she came crawling back. How he left her and in her mind she called out woefully, Robbie, come back! Robbie! Robbie! Come back! And then she went after him and found him all miserable, perched on a fence, and she went over to him and begged him not to be mad at her. She never saw me perched on a fence. No matter how many times I sat there all miserable. And she never came after me. And she never called out in her mind, Danny, come back. Danny! Danny, come back! I just had to listen to it all, all those stories filled with everything I didn't have and desperately wanted to have, listening to it and wanting to hear more and more, I must have wanted it, how could I not have wanted it, and making like it didn't get to me. Listen to it. Listen to it. Keep listening to it and thinking about it and imagining it ...

Imagining it. That's all. Losing my whole life and nobody cared. I was all alone with it. In the end, nothing could be done, no way to make it better, not even Líza saying, "I know, I believe you, I know how bad you feel," when I felt bad. Terribly, awfully bad. Even sympathy didn't help. Nothing could help. No tender words, no nothing. I curled up under the comforter and surrendered to my misery. I was freezing again. Nothing broke the silence. Immersed in that silence, I finally fell asleep from sheer exhaustion.

During the night, the temperature dropped and it was more than evident in the monastery cell. The cold woke me at about two in the morning and I lay that way till dawn, curled up in a fetal position, as closely bundled up in the comforter as humanly possible, frozen numb and listening to the syncopated concert of my chattering teeth. The silence crystallized into degrees centigrade plunging on the thermometer. All I could think of was morning, and how soon it would arrive. Finally, it did. From the window, a barred strip of pale daylight fell across the cot and touched Christ's waxy profile. As the light of the sun rose golden, his Jewish face gradually emerged from the gloom, impervious to the frost that was even settling in tiny crystals on my comforter. At seven I tried getting up. The best I could do was to fall out of bed. Overnight, the lubrication in my joints had stiffened my knees and elbows into balls of ice. From somewhere deep in the monastery came the strains of distant monotone singing. I got up off the floor, and launched into frenzied motion. *Asperges me. Domine.* Four or five voices keened plaintively through the frigid monastery corridors. I began to regret having undressed the night before. With extreme self-control, I put on my clothes. I wasn't thinking about Líza. Even she couldn't expect that of me. What I was thinking about was that I had to find myself a place to live. A heated place, with central heating, a metal radiator that just sits there, unobtrusively diffusing heat. Or at least with a stove and a heap of coal in the cellar. I fled the monastery and trotted down the street toward the town square. Picturesque little clouds floated across a frosty blue sky and Hvězda mountain was festooned with wisps of mist. At its foot, windows of minuscule cottages mirrored the rising sun. It occurred to me that this was how it looked in movies about the Alps, the charming little villages in the snow and the clouds drifting past rocky peaks. And with an intelligent-looking vicar or teacher and a lovely country girl. In a warm movie house. Never cold. Here, it was twenty bitter Broumov degrees below freezing, and children gambolled across the square, shouting happily, deliberately clambering on the highest snowdrifts, throwing snowballs. The boys at the girls, the girls at the boys. Merrily, merrily. They called out to me, "Hello, teacher!" and I had to answer them. A small girl, awfully pretty in a short skirt, said hello. She had no idea what she had to look forward to. If only she were older, so I could sleep with her. Good God, I was an educator.

Then I taught, and, standing in front of pupils who followed me with ingenuous eyes and respectfully answered my questions, I pronounced stupid clichés about politeness and silence and applying oneself, and it made me sick and I couldn't be a teacher, I had to be a decadent dirty old man, the foul-minded Danny Smiřický, Dannykins, wooer of Líza, and so, during history class I recounted what Leda had done with the swan, and about pharaohs marrying their sisters, that was to the fourteen-year-olds in the third year, and in geography in the second year, what Greek mythology said about the origin of the Milky Way, and so on, until I wound up my teaching day in zoology in 3B with a comprehensive discourse on the forms of hermaphrodism in nature. And in each room I picked a girl, always the prettiest one, and ogled her with narrowed eyes the whole class long, and posed questions with double meanings. They had what they wanted. I was no educator. Teaching was something I had never wanted to do, and now they had me. I could tell how it aroused the teenage girls, and how we connected. Oh, no, they were no innocents. Right off, they had my number. From the very first day, a tacit bond formed between them and me.

All this went on against the backdrop of one overpowering resolve: keeping warm. As soon as the final bell rang in the afternoon,

I bolted from the school, consumed with a plan. Somewhere in Broumov lived a certain Mr. Knittel. Knittel used to be a civil servant in Kostelec during the war. He'd have to help me out. I hurried to the police station, impelled by the cold penetrating my gloves. A fellow hunched over a desk reluctantly looked up the Knittels' address for me. It was on the outskirts of town.

The snow on the road sparkled in the wintry light and I set off on it, down the hill toward the villa district called Spořilov. As in a fairy tale, the landscape around Broumov lay sleeping sweetly under a blanket of snow. The cliffs on the horizon glowed purple and the blue sky was streaked with orange clouds. I was leaving the town and everything behind, convinced that where I was going, I'd meet with success. My despair faded. At that moment, I didn't feel like an exile, and I didn't happen to be sexually troubled, nor was I standing before a classroom full of randy kids or in a dingy faculty room. I was striding down the road in an easterly direction, alone. Alone, in a new adventure, without Líza. I started thinking of how I would tell her about it when we got together again, maybe during the midterm break, and how nice it would seem in retrospect when I'd relate it to her. That's how it always is, in life. Through and through, life is purely a matter of the past. There is always something bad about what is going on in the present, but as soon as it slips into the past, it turns into something good. Or, all I had to do was think of Líza and how I would tell her about it, which put it into the past, and made it better. I walked by a vacant little house with a neon sign that said Eden Bar, and turned toward a cluster of three villas, surrounded by gardens, not far from the road. They were large German homes, with gables and balconies and glassed-in verandas. I could just feel the warmth emanating from them, the warmth I craved. I opened one garden gate and shuffled through the snow. There were two nameplates by the door. I had found the right place. Josef Knittel, Director, M.S.T. I didn't know what M.S.T. was, but it was the right Mr. Knittel. I rang the doorbell. In a while, the door gave a soft click and I walked in. A wave of tropical air hit me and I found myself inside one of those glassed-in verandas. In a gilded cage perched a yellow-capped white parrot that gave an unintelligible croak at the sight of me. Broumov disappeared as the warmth poured over me like spring sunshine. A sense of security filled my soul. Here I wouldn't get thrown out. A glass door opposite opened and filled with green: in a green Japanese kimono embroidered with colourful peacocks, it was Mrs. Knittel, holding a lorgnon like something out of an old song. She looked exactly like she used to look during the war in Kostelec. Except maybe that her upswept hairdo, dyed black, wasn't as meticulous. She raised the lorgnon to her eyes with a chubby hand and she looked at me.

I offered a polite smile. "How are you, Madame."

She stretched her neck and looked me over intently. Then the light dawned. "Ah, young Smiřický!" she sang out, "Fancy meeting you here! Whatever are you doing here?"

She reached out a hand. I shook it. I considered kissing it, but changed my mind. "Madame," I said, smiling again.

"Come in, come in!" she said, dropping her voice by a fifth. In profile, her bust nearly filled the doorway, but I slipped past somehow without touching it. Beyond the veranda was a dimly lit study, with a clock and paintings I couldn't see, but I knew were there.

"Come on in!" She held the door open for me. I walked in and suddenly felt perfectly fine. This was the world I used to live in, with ladies and lorgnons and salons and teas, and I was always a huge success with older women. They perceived me as sensible and always said what great company I was, so entertaining, and they were right, I was. There was always something to talk about with elderly ladies, a fellow didn't have to worry about boring them or making a fool of himself, he could prattle on about anything, about acquaintances or about the political *status quo*, mainly the *status quo*. I had no doubt that Madame Knittel would bring up the *status quo*. In this world, I felt comfortable. Like back when I met Líza. And now, the parlour I was standing in gave off a breath of that old, different world, nothing like Broumov with its winter and dirt and Stalin in shop windows. It was a square room with a bay window on one side, and in it a nook with four armchairs in a fabric with a matte sheen, velour or velvet or something. They were set around a low coffee table, and the heavily draped window gave only a glimpse of Broumov snow, the only—extremely remote—piece of that other world that invaded the ambience. Inside the room, a wonderful warmth emanated from a tall tile stove, its ceramic tiles embellished with bas relief profiles of emperors. Against one wall was an overstuffed sofa with pillowy arms, opposite a china cabinet with crystal, porcelain, and silver on display behind a glass door. A tall grandfather clock ticked away the time and a painted Chinese screen blocked off one corner of the room. The lavender walls were decorated with paintings. Like a swan, Madame Knittel sailed into all that opulence and gestured to me to take a seat on the sofa. I took a seat.

"Fancy meeting you here," she warbled once again, and turned to open the china cabinet. "So tell me all about it. What are you doing here?"

"I'm looking for a flat, Madame."

"A flat? You're working here?" She turned to face me with a bottle of eggnog in her hand. I hadn't had any eggnog since the war, and it caught my attention.

"Yes," I nodded distractedly. My mind was on the eggnog, I was really looking forward to its vanilla sweetness in this room that was the shadow of another world.

"Good heavens, what a surprise!" She set a gold-rimmed cut-glass goblet in front of me. "And what is it that you're doing, Mr. Smiřický?"

"Teaching," I replied.

"At the high school?"

"No, the basic school."

"But I had no idea—"

I hurried to interrupt her, it would be a shame if she were to rank me in some lower slot on her social ladder. "I really should be teaching at the high school, but you know how it is." I gave her a meaningful look.

"There are no positions?"

"Not for *me*, Madame. They don't have a position *for the likes of me*." I could tell right off that I had aroused her sympathy. And also, a wave of righteous indignation. She understood what I meant. What I meant her to understand that I meant.

With a worried expression, she said, "So that's what all this has done to you!" Her mousy eyes filled with annoyance and the urge to bemoan the *status quo*.

I gave another gallant smile. "What can I do? For the present, what can I do?"

"Yes, yes," she said, looking fretful. "The way they're carrying on. And just think of all the unhappy people already, Mr. Smiřický, all those people!"

"I know," I said tragically and laconically.

"You know, our son Joey, Mr. Smiřický," she continued, "he had to join them, his livelihood was at stake. And I'm terribly frightened of what people will do to him when it all turns around."

Aha, I thought to myself, but out loud I said, "But everyone knows why he had to. And besides, he's not the only one, practically everybody is joining them."

"You really think so?"

"Certainly. You don't have a thing to worry about, Madame."

"God willing," she said, and finally poured the eggnog. "Help yourself!" she said.

"Ah, thank you, Madame," I said, seizing the goblet. "So—shall we drink to what we are all hoping for?"

"God willing!"

I downed my eggnog. It was a little disappointing crossing my tongue, but in retrospect, it was good again, and besides, it went with the wallpaper.

"And what about your Oldřich?" I asked.

Madame's worried look came back. "Would you believe, they fired him? He used to work for the Office of Economic Control, you know?"

"Yes," I nodded.

"Well, they gave him the sack."

"For political reasons?"

"Of course, what else. And after that, it took him a long time to find work. A long time, almost half a year. But now, thank God, he has another job, and a good one."

"Where?"

"In Liberec. In a lamp factory. Used to be Taussig & Schreiber."

"So now, he's doing quite well, isn't he?"

"He's not complaining. But you see, Mr. Smi—Professor," she said, and I was pleased, she had finally ranked me, and ranked me favourably. "You see now," she continued, "how all of us are hard-hit."

"I do." I thought about bringing up my living circumstances. The time seemed right. "They've driven us out of our homes, away from our parents. Take me: they assign me here to Broumov and don't give the slightest thought to where I should live or eat or anything."

"So, you have no place to live ..." she mused. She caught on right away. I could tell she was formulating a plan in her mind. I knew it, oh, I knew I had come to the right place. I was beginning to feel perfectly safe and sure of being warm. I watched the lines on her face furl pensively, and then I saw them unfold amid a conspiratorial flush. "Listen, professor, I might know of a place!"

"Oh, Madame! If only it were possible—" I meant to continue as sincerely as I knew how, about how grateful I'd be, but she jumped in, following her own train of thought.

"There is a gentleman living upstairs, a certain Mr. Kolrt. You may remember him, he used to work with our Oldřich in the district office in Kostelec."

"I'm sure I do, by sight." In fact, I didn't have the foggiest notion.

"Yes. Well. And he lives there all by himself in a beautifully furnished four-room flat."

"And you think he'd sublet a room to me?"

"Of course! He'd be delighted, Professor."

"And—what does he do?"

Madame Knittel tilted her ebony head toward me. "Nothing!" she said softly.

"Nothing?"

"Nothing."

There was a momentary pause. Then I said, "How come?"

"He just decided not to work."

"Not to work?"

"That's right. You may have heard about his case."[10] She was setting the stage.

"No, I haven't."

"Well, he got ordered to pay a huge amount of alimony and it turned out to be most of his pay. So he got mad and said he wasn't going to pay anything at all, and he quit working."

"Interesting," I said.

"You see, Professor, the woman he married was a Jewish girl straight out of a concentration camp, and she used to beat him. That's why he divorced her."

"But why the alimony, then, if she was the one at fault?"

"Well, according to the court, the fault was his." Madame was enjoying herself. "You see, one time, when he couldn't bear it any more, he struck her, and she rushed off to the doctor's with the bruise and had it confirmed in writing: criminal assault. And so she won."

"Interesting," I said. "And so now he's not working at all." I wanted to get back to the subject of the apartment. Mr. Kolrt's personal life didn't particularly interest me, but his nice warm flat did.

"No, he isn't," nodded Madame.

"What does he live on?"

She shrugged her shoulders and tipped her head to one side again. "God only knows. He never goes anywhere. Maybe he had some money saved up."

"And you think he'd take me in?"

"Why not, Professor? He'd be more than happy to!" she insisted. "He won't be so lonely."

"Well, Madame, I'd be truly grateful."

"Why, of course. You can count on it. He'll be more than happy," she repeated.

"And—" I had to ask her. "Do you think you might approach him about it, Madame, you're so good at—"

"Don't worry, Professor. I'll see to it for you."

"Thank you so much, Madame. And—if you wouldn't mind—"

"Mind what?"

"If you could find the time—could you possibly speak with him now? You see, I'm staying at the hotel, and it's running into money—"

"No problem! I'd be delighted, Professor," she said eagerly, and stood up. I could tell she actually was delighted. She must be awfully bored with her life in this lonesome frontier luxury of hers. Nothing in her house, for that matter nothing about her, fitted in with Broumov, with this dull hole. She was transplanted from busy, social, gossipy Kostelec, she and all her opulence and accoutrements and ambience. I stood up too.

"Thank you so much, Madame."

"Don't get up, Professor," she ordered. "And help yourself." Pleased, I watched her pour me another eggnog, and I was even more pleased when she left the bottle on the table. "I'll go get him." She turned to go, displaying in all its glory the peacock on the back of her kimono.

"Thank you," I said again, and when she was gone, I stood up. I stretched my limbs, now pleasantly warm and loose, and set out across the room. The plush carpet was soft under my feet. These people. Living here with cushy armchairs and radiant tile stoves and still not happy. How then should I be happy and content? What more do they want? They clearly have everything they need to be happy, food, heat, eggnog, and still they bitch. I have nothing, not Líza, not even the chance of seeing her and speaking with her, not even once a week. Not even the option of not working. How am I supposed to be happy? I longed to be happy, but I wasn't. I thought of a booklet I'd seen in the faculty room: *The Sayings of Masaryk*. "He who deliberately seeks happiness has already lost it."

So says Masaryk.[11] He pisses me off. Easy for him to say. Or
Mayakovsky.[12] "Youth does not mean spending all one's days
immersed in romantic novels." Easy for them to talk, when they
came by their happiness easily and comfortably and effortlessly,
in politics and academe and poetry and revolution. With an
American wife and their picture in any newspaper they opened.
And besides, Masaryk could sit and make noble-minded conversation with the noble-minded Karel Čapek[13] about God and
immortality, while other people had to go begging for relief, at five
crowns a week. Why didn't he go preach to them that they should-
n't go for happiness if they didn't want to lose it. That was his philosophy in a nutshell. Just because for him it came out of the blue,
because he happened to be born in a time when a poor boy could
become a millionaire or take off for America, or not do anything
if he felt like it, he concluded that people needn't seek happiness
because it would just come to them. Me, I didn't seek it and they
shipped me off to Broumov. And the ones who did were sitting
warm and dry in Prague. Stupid Masaryk. All those fearless
humanists—stupid. I downed the eggnog and poured myself
another. I was feeling bitter. And all of them telling me, you're not
the only one, as if that would make me feel better. As if it could
help a person to tell him you're not the only one who has cancer.
Lots of people have died of it, mister. You're not the only one. Or
Líza saying, What about Petr Hladký? She told me, he doesn't have
a girl at all, and look at you, whining because you don't get to sleep
with me. As if I gave a damn about Petr Hladký eating his heart
out. All that mattered to me was that Líza was sleeping with
Robert and not with me. Everyone always envies the ones who are
better off. And anybody who's happy because others are worse off
than he is, well, he can only be a moron. Right. It wasn't about the
magnitude of the suffering but whose it is. Mine. I poured myself
another glass and sat back down. Everything in the world is stupid. Dumb, stupid life. Better to die.

Footsteps sounded behind the door, and then it opened. I
turned. A short, scruffy fellow came in the room, unshaven, his

shirt unbuttoned at the neck under a shabby sports jacket, the cuffs on his baggy knickerbockers down to his ankles. He gave a guilty smile.

"Good day," I said.

The fellow stopped by the tile stove. Madame swept past him and said, "Here he is. Mr. Kolrt, this is Professor Smiřický."

"Smiřický," I said, reaching out my hand. He giggled and took it limply. His hand was icy cold, and he didn't meet my eyes. I felt a shiver go through him. His nose was red from a cold, and when he opened his mouth, he showed yellow teeth sorely in need of a dentist. Damn, I thought, what an unsavoury roommate.

"Pleased to meet you," I said. He didn't respond.

Madame addressed him in a motherly tone. "Come now, Mr. Kolrt. Are you in agreement?"

He gave another giggle.

"Come now, Mr. Kolrt," Madame repeated. He stood there with his silly grin. It seemed to me that I ought to intervene.

"If you would be so kind, I'd be very grateful. I truly have no place to live."

It seemed to me that he squirmed a little, as if he were trying to wriggle out of it. In his eyes I saw reflected vulnerability, along with an intense reluctance to take me in. Mr. Kolrt was a nutcase. No doubt about it.

"Really, I wouldn't ask such a thing of you," I went on, "but I truly can't find a place to live anywhere."

He snickered.

"Come now, Mr. Kolrt, say something," said Madame, in an effort to help me draw him out.

Finally he opened his mouth and said, in a timidly hesitant voice, "Yes, well, if you say so, but it seems to me, I don't know, but after all, a fellow shouldn't be, you understand me—"

The sentence had no end. He fell silent. I didn't know how to react, but Madame saved the day. "Of course the professor understands. But all he wants to know is whether or not he can stay with you."

He was grinning. "I, you have to understand, I don't understand anything, I just know that, it seems to me, if I want a place to live—"

"Look here, Mr. Kolrt," interjected Madame. "You've got a four-room flat and you live there alone like a hermit, and all you think about is your troubles, and that's not good for you. And the professor here, if he lived with you, it would take your mind off things, Mr. Kolrt—"

"Understand me—" He raised his voice, interrupting Madame in turn. Madame stopped short. He paused for a moment and then continued, "Understand, I don't get it, but when I move in somewhere, it isn't right, understand me!" Now he was almost shouting. "I don't know anything, but it seems to me that the thing to do, when a fellow moves, do you understand me—"

His sentence hung unfinished in the air, leading nowhere. Madame looked at me. It was my turn to step in. Echoing his monotone, I said, "Mr. Kolrt, I don't want to be any trouble, but if it were only possible—"

"Of course it's possible!" Madame exclaimed. "The professor will simply move in tomorrow, you'll help him with his bags, Mr. Kolrt, and you'll see that in the end, you'll be glad you did. A healthy boy like yourself, throwing your life away like this. Where will it lead, Mr. Kolrt, where is it going to lead?"

He snickered again.

"At this rate, you're never going to get anywhere, Mr. Kolrt! You ought to find yourself a job, make some money. I only want what's best for you. How many times have I told you. Am I right?"

Another giggle. I was getting annoyed, it was starting to look as if it wasn't going to happen. I wasn't sure whether the fellow was really that stupid or just pretending. Either way, he obviously didn't want me in his flat, and that thought reawakened my intense dread of the cold. I just had to get into that place of his. At any cost.

"Mr. Kolrt, I would truly be genuinely grateful—" I said, and Madame chimed in again.

"Mr. Kolrt, listen here. You know I've always given you good advice, haven't I? The professor here is a young person too, you could have fun together, the two of you."

His response was a giggle that turned into a frigid shiver. Madame picked up on it. "Are you warm enough up there, Mr. Kolrt?"

His only reply was a silly grin.

"Don't tell me you have no coal."

He didn't say anything.

"Don't you have any coal?"

"I have a little," he said vaguely.

"Don't lie to me, Mr. Kolrt!" Madame snapped at him. Damn. My mood plummeted. He had no coal, and here I was pushing so hard to move in with him.

"But you're entitled to a coal quota. You have a coal ration certificate, don't you?"

He grinned.

"Have you got a coal certificate, Mr. Kolrt?"

He nodded his head.

"So why didn't you come to me and say, 'Mrs. Knittel, would you lend me some money for coal'?"

He raised his hands in refusal. "No, please, I don't want any, no thank you, please, understand me—"

"Understand me, understand me! How are we supposed to understand you? You're up there shivering in the cold like some animal, you're not working, how are we supposed to understand you, Mr. Kolrt?"

It sounded to me as if Madame was losing her grip. I had an idea. I stepped over to the lunatic and spoke to him in a tone he would have to answer. "You are entitled to a ration of coal, aren't you?"

He looked at me and suddenly tears welled up in his eyes. Then he nodded his head. I gave a quick glance to Madame, we made eye contact, but she didn't catch on.

"And you still haven't drawn against it?"

Then she caught on. She spoke up. "How much are you entitled to, Mr. Kolrt? It must be at least fifteen hundred kilos, isn't it?"

He started trembling again. Madame leaned harder. "Where

have you got that coal certificate of yours? Show it to me. I'll have a look."

"Understand me," he babbled. "I don't want to, I'm not up on things like, but—"

"Mr. Kolrt, bring me your coal certificate," It was a peremptory command. The lunatic caved in to the chill in her voice. He pulled away from the stove, turned and walked softly to the door.

"And don't you dare stay up there! Or else I'll have to come and get you!" she called after him.

He left a snicker in his wake and slipped out the door. Madame fell back heavily into her armchair and stared straight ahead. Her face took on an expression combining exhaustion with concern over the crazy man's lot in life.

I sat down too and said, "Oh, my God."

She was quiet for a while, then she sighed. "Poor man."

I was fed up with the lamentations. "Is he always like that?"

"Yes. But he didn't use to be. It's only since he came home from the hospital and quit his job."

"What was wrong with him?"

The worried expression faded as Madame launched into the story. "He shot himself. He wanted to commit suicide."

"Good Lord."

"He found the rifle our Oldřich left in the garden, a .22, and shot himself with it."

"Where?"

"He was aiming for his heart. Fortunately he missed. The bullet hit his lung and it's still in there."

This fellow was growing more revolting by the minute. Jerk. If he was going to do it, why couldn't his aim be better? The fact that he had wanted to do it impressed me, but his failure disgusted me. True, there was a time when I also considered a neat little unsuccessful suicide attempt. Deliberately unsuccessful. Slash my wrists, when they would find me in time. So people would whisper and the word would get back to Líza. But this one apparently wasn't deliberately unsuccessful.

"I've talked myself blue in the face, Professor, but he's like a mule."

I looked at her. She resumed that half indignant look of concerned martyrdom. Oh, yes, the old crow knew he was crazy. And I could tell that it amused her to torture him. She kept him up there, cold and hungry, like a life-size toy. She had no lady friends here, and she was too old for a lover. So she had herself a fool. But that was none of my business. I needed a place to live and I decided I was going to have it, along with the fool's ration of coal.

"And he used to be so jolly! He and Oldřich used to play ping-pong together. And he just hated the Communists. Now he's petrified that they're after him, and that's why he doesn't want you there."

"He was politically active?"

"Oh, no, Professor, but he'd babble to God and anybody who'd listen about how much he hated the Communists. I always told him, Mr. Kolrt, hold your tongue, one person can't change things. But he wouldn't listen. And now he's terrified."

The door gave a creak and he reappeared in the doorway. In his hand was his coal certificate.

"Here, Mr. Kolrt, show me." She took it out of his hand and raised the lorgnon to her eyes. I watched him. He cut a strangely wretched figure in those floppy pants down to his ankles.

"Great heavens!" Madame exclaimed. "He has a quota of two thousand kilograms. And he hasn't drawn a single one! Mr. Kolrt!"

He tittered.

"Why didn't you come to me and say something. What a waste! Or why not transfer it to someone else if you don't intend to use it yourself?"

"Understand me," said the fool, "I don't want, they don't allow, if a person has a quota, I don't know about all that, but—"

I broke in, "Look here, Mr. Kolrt. I'll make you a proposition. I'll buy the coal and you'll let me have one of your rooms. And we'll take the price of the coal off my share of the rent, all right?"

He squirmed. "Understand, I don't know about all that, I think—"

Madame interrupted him. "Now, that's a good idea, isn't it, Mr. Kolrt! Come now, you can't object to that, can you?"

"Understand—" he tried to say, but she rode right over him.

"That's something you could have done a long time ago. You could have sublet to someone, or even two, they'd pay you rent and you'd have money."

"Understand me," he tried again, plaintively.

"And you wouldn't have to suffer like this."

"I think it's an idea that would benefit both of us," I said.

"Are you listening, Mr. Kolrt?" Madame bore down on him. "So give him an answer. Do you agree?"

I chimed in. "I don't want to pressure you, but it seems like a pretty good deal, both for you and for me."

"Of course it's a good deal. It's the best thing you could do, Mr. Kolrt," said Madame.

I said, "I really don't mean to pressure you."

"The professor has the best of intentions," said Madame.

He reached for the coal certificate. Madame put it down on her lap.

"So, do you agree, Mr. Kolrt?" she said.

"Understand me," said the lunatic.

"So the professor will move in with you tomorrow, all right?"

"Understand me—"

"And he'll buy the coal and by tomorrow night you'll have a fire going in your stove."

The tension was escalating. I could sense his desperation. The whole thing was starting to get interesting.

"I really will be extremely grateful. I truly have no place to live," I said.

He choked a sob. "Understand me—"

"And then, Mr. Kolrt, you'll find yourself a job," said Madame. The crazy man's gaze flittered around the room. He hunched his shoulders. Madame persisted. "Otherwise, where will it lead, Mr. Kolrt? Haven't I always told you? What will you do when you run out of money?"

At this point, I backed off. I just watched his resistance crumble.

"What will become of you? What do you expect to live on, Mr. Kolrt? You have to work. Everybody has to work."

"Understand me," the lunatic burst out, "the coal—"

"What about the coal?" Madame cut him off. "What are you talking about? The professor will simply buy it, and give you half of it instead of rent."

"Certainly," I said.

"Understand—me—" The fool wailed so wretchedly that he silenced us both for a moment. "I don't know, but after all, for all I know, it isn't permitted, when I move, I mustn't, I think, understand me, my coal ration, understand me, sell my coal quota."

It was the first semi-comprehensible thing he had said. And Madame burst out laughing. "So that's what he's worried about. Look here, Mr. Kolrt, you're not selling anything! The professor here will give you money to sublet a room from you, and you'll use it to buy yourself your own coal. You'll buy it yourself, with your own money."

"Certainly," I said.

He opened his mouth but Madame didn't let him speak. "There's nothing illegal about it, Mr. Kolrt. That's the way it's done."

"Understand me—" he gasped.

I said, "If it doesn't seem right to you, then I'll just lend you the money. When you get a job, you'll pay me back."

"Lend, lend, why should you lend?" exclaimed Madame. "The professor will pay you for his room and you'll buy the coal out of that, do you understand me?"

"I—I—" said the lunatic.

"And you'll both be warm. The professor will be glad of the company."

"Certainly," I said.

"I—" said he.

"So, Mr. Kolrt. Is it a deal?"

"I—"

"Mr. Kolrt! You know I only want what's best for you. But talking to you is like—"

"Understand me—a ration of your own ..." He tried again.

"But the professor doesn't have a coal ration of his own. He's not here permanently, he just wants to sublet. They'd never give him a quota."

"Or it would take much too long. The winter would be over." I smiled.

Suddenly, he straightened up. The desperation in his eyes vanished and it seemed that he had arrived at a decision. He took a step backward.

"Wait, Mr. Kolrt!" called Madame. "Is it settled? Do you agree?"

"I think you ought to," I said.

He started fishing for something in his pants pocket.

"The professor's intentions are good. It's the best thing you could do, Mr. Kolrt."

"Yes," said the lunatic.

"If you'd like, I can give you the money right now," I said.

He pulled his hand out of his pocket. He was holding a bunch of keys on a ring.

"No, no, thank you, I—"

Madame spied the keys. "Now, that's what I like to see, Mr. Kolrt! Good for you!"

I watched his hands. His fingers trembled as he tried to remove one of the keys from the key ring.

"You'll give the professor a key—"

Just then he finally succeeded in separating the key. "Here—" he said, reaching his hand out to me. "I hope—you'll be—happy—"

"Of course," I said, taking the key. A slight frown flickered across the crazy man's face, as if I had distracted him.

"Understand me—" he said, but this time there was something determined, something ominous in his tone. Both Madame and I were taken aback. "Tomorrow," he said, "it will all be—in the hands of the court."

"What?" Madame sounded stunned.

"Tomorrow I'll put the whole apartment—at the disposal of the court."

"But why would you do a thing like that, Mr. Kolrt?"

"I know which way the wind is blowing." Now he was speaking firmly and clearly. Even Madame couldn't rattle him.

She said, "Mr. Kolrt, don't be crazy!" All the while, he was maintaining eye contact with me. I recognized what was behind the look. I had been there myself, on occasion. Suddenly I wanted him to go ahead and do it. The miserable, shattered wretch disgusted me, I wanted nothing more than for him to get out of my way. All I was interested in was his flat and his coal. I really wished he would do it.

"I understand—" he was saying, retreating toward the door. "You don't have to say a word. I know which way the wind is blowing—"

"Stop it, Mr. Kolrt." Now Madame wasn't smiling.

"I know, tomorrow it will all be in the hands of the court, at its disposal, I won't be around, understand—"

Madame exclaimed tearfully, "Wherever would you want to go, Mr. Kolrt?"

"I know what they want from me, but I won't stay ..." He was at the door.

"Where would you go?"

"It's here I won't stay," he said, with sinister emphasis on the word "here." He was being terribly obvious, and I had to smile.

"But if you won't stay here, where will you go?" asked Madame.

The crazy man measured her with an indignant look, and then he spoke in a tone so surprisingly fierce that her mouth fell open. "*I know*—" he exclaimed, "what they're after." Then he opened the door and continued, a little more mildly, "Understand me—" A baleful pause followed, in which the clock ticked loudly, and then he declared, slowly and emphatically, "I won't stay—*here*."

We stared at him in silence. He looked from Madame to me, as we stood there wordless. Then he gave a little bow in my direction and slipped out the door.

"But, Mr. Kolrt," said Madame weakly. He was gone. Even his footsteps on the carpet were inaudible. Madame sank back into the armchair and stared straight ahead. I turned back to the coffee table and my glance fell on the empty eggnog glass.

"Good God!" I said, and poured myself a drink. Madame turned and glared at me, but said nothing. I sat and downed the eggnog. "That fellow really troubles me," I said. Madame sighed. I continued philosophically, "Amazing how a woman can destroy a person."

I thought of Líza. If Madame only knew. And to think how much worse off I am than that lunatic. At least, he can do something. Shut himself up and go cold and hungry and let his whiskers grow. Not me. All I can do is suffer and suffer. But that wasn't something I could bring up. Madame didn't say a word. I was annoyed, I wished someone would say it. But Madame just sat and sighed.

I decided to broach it. "It looks like maybe he's planning on hanging himself in the morning."

She nodded. "Yes," she said.

Pause.

Then I said, "Poor fellow. And you say he used to be jolly?"

"Used to be. Very. But it's all on account of that woman. Her, and the Communists." Madame sighed again.

I decided to put an end to it. I looked at my watch. "Well, I'm going to have to go," I said. I was curious whether Madame would do anything.

"I'll send his sister a telegram," she said.

"He has a sister?"

"Yes, but they're on the outs."

"And she's not in touch with him?"

"No. But I'll wire her to come."

I could tell that she was already planning the dramatic scene. Enter the sister, and exit the brother, by his own hand in his own room. I got a nasty idea. "If you like, I'll send it off for you. I'll be passing right by the post office."

"Yes," she said absently. "What a fellow. And to think of all the talking I've done." She was clearly changing the subject. I was right, she had no intention of sending that telegram. She was fed up with him, her little puppet, and she was in the market for a new sensation. I could see right through her, into her very soul, and it wasn't in her genitals any more. Maybe in her brain or in her eyes. I could see her imagining the next morning, herself pounding on the door, then its being broken down, and the lunatic's feet dangling motionless a little way above the overturned ottoman.

"I believe you. But these people, they usually won't be talked out of it."

"Professor, if you only knew"—she waved a hand—"but, what's the use?"

"I understand. Anyway, Madame, if you'd like—"

"And my husband found him any number of jobs. But he'd always quit." She was hell-bent on having a corpse. Well, I was hell-bent on having a room and some coal. Implausibly, I imagined myself inheriting that four-room apartment, fully furnished, along with a two-thousand-kilogram ration of coal. Another image followed from the first one: me bringing girls up there. Maybe the pretty little preppy in the fourth year class. Or even Líza. Maybe I'd finally seduce her, in an apartment like that, with a painted screen and wallpaper and far from Prague, if she'd come. Yes. Madame would surely corroborate my testimony that I'd rented the place from Kolrt, and then I'd take it over. The rent would be cheap, here in frontier country, and—but I didn't want mundane complications to spoil my seductive imaginings.

"Well, I guess I'll be going," I said, rising with finality. Madame stood up too. I picked up my overcoat from the chair beside me and put it on. "Madame, can I have the coal certificate?"

"Certainly, certainly, Professor," she said, handing it to me. I stuck it in my pocket.

"Well," I flashed her a final polite smile, "I'll be going now. Adieu, Madame."

She smiled broadly and shook my hand. "Au revoir, Professor."

"If you'd like, I'll post that telegram—"

"Thank you, Professor. I'll have to talk it over with my husband," she said sweetly. Yes, she wanted a corpse, nothing but a corpse. Nobody was going to spoil it for her if she could help it.

"Well, adieu," I said one last time, and turned to leave.

"Au revoir, Professor," she chirped.

I passed through the study and out onto the veranda. It was already dark. Outside, I was hit by a sharp freezing wind. I rammed my hands in my pockets and trudged toward town. The stars shone sharply overhead and the cold wind cleared my mind of all thoughts. The walk to the town square was unexpectedly long, and when I arrived, I decided to spend the night in the hotel. Another night in the monastery was unthinkable. I headed toward the corner of the square and the lit windows, and went inside. It was pleasantly warm. In the lobby stood a rubber plant in a barrel and three rattan armchairs at a round table. Beyond them were stairs with a red carpet held in place by brass rods. The atmosphere had all the cosiness of a small-town hotel. I walked through into the taproom and asked to rent a room. The waiter gave me a key attached to a wooden ball and I climbed the stairs. The room was practically empty, just the bed, a table, a chair, a nightstand and a coat rack, but it was warm. I undressed quickly and climbed into the bed. The tower clock out on the square was just striking seven, but I was sleepy already. Not a thought of food. I lay in bed with my eyes shut while my thoughts fell gradually into place. Once, long ago, said the voice in my head, once long ago, even before I knew Líza—but I wasn't sure just what it was I had intended to think about. Then it dawned on me that the adventure was over, and that all I could look forward to was school days. Long days upon days of school. But there was still the lunatic. I wondered if he was hanging himself already. And then I thought of Líza again. And then the big warm apartment in the villa and the girls I'd bring there. And bringing Líza there. And her sleeping with me. Of her breasts under her pyjama top and her legs and her lips. And the window filled with desolate winter stars. And how I'd lie beside Líza in bed and embrace her and unbutton her pyjama top. And how happy I'd be. Finally. Me, happy, for once. And then, abruptly, my mind flip-flopped. The lunatic dangled in front of me with a noose around his neck, and it came to me what I was doing. The impermanence, the ambiguity, which at least in front of people, at least in front of Líza, I was obliged to call life. The whole big empty useless zero, the futility of days in classrooms. And I realized that we were interchangeable, the nutcase and me, that it was just a matter of time until I'd be the one looping the curtain cord over the peak at the top of the tall tile stove. Or, more likely, gently drawing a razor blade across my wrists. Not that I would first have to become what he had become. But I would wind up being what he was now, this minute. This night. With the noose around his neck. I thought again of Líza. The image of her lovely white body, her skin silky all over, turned me inside out. It was all lost. Everything. All of life. All of life in romantic novels. In one particular romantic novel. To hell with Mayakovsky. And besides, he shot himself too. I curled up under the covers and pressed my hand to my sex. A wave of atrocious pain ripped me to shreds. All of life, Líza, all my life, all of it irretrievably lost. And there was no way I could stave off the pain, because all my desire was concentrated on one, single, solitary thing. An unrelenting ache was eating me alive, from the inside out. I squeezed my eyes shut until tears spilled out of them. It was a lost cause. Líza. And she'd never know, never find out what all this body, this soul had to endure. Never. I wanted to die. I didn't want to stay here. I wanted the pain never, never, never to ease up. And I wanted nothing more than to escape it. All of it. Life.

1949

1. *After the Czechs evicted the Sudeten Germans from the border regions, including the Benedictine monks, the Church assigned another group of brothers to the monastery—all of them Americans of Czech origin.*

2. *Under the Communists, educators did not choose their jobs, but were assigned them, usually based on their political profile. The less "reliable" a teacher was, the further from Prague his or her assignment. The least desirable assignments were in remote border communities.*

3. *Upon completing five years of elementary school, pupils were split into two streams. The privileged and academically talented proceeded to an eight-year classical high school called "gymnasium," similar to the lyceum in France. These were perceived as elite schools. The other children went on to a three-year basic school to finish their eight compulsory years of education and then usually moved into apprenticeships or the workforce.*

4. *"People like us" included anyone who did not actively support the Communists: people considered "bourgeois," real bourgeois, Jews, Catholics, Germans, non-Party members and other "unreliables."*

5. *Lidice: the small Czech town razed to the ground during World War II by the Nazis, in arbitrary retaliation for the assassination of Reinhard Heydrich, the Reichsprotektor.*

6. *Klement Gottwald, the Communist president of Czechoslovakia from the putsch in February 1948 until his death in 1953.*

7. *At that time, an "ordinary teacher" graduated from a one-year teacher training course immediately upon completing secondary school, and was only qualified to teach in an elementary school or a basic school. A professor, on the other hand, had earned a university degree and could teach in an academic secondary school, the "gymnasium."*

8. *"Dark Blue World" (Tmavomodrý svět) was a hit song from a pre-war musical of the popular Liberated Theatre, known for its left-leaning productions, hilarious with biting political satire. The unique voice singing it on the record is that of Jan Werich (1905–1980), satirist, comic actor, writer, director, and co-founder (with George Voskovec) of the Liberated Theatre.*

9. *Jaroslav Ježek (1906–1942), outstanding Czech composer of jazz and pop music in the 1920s and '30s, a contemporary of Kurt Weill. Composer for the Liberated Theatre.*

10. *Under the Communists, it was illegal for someone capable of working not to have a job; he was considered a social parasite and could be arrested.*

11. *Tomáš Garrigue Masaryk (1850–1937), first president of Czechoslovakia (1918–1935), philosopher, educator, author; married an American woman, Charlotte Garrigue, and took her name.*

12. *Vladimir Mayakovsky (1893–1930), the Russian poet, an ardent supporter of the Communist cause.*

13. *Karel Čapek (1890–1938), Czech novelist, playwright, best known in the English-*

speaking world for his plays *R.U.R. (in which he coined the word "robot") and* The War with the Newts. *Čapek was part of President Masaryk's inner circle in the period between the wars. He wrote a popular book about the president,* Conversations with Masaryk.

Filthy Cruel World

... the present time is not pastoral,
but founded on violence, pointed
for more massive violence: perhaps
it is not perversity but need ...
—Robinson Jeffers

The whole evening was a screaming bore. It grew harder and harder to force my cheek muscles into a smile, and the expression on my face felt stiffly unnatural. By half past eleven or so, I could tell that Jesenin was concentrating desperately on stifling a yawn. As I watched his mouth contort grotesquely, I felt myself crumble under the weight of the emotional deficiency of my ridiculously lonely life, and suddenly I couldn't stand it any more. The whole time we were in the pub, sitting under a plaque proclaiming that two nineteenth-century writers had sat there, all I was interested in was whether Jesenin, Ferdinand, and Jana were as cheesed off as I was at having to be there, nattering about stuff we'd nattered to death a thousand times over. And if they were, why in the world were we all sitting there, who was forcing us? And for that matter, why do people insist on getting together at all—when all they can come up with to talk about is the absurdity of socialist realism and the socialist regime, scuttlebutt about the relationships of other people or high-handed judgments about their character, competence, inclinations, and appearance; political reflections on where the world is going; and other such inanities.

True, it is remotely possible that they actually enjoyed it, the idiots. Me, I was furious with myself for being so spineless that I'd agreed to come with Jana, because I knew how much it meant to her. Now that we were there, over an empty bottle of wine—we couldn't afford a second one—and now that we'd covered all the absurdities of socialist realist productions old and new, and everyone we knew, and now that even Ferdinand had quit trying to be clever and his appearance, normally deliberate, meticulous, and showy, had wilted into banal mediocrity, and now that even Jesenin's eyes were turning glassy with boredom, I couldn't figure out why it was so important to Jana.

I found out later, though, standing with her on the bridge, with the immaculate sparkle of the Vltava River under us like a black dissolved mirror, and above us nature's finest display of costume jewellery, the starry autumn sky. There, tremulously, she informed me that ever since she'd met me, things between her and Marty had been unravelling, and, long story short, that she loved me. True to the old rule about never telling a girl you love her, even when it's true, and especially when it isn't, I answered evasively, in a convoluted sentence, and then in long run-on sentences interspersed with pauses and unfinished phrases, covering my behind by implying some great and tragic love that kept me from loving anyone else. The costume jewellery overhead seemed to call for me to kiss her, and she apparently expected it, so I did, but the intensity of her response made it less than pleasant. That was why I didn't drag it out and went home to bed.

She had invited me to her place for the following evening. When I arrived, Jana wasn't there. Instead, I found a buxom, remarkably unintelligent brunette eating cookies, who entertained me with the story of a book she was reading about a tribe on Borneo that still practised cannibalism. Jana was taking a bath, the busty beauty told me, stuffing her mouth with cookies. After a while, Jana showed up, dressed in sweats. Good thing I hadn't come any sooner, she told me, I'd have seen quite a sight. And what would that have been, I asked, without the slightest hope of hearing anything interesting. She said she had been squeezing the blackheads on Hedvika's back, and I had rung just as Hedvika was putting her clothes back on. I didn't say anything. Conversation stalled. Hedvika hung around a bit longer, apparently hoping to learn more about me. But I wasn't talking, I was watching Jana, try-ing to decide whether it would be pleasant or not so pleasant to sleep with this Jewish girl, who was sometimes more attractive and sometimes less.

Finally Hedvika left and I sat down beside Jana and started in right away. Just as I thought, she was naked under her sweatsuit. I turned off the lamp and the room got dusky, with only the street lamps shining in through the window. In the silence, the sofa creaked like crazy. I was reminded that my absurd old malady had resurfaced again that morning, but by then, it seemed kind of dumb to stop.

Afterwards she told me that it hadn't been good, that it was over too fast. Of course it was, dummy, I said to her in my mind. If you were me, with that absurd nuisance of mine, I wonder if you'd be making such a big deal of it. Besides, I could feel the symptoms coming on and it was getting to me. She asked me if I'd marry her. I said I wouldn't. She asked if it was because she was Jewish. Pissed off as I was, I said yes, even though that was the one thing about her that didn't bother me at all. She believed me and barked a bit-ter, angry laugh. Meanwhile, my mind was on that nuisance of mine and about not having the requisite pharmaceuticals to deal with the symptoms.

Lights from passing cars slid back and forth across the ceiling and I was beginning to feel cold. I got dressed, she put her sweat-suit back on too, turned on the light and then came up with some photographs to show me. It was the history of a life. A snapshot of a pretty skinny girl just home from the concentration camp at Terezin; a picture of an attractive fleshy woman posing for a painter who hid his lack of talent behind modernism; some showy and flattering professional portraits of her as a *femme fatale*; can-did shots of seven or eight lovers; and then the reality I had before me, an aging "girl," sometimes quite pretty, sometimes less so, with the post-war inferiority complex about being undereducated.

She brought up the previous evening, how smart Ferdinand was; what a bastard Jesenin was, but smart; and what a swine Marty was, but smart; and Rick, how schizophrenic he was, but smart. Then I went home so I could minister to my wounds.

It was cold in my place. My landlady hadn't lit the stove, she hadn't set up for tea. She never did anything unless I expressly asked her to, and even then she usually forgot. In the morning it was even colder, a lot colder, and I couldn't find any socks or a clean shirt. Come to think of it, I didn't have any clean ones. Then, a boring day at the publishing house. That evening, I had a date to play ping-pong with my colleague Pepík, but because the husband of some girlfriend of his in Dejvice had been called away on a business trip, Pepík had to seize the moment and deliver his load of spermatozoa to Dejvice. He called his wife from a public phone to say we were playing ping-pong, hung up and hurriedly took his leave. There I was, left with a free evening. What to do with it? I looked through the movie listings—dullsville. The same for theatres. Concerts bored me. I considered dropping in on Marty, but the idea quickly lost its appeal at the thought of another evening wasted gabbing—about art, the absurdity of socialist realism, the socialist regime and other people—and also because his current girlfriend, the one he had after Jana, had cheated on her previous lover with me. I thought of dropping in on Líza, but what good would that do? She didn't love me any more, I didn't love her either, and besides, she wasn't inclined to things physical, never had been. And the thought of returning to the damp cold and bedbugs of my burrow in Smíchov, to bed with some book or other, no, that turned me off. So I wandered the streets, irritated by people all dolled up to go to cafés and theatres, obviously having fun; I was desperate in my loneliness, both physical, which could easily have been remedied, and emotional, for which there was no remedy and which was eating me alive like a cancer. I found myself in front of Jana's building. I looked up and her light was on. I went upstairs and rang her bell. She came to the door in a skirt and blouse, pale, powdered, and rather pretty. Better than the loneliness. Maybe. I wasn't sure. Surprised and pleased, she asked me in and made tea. I talked knowledgeably about art, and after a cup of tea, I laid her back on the couch, but because yesterday's nuisance was still painful, all I did was kiss her and pull off her blouse and brassiere and fondle her breasts until her teeth started chattering and she begged me to quit torturing her if I didn't intend to go any further. I explained that I'd be glad to go further but that I couldn't, and why I couldn't. She asked me if I'd have sex with her again when I could. I said yes. Lots? I promised. She asked eagerly if we would ever go to the country, to a cottage, that's great for lovemaking. I promised her that too.

Then she talked about Terezin and her life afterwards. She made some more tea, she stoked the fire in the stove and the room started getting warm. I went out to buy a bottle of rum and we made ourselves some grog. She drank like a trooper. Pretty soon it got really hot. We kissed some more and I undressed her so I could have a look at her. She was twenty-eight, and attractive. She had a better body with her clothes off than with them on.

When I got home, the stove was still cold and the tea wasn't set up for either. Before falling asleep, I remembered her asking if I'd marry her. What if I did? After all, she had that apartment, it could be furnished to my taste, I could bring my upright piano there, which wasn't allowed in a sublet. The fire could be lit, I wouldn't have to go to the trouble of rounding up bedmates, and paying for two rooms in a hotel because the regime was so puritanical. But living with her? I didn't have any feelings for her, no love, not an iota. Sell out? For what—for the flat? For a flat, surrendering the dream of the fantastic world I used to have with Líza, the dream of regaining it, perhaps with some other girl? Or did I even dream of it, still? Well, I knew I was capable of various things, but marrying someone I didn't care for, out of some silly notion that it would help kill the memory of how life could have been, and might be again? No, nothing that foolish, not that.

When I was at Pepík's the next afternoon, he fell into one of his fits again, carrying on about his lady friend in Dejvice. I lost track of what he was saying but the gist of it was that she was emotionally involved with him but he wasn't any more, it was beginning to pall on him, and how awful it was, he had done it all so many times it was no fun now and it bored him. "So why do you do it?" I asked. "What am I supposed to do?" he asked me. Then his wife came home and he was much too attentive to her, as if he had a bad conscience. Which, of course, he didn't.

That night Jana and I went to the Mrázek tavern with the Procházkas and got plastered. On the way home, Zuzana had to hold on to Ríša, he kept wandering off, pissing on the sidewalk. I wanted to go to bed with Jana or somebody, alcohol always did that to me. We went to the Procházkas for coffee. Zuzana made the coffee, we sat across the room from Ríša's sculptures, one of them was in some kind of red stone, a nude woman with a disproportionately long forearm, its two fingers holding one of her eyes open, an eye that seemed to meet mine with a steely stare. Ríša fell asleep over his coffee, Zuzana moved him into the next room and opened out the bed in the studio for us. We climbed in bed and started in. Jana's teeth were chattering, she called out, "More, more, oh God, yes, yes, so good, wonderful, oh my God, oh how wonderful." I listened to her with interest but I had trouble coming. I was drunk and to hell with the absurd nuisance. And not just the absurd nuisance.

In the morning, we got up around eleven. Jana shivered with the cold as she put on her clothes, she didn't look so pretty with goose bumps and a hangover. We walked across the bridge, below us the chilly fog swirled across the river's surface, while Jana fussed about "what if something comes of it." I felt rotten, the way you feel after boozing. Surprisingly, my symptoms seemed to have let up, but the whole world was still cold, mizzly, and unfriendly; I was alone in it and alone inside myself too. Líza was long gone, everything was a lost cause, I didn't have anybody anywhere and I couldn't expect anything from anyone and nobody was waiting for me anywhere. I didn't feel at ease in this world. "What are we going to do if something comes of it," Jana wailed, "I'll have to get an abortion and that's nasty, why weren't you careful?" "Nonsense," I told her. "You'll know in a month, and if you are, I'll marry you." And it was out, I'd said it, I don't even know how, and at the time I didn't really give a damn. She asked me to repeat it. I didn't give a damn and repeated it, "I'll marry you, silly." She giggled and cuddled up to me, and asked me when. I said, "Right away, say, after Christmas."

That was when it all started. She was transformed into a bride. I had to write my father that I was going to bring her home for Christmas. She carried on about furniture and cohabitation. She kept telling me we'd be happy together, and usually I'd just give a vague mumble, and then she'd start to pester me about whether I loved her. The very first time, I said no, and from then on I kept repeating it. "I'll marry you, but I don't love you. I don't love you but I'll marry you." She was furious. "Why do you want to marry me, then?" I said I would marry her, I never said I wanted to, or that I loved her. Just that I'd marry her, because I wasn't swine enough to say I didn't want to. In a passageway she told me, "You're a swine, but I love you."

And all of a sudden it began to scare me. True, I didn't give a damn and I had nothing to look forward to, nobody cared about me and so I didn't care about anything. The only love I'd ever had was over and there was probably nothing else like it for me in this world. But tying this exasperating woman around my neck? Forever being interrogated about whether I loved her, and being told what a swine I was for not loving her? I had enough to deal with without her. Couldn't she be glad I'd promised to marry her and just leave me alone?

I began to make excuses, I was busy, no time, or there was something Pepík and I had to work on. I almost didn't see her at all. She kept hounding me by telephone. One night when I was over at Pepík's, the phone rang. It was her again. "I want to talk with you," she said, her voice quivering. "I don't have the time," I said, "we're pushing a deadline." "So you won't come over," she said ominously. "I can't," I said. "Well, then, don't bother to come over ever," she said, "nobody needs to bother to come over at all any more. I can't stand it, I've had it. I'm going to end it," she sobbed, and hung up. I was annoyed, and a little worried. She was hysterical, she might really do herself in. I didn't want that. On top of what people would say, I didn't want to have her on my conscience. I went over to her place. She was putting on make-up in front of the mirror. "Jana, don't be mad at me," I said. "I'm over it," she said. "I'm going over to Ferdie's." "How about I escort you," I said. "All right," she said. In the streetcar, she asked me if I really didn't love her. "No," I said. "And quit asking me all the time." She said, "But you will marry me?" "Yes," I said. She kept pushing it: "And do you want to marry me?" "I told you already." "Tell me if you want to or not," she insisted. "You don't really want to, do you!" "Come on, Jana," I said, "cut it out." She locked eyes with me. "Tell me, do you want to or don't you!" People in the streetcar were staring. "All right, Jana," I said, "I don't want to." "So you won't marry me," she wailed. "All right then, if that's what you want to hear, I won't," I said. She exclaimed, "You're serious! And you're only just telling me now? You have the nerve to wait until now to tell me? Oh, I can't take it any more," she gasped great sobs like I'd never heard before, then she slapped me in the face, got up and started shoving her way to the exit. People watched us with interest. I rushed after her, almost knocking her off the streetcar step and jumped down after her. She howled, "Don't touch me!" And then, "I can't stand any more. This is too much, too much already." "Oh, come on," I said, afraid she'd really do herself in. "Well then, I will marry you, don't be a crybaby," I said, like Líza used to call me. Crybaby. And it seemed like I was desecrating that gentle word, crybaby. "I'll marry you, I was just shooting off my mouth because I was mad." She turned to look at me with solemn eyes that had always been pretty. "Danny," she said, "you've got to marry me. You've just got to, I can't stand this life any more. Nothing ever comes true for me. It's all filth and shit. Danny, you have to marry me." I almost felt sorry for her. If it weren't for the war, if it weren't for the fact that her family had never come back from the camps, she'd still be a wealthy manufacturer's daughter, she'd marry into her faith, some rich guy, she'd have a dowry and she wouldn't have to beg a nobody like me to marry her. "I'll marry you," I repeated. "And will we go visit your folks?" "Sure, sure," I said. And so I was in it, up to my neck. It was awful. All on account of my silly fear that she might kill herself. And actually, what was I afraid for? Wouldn't it have been better if she actually did do it? After all, what did she have to look forward to? And what earthly good was her life, anyway? But still, I was afraid. Afraid of feeling guilty, and that was more important than all the suffering the girl would still have to endure in her life if she didn't end it soon. So I assured her I'd marry her. I figured nothing could happen before Christmas, and after that, we'd see. My aversion to marriage with Jana—which had turned pretty much absolute—made me sure I'd find a way to get out of it somehow.

The day before the Christmas trip, I ran into Marty. He was drunk, of course he had heard about me and Jana but it didn't matter to him, and he hauled me up to his place. "That slut," he whined, "she took me again, plucked me like a chicken, I haven't got a cent left, the slut." I asked, "Which slut?" "My wife," he said. "But you're divorced," I said. "She still keeps coming around," he said, "I still love her, the slut." He swilled some more rum. "So why did you divorce her?" I asked. "She left me. She said I was sexually repulsive. She moved in with that pervert Kolenatý." Surprised, I asked, "You mean he's not sexually repulsive?" "No, not him," said Marty, "but I am." "Send her to hell," I said. "If only I could," he snivelled, "but I can't refuse her anything. She shows up for the night and I'm a goner. Yesterday I gave her my whole pay, and now I'm going to have to moonlight, playing at the club every night this week. I don't know when I'll find time to sleep." Listening to him made me think, I'm as much the victim of a woman as he is. Líza. Why didn't she love me while I was still in love with her? It wouldn't have had to come to this. I could have been better off. Much. I don't know how any more, but back then I knew.

And now all I had to look forward to was a trip out to my father's with Jana. I poured myself a drink. Marty fell asleep, pretty soon I was drunk too and I went home.

So we went to visit my parents. It was cold at the railway station and she was shivering, she kept telling me how her legs were actually naked all the way up and how it's drafty up there. Then she wanted to know what my father would say to me for bringing home a Jewish girl. "He'll be beside himself," I said. She was offended. Why did she ask me, then? What did she want to hear? If I said he wouldn't mind, she'd accuse me of lying. So just what did she want me to say? Did she actually think my father would be pleased?

Father acted as if he didn't notice a thing, but it was all over his face how stunned he was. And to top it off, as soon as we arrived, Jana asked for black coffee, pulled out her cigarettes and offered him one. She did that deliberately. My father's wife turned stony. He tried being jovial, he called her dearie, you could tell how taken aback both of them were and how much restraint they were exercising. Embarrassing. They put her in my old bed and I was to sleep on the couch in the kitchen. "Come to me, after," Jana said. As soon the light in their bedroom went out and they were quiet, I snuck over to the room and into bed with her. "They're stupid," she said. "Your old man's an anti-Semite, it's as plain as the nose on his face." "He is," I said. "And this stupid apartment, no privacy anywhere, when you go to the toilet they can hear you everywhere. And your old man walks around in his underwear and he's not the least ashamed in front of me." "Mmhm," I said. Then she said, "Love me." Which meant I should have sex with her. It was awful. There were moments when I thought she'd gone crazy. It was like it was almost a matter of life and death. And this was the hell I was getting myself into. No way. Never.

Toward morning, I went back to the kitchen couch, a total wreck. After that I was safe most of the day, my father's wife gave her an apron and made her cook. It was apparently to see if she knew how, even though it seemed like a futile hope. At least it gave me time to think. I sat in an armchair in the other room and stared straight ahead. I felt like nothing in the world would ever get a rise out of me again, because I didn't care about anything. But then, thinking about it, I realized I did care, I cared more than anyone. Other people only cared about things like clothes and wives and jobs, while I cared about everything. Life. And I had no idea how to salvage my own. The one who kept forcing her way into my mind was Líza, the witch. Why had she dropped me back then? Why did she defend her little hotbox of delight from everybody but that idiot Robert Hartl? Líza didn't care for me. I amused her, I was good enough for that. She swore she loved me, she insisted that her intentions were good, that she didn't mean anything bad, that she wanted me to be happy. And all the while she didn't care the least bit about me and even less about whether or not I was happy. All she cared about was getting a letter from me every day, and when I was with her that I not talk about anything but how beautiful and how brilliant she was and how I loved her. That's what she cared about. Not about me. Otherwise she'd have taken pity on me, wouldn't she, and given Robert the boot. Or at least gone to bed with me. She wouldn't have let me quit loving her. And I never would have, if I could have been with her. But the way it was, there was a law for it, a cruel law of nature. You can love like crazy, but you can't love forever if you aren't allowed to attain love's sole purpose. And if you aren't loved back. And I wasn't, because otherwise I'd have attained love's sole purpose, wouldn't I?

Jana came in from the kitchen, pretending to stagger, she stuck out her tongue and didn't look very pretty. "Old sow," she said, "I've got to keep working, this is no fun." "Forget it," I said, and she answered that she'd like me to tell her just how. "It's Christmas," she complained, "all the time work, work, work!"

In the evening it was time for the awkward gift-giving ceremony. I had explained to Jana in advance how frugal my father and his wife were, but all the same, she was shocked. "Your old man is really stingy," she told me later, holding a comb worth twenty crowns and a minuscule bottle of toilet water.

At Christmas Eve dinner, my father got loaded. I was bored, Jana drank and drank but couldn't get drunk. Father turned dreadfully witty. He kept bringing the conversation back to Uncle Kohn who had married my Auntie Marie. He apparently thought he was proving how little he cared that Jana was Jewish. Of course, the only thing he proved was that it stuck in his craw and that he couldn't stop thinking about it and, because he was drunk, talking about it. That night I had to go to Jana again, although when I got there, I told her I couldn't. And I really couldn't. But there was no stopping her. She made me do all kinds of things I could do. It reinforced my horror of matrimony.

The next day we returned to Prague. All the way home she carried on about how stupid my father and his wife were and what a swine I was. I couldn't understand why she wasn't tired of it yet. I carried her suitcase up to her apartment for her, and in the darkened room she tripped and fell flat on her face. She was so mortified that she burst into tears. As for me, I was just embarrassed.

After that, things got even worse, because she started hauling me around to visit her friends. One evening it was a horrid, gawky, voluble woman dentist, Jana described her as beautiful and smart—all her friends were "smart"—but she seemed ugly and dumb to me. Jana told me her story: it seems that she wanted a divorce but her husband wouldn't give it to her on account of some kid, and so she was living with the husband of some woman who was also unwilling to turn him loose. The next afternoon we went to see a fellow who manufactured some kind of machine parts. She explained to me that nobody in the country was making them any more, so he actually had a monopoly on them and supplied them to nationalized factories. The guy was a red-headed pipsqueak who hardly said a word, while his busty woman—who took up almost two seats—carried on a discourse on literature with me. She was his brother's wife, Jana explained to me, the brother had run away to the West and now she was living with this guy. She asked me what I thought of that. "Nothing," I said. That evening she made me go with her to the Procházkas. Říša was sprawled on the floor under the red nude sculpture, beside him lay an epileptic called Zázvorka, and they were having a boozy argument about which poet is greater, Seifert or Holan. Zázvorka's date was a captivating brunette with an exaggerated hairdo. She spent the whole evening trying to get him to leave, and finally succeeded. The whole time, Zuzana had her eye on the girl. When they left, Říša fell asleep while Zuzana and Jana spent the next hour gossiping about the epileptic and how scared they had been that he might have a fit right there on the spot. "Milena is wild about him," said Zuzana, "but he has no intention of marrying her, he just lets her hang around because he knows he needs someone to take care of him." When we left, Jana insisted that I accompany her to her place, although the Procházkas lived just a few doors down from me. She carried on about what a genius of a painter Zázvorka was and how he'd fallen in love with an artist's model called Demartini, who didn't give a fuck about him. I didn't know what made Zázvorka a genius, and I didn't like Jana using foul language. "Besides," she said, "there's a wedding in the offing." "Whose?" I asked. "The Demartini girl, of course," said Jana. "Don't you think it's awful, I don't know of one marriage where everything is okay." It didn't seem awful to me, or peculiar or even interesting. After all, that's the way it is everywhere, and so it seemed perfectly natural. The basis of society, the basic unit of the human race isn't the matrimonial twosome but the matrimonial triangle. No doubt about it. By the time I caught the streetcar for home, it was midnight. When I was changing trams at the National Theatre, I ran into Marty. He said I should come with him. "I'm pooped," I said. "Baloney," he said, come on, just for a little while. We struggled up the steep Pohořelec Hill and he led me down into a basement. The only light in the room was a single candle, a long-haired girl was banging away on a piano, and some guy was leaning on it, making eyes at her and naming compositions for her to play. There were coffee cups all over the place. Another fellow was sitting on an antique loveseat with a woman, and Sobíšek, the organist, rose from an armchair to greet us. Someone poured us coffee. I just wanted to go to sleep. Marty, whispering in my ear, asked what I thought of the girl at the piano. "She's all right," I said. "She's nuts about Sobíšek," said Marty. "So what?" I said. "But Sobíšek's homosexual," Marty said, "he's living with the guy at the piano as man and wife." "Which is which?" I asked, but it was all the same to me. All I wanted was to go to sleep. There was a discussion about art, the absurdity of socialist realism and about the surrealists. I felt a helpless, furious rage at everything. Such was what was officially referred to as life.

It was five in the morning before I got home. I had to be up by seven. And in the evening, more socializing. I would have happily murdered Jana, but every time I objected, she went into hysterics. This time we called on some woman writer. She sat there in a little room, fat, in a purple dress, Jana said how elegant she was—you couldn't prove it by me—and that the reason she was sad was because they had just taken her husband to the nuthouse that morning. Attempted suicide, Jana said. Actually, he wasn't really her husband. And he was married too. What a surprise. Weepily, the woman showed us his latest unfinished paintings, tears flowing to prove how much she loved him. Jana gushed over the paintings. To me, they looked like a lot of paint-slinging. We drank several bottles of wine. It was half past three when we got up to leave. We stood around waiting for a streetcar way the hell out in Vysočany for almost an hour. I had a miserable headache. I hoped she wouldn't expect me to take her home. Naturally she did, and when I tried to say no, she burst into frantic tears. I couldn't stand it, so I stayed with her. It was another half hour before we got to her place. Then we stood downstairs in the hallway for a long time. The headache and lack of sleep made me groggy. I couldn't quite follow what she was saying. It was more stuff about would I ever love her and when I assured her that I never would, she started in again about how I was a swine but that she loved me anyway, and on and on. I interjected, perhaps redundantly, that I didn't love her, though. She hissed with pain and rage. "If you keep saying that," she said, "I'll get over it and quit loving you." God willing, I thought to myself. "And then I'll show you," she continued. "I'll sleep with everybody I meet." I thought to myself, if only you would, I'd have some peace and quiet. How come she couldn't see that I didn't care about that at all, that I didn't care about her at all? How come she still didn't catch on?

The next day she showed up bright-eyed and bushy-tailed. She said she had tickets for a film screening that night, and did I know what movie they were showing? I told her I didn't, and that I was terribly sleepy. "That's all right," she replied, "this is something you just mustn't miss, it's *The Best Years of Our Lives*." "What time?" I asked. "Ten," she said. That was too much. But she dragged me there anyway. The audience was totally international, Hungarians, Slovaks, Bulgarians, Chinese, students from the Film Faculty at the Academy. There was a wild scramble for seats. At the beginning of the movie, I felt like falling asleep, but then I got into the story. The characters were simple and ordinary, with simple, ordinary problems. The cripple's problem was whether his sweetheart wanted to marry him out of love or out of pity. Then there was the fellow whose wife had left him after they'd married in haste during the war, his problem was whether the beautiful young girl from a wealthy family would overcome prejudice and marry him. She did. And the cripple's sweetheart really did marry him out of love. It just blew me away, all of it. I was charmed by the pure little face of the actress playing the banker's daughter, and the touching loyalty of the cripple's bride. That's how it ought to be in life, I thought, slipping out of the world I lived in, back into the fresh, bright, and impressionable world of my lost youth. When the movie was over, Jana said she didn't like it. "Why?" I asked. "Because that's not the way life is," she said, "and I don't like stories that sugar-coat reality." Irritated, I asked her, "What makes you think it isn't like that?" "Because life is much crueller," she said. I retorted, "Americans are different. Simpler." She shook her head. "I think not." In my mind, I told her, You can think whatever you please. You believe that your own shitty view of life is the rule in the whole world, do you? You believe that everyone everywhere is

like you and me and Ríša and Zázvorka and Pepík and Zuzana and
the Demartini girl and Sobíšek the organist and that dentist
woman of yours and that nutty painter and his literary concubine,
all of them? They aren't, that's the thing, they aren't, I said to myself,
and I was still saying it at three in the morning on my way home
across all of Prague. That's just it, they aren't. They can't be.
Somewhere, I didn't know where but somewhere people have to
be living better lives than we are. Somewhere there must be other
plot lines, other loves. It can't all have perished with Líza. But I did-
n't know where to look, and it made me sick, sick to my stomach
and sick at heart.

The next day was New Year's Eve. We were supposed to get
together with Pepík and one of his paramours, a recently divorced
lady, and all of us were to spend the night at Pepík's place because
he had sent his wife and daughter to the mountains. Jana came to
meet me at the subway, but she said she had a terrible headache
and was going home. I didn't try to talk her out of it, and she,
amazingly, didn't insist on my taking her home. I was pleasantly
surprised. Pepík, on the other hand, made a sour face when I
showed up alone. His lady, dressed in a fur coat, kept whispering
in his ear, on the way to his place we met Jesenin with two bottles.
Pepík gave us the key and said that the two of them had to go
someplace first and that they'd come later, meanwhile we should
go upstairs. Of course, they didn't show up, so Jesenin and I sat and
drank. Jesenin talked about women, I listened. At one, Pepík
arrived, turned on the record player and for a while tried to cheer
things up. It was no use, the mood was shot. *Sometimes I love you,
sometimes I hate you*, sang the phonograph, *and when I hate you, it's
'cause I love you*. Then we went to sleep.

New Year's Day I had a date with Jana at her place. When I got
there, nobody was home. I waited out front in the freezing cold
until five, then I went over to the café on the corner for a cup of
hot tea. Jana was sitting there with a young punk dressed like out
of some movie. I sat down at their table. The punk quit talking and
never said a word the whole time I was there. Jana looked as if I'd

caught her *in flagrante*. I joked around, brimming with cheery sociability, and my heart was light. We had planned to go to the theatre that evening. I offered them the tickets I had bought in advance. Jana declined with a sheepish smile. "No matter," I said, "on New Year's there's always somebody who'll buy a ticket. Well, so long, Jana, give me a call sometime, if you feel like it." "Yes, I will," she said. Now she could phone me all she liked. I had my reason for breaking up with her. Besides, I knew that now she wouldn't do herself in, and if she did, it wouldn't be on my account. From then on, my conscience was clear. Actually, I had played fair the whole time. I never quit saying I didn't love her. I never even told her I wanted to marry her. I just said that I would. I'd played fair from the word go. She was the one who kept pestering me. It was always them who pestered me, I never pestered anybody. They were always the ones who wanted to meet, chitchat, confide, make love, get married. I never pestered anybody like that, I preferred to bear the burden of my stifling loneliness alone rather than pester anyone with it. The only one I ever pestered was Líza. But that was because I loved Líza. Love justifies everything, in love there's no pretending, there's no running away from anything, anywhere, in love you float out of this world of filth and trash and up into little white clouds, from this inferno to a pastoral idyll, from this tangle of idiotic passions and nasty indifference to the green meadow of genuine feelings. Love justified, even demanded pestering. Boredom, desperation did not, nor did the need for deliverance. That was selfish, inconsiderate. That wasn't the purpose of love. Love was only for itself, or for attaining its sole purpose, its sole reward: the melding of souls at the moment of physical union. None of that was possible with Jana. That poor unfortunate wanted deliverance. From the outset, she saw in me a means of her deliverance. Even if she never admitted it to herself. I could see it all clearly now. And in the end, when she had almost won, whatever it was that was honest in her had gotten the better of her, and she turned to someone she couldn't expect deliverance from, the punk who dressed like in an operetta. I felt sorry for her, but I had no intention of being anyone's deliverance, and now it was clear to me that I didn't even want to be my own deliverance. That what I wanted was to die if I didn't find love. That I wanted nothing but to once again feel my heart muscle fill with that incredible, super-human, supernatural thing that allows a person to see beauty where there is nothing but skin, mucous membranes and fat deposits surrounding mammary glands. And that I wanted it, not for deliverance from death, but to find life again. And that I wanted to find it an awful lot.

I didn't hear from Jana for about a week. The whole time I con-centrated on work. Then she called to ask if she could see me. We met at the foot of Wenceslas Square, she was docile, proper, she mentioned ailments but she didn't nag. I noticed how wasted she was, how shabby her coat was, the greasespot on her shirtfront. We talked about art, the absurdities of socialist realism, the absur-dities of the socialist regime. She didn't touch on what we were both thinking about. So I didn't bring it up, but still, I wanted to have it all confirmed verbally, there and then. Finally she began dropping hints, testing the waters. I responded as if it were all done and over with. As far as I was concerned, it was. Then she told me that she could get her hands on two vouchers for a stay in the mountains. If we had gotten married, she said, we could have gone there together. Delighted that now she was using the conditional when she talked about our getting married, I said cal-lously, "So why not go there with your buddy-boy?" Nervously, she asked, "So you're not going to marry me?" "No," I said. "I know I'm dumb," she said, "but I can't help it. I always do that." "You do?" I said. "It's all crappy," she said, "life is crappy. Hitler, and then after the war, and now this. But it might have been nice if we had gotten married," she said. "I think not," I said. "Really?" she said. "Really," I said, "Jana, I couldn't have loved you anyway." She said, "I know. There would always have been Líza standing between us," she said, looking at me hopefully. Poor thing, she wanted a rationale. She had given me up, simply surrendered. The thing with the punk wasn't a fling, not a surrender to uncontrollable lust, but rather a deliberate deed, in fact, a heroic deed. She had so craved deliverance, yearned so much to be married, and she had failed. She recognized it, and capitulated. She gave me my freedom. But she wanted at least to have some kind of romantic rationale, so she'd have something left, some justification to comfort herself with afterwards. I took pity on her. I'd give her her rationale. Fine, I thought to myself, if that's the way you want to see it, girl, if that's how you want to explain away the fact that you never could have aroused even a spark of love in me, so be it. "Yes," I said aloud, "Líza would always have stood between us." "I knew it," she said. She didn't believe it. And it wasn't the truth. Líza couldn't have stood between me and her, because I'd never loved Jana. But some folks can't look truth in the face, in fact, there are times when everyone is unable to look truth in the face.

After that, my life was easy for a while, predictably, after those weeks of horror. I wanted to make it last, so I focused on work with Pepík, and was quick to change the subject when he fell into one of his fits, carrying on about how things weren't right any more and how he had nothing to look forward to and how miserable it all was. Then one afternoon I found Robert waiting for me. I could tell that he was anxious to spill his guts. "I'm ending it, man, or else I'll go crazy. I'm getting a divorce." I told him not to bullshit me. "No shit," he said. "I'm going to the lawyer's first thing in the morning." "Bullshit!" I said again. He insisted that was the way it was, that he was really ending it, and then he launched into a tirade. "She admitted that she'd spent the whole night naked in bed with Borůvka," he said. I said, "So what?" "That jerk told her," said Robert, "that he was in full control. Naturally, she believed him. And naturally he wasn't. In control." Well, there I certainly could believe Robert. How could Borůvka have stayed in control, in bed with a naked Líza? Once again I imagined Líza's body, and the pain a person never confesses to anyone, pain he suffers and bears alone until he drops under the weight of it, or else he comes out the other side with nothing left but futility. "Well, buddy, that's not so bad," I told him. "After all, you cheated on her with that

woman in Milovice, that Venus, remember, back in the army?"
"Oh, that wasn't everything, it was just the last straw. She's never
home, she's forever running around, God knows where, and when
a fellow asks her where she's going or where she's been, she just
snaps, 'What's it to you?' and says 'I can do what I please.' There isn't
an ounce of feminine tenderness in her, not a particle of thought-
fulness, not a bit of interest in a fellow. You wouldn't believe how
little she cares about me. I can't remember when she did any
housework, not to mention cooking dinner. But it's not dinner I'm
talking about, what I mean is why can't she, just once, stay home,
so we could sit around together, maybe share some wine, make an
early night of it. But the way it is—it's destroying me, man. I'm
always waiting for her someplace, waiting and waiting and in the
end she shows up at ten instead of five, or not at all." Listening to
Robert's litany, I was thinking, What about me, I've been waiting
for her a whole lifetime and she never came. And won't ever come,
now. And I don't even love her any more. How am I supposed to
feel, Robert? And you can't even appreciate the fact that you get to
sleep with her. Find your tenderness somewhere else, stupid. And
dinner and the rest. Be glad you've got Líza. You'll never divorce
her. Out loud, I said, "Bullshit." "No, Danny, no bullshit. Just wait
and see." "Well, Robert," I said, "I'll wait but I won't see, because
you're full of shit …" And in my mind, I continued … because she's
in you, and you'll never shuck her. Never in hell. He said I was mistaken, and I replied that I knew it as sure as death. He fell silent
for a while and then he said that sometimes a fellow has to feel
sorry for her, that she's essentially vulnerable, with all her sorrows
and troubles. He didn't mention divorce again, the idiot. No way, I
knew it. He'd never, ever be able to leave her. He just had to get it
out of his system now and then, and of all people, picked me. But
that was him all over. He had her under his skin like a splinter, he
had her in his gut like an ulcer, she had him in the palm of her
hand, he had her in his soul like a conscience, like original sin.

After that, I was overwhelmed with loneliness, the worst kind
of loneliness, the kind that, with inexorable logic, opens your per-

sonal ledger to show you a wasted life. Thirty years of it, I thought
to myself, thirty years, and before them and after them, why? Did I
ask anybody to bring me into the world? What gave them the right
to spawn me? Couldn't they afford birth control? How could they
have been so selfish as to bring into the world this wretched bag of
misery that was me, for the dubious pleasure of gratifying their
parental instincts? And inevitably, then, I had accomplished nothing. At thirty, I was none of the things I'd wanted to be. I wasn't a
great musician, just a second-rate saxophone player. I hadn't seen
America, I'd never even been out of the country. I hadn't accomplished even those relatively inconsequential things. And what
about the foundation of man's absurd existence, a mate, a person
to share it all with? What about that? Where was that someone I'd
be first in the world for? Who would put an end to the loneliness
that was killing me? But it could only be someone who would be
first in my world too, someone I would love. It could have been
Líza. It wasn't.

And so I walked the streets, thinking of Robert, who had been
granted this opportunity and, by his own incompetence, indul-
gence, idiocy, had blown it. And thinking of Pepík, drifting like a
mayfly from one fractured soul to another, frittering away his
immense talent on stupid love letters. And of Marty, gradually losing his hearing, throwing his money at a slut who spent it with
other guys, leaving him nothing to show for it. Of Jesenin, who
was becoming better and better as a poet and worse and worse as
a human being, headed for the same fate as me, loneliness without a partner, without a soul. Of Jana, how I had hurt her and how
she was rushing, falling headlong into God only knew what.
Walking, thinking, my mind flooded with shades of all those
drunken, cankered, drivelling, redundant and unhappy people.

Then I ran into Líza, wearing blue slacks and a blue blouse with
a red scarf, her eyes sad and tired in her delicate face. "Come along
with me, Danny," she said. We walked through the night, up
toward Kobylisy. I said, "I hear you're getting divorced." "Did Hartl
tell you that?" she asked. "The idiot. I hate him! How could I ever

have been stupid enough to marry that idiot?" "You're not going to break up with him, Líza," I said, "you love him." She exclaimed, "Hartl? You're out of your mind!" "Well," I said, "maybe you don't love him, but you're gone on him, you're used to him, he's got something that gives him a hold on you. You simply won't leave him." "Sure I will," she said. "Easily, wait and see." I said, "And then will you marry me?" "Sure," she said. "Bullshit, Líza." "No," she said, "I will marry you." I said, "Líza, I love you. You know I love you. I've always loved you, and nobody else. Everyone else was a mistake, when I was with other women, I never loved anyone but you." She said, "Are you sure that's not bullshit?" "It's not," I said. "I swear. Marry me. Even if it costs me my soul, marry me." I hugged her and went to kiss her, but she ducked her head so I only got to kiss her soft, smooth cheek. She never would let me, she used to say that kissing is a start, and you shouldn't start anything you don't intend to finish. It's immoral, she'd say, cruel, sinful. And this time she ducked again. I knew it. She'd never break up with him. I let go of her, she asked if I truly loved her, I assured her I did but she didn't believe me, she's no fool and I didn't know if there was anything left inside me or not, I truly didn't.

I didn't know anything. Everything made me sick, I wanted to die, I considered suicide but I knew I wouldn't go through with it because I was a coward. I lived between work and bed, I turned into an animal, livestock, the only difference being that I wouldn't be any good to anyone after the slaughter. Bibi stopped in, she was getting a divorce. Her husband had been fired from the hospital for drunkenness and indolence, he was living with some nurse and kept trying to cadge money from her. She gave it to him, she said she felt sorry for him, he was so dopey and out of it. But her story was just a tiny if telling detail in the picture of a world that was all like that. Bibi flattered me, one compliment after another. "I feel good when I'm with you," she said, "you make me feel natural, with you a girl doesn't have to talk about anything, doesn't have to play any games, Danny. I miss you." I didn't know if she wanted me to sleep with her, or to marry her, or whether she actually wanted nothing but this friendship, and I was reluctant to ask. I hung around with her and she kept talking about how miserable she was when she was alone, how she was a loser in the game of life, how she wished she could be a little girl again, how she wanted to fall asleep and never wake up. Sometimes she'd say something amazingly wise. "You know," she'd say, "there's only one way to find happiness: for people to meet when they're young enough, go together for a while, and get married early enough and have a child. Otherwise it always ends up like this." Yes, Bibi, I thought to myself. It's an unpleasant egotistical gamble, life is. Get to know each other early and have a child together. That's the only source of happiness. But as for what becomes of the child, there are no guarantees. And aside from that, what is there but a futile chase after success on the job, which you generally don't achieve, or if you do you find that it's just a few terribly fleeting moments of elation and after that, back to nothing, just the stress of trying to maintain it or match it. Or else the everlasting quest for someone with whom to create a selfish union of happiness that can immobilize death and all thought of it. That was Jana's desperate pursuit, and it had been mine. It was clear to me now that pursuit wasn't the way. It would either happen or not. By itself. And I didn't want what Bibi may or may not have wanted: the union of two losers. That would be admitting defeat, humiliating myself. I wanted to either win at life and live, or lose and die. But not to humiliate myself. Not to double my loneliness. Not to have a person for whom I might be first in the world but who might well be last in mine, not someone I would happily trade in for the one I'd been waiting for all my life. I hung around with Bibi but I would have preferred to be home sleeping, because I wasn't getting anything out of it. Maybe she was, for all I knew it brought her some relief, she was a woman and didn't know how to be alone. As for me, it just tired me out.

In the meantime, Líza naturally wasn't getting a divorce and I didn't feel the need to see her. Once I encountered Kamila, we went and sat down together in a café, she nattered on about some Jirka loving her and about going with some Václav and having a crush on some javelin champion called Biebl. "What a hunk," she said, "when he takes me in his arms my bones crunch and I have to tell him, sweetie, take it easy." She said he wanted to divorce his wife and marry her, but she was going to wait for Václav, he was getting an engineering degree, he'd introduced her to his folks and she had stunned them when she lit up a cigarette and chugalugged a glass of wine. And then lately there was a certain Ivan, a priest in the Russian Orthodox church. "... really cute, he took a two-month course for it and now he just putters around in that church where the SS killed those parachutists."[1] I asked her point blank whether she had slept with the Russian Orthodox priest, and she made a coy face and said I had a filthy mind and that I always had, but she had a weakness for me, from way back when I taught her political economy in Jičín and we used to go to the Prachov Cliffs together and party. She told me that Jirka had found out about Ivan, and Václav had picked a fight with Biebl, I could barely follow her, only partly because it turned out that there were two or three Jirkas, I listened to her pleasant if rather crass voice, she reminded me of Maggie from long ago, Maggie from the White Swan department store. Kamila talked about honeymoon nightgowns, some girlfriend of hers was getting married and kept referring to two souls becoming one, and making herself out to be chaste and Catholic and buying a slinky transparent nightie for her honeymoon. She mixed lies and fantasies and half-truths and rumours, I wasn't all that interested, but she was pretty, nice to be seen sitting around in a café with. "How are you fixed for money?" I asked her. "Not so hot," she said, "I bring in less than six hundred a month." "And what about your Václav or whoever?" She said that he had a scholarship of a hundred and fifty. I invited her over for the next day but one, my landlady's day to go to the theatre. I gave Kamila a hundred-crown bill when she arrived. I didn't care about the hundred. Some other time I might have thought twice, but now it wasn't important. When we were in bed together, I switched on the lamp and looked her over. She said, "What are you looking at?" "Just looking," I said. "You're beautiful, Kamila." She giggled and started telling me about her day at work at the hospital, how the doctors in gynecology had nabbed her and dragged her into an examining room and, against all her protests, undressed her and after examining her, they told her it had been a bet, that Dr. Kovář maintained that she looked like Lollobrigida, but they said that beside her, Lollobrigida was nothing. I said to her, "Kamila, stand up." "Why?" she asked. "I want to see you," I said. She climbed over me, got up and stood there with her weight on one leg and her arms akimbo. The soft light from the bedside lamp smoothed out the flaws in her skin, illuminating her firm body, fair and tanned, her breasts like little apples, and the crescent of shadow under her tummy. She was lovely. But what I needed in her was a different soul. I thought about what kind of a life it would be, to possess this body but containing the soul of my dreams, a soul that existed somewhere, maybe had existed once upon a time in Líza, and surely still did somewhere outside Líza, in some other body that I would meet some day. But I knew in advance that it would be futile, that it would go wrong somehow, that something would make it turn out impossible, unattainable, hopeless. All I could do was speculate on how much I could love someone like that, curvy and sexy like Kamila with a wise, gentle soul—unlike Líza's, hers was wise but cruel, and sometimes also desperate and vulnerable. I knew I was being unfair to Líza, that she was unhappy too, deprived by a cruel quirk of destiny of the ability to deal with life. And me, all I could have was this body, for a hundred crowns, maybe even for nothing, I didn't ask. "Well sir," she said, "are you finished examining me?" "I am," I replied, "you're beautiful." "The gentleman is chivalrous, and an authority," she said. "No," I said, "even a blind man could tell." She asked, "How's that?" I played along with what the conversation seemed to call for. "By feeling," I said. She smiled. "Ah, the gentleman is a punster." Then she sat down on the edge of my bed and took me by the hair. "Well, I'm going to have to go," she said. "Go ahead, Kamila," I said. "And come again, but after the first of the month." "Danny, don't be like that," she said, but she wasn't really offended. "You don't think I'm here on account of the hundred, do you? I can always make that, and maybe ten times that if I want to. But that's not how I am, you know? You don't know, do you? I always had a weakness for you, even if you never loved me, the way Václav does, or Biebl." I said, "Oh?" She said, "You do know, don't you?" Maybe she was genuinely fond of me. She'd probably have to be. Maybe she was a better person than I thought. No playing hard to get if someone appealed to her, and if he didn't, she let him know it right off the top. Dear, good Kamila. I went with her all the way to the suburb of Krč. On the streetcar home she gabbled about those tangled relationships of hers, and it was pleasantly soporific. I got home around three o'clock. The next morning, Souček came by. "My liver's shot," he said. I asked, "How come?" "An abscess, and the parasites I brought back from Korea," he explained. What could I say? If he said so, he ought to know, he's the doctor, not me. "You find out who your friends are," he said. "They all turned their backs on me. And the girl I was going with, she hit the road when my bankbook hit bottom." "No kidding?" I said. "That's right," he said. His sallow jowls quivered. "The little while I have left, I'm spending looking for a decent gravesite. Do you know of a nice cemetery?" "The new Jewish one," I said. "They won't put me there," he said, "I'm Catholic. I'm going to Karlovy Vary to take the cure,[2] but it's not going to work anyway." "Well," I said, "I know they have a graveyard for dogs there, and Bibi is there. Say hello to her for me." "Which Bibi?" he asked, "Bibi Marečková?" "That's the one," I said. "She's in Karlovy Vary?" "Yes, she's a neurologist up there. And she's getting divorced." "Divorced, you say," mused Souček. He left. Not long afterwards, I got a letter from Bibi. She wrote that he had proposed to her. That he'd told her his liver was shot and she, Bibi, needed someone she could respect and look up to. She wrote that she couldn't tell if she was supposed to look up to him on account of his shot liver. And that he didn't expect an answer right away, he'd come back for it. Bibi was upset. How was she supposed to turn him down? And to make it worse, her husband was jealous of Paul, the psychiatrist she was attracted to, but he was four years younger, so the whole thing was pointless anyway. And her husband was making scenes about it. His daily schedule consisted of spending nights with the nurse, mornings coming to the hospital to make a scene for her, afternoons getting drunk with someone who'd pick up the tab and then back to the nurse's for the night. I wrote her to simply tell Souček that she didn't want to marry him because it offended her that he'd known her all that time and hadn't cared about her but now that his liver was shot, she was good enough for him. I mailed the letter knowing I was being unfair to Souček, after all, he couldn't help it that he was fat, bloated, but we're all cruel and unfair— deliberately or accidentally, consciously or barely so, or totally oblivious—mostly by being an inaccessible object of desire. Every pretty girl is cruel to all the dozens of insignificant homely guys who reach out to her, every rejection is cruel, the world stands on filth and cruelty.

Then I ran into Robert with Líza at the theatre. He held her hand and she called him darling, every time she said it he gave a shiver of rapture. So much for his divorce, and as for the teacher he had been two-timing Líza with out of desperation and self-indulgence, she was long deserted and forgotten. All Líza had to do was snuggle her butt against him and he was a goner, her obedient puppy. When Robert left to buy cigarettes, she said, "Danny, you're a fine one, you never come around, in spite of all your promises about 'always and forever, Líza.'" "No, Líza, not me, you were always the one who didn't give a damn for me," I said. "Rubbish," she said, "just remember what all I did for you." All you did for me? I said, but only to myself, because by then Robert was back with the cigarettes. All right, so you wangled a few vouchers for me, ran some errands for me at the faculty when I was teaching up in Broumov. But what about all your promises, Líza love? What about all the evenings when I was in the army, and I came home on leave to you and instead of me you were off somewhere fooling around with Colonel Fábera, or that kid of his, with Ferdie, or Ivan the surrealist or Krocan the realist, that klepto Ríša, that pervert Engandin, Novotný, Hrubý, and God knows who else. What about that, Líza? And what about all the other stuff?

So I lived like that, in a vicious circle between Pepík and Marty and the Procházkas, Jesenin, Kamila, and that whole pack of buddies, and in time I started feeling unwashed, the whole world seemed grimy, unclean. And boring. Desperately boring. One time Jana phoned me. "I have to talk to you," she said. We met in a café, it was empty when she arrived. Her mouth looked swollen, she seemed small, not very pretty. "Good God," she whined, "I'm losing my teeth already. It's all from Terezin, that is where my teeth started rotting. And what about you, Danny? What are you up to?" "Same old stuff," I said, "you know, working. And how are you doing?" "Lousy, you know how it is. We've had it, you and me," she said. "Life isn't worth shit. Crap, crap, crap," she groused. "Now I'm going to have two front teeth pulled and that's the end of it. A woman with false teeth. It's a stupid, crappy life. God really fucked it up. But there is no God anyway. It's all a bunch of shit."

I sat opposite her, the café was awash with the white light of late winter, bouncing off the marble tabletops that had heard so much, all that and more. She was right, but just partly. It was only us whose world was crappy, ill-made. There were others whose world wasn't like that. Another world. If there weren't, even this café couldn't be here, nothing, nowhere. There were others who knew how to hide their troubles, they didn't talk about them, they didn't cave in to them. But maybe theirs weren't as bad, I thought. And besides, they couldn't take credit for it. They're the ones who met when they were young enough, knew what they wanted, and hadn't the slightest idea what a miracle it was, meeting like that, what an invaluable, unwarranted piece of luck. They had their picture-perfect children in time, and never dreamed how bad it would be not to have them. Children who some day might lose their way in that dear, fine, clean, strict, self-controlled world of theirs and tumble, cherry cheeks and all, into the cesspool to join Jana and Líza and Marty and me. All it takes is some little tiny Freudian emotional trauma at the age of thirteen. All it takes is an attractive sex partner. All it takes is, I don't know, something so trivial a person doesn't even notice it. Or just barely. I asked Jana if she was still seeing that dressed-up punk. "Well," she said, "he's very nice, but it isn't going anywhere." "Why not?" I asked. "Well, he wants to marry me, but he's just a kid." "That's all right," I said. "Come on," she said, "I could almost be his mother." And where do I find anyone? Probably nowhere at all. Or maybe, I thought, hidden somewhere behind the wall of prejudices, destiny, the cruelty of the world. Someone who wants to be loved a lot, more than the ones who meet early enough.

A person's capacity for loving increases as his capacity for living diminishes. The way all capacities grow with the approach of death. As the lovely landscapes of possibility recede, life turns into an increasingly awkward economic and patho-biological affair, and the capacity for love becomes stronger, more fantastic, more selfless, more desperate. I would like to meet someone who wants more than the fine, solid, custom- and tradition-based, sanctified and dependable unions of the spotless world, someone who yearns for a soul that conceals secret surprises and everything that can't exist in the clean world. But did I have a soul like that?

And it came to me that I didn't have a soul like that, that I had nothing, nothing, nothing at all. Nothing raised me above the lucky people in that better world, it was all wishful thinking. Reality was reality, I was in fact a worthless person, doomed in nature's struggle for survival. But all the same, I still wanted to meet that someone, wherever she might be. I wanted to experience my destiny, no matter how cruel. There was nothing but cruelty in this world of mine. And if a ray of light should ever happen to break through, it would be extinguished by cruelty. I might catch a glimpse of it but the cruelty of my world wouldn't let it near me. All the same, I wanted it to break through. Break through, light ray, even if it should cost me my life, break through. I knew in advance that I'd be unhappy, that I'd spend more nights writhing with pain, jealousy, despair. But I wanted to live everything that destiny had in store for me. Desperately, I wanted that. I was a damned and defective and inferior individual. I was, because I lacked the capacity for living the life they lived in that other world, a world I knew existed but didn't know how to find. And so I wanted to experience everything, even if it killed me, because the way it was now, none of it mattered at all. And over and above all the filth, decay, indifference, all the injustices committed against me and committed by me, I found that I had something incomprehensible, absurd, amazing, and incredibly silly: I had hope.

Just as Jana and I were saying goodbye, it came out that she still wanted me to go to the mountains with her. That'll be the day, I thought, you go and take your punk to the mountains with you. I'm not going to fall into that all over again. She was clearly taken aback and that made me feel sorry for her. She stood up, she wouldn't let me pay her bill, though I noticed that her billfold was practically empty. She put on her shabby coat, shook my hand. "So long, Jana," I said. "So long, Danny, so long." "So long," she said out on the street, and took off after a crowded streetcar. As she ran, I saw the dried mud on the backs of her stockings.

I turned and walked down the street against the flow of traffic, the lights going on in shop windows and people walking, hurrying, laughing, as if everything were all right. And everything was all right. The Law of Cruelty was operating flawlessly. There is no other law. And so everything—according to that law—everything was totally, undisturbedly, inexorably, inevitably all right. So all right that it was beyond human reason.

1955

1. *The parachutists were the members of the anti-Nazi underground who killed Reinhard Heydrich (1904–1942), Reichsprotektor in Nazi-occupied wartime Czechoslovakia.*

2. *Karlovy Vary (also known as Karlsbad)—a spa in the north of the Czech Republic known for its various healing mineral waters.*

Song of
Forgotten
Years

The singer had a fabulous mouth on her. Fabulous and huge. When she opened it up for that final open vowel that feels so great to sing, her face seemed to melt into it, except for the still slightly flustered green eyes. The white, pearly, youthful teeth gleamed in the pink cavern:

You and only you,
you and only you,
you and only you,
my baby lo-o-o-ove

In the obligatory finale, she leaned back with both arms raised to the gilt ceiling of the hall, and the quartet of youths surrounding her stood on tiptoe and bent slightly forward to synchronize that highly effective final spread chord, while the deadpan young man on the electric guitar stumbled over the last break, and the organ shrilled *fortissimo*. After that, everything was drowned out in the enthusiastic frenzy of the crowd.

Looking around, I began to feel increasingly out of place. When you're only forty, it seems doubly incredible that these near adult guys, and these cute chicks all gussied up in their miniskirts, grooving on the twist as if it were the annunciation of the Messiah, hadn't been born yet when we were already sweating the hot ad lib solos in pieces by Emil Ludvík and Count Basie. But that's how it is. And somehow it's very sad. For us, I mean.

The Big Beat group on the stage took a bow. Woodenly and awkwardly. Not a bit professional, just as there was nothing professional about their playing and their singing. But they were young, electrified, with the green eye of the amplifier glowing from behind them, all three guitars gleaming with polish, the tenor sax player's instrument shining golden. They had a glow about them, their instruments as well as their faces, and the singer with the fabulous mouth bowed in a happy daze. She was wearing a home-made gown, her cheeks coloured with pure and unaffected joy, her eyes still a tiny bit flustered, and the crowd just kept on stomping and cheering.

"Sensational, eh?" said Rudi, sitting next to me.

"The girl or the music?"

"Why, the girl, of course."

"A little off key, don't you think?"

"Ah, but doesn't she swing, boy! And she's only a beginner. You wait till next year—I tell you she'll be a second Eva Pilarová.[1] She's just signed with the Radion band, for this fall."

Hmm, I said to myself, taking another look around the packed hall. A typical, predominantly teenage crowd that thrived on records, top-ten radio and the latest hits on TV. She may really turn out to be a second Pilarová at that. The first, the one and only and inimitable one, can't handle the demand all by herself anyway. New bands and groups are springing up all the time, they need more and more numbers, more and more singers, more and more twists and madisons and I-don't-know-whats ....

The Big Beat was slowly bowing its way out. There was no TV when *we* were twenty. F.A. Tichý[2] was all the rage, and if you wanted to buy a record, you had to bring an old one in exchange, or slip the salesclerk an extra hundred crowns or so. The music *we* played was slightly more complex. Swing, and then we took a stab at bebop. Except that by the time bebop arrived, I was about done with being an active musician. The frenetic orgy of applause in the hall was dying down now and another band was taking the place of the youngsters on stage. I had never heard this group play, but I vaguely knew of their existence. They were just a common or garden-variety jazz band that never made any records, the kind that came in to fill up the program.

They launched into some foxtrot or other, and a stout, not-so-young singer stepped up to the mike. About my age, I guessed, maybe a bit younger, thirty-six or thirty-seven. In a small but flexible contralto, she launched into some nondescript lyrics. She looked familiar. I couldn't place her, though.

"Who's that?" I asked my Prague friend, who in spite of his forty years still managed to stay on top of the new music scene. An aging bachelor with no position to speak of, with nothing left but these eighteen-year-old chicks, their pastel-coloured trench coats hanging in the cloakroom of the Julda Fulda during afternoon tea dances like so many tropical flowers.[3]

"Venci Kavanová," was his automatic reply.

Venci Kavanová. Nobody I know. Or rather, yes, I did know her, vaguely, the same way I knew the band she was singing with. I'd heard that she sang somewhere—was it the Baroque or the Pygmalion, or some other nightclub?—and I had even glimpsed her slightly crumpled photograph in some passageway under the antique-looking emblem of the Tabarin bar, one of those faces that have not become second or third Pilarovás, and never will.

But now she seemed personally familiar to me.

And then she cut loose with some scat.

And all of a sudden I knew who she was.

It was back in 1951—it was a regulation screw-up. They interrogated us at Division HQ, first individually and then the whole lot of us together, and the *politruk*[4] acted as if we'd all committed high treason. But it wasn't high treason, it was all quite innocuous, and we hadn't even meant anything the least bit subversive by it. We had simply taken the liberty of doing a swing arrangement of the well-known army song "Marshal Buddeny."[5]

When all's said and done, they had nobody to blame but themselves. They shouldn't have insisted on our engaging in what they called "mass activity." Instead of that charming *contradictio in adiecto* known as organized leisure, they should have given us passes to go off-post to the town of Pilovice, and the girls in the five local taverns and the Youth Union[6] club room would have occupied us and it would never have occurred to us to make "Marshal Buddeny" swing. As it was, after a whole day at the tankodrome,[7] with nothing to look forward to but an evening in engine shop, we really had very little choice but to go in for "mass activity" and the optimistic songs of Radim Drejsl.[8]

The jazz band we pulled together wasn't half bad. (I meant to say the army musical ensemble we pulled together.) Four saxes, two trumpets, and one proper tailgate trombone that a reserve lieutenant poured his heart out into, having been called up under the newly invoked Recall of Reserve Personnel Act. Of course, for Drejsl's stuff we switched to clarinets, violins, and a tremulous flute, but otherwise our pianist arranged a number of cantatas to J.V. Stalin and odes on anti-aircraft guns and other laudable weaponry in the style of Glenn Miller. I imagine we were the only orchestra of the time that paid homage to the Generalissimo with *glissando* chords on the saxophone. And of course, Marshal Buddeny as well.

Our piano player had also got hold of a singer, a girl in her third year at the Prague Conservatory who was spending the summer vacation in Pilovice, and she joined our group to sing the "Ballad of a Korean Girl" in a pleasant, clear contralto.

It goes without saying that a girl, and a rather pretty girl at that, inside an army camp on a pass to sing with the unit band will be the object of general admiration and secret, unrequited love. But she really did sing well. Extremely well. And what's more, her name was Venus. Venus Paroubková or something like that. But Venus. The name itself took my breath away; it was as if a girl with a name like hers was running around with nothing on, and no cause to be ashamed, either. If there had been an Eva Pilarová then, I would certainly have said that Venus would some day become the first-and-a-halfth Pilarová. But there was no Pilarová in those days. In those days the jazz musician Karel Vlach, like the last of the Mohicans, was stubbornly continuing to exist while bleak experts used the authority of official decrees to try to replace the saxophones in dance bands with cellos. No one did the twist back then—Russian folk songs were the order of the day, and stuff that sounded like the work of a twelve-year-old Smetana, or perhaps the secret compositions of Mrs. Dvořák, or something like that.

Fortunately, our commander was a complete musical illiterate who couldn't tell a guitar from a kazoo, while his politruk had been raised on theoretical brochures and had no idea that something played in a tank corps uniform and not a white jacket with a narrow bow tie could be jazz. The commander even had proper music stands made for us, according to my design, regular jazz stands except that their front panel was in the shape of a pentagonal Hussite shield with a gilded mace in the middle.[9] And it was over these revered symbols of Hussite military glory that our swing version of "Buddeny" sounded at an Army Day concert. And to cap it off, it was sung by Venus Paroubková, and she improvised one chorus in scat.

Today, I don't know which was the worse mistake, the scat or our jazz-style music stands in the shape of Hussite shields. But the biggest mistake of all was that it took place with an army art corps general—or some such brass, something that walks around fetchingly trimmed with gold braid—in the audience. He wasn't fooled by our tank corps uniforms. He could tell the music of spiritual decadence when he heard it.

There was absolute hell to pay.

"Those music stands are over the line!" fumed the big brass. "You think you're in some nightclub, do you? You're in the army, comrades! A sacred military symbol, consecrated with blood, and you take and use it as if you were R.A. Dvorský and his Melody Boys!"[10]

Those music stands stuck in his craw worse than anything, maybe even more than the syncopated Buddeny. "Nobody's going to smuggle decadent music into *this* man's army, comrades. We'll make short work of anybody who tries. We'll show them what for. Understand, comrades?"

"We understand, Comrade General!" (or Colonel, or whatever) we replied in unison—whereupon we were made short work of.

That name—the Melody Boys—stuck with us as we swept the grounds and scrubbed latrines and dug sewers behind the newly erected officers' quarters. All of us except the reserve lieutenant, that is. He was the only one to benefit from the whole affair since he was lucky enough to get kicked out of the army.

As for Venus, she was a civilian, and so it wasn't really her affair.

The plump singer on stage scatted on. It was mellow. She sang precisely, freely, with a real swinging beat. But she was fat, with a pleasant face framed by faded thinning curls.

A couple of teenyboppers in the next row broke into snickers. A smart-ass seventeen-year-old nerd croaked, "That's what I call heavy artillery!" and the teenyboppers tittered aloud. The pimply joker outdid himself. "Get a load of her! Butterball, or what?" I bit my lip. I felt as if it was me they were making fun of.

She finished singing and a smattering of lukewarm applause sounded here and there. Where are you, I thought, you magnanimous Americans, who'll applaud a fat old black woman till your hands ache? This so-called nation of musicians only goes for younger meat. Beyond the footlights, another Big Beat group charged impatiently on the stage, their electrophonics already set up and waiting. I rose, mumbled to Rudi, "I've gotta go," pushed my way down the crowded row and turned under the gallery to the door leading backstage.

Venus wasn't there.

"Who, Mrs. Kavanová? Oh, she works downstairs, in the club," said a fellow in a purple jacket with silk lapels and a saxophone sling around his neck.

"She was just singing here a minute ago," I said.

"Oh, she just does a gig up here now and then," he replied, "she just popped up here for that one number. Her regular job is singing in the nightclub downstairs."

Downstairs had the dim lighting of a bar, and an international clientele. Ladies whose virtue tends to loosen with offers of foreign currency, swarthy Levantines in tuxedos, inebriated holders of expense accounts. Venus was sitting on a chair beside the pianist, gazing at nothing.

I circled the dance floor and looked at her. She felt my scrutiny and flashed me an indifferent glance.

I grinned. "Hiya, Venus!"

"Yeah, same to you," she replied. She apparently thought I was tanked.

"Don't you recognize me?"

She looked me over. Her eyes were the same green as the eighteen-year-old twist-baby upstairs. And she had the same fabulous mouth, too. But it was all surrounded by incipient wrinkles, and it was all well over thirty. And still not so much as a glimmer of recognition in those eyes.

"Nope," she said. "Should I?"

"Damn right you should," I began, and then I realized that she really shouldn't. She had been the pretty girl at the mike, while I was just a near-sighted sergeant, one of four sax players. Eleven men and a girl. And she had only had eyes for the piano player. She was still staring at me without so much as a spark of recognition.

"Okay," I said, "so you shouldn't. I'll give you a hint: Pilovice."

Her eyes narrowed. "Wait a minute," she said. "Yes, I remember you, you're ... Kálecký—"

"Lavecký," I corrected her. "Miroslav Lavecký."

"Hi, Lavecký," she said amiably, shaking my hand. "Well, the earth sure has taken a number of turns since those days, hasn't it?"

"Sure has," I grinned at her. "Say, can you have a drink with me?"

"We break after the next number," she said. "I'll meet you at the bar."

She sang one more number. "Oliver Twist." I listened attentively. She was no worse than the little twist-princess upstairs. Better, if anything. But this wasn't the right audience for that sort of thing—the Levantines, the expense accounts, the business girls. And upstairs, it wasn't the audience for the kind of song she usually sang.

"So you stuck with music, did you?" I said when she sat down beside me at the bar.

"Mm," she replied. "Didn't you?"

"No, not me," I said, with a note of regret. "I'm a planner in a factory in Liberec."[11]

"Married?"

"Sure, you know how it is. How about you?"

"Me too. Three kids," said Venus.

"That's swell." I didn't know what to say next.

She asked, "You don't have any kids?"

"One, a girl. She's just starting sixth grade."

"Same as my oldest. Listen—it must be eleven, twelve years already."

"Twelve." I tried to change the subject. "I didn't know you were Venci Kavanová. If I had known, I'd have come to hear you long ago. I'm in Prague fairly often."

"Yup, that's me all right," she said.

"Your husband's a musician too?"

"That's right," she said. "He's the bass player, maybe you noticed him."

"Here in this band?"

"That's right."

"Oh, I see, that explains—" I stopped, again not knowing where to go from there. This wasn't exactly a prestige job for a graduate of the Prague Conservatory of Music. "I mean, I thought you were going in for opera. Couldn't get work, I guess. Too many singers and too few slots, I suppose ..."

"But they kicked me out," she said matter-of-factly.

"What do you mean, kicked you out?"

"Kicked me out. Expelled me from the Conservatory. After that concert of yours."

"What?"

"After that 'Buddeny' affair," she said, and my heart stopped.

"Somebody ratted on me at the Conservatory and one of the girls on the Youth Union Committee took it on as a cause."

"On account of the swing version of 'Marshall Buddeny'? They expelled you just for that?"

"Sure. Don't you think that was enough? Didn't you know?"

"No, I didn't. I got in some trouble after that over an AWOL— they tossed me in the can—"

"Well, I was suspended for a year," said Venus, "I was supposed to go to Ostrava on a brigade.[12] To be re-educated, you know? But in the meantime I got married and had a baby, and I never did go. So I couldn't get back in the Conservatory."

"So you began singing with a band?"

"No way. Remember, there were hardly any bands back then. And no twist fever, either. And even if there had been, they'd have cooled it right down, and fast! No way."

"So what did you do?"

"Well, for a while I sang folk songs with Trávnice,[13] a friend of mine got me in, a former organist who switched over to the cembalo in a hurry, but they dumped him for some silly reason or other, disrespect for the collective or something, so I wasn't long for that world either. Then I had my second girl and then my boy, and after that I started singing with the band. Jazz was coming back in style. Now and then a gig upstairs or at Julda Fulda, like that."

It kind of took my breath away. Kind of a lot. For something to say, I asked, "Do you do any TV? I've never seen you."

"Not much. You've got to remember, I'm an old bag now."

"What do you mean? You look terrific."

"Not bad, I suppose, for a mother of three."

"No, really, you look great."

"But to the twist kids, I'm an old bag," she said. "And the twist kids make up ninety percent of the audiences these days."

"But you do sing up a storm," I said, awkwardly. "Even better than back then."

She laughed. "Whatever good that does me," she said. "I'm not the type for *chansons*, and that's all there is for someone my age. No, for me, it's got to be jazz." She turned to the bartender. "Tony, give me a double. How about you?" She turned back to me. I nodded.

"You know, Mirek, if for nothing else than for the jazz, I'd like to be twenty again. Now, in the year nineteen hundred and sixty-three. Not then. We were born at a dumb time."

I don't know why, actually, but the image of those sniggering teenyboppers upstairs flashed through my mind.

"We'd have turned up the heat," Venus said.

"Ain't that a fact," I said, and my fingers started tingling. Left index finger, middle finger, ring finger on the B, A, and G keys, pinky on the grooved G-sharp and thumb on the octave key. But it was too late. I started, realizing that I wasn't the young jazz fiend, no young Gable look-alike, I was the sober comrade Lavecký, planner with Kablona, N.E. in Liberec.[14]

Out of the blue, I said, "Do you remember the number you used to sing with us all the time?"

"You mean 'Buddeny'?"

"No, I don't mean at concerts. I mean at rehearsals, fooling around. 'Annie Laurie'. Like Frankie Smith."[15]

She smiled. Venus. Back then she had thick blond hair, probably done up in a way that would seem hopelessly out of date to me today. But back then—the piano sounded a few notes, the band was back from its break.

"'Annie Laurie'." Venus smiled dreamily. "Another folk song done up in swing."

"A Scottish one, though," I remarked. "They didn't fall under the jurisdiction of the folklore protection patrol."

"Wait a minute!" she exclaimed eagerly. She jumped down from the bar stool and ran toward the stage. She was solid and stocky, like a little barrel. Her sequined dress was designed to hug the overly rounded vestiges of her once-fine figure. Venus. With a name like hers it was as if a girl was running around with nothing on, and no cause to be ashamed, either. She was explaining something animatedly to the piano player, then she straightened up and grinned over at me across the dance floor. The trumpet player blew the familiar introductory break over the swish of the drummer's brushes, and Venus stepped up to the mike. Her fine clear contralto filled the dimness of the club.

> *Maxwelton, Maxwelton's braes are bonnie*
> *Where early, early fa's the dew,*
> *And 'twas there that Annie Laurie*
> *Gave me, she gave me her promise true!*

I shut my eyes. It was long ago. It was so awfully long ago. It was a blood sacrifice, a different, less conspicuous one, on behalf of a better life for that generation of twist-crazy teenyboppers upstairs. Baloney, I said to myself. Quit it, you're being as mushy as an old whore. I opened my eyes.

Venus, a rather well-padded Venus, was singing—in a forgotten voice—that song of years so quickly forgotten.

1963

1. *The most popular and durable Czech jazz singer.*
2. *Leader of a polka-and-waltz orchestra.*
3. *Popular slang name for the Julius Fučík Park of Culture and Recreation, an entertainment venue named after a Communist journalist executed by the Nazis.*
4. *Army abbreviation for political officer.*
5. *Well-known song honouring one of the Soviet Union's first military heroes. Playing it in swing time constituted grave heresy.*
6. *The Communist organization of young people.*
7. *Exercise grounds for training tank crews.*
8. *The best-known Czech composer of political songs of the Stalin era. After his first visit to the Soviet Union, he committed suicide.*
9. *Hussites, followers of John Huss (Jan Hus), a Czech disciple of the fourteenth-century religious reformer John Wyclif. The Hussites were a radical religious movement with strong social overtones that made them acceptable (retrospectively) to the otherwise atheistic Communist regime.*
10. *A famous pre-WWI dance orchestra, viewed by the Communists as the epitome of bourgeois decadence.*

11. *In a socialist company, the person responsible for checking on how quotas were being filled.*

12. *"Volunteer" brigades, which did unpaid work in agriculture, mines (men), and heavy industry (women), were on one hand the way people who committed any sort of minor political "crime" were "allowed" to atone, and on the other, the way ordinary people made themselves some points in the eyes of the regime. Early on, enthusiastic Communists actually did volunteer to go on these brigades.*

13. *One of several professional folk song and dance ensembles of the Stalin era.*

14. *Abbreviation for Kablona National Enterprise. A "national enterprise" is a state-owned company.*

15. *A black singer who performed in Prague with a British-based black jazz band in the years between WWII and the Communist putsch in 1948.*

Pink

Champagne

We stood in front of the window, eyeing the gold-buttoned slicker picked out by Líza Pecáková-Jánská, and it started to rain. An evil omen, I guessed at once. The rain quickened and soon it came pouring down. There was some edgy last-minute jabber that settled nothing, and we herded ourselves into the Swan, drenched and confused. Rico's cape puffed up like a soaked sponge. Assback groped with steam-covered glasses and almost knocked over a naked mannequin. Everything was balled up; we should have dropped the whole business then and there. But Líza was waiting, and the Grand Scheme was actually quite sound: (1) Assback to banter with saleslady; (2) me to start wailing about theft of wallet containing five hundred crowns, thus fixing all eyes on myself and away from (3) Rico, who liberates slicker from hanger, stuffs it under his cape and proceeds to home base.

But destiny ruled otherwise. Assback became nervous, and when he's nervous everything comes out backward, the saleslady got scared, and as she looked around for help, the supposedly inconspicuous Rico stood out in his puffed-up cape like a fuzzy exclamation mark. Furthermore, somehow or other I didn't quite have the appearance of an Owner of Five Hundred Crowns, but I didn't realize this until I started to sound the alarm. Finally, the slicker had a lining, which Rico hadn't taken into account. So when they nabbed him, the *corpus delicti* bulged from underneath his cape, its gold buttons signalling merrily. Before he could even think of dropping it, they were leading him and his booty to the director's office. Me, too—and that was another planning error. I couldn't

260

just get lost, because if I didn't sob for justice they would have wised up at once that the five hundred was a fiction. So they led us along side by side, thief and victim, and of course they established a connection between us, even though the wrong one: that Rico, caught with the slicker, also stole my five hundred. Naturally, when they searched Rico no five hundred crowns showed up, and the director was just about to apologize that another thief must have done it, when some kind of assistant manager entered the case. All this time he had been standing in a corner like a plaster dwarf, next to the big picture window with its grand view. And it was a Grand View, a director's view, Jan Zizka on his prancing steed, streaming with rain, roofs aglow with neon lights, Prague spread out below like a dish of cranberries and cream. And this assistant manager was tossing us his insulting squint, the kind of squint that leaves a guilty smudge on the most innocent of faces. And he says, "Wait!" And there I was—just about to exit, having given them a nonexistent name and address where the nonexistent five hundred were to be sent, but when that bastard functionary said "Wait!" I froze in the door, even though my brain whispered, Get lost, jerk! Nobody will catch you down that stairway. Remember you won that sprint down the Petřín Tower, and this clown here has one leg shorter than the other and he probably has other defects besides, this type always does. All the same, I froze like Lot's wife. And the assistant manager says again, "Wait!" And he starts to innuendo me in a deadly familiar tone. "So you had a wallet with five hundred crowns? And you found out you lost it just exactly at the precise moment when this one"—he pointed at the soaked Rico—"just when this one was busy carting off national property? That's kind of odd," he says, and steps out of his plaster dwarf corner and plants himself right in front of the picture window with that beautiful abstraction of Prague in the spring rain. He stands there just to spoil the view. "Very odd," he goes on, "it looks like conspir ..." I didn't hear the rest, because I successfully traced a fiery spiral down the stairway, getting a glimpse of Assback through the glass doors on the second floor. He was no longer with the saleslady, but between two pained-looking chaps with green stars on their lapels. This was a new one on me—the stars were on the outside instead of the inside the way cops wear them, but this only occurred to me later, back at the Boathouse.

Assback showed up a half hour after me, a jabbering idiot. "Esperantist Russian a for me took they," he said, and I asked him to shift from reverse. He shook a bit and then rattled, "Christ, that was some sweat! They were Esperantists. But when I unwrapped the Russian, they took off." "Ass-backward, eh?" I asked. "You bet, jerk," he said. "I was scared, and when I'm tight like that everything comes out the same—Czech, Russian, it's all one salami." "Jerk," I said, "you sure know how to sweet-talk a woman. That saleslady didn't even notice you. You know where Rico is right now, all on account of you?" "But he's got a cert," said Assback. "Sure he has. But who knows if the cert covers such expensive stuff. Remember last time, that whisk ..." "Sure," interrupted Assback. "But that's because we drank it. There was damage which had to be made up." "Right," I said. "That's just my point. Now there's no damage, ergo nothing to be made up, ergo they'll get frustrated and throw Rico in the clink."

As it turned out they didn't lock him up, but all the same he didn't show till six-thirty. He would have made it sooner, the director would have been satisfied with the cert, but that bastard assistant manager wouldn't give up. Not even the official seal of the clinic impressed him. Kleptomania, he said. "So you suffer from kleptomania, comrade, as certified by Comrade Dr.—I can't quite make this out—Dr. Chroust? Chroust, eh? And that other comrade, the one who lost five hundred crowns, why did *he* run away? Eh? Why?" "I don't know him," said Rico, but unfortunately his voice happened to break just then, and the whole thing sounded highly unlikely. The assistant manager grimaced and expounded his theory on the misuse of kleptomania—"If indeed it's a question of kleptomania at all, which we will find out pretty soon, comrade, and not from Comrade Dr. Chroust, but from Professor Šťáhlava himself. There have been known cases where our comrade doctors have certified various gold-bricks and sadist pals of theirs non compos mentis, just out of plain comradeship. The devil knows, but it looks to me like you are consciously exploiting your defect—if indeed there is a defect—for criminal purposes." He turned to the director, who in the meantime had exchanged places with him and stood silently in the dwarf corner. It was getting quite dark outside, drops of water burst like shrapnel against the tin gutter and formed miniature rainbows, prettier than the six reincarnations of Lenin. "You understand their method," the assistant manager said to the director. "One of them starts to raise a commotion at one end, and in the meantime the other ..." In short, they bounced Rico back and forth between them until he confessed, so that he could go and see Líza. He didn't tell them the real truth. He said he was bribed to steal the coat for a sum of fifty crowns by a certain Emil Růžička who wanted it for his girl, which screwed them up at least a little bit, because Emil Růžička is a real person and a stupid ass, and his father happens to be in the cabinet. But, of course, in the end they'll get Rico anyway, naturally he had to give them his own name, too. Still, for the moment he was free to see Líza. The bells were just chiming seven, the shops were lit up but closed, and, except for Assback's tape, we had to go before Líza empty-handed.

We had promised her the slicker, and the tape hardly made up for it. Besides, our bad luck had no end. The tape featured Assback's recording of a work by Stanislas Kostka, a poet whom Líza couldn't stand. But since Assback's mirror renditions of the Czech language always brought Líza to a state of ecstasy, we thought that this reverse version of the Kostka poem might make an appropriate birthday present. The problem was that Líza's tape recorder was busted; it turned too fast, and Assback sounded like a rheumy Mickey Mouse. Líza watched intently as Assback laboured to slow down the spool, and we watched Líza to learn what she thought of all this. She was frowning. Finally she turned off the machine with Mickey in mid-squeak, and said, "That's quite a gift you have brought before God's Only Daughter on her xtieth xday. A stupid tape, badly recorded, and that's all. I must say that your gang has a most peculiar way of expressing respect and devotion! You can all go to hell—I am giving myself to Professor Friml."

It was dark, in the gas fireplace small flames flickered economically, and behind the wall Líza's daddy complained about the times with so much conviction that we heard every word. "It's all sliding downhill to hell, everything's going from tens to sixes and getting worse and worse. Holy Mary of Svatá Hora, how can you stand to look at this mess!" Líza's dark eyes are bright. She says, "This wall is only plaster; the one on the other side of the kitchen is brick. Lucky." And her dad shouts, "The plague on them! A-bombs on them! Hydrogen bombs!" It's hard to believe that even a brick wall could ever muffle such a majestic voice, and we gawk at Líza in her mini and we wonder how in the world a girl can wear such long stockings without showing even a peek of garter. Líza stretches herself in front of the gas flames, her legs shine with a nylon glow, and she says, "You are some gang! You're nothing but a bunch of cripples. I'll go with Professor Friml and, for your information, he will *buy* me that slicker."

Lord in Heaven! Surely our transgressions do not call for such dreadful punishment from the Divine Daughter! We fall on our knees, the gas flames illumine our desperation. "Not that," we shout. "Anything but that, holy virgin of virgins!" Líza blinks, crosses her legs, the gas flames flicker in her eyes like tears of honey. "All right," she says. "You can swipe that slicker for me for All Souls' Day, but now I need something else, namely a push-button switch because I am fed up with these." Her long, shapely arm points at the wall, a tender halo of delicate golden hairs outlining her limbs, and her thin finger with its silver nail points accusingly at a hideous, black, old-fashioned post-office-type switch. There is a moment of silence, then Assback says gloomily, "They've got the kind you want in Psychiatry. Pea-green in the big lecture hall and pink in the smaller one." "I want pea-green," says Líza. "Pea-green goes with everything." We look at each other, more silence. "They can be screwed off," says Assback. "Two screws." But Rico says, "Yes, but not Psychiatry. I can't do that to old Chroust. Like that assistant manager said, comradeship. Besides, Chroust is about to spring a tremendous scoop: he sticks people into a special liquid with the same specific gravity as the human body, and they float in it like birds in air. Suppose I spoil this scoop for him? What then?" Another moment of silence. Líza stretches and decides, "All right, it will have to be done by Assback. I am sorry, Rico, that for my sake you are not willing to risk the comradeship of some jerky Chroust, and you are hereby struck from my grace. Assback will do it."

Assback bares his yellow teeth. "I am no good at stealing, but I'll do it. In fact, I'll do it with gusto. Do you know that the bastards refused to pay me for my psych demonstration? And in all of Prague nobody but me has this defect; the nearest one lives all the way in Košice. They used to pay me, now I'm supposed to demo for free, that's what the Dean told me." He pauses, and from behind the plaster wall roars the mighty voice of God the Father: "They'll ruin us! They'll rob us blind! They'll make a fiscal reform on us!" And Rico says to Assback, "You lousy esophagus! You hungry gullet! Don't you know that in this day and age nobody pays for *anything*, not even a blood donation; everything is done in the spirit of sacrifice and social consciousness, and you want to get rich without working just because you've got a shitty defect." "I can always go to a burlesque theatre," exclaims Assback. "Or the circus! They'll be glad to pay me in gold." "Bull," says Rico. "Forget it. Your defect has no drama, and you can't handle it well enough. It wouldn't work in a circus. Believe me, your thing's no good except for a science lab. Maybe if you were a talking horse—but then you'd be better off talking normally. A horse that talks ass-backward is no big deal either." And Líza smiles her pearly smile, turns her behind to the flames, and suddenly the doorbell rings.

For a while nothing happens, then God the Father is heard shuffling his slippers and clearing his throat in the hall. The doorhandle clicks. "Well, look who's here! Česťá," shouts the voice of

God the Father. "What a pleasant surprise!" Líza springs up like a cat, opens the window, and we jump one after another into the cold rain, right into a begonia bed. Second Lieut. Čestmír Pecák, MD, had evidently wangled a pass so that he could join his wife's birthday celebration in the family circle. That should make Líza very happy.

We crawled out of the begonias covered with mud, and it was half past nine; we decided to go to the theatre and hang around to watch Kubišová leave. But on the way, on the corner of Gawker Street, Rico got the idea of showing us how to rob a cigarette machine. He rolled up his sleeve and said, "This way. You shove in your arm like this." He stuck it into the machine up to the elbow, and it stayed there. Fortunately it was dark out, but that didn't help much. He tried everything, twists, gentle pulls, sudden jerks; we pounded the machine from all sides and in the end Rico even suggested that we drop a crown into the slot, but we didn't have one. So there was nothing for Rico to do but stand nonchalantly in front of the machine, whistle to himself like he's just watching the world going by, and I planted myself a little bit to the right of him like I'm taking in the street scene, too, to cover Rico's arm with my body. We sent Assback to Holešovice to get Platýz, who has a portable blowtorch.

So we just stand there, watching life, which at this hour in Gawker Street is pretty monotonous. The local dog had died, and now the street was overrun with cats. A solitary lamp was swinging in the wind, throwing unsteady shafts of light across dead doorways. Assback had only been gone a few minutes when an old crone suddenly peels out of the darkness and makes for the machine as if a smoke is all that stands between her and the devil. But she has no small change; in fact, she has no big change, either, so she starts to beg. We try to give her the rush. "Get lost, countess," says Rico. "Try to make a few quick sous off the Gypsies and leave our machine alone. We haven't frisked for a month because we were in a frisk, but tonight we'll be frisking it to the hilt," he says, "so turn your forehead rearward and it's hup-two-three parade-march up your arse." The crone seemed surprised; she kept watching us suspiciously. She waddled a bit to the side to get a better look, but I blocked her view and yelled at her, "Are you deaf, queenie? Abscondate yourself, your higherness, or ..." These foreign-sounding words must have scared her, for she beat it in a hurry. But she spat some weird glances over her shoulder at us.

We waited some more. It was dark like a coal mine at Christmas, and the parade of characters on Gawker Street resumed. We hear some kind of syncopated footsteps, and a drunk turns the corner, picks his way among his hallucinations till he reaches the machine, focuses on me, and says, "Out of my way, young whippersnapper." Like something out of the last century. He gives me a shove, sees Rico's arm in the machine, and whispers furiously, "Leave her alone! That's no place to stick it! Aren't you ashamed? Pull it out at once!" And then he forgets all about it like a typical drunk and begins to preach to us. "Boys! Here you see four one-crown coins. I believe in the honesty of our social system. As proof of my faith I will stick these four crowns into this slot, I pull this knob, and what happens?" What happened was that Rico's arm fell out, followed by such a mountain of coins and buttons that we stared like madmen. "What's this?" says the drunk. "You see this, boys? It's a shame, a damn shame. Our social system has failed me again. The faith of a simple man should not be broken. Where are my Partyzans? Where are my cigarettes? Money," he said, and snorted with contempt. But when we tried to put our hands on the loot he turned on us furiously and hit Rico on the side of the head. Then he stood at attention in front of the machine, his feet planted in the coins, declaring that he would remain on guard because he was a loyal citizen, though betrayed and disappointed a thousand times over. He sent us to look for a cop. He was soused to the gills.

It was still rather early; we went over to the theatre to wait for Kubišová, but the place was closed. So we went home. I was already lying in bed when it occurred to me that we should have waited for Assback, who had gone to get the blowtorch. But it was too late for that. By now, the boiled guardian of the social order must have fallen asleep on his carpet of coins. On the upper deck, Kalabis seemed to be having heavy dreams and tossed back and forth. My thoughts drifted to Líza Pecáková-Jánská, and I pictured what was probably going on at that moment between Dr. Čestmír Pecák and the Divine Daughter. I became so jealous that I blacked out.

The next day, Assback told me that when they went back to the cigarette machine during the night, the drunk was dead; he had been hit on the head with a blunt object. They notified the police, and the cops kept them in the station overnight because, upon examining the scene of the murder, they found that someone had robbed the machine. The pile of coins must have attracted some covetous bastard, and that idiot of a drunk laid down his life in defence of the social order. There was a story about it in *Evening Prague*, but Assback's name appeared only in initials.

All the same, Assback hadn't slept all night and therefore wasn't in proper shape for the job the next afternoon. We surveyed the scene around the psych lecture hall to find out how much of an attendance there would be for Professor Šťáhlava 's lecture. The attendance seemed to be shaping up fine, but Assback could hardly keep his eyes open. We trailed in behind the crowd and stayed in back near the door, right under the switch. The lecture hall was mobbed, some students busily opening notebooks and others using the close quarters to feel up the girls. There seemed to be quite a few people who weren't exactly med students, a lot of veteran types and the kind of smoky ladies who attend intellectual affairs but not because they're particularly interested in the subject. In came Professor Šťáhlava, a stick with a goatee on top, and delivered a learned address, half of which seemed to be in Latin, while the ladies in the rear conversed in lowered voices and Assback began his work. Dusk was falling. They put on the lights, but only in front at the podium, and in the darkness at the rear Assback furiously scratched with a screwdriver trying to hit the groove. He missed again and again; he simply was no Rico. Fortunately, the professor gave science short shrift and the cabaret began. First they brought in a fellow who went crazy out of an honest habit of taking everything too literally. He had pondered the problem of reducing national expenditures, and finally hit on a perfectly plausible plan for hiring orangutans in place of police-men. The ladies found this so amusing that Assback could work undisturbed.

It was raining, and I glanced out of the lecture hall window toward the garden full of tall pines. Inside the Gothic silhouette of the maternity hospital across the park, little yellow eyes opened one after another until the building shone like a Christmas tree and warmed the darkness at the back of the hall with a hazy yel-lowish glow. It was a pleasant city and a pleasant time, and it was good to serve the Divine Daughter, and that was the most impor-tant thing of all. Something tinkled, probably a screw dropped by Assback. The political moron on the podium was replaced by a madwoman explaining how her husband brought home a differ-ent mistress every night in his briefcase; the whole thing really smacked more of a burlesque show than of psychiatry. The mater-nity hospital radiated its megawatts, apparently a crop of babies was popping out all at once like tiny turtles cracking their eggshells—and suddenly darkness. The lecture hall, too, had become pitch black. Behind me, Assback screamed, "Yeeow!" White stars exploded behind the windows, everything was confusion.

Somebody opened a window and cold droplets blew into the hall. Voices became panicky, the madwoman wailed. I felt Assback crawling around my feet. "Have you got it, jerk?" I asked angrily, and Assback replied: "Jerk, I got a shock. I must have touched off a short at the maternity. The switch is somewhere around here on the floor, careful you don't step on it!" and he continued groping on the floor. The girl medics wailed, apparently abused by stu-dents and non-students. Here and there around the hall matches flared up, and suddenly somebody opened the door behind us, a heavy foot in a heavy boot strides in and, naturally, steps precisely on the pea-green switch lying on the floor. There is a crunch, and it's all over. And this somebody grabs for the switch and, of course, gets a shock like a cannon-shot and screams furiously, "Yeeow!" Our instincts take over, we both try to vanish; I succeed. But Assback, dopey from lack of sleep, stupefied by the cops and the electric shock, gets caught in the net. They nab him. Somebody lights a cigarette lighter, somebody else a second one, and between them they lead Assback off, who blinks and tries to explain, though naturally ass-backward so they take it as a provocation. The hall, meanwhile, is dotted with the slowing tips of cigarettes; the smoky ladies are waiting for somebody to come and fix the electricity.

I waited for Assback almost an hour in the arcade facing the loony ward, right across from the department where bimbos specializing in the tourist trade are treated for various sexual maladies. They were obviously bored there and put on a Chinese shadow-play for me. They had a broad window like a 70-millimetre movie screen, and when they noticed me gawking, they drew the curtain, undressed, and performed some kind of lesbian tragedy. Of course I peered my eyes out without blinking. It was very nice of them to do all this just for me; they had no other audience in this lonely alley between the syphilis clinic and the rococo house supposed to have been occupied in the eighteenth century by a physician-cannibal; nobody ever walks here, especially in the rain, except perhaps a Dr. Jekyll or a Mr. Hyde. I stood there all alone. The nude bimbos behind the curtains fascinated me so much that when Assback finally showed up I was drenched to the skin.

We aimed for the centre of town and along the way Assback reported on the final act of the pea-green switch incident: he tried to explain his behaviour as an attempt to tighten a screw that had come loose, but he was unable to explain why he happened to be in the possession of a screwdriver, an object not normally carried to lectures by philosophy students. On the other hand, why on earth would a philosophy student want to unscrew a switch in the lecture hall of the Psychiatry faculty? They couldn't figure it out. The whole thing began look like a case of mental aberration and thus favourable for Assback. But up till this point the proceedings were carried out in the light of cigarette lighters. Then somebody fixed the wiring, and when they got a clear view of Assback they recognized him as the demo case with a unique speech defect. Their professional pride was hurt; they told him not to come to demonstrations any longer—they'd rather pay the carfare of the psycho in Košice than bother with a questionable, irresponsible character like Assback. It was clear we wouldn't be able to get a switch for the Divine Daughter, not that day, anyway. It continued to pour.

On Poříčí Boulevard we were joined by Rico, and the power of desire drew us to the show windows of the White Swan, shining into the melancholy night. Behind the glass in the middle window was the slicker, on a mannequin with a wooden ball in place of a head, but with a figure almost matching that of Líza Pecáková-Jánská. We pressed our noses to the glass and in each of our skulls the same disgusting scene was being transacted: the slicker is handed over the counter to Professor Friml, expert on Old Church Slavonic, in return for his ill-gotten cash; then it is being carried to Radlice; it is tried on by the Divine Daughter and then it drops to the floor, and soon the mini drops to the floor too as a reward for the degenerate savant. All of us reached this point simultaneously in our independent imaginations. We stepped away from the pane, and in unison uttered, "Shit!"

Ahoy there, a cheery voice greets us, and it is Polly, a medical student and a fellow member of the gang, a blonde with long hair in the back, in a black-and-white-checked mini and shiny white boots; she was just tooling around the Swan with a melted-cheese sandwich in her hand and a lunchbox slung over her shoulder. "Ahoy there, ahoy, crickets, what's new?" In sorrow, we told her all our troubles. The rain pours down on us; we are one hell of a soaked gang. Polly's hair hangs down like wet straw and rivulets of water stream to the sidewalk. We have one crown twenty-five between us, and that's why Polly's information wasn't worth very much to us. "Pea-green switches? I just saw some on the third floor," she announces. "Where?" "Right here in the Swan. Seven crowns each." She notices everything. "Go on, chum," says Rico. "Are you trying to tell us that in the White Swan they sell pea-green push-button switches? How come? Where do they get the nerve?" Rico is getting excited, quite justifiably. "God almighty, how can they have the gall in this day and age to stock pea-green switches?" Now he is shouting: "What kind of system is this? How can they ignore the public and sell push-button switches?" "Bastards!" yells Assback. "Criminals! Irresponsible gang of thieves!" Assback shouts hoarsely, shaking the recently electrocuted arm. "They just calmly go ahead and sell them, like soap or dish towels!" "Criminals! Swine!" we shout, one on top of the other; people begin to gather and to mumble. And then we suddenly see a cop coming down the street and we break into a barbershop quartet version of a blues, Polly an octave higher, and we harmonize:

Champagne, champagne,
Mellow, mellow wine!
Pink champagne, you
Made me feel so fine!

The cop draws near and is on the verge of questioning us, when Polly says, "Comrade police, we English students on the peace marching to Cairo," and she hands him the lunchbox and he almost makes a contribution, but then he regains his self-control and says, "All right, break it up," but without any conviction, and the bystanders begin to sing along:

Pink champagne, you
Left me feelin' blue ...

The coins jingle into the box. Amazing that we never thought of this before!

Pink champagne, you
Left me feelin' blue!
Pink champagne, you
Broke my heart in two!

Altogether, we collected twenty-three crowns sixty, enough for three switches and a garlic salami for Polly thrown in. The rain stopped. The Swan sparkled into the dark Prague night, and all at once a happy mood took hold, a festive mood. But Polly, the medic, got a medical idea, and none of us jerks thought it through to the end, none of us had enough brains to realize that on this ill-starred day disaster was sure to crash down on our heads. This was Polly's idea: to attempt a therapeutic intervention against Rico's kleptomania. Medicine was beginning to affect her reason. "Let Rico *buy* those switches," she says. "Rico hasn't bought a blessed thing in the seven months. He has had his cert, he's been stealing everything he needs. Buying will break the klepto habit," Polly says. And Rico nodded his small blond head, too small for his body, and stepped into the lit-up entrance of the Swan like a sleepwalker, a gentle lamb back on the road of virtue. That's the only way I could explain it to myself. Maybe he had gotten so used to stealing that buying now seemed an interesting oddity. He entered the store, and disappeared into the crowd.

We stand around, waiting, Polly gabbing about modern learning theory and principles of negative reinforcement and it starts to rain once more. That is, of course, a black portent. Soon a second omen becomes manifest in the form of the crone from Gawker Street. A Baba Yaga straight out of a fairy tale, she fixes us with a bloodshot eyeball and then disappears into the Swan. And on top of that, who passes by but Professor Friml, decadent Slavist, holding a black umbrella with flower-power lining in one hand and a ravishingly beautiful third-year medic in the other. Three evil signs: a pestilential conjunction. I got scared and ran in after Rico to prevent a disaster. Assback tagged along after me.

The moment Polly stood alone in her checkered mini she was addressed by a spiffed-up Negro: "Hey, baby, how about comin' with me to the Yalta!" So at least in my anxiety I am solaced by the knowledge that Polly's dinner is assured, in the Yalta no less, which is beautiful because the W.C. lady there is a very pleasant old reactionary, the former Mrs. Councillor Blahníková. Polly and she are in cahoots. As soon as Polly fills up on squirrel soup and peahen goulash, she goes to the W.C. and the good Mrs. Blahníková lets her out through the fire escape. And then her black friend can rage all he wants. Mrs. Blahníková loses her tip, of course, but what wouldn't a person do for sweet Pollynka.

The thought that Polly was staked to a first-rate dinner warmed my soul, and I rushed to the third floor, the electric appliances department, but I got there too late. Assback bumped me from behind, but Rico was already in custody. He was standing at the switch counter with limbs spread apart like a scarecrow, a pair of salesgirls holding each arm, the assistant manager facing him, and the Baba Yoga approaching from the flank. Only Professor Friml was missing to complete the tableau.

There was nothing we could do to help. The director strode in our direction, and though he didn't recognize us he had us pegged pretty well, and told us to get lost. In my last glimpse I saw Baba Yaga bending her head toward the assistant manager. She blinked suspiciously at Rico and then suddenly a devilish insight came upon her and evil cybernetic connections hooked up in her brain. Then a Judas-like whisper into the assistant manager's ear and a funereal black nail pointing at Rico.

We waited in the Boathouse until nine. At nine some beery types got into a fight over a soccer match. One of them broke off a chrome column full of pipes, and beer poured out all the way to the sidewalk and down the drain, and later that night drunken rats chewed up an unconscious pensioner who had fainted from hunger. We beat it, even though the cops don't usually bother with soccer brawls. Rico's case was written up next day in *Evening Prague*, to the effect that law student R.N. was arrested at the

White Swan as a suspect in the murder of locksmith Joseph Benedikt the night before on the corner of Gawker and Pusher Streets. Witness J.B. had identified the suspect as the man who had rudely chased her from a cigarette machine that she had intended to use (I'd like to know how—she didn't have a brass button) near the spot where the murdered Benedikt was later found. And so it began to smell like the gallows for Rico, unless kleptomania is considered an extenuating circumstance even in the case of murder.

As yet, of course, we had no inkling of these developments as we made our way from the Boathouse to Radlice, after an unsuccessful attempt to hitch a free ride on the automatic tram. It was around midnight, and we gently tapped our code on the first-floor window of the Divine Daughter. It was pouring again.

A different window opened, the one to the left of the entrance, and Mrs. Jánská looked out. She became frightened—we looked like dead Beatles pulled out after two weeks in the Thames—but then she recognized us and informed us that Liduška was not at home. No? And with whom is she? we asked, figuring that on the basis of this information we could deduce where she might be, but Mrs. Jánská said: I don't know this one yet. He's tall, sideburns like Kaiser Franz Joseph the Second, may his soul—*rest in peace*, we finished the phrase in unison—and good night. There was no point in asking any further. We didn't know him either. A newcomer.

Mrs. Jánská closed the window, and once again we trotted through the rain and the darkness and gazed at Prague, glowing like a dying bonfire, floating in light, so many embers, and behind one of them is the Divine Daughter right now, but which one, and with whom? With a sideburned one, but who is he? Polly was in good shape, anyway, she was no doubt sweetly dreaming away in her nest on Strahov, full of peahen goulash, her black suitor perhaps sleeping off a binge in a first-aid station, but what about us, in the rain and the dark and our stomachs grumbling, slickerless, Rico-less, without even a single pea-green push-button switch. How can we face God's Daughter?

The next night we screwed up our courage and shuffled to her place. She was again warming herself in front of the gas fire, in a mini and long stockings, and she didn't say a word about switches. A copy of *Evening Prague* with the item about Rico lay on the tiger rug beside her, and God's Daughter was no longer interested in the slicker but in how to get a ticket for Rico's upcoming execution. She didn't believe us when we told her that no such tickets were available. After all, with a little influence one could get anything, she thought.

It was ten o'clock, God the Father behind the plaster wall was tuning in Radio Free Europe, and Líza remarked crossly that perhaps they should give him a special medal as the last faithful listener and the only listener who still preferred politics to jazz music; Assback suggested that perhaps such an award could be arranged through one of those Munich-based Negroes who seem so attracted to our lesbian friend, and the words were no sooner out of his mouth, speaking of the devil, then there was a gentle code-knock on the pane. We opened up and, there on the sidewalk in the moonlight stands Polly, the blonde medic, her belly full of Yalta cuisine, the second straight lucky day for her. We let her in. She laid her soaking wet lunchbox on Líza's botany notes; she and Líza embraced and stuck out their behinds toward the gas flames and Polly launched into a typical med-student story of some idiot who during practical exams in plastic surgery cut off his own ears and sewed them on backward, so that now he hears everything the wrong way. The gas flames danced over the imitation logs, which looked more like dinosaur faces than firewood, and God's Daughter opened up a bottle, the last from the supply stolen for her by the soon-to-be-deceased Rico. The evening mellowed; warmed, we were once again the old gang of the Knights of Líza's Grail.

Champagne, champagne

we sang, Polly's voice ringing out an octave higher.

Mellow, mellow wine!

Even God's Daughter sang along, a little off key, for she has no musical ear, and behind the plaster wall the Lord himself joined in, too. After so much bad luck, things were once again quite OK.

Pink champagne, you
Made me feel so fine!

1967

V
Another Interlude

The
Mysterious Events
at Night

From the cassette recording by Derek MacHane, kindergarten student at the Dwight O'Mackay Public School in Etobicoke, Ontario.

After he was told by Mummy that he was putting on weight, Tentvůj signed up at Weight Watchers. He got himself a scale to check up on his calories. Also *mrkefs*, which are a lot like carrots, except in the Czech language. And celery stickers and other *vedzhtebels*, as he calls them. Tentvůj is my dad. That's not his name, really. But that's what Mummy's friends always call him, "Tentvůj muž," when they talk to her in our language, and when I was little I thought it was his name. It means That-Husband-of-Yours and sounds like Tant-Vooey. Sometimes I call him Dad but I always think of him as Tentvůj.

Every morning Tentvůj weighed his food for the whole day. All the time he was being watched by Kokour who was sitting on the table, although Mummy kept throwing him down, but he kept coming back up all the time, because he was very interested in the weighing.

Kokour is our biggest cat. When we went on vacations to Florida, Mummy wrote down for our cleaning lady, on a slip of paper, *Don't forget to give Kokour his food every day!* When we came back Kokour was twice his old size. Mummy was shocked, thinking he was pregnant although the vet told us that he isn't a girl cat but a boy cat. But Mrs. Bottomrider said (in English), "Oh, no! He's a regular fatso. I gave him three cans every morning all at once. You can't expect me to serve Mr. Kokour his food three times a day! I live all the way in Cabbagetown and that's a half hour by sub-way!" Mummy forgot to inform Mrs. Bottomrider that Kokour is on a diet of one can a day.

Kokour is quite stupid and he let himself be fooled up by his original owner by a stupidly simple trick. In those days we still lived in the furnished apartment on Charles Street right across from the post office. One day in the wintertime I was watching out the window and I saw a gentleman with a big tomcat on a leash. In front of the door to the post office he unhooked the leash, said something to the cat and stepped inside. The tomcat, which was white with black spots, waited in the snow outside. But from the window of our apartment on the twelfth floor I could see into the alley next to the post office, into which the back door opens. While the tomcat waited at the front door, the gentleman left by the back door and quickly disappeared down the alley. But the tomcat kept sitting. Every time somebody left the post office, he went up to him, put his nose up against his pants or shoes, and then went back to sit some more.

The next morning I looked out the window and the tomcat was still sitting in front of the post office, putting his nose up against the pants of anyone leaving. At noon he was still there, and he was still there when it started to get darker. I went to the fridge and got myself some ham, which was meant for sandwiches. I took the elevator down and crossed the street to the tomcat. He put his nose up against my pants, but when I offered him the ham he started to eat so furiously that the ham disappeared in no time. Then he sat down again and licked himself. That night Tentvůj was mad because when he wanted to fix himself a sandwich as a bedtime snack, but couldn't find any ham in the fridge, I admitted that I gave it to the tomcat who was still sitting by the post office. It was already dark but we all went to the window and there he was, just sitting there. We saw him clearly because light fell on him through the glass doors of the post office.

"Chudáček pitomá!" Mummy said in Czech (but that was the wrong word, because our teacher Mrs. Pochopena-Nutney teaches us at Saturday Czech school that *chudáček* is of the masculine genre, as is tomcat but *pitomá* is of the feminine), and next morning she bought the tomcat pet food in cans from the supermarket. For the next few days, every morning and evening, I opened a can of pet food and took it out to him. He became so used to it that as soon as he saw me, he would run toward me, to the end of his leash, and meow.

I did that all week long. Then, on Saturday, we were coming back with Mummy from the St. Nicholas Day children's party. There had been a terrible blizzard: the snow was three feet deep, and untouched because no one had ventured outside. The light shone through the large doors of the post office and the untouched snow sparkled like diamonds. Above it, in front of the door, there was a small white hillock. It was the tomcat who was still sitting there, waiting for his master.

Mummy picked him up and brushed off the snow. Underneath, the tomcat's fur was all crusted with ice. But when we brought him to the apartment, he thawed out, ate the ham that had been bought for Tentvůj's sandwiches (there were no cans of cat food left) and then made a mess on the white mat in the washroom. From then on he stayed with us. Mummy bought him his own washroom with litter and we called him Kokour ("Tomcat").

That spring our family moved into a new place, our very own house, and Kokour moved in with us. The house was roomy and Kokour walked around it all week, looking sad. And he was meowing all the time.

"He's looking for a girl cat," said Tentvůj.

"Will he find her, Dad?" I asked.

"If you keep him in, he won't," Tentvůj said.

"If I let him out, he'll run away," said Mummy. "He hasn't gotten used to the new house."

"That one? Run away?" sneered Tentvůj. "Three months with us and just look at the size of him. You know what that says in cat language? Damn good living!" Actually, Kokour never said anything. He only meowed.

That evening Mummy decided to let Kokour out into the garden and in the morning he didn't come back. The next morning either.

"You see," said Mummy, with tears in her eyes. "I was sure he'd run away. He's probably standing in front of the post office again."

"Don't be daft, Vicky," said Tentvůj. "He'll be back for sure. He just off somewhere catting. Don't worry!"

I asked what is *catting* and Mummy explained that he was looking for a girl cat. Kokour looked for one more day, but must not have found one, because he came back home. He ate three cans of food and then slept for two days.

I decided to find him a girl cat myself and set out to search for one. Three blocks from our house I saw an old lady sitting in a rocking chair on a porch with a cardboard box on her lap. A black cat sitting on a banister next to the steps was watching her. When I moved closer I saw three kittens in the box.

"Oh, aren't they cute!" I cried, to endear myself to the old lady.

"Aren't they?" she said.

"Oh!" I repeated. "Could I have one?"

"You could, if you promise to take good care of it," said the old lady. And that's how I found Jůlinka for Kokour.

She was still a kitten, all grey with green eyes. I put her down beside Kokour and he sniffed her. She started to poke her nose into his belly and also to paw him there. Kokour didn't like that; he smacked her three times with his paw. Soon after that Mummy came in with Tentvůj and he started in right away talking about what a bad idea it was to have Jůlinka. But Mummy lifted Jůlinka up to her face and said, "We can't put such a helpless creature out into the cold!" Although it wasn't cold, because it was spring.

Jůlinka bit Mummy's nose. She had sharp little teeth, like pins.

"Helpless creature!" said Tentvůj. "And besides—" he pointed towards Kokour "—soon he'll knock 'er up and the place will turn into a regular cathouse!"

"He knocked 'er up already," I said.

"What?" Mummy shouted.

"He knocked 'er up three times, when she stuck her nose into his belly," I said.

"Oh, I see." said Mummy and turned to Tentvůj. "She's just a kitten. She can't even pee on her own."

But Jůlinka could, and Mummy had to put her new dress in the washer.

Jůlinka and Kokour soon became friends. She would growl and jump on him and he would knock 'er up every time, but not very hard. Then they would lie next to each other and Jůlinka would lick Kokour's face, and vice versa.

But one morning, while Jůlinka was sitting on the fence in the garden, a big strange dog came along and started to jump up at the fence. Jůlinka was shocked and ran away along the fence and across the garage roofs in the alley. She didn't come back that evening, or the next day, or the day after that. Kokour was sad. He walked through the house looking for her.

Jůlinka was gone for three weeks and Kokour became so thin that Mummy was shocked and worried that he might harm himself.

Tentvůj chuckled.

"Don't laugh," said Mummy, "there are cases. Sometimes, when a dove dies, her mate deliberately flies against a rock and commits suicide."

"Birds are monogamous," Tentvůj informed her. "But that egotist?" and he pointed at Kokour who was eating a fresh smelt that Mummy had bought for him instead of pet food, so he wouldn't be sad. "He only thinks of himself. He is Czech through and through. The only thing he'll ever fly up against will be another cat!"

Mummy decided that we would get him one, so he'd have one to fly against.

For the new cat we went to the Humanist Society. There in cages sat many cats and doggies, mostly crying. When we walked among the cages, they all threw themselves against the bars, stuck their paws through them and made sounds that sounded like "Take me! Take me!"

"What do you do with them?" Mummy asked the attendant in a shaking voice.

"They stay here for three weeks. If no one takes them, then—"

"Then what?" Mummy asked, her voice again shaking.

"Research laboratories," said the attendant. "At the University of Toronto."

Tears came up in Mummy's eyes. She looked around and saw a black kitten with big yellow eyes sitting in the corner of a cage. She was looking at Mummy.

"Oh!" Mummy said in our own language. "*I can't stand the thought. Gimme that one!*" and pointed her finger at the black kitten.

That's how we bought Buba. She cost us five bucks, shots included. Mummy gave her the name Belzebuba, but it was too long. We started to call her Buba and it stuck with her.

She also put her nose on Kokour's belly and pushed him with her paws and he would always knock 'er up. But they became friends and licked each other's faces.

When Buba was with us for two weeks, one morning I was looking out into the garden, and suddenly, there was Jůlinka running along the fence. Although I first thought it was only Jůlinka's ghost. She was so skinny that you could see all her ribs and I was afraid they would poke out through her fur. I opened the sliding door to the kitchen. Jůlinka ran up to me and started to swear. She swore a lot. I quickly gave her three cans of pet food and she gobbled it up. Then she ran over to me and complained some more, and then ran back again to the dish with the pet food to gobble some more. It was as if she couldn't make up her mind if she should swear or gobble.

Then she saw Buba.

Her back turned into the letter U and she hissed like a snake. Buba came up to her and stuck her nose up against hers. Jůlinka knocked 'er up with her paw, with her claws sticking out. Right in her nose.

Buba is as black as coal, so that when it's dark you can only see her eyes. That's why Tentvůj sometimes calls her "Eyes." When Jůlinka knocked 'er up across her nose with her claws, she had a surprised look.

Buba always wanted to be friends with Jůlinka, but Jůlinka always hissed at her like a snake.

"She's jealous," said Tentvůj. "When she was lost you got Kokour a concubine, so she's jealous."

Buba was just licking Kokour's face.

"And have them both spayed," said Tentvůj. "Otherwise we'll really have a cathouse here soon."

"Buba's just a kitten," said Mummy.

Soon after that Buba started to get fatter.

"What did I say?" said Tentvůj. "He knocked 'er up!"

Kokour's face was just being licked by Jůlinka. Buba walked by carrying a Kleenex in her mouth, which she'd found in the garbage.

"Look! She's nesting already," commented Tentvůj.

"*Oh, no!*" said Mummy.

"*Oh, yes!*" mimicked Tentvůj. "Or do you think she caught a cold?"

Next day Buba had three kittens. A few weeks later one of them was taken by Mrs. Pochopena-Nutney for their Deborah, and another one by Mr. Tabborski, the film director. That kitten, who was a real tomcat, later ripped up Mr. Tabborski's diploma from the Venice Film Festival.

One cat stayed with us but she took after Kokour. She was very stupid. Tentvůj gave her the name Blbeta, which means Silly.

That's how we acquired four cats. They were all spayed, because Tentvůj insisted.

The news soon spread among the cats in the neighbourhood that there was lots of pet food to be had at our place. The alley cats tried, successfully, to horn in whenever the sliding door from the kitchen to the garden was left open during the summer. They snuck inside, but always kept distance from Mummy and me, and Mummy gave them names. A large alley tom came most often. He was very hairy, especially on the face and around the eyes, and Mummy called him Brezhnev. But others came too, for instance a tabby with a fluffy tail like Blbeta's, whom Mummy called Daddy (referring to Blbeta's uncertain paternity). Another one, which bleated like a sheep, had one blue eye and one green eye. That one was Cocktail. Kokour and Jůlinka hissed at the alley cats, but Buba only sniffed them and had a surprised look. Blbeta was scared and hid under the sofa.

Blbeta was so stupid that she thought people liked to eat worms and insects. Every night she brought something in from the garden: a caterpillar, a mosquito, or a dew worm. She always left them on Mummy's blanket, usually still alive. Once a caterpillar crawled into Mummy's ear. She woke up and screamed. After that Blbeta was locked out every night and she always peed on the screen door out of revenge.

That's what most likely attracted many of the animals who assembled at night in our garden in front of the screen door. We weren't aware of it because every night we fell fast asleep. But one night I had a stomach ache from eating too much pecan cake— and that was the night the mystery began. Awakened by the belly- ache, I burped and remembered that Tentvůj had Alka-Seltzer in the kitchen for his morning hangovers. The cuckoo clock in the living room had just announced midnight when I went downstairs in my bare feet. But I stopped because there was a light on in the kitchen. I kept quiet and watched Tentvůj sitting on a chair in front of the open fridge, helping himself to the fresh bread that Uncle Peter, who is the delivery man at a Jewish bakery and delicatessen, brings to us, despite Mummy's protests that bread is a caloric bombshell. But the Jewish bread is very good. I eat it, and that night Tentvůj was eating it too, in secret, spreading it with butter. On the floor behind his chair sat Buba, eating a long dew worm.

I snuck back upstairs and went out on the sun deck to wait until Tentvůj had satisfied his hunger and gone back to bed. There was a harvest moon and a light breeze. I looked over the railing into the garden. On the lawn in front of the screen door sat Kokour and Jůlinka. The alley cats formed a circle around them, and around that circle, in another circle, sat squirrels and raccoon kittens with the mother raccoon. She was holding the remains of a large rib roast in her paws, just like the one we had for dinner that night, which Mummy then threw in the garbage can. The mother raccoon tore pieces off it with her fingers and gave them to the raccoon kittens. The garbage can was tipped over and the garbage was spread all over the lawn.

I watched the scene for a long time and I saw that right in front of Kokour and Jůlinka sat the other three: Brezhnev, Daddy, and Cocktail, staring at them without saying a single word. Suddenly the door creaked open and Mummy came on the sun deck in her white see-through nightgown. She had curlers in her hair and her face was all white from night cream.

"Derek! What are you doing here at this time of night!" she yelled at me, in our language, and I said, *"Shh, Mom!* The cats are having a spiritual seance down there!" and I pointed my finger over the railing.

Mummy looked. The alley cats, squirrels, and the raccoons sat in the moonlight in the circle around Kokour and Jůlinka, completely silent. At that moment Buba crawled in through the fence, carrying another dew worm in her mouth. She sat down and watched the scene with a look of surprise.

"A spiritual seance?" said Mummy. "Poppycock! They are having a meeting. They're screening Kokour and Jůlinka, 'cause they've just moved in."

"What is 'screening'?" I asked.

But Mummy didn't answer and chased me back to bed.

In the morning Mummy made a ruckus when she took uncle's bread from the fridge to make me a peanut butter sandwich.

"Otto!" she addressed Tentvůj in a strict voice. "Yesterday there was a whole loaf and today there's barely a third. Can you explain that to me?"

Tentvůj, who was sitting at the table weighing calories, closely watched by Kokour, was obviously startled.

"I didn't eat it!" he said. "It was probably—probably the cats, or maybe …"

"Oh yes, the cats!" said Mummy ironically. "I didn't know we had bread-eating cats. I thought that cats were meat-eaters. Ours must be unique."

Before Tentvůj could say another word, Buba arrived with a dew worm. She jumped up on the table and offered the worm to Kokour. The worm started to curl up.

"Phew, Buba!" said Tentvůj. He wanted to throw the worm out into the garden, but Mummy stopped him. She sliced two thin slices of uncle's bread, picked up the worm with a fork and placed it on one of the slices. Then she put the second slice on top and said:

"Here, Buba! Eat! *An earthworm sandwich!*"

Buba tilted her head to one side and cast a surprised look at the sandwich with the earthworm. The worm wiggled himself partway out of the sandwich. Buba pulled him out the rest of the way and ate him.

"It seems she doesn't take to bread," Mummy said. "I wonder who took to it last night?"

"It wasn't me! *Cross my heart!*" said Tentvůj, afraid that Mummy would scold him. But he was lying. I saw him eating the bread at night, with my own eyes.

"I wonder how the cats opened the fridge?" Mummy went on. "Actually, how did they even get inside when we put them out at night, now that it's summer? All the windows have screens. Do they know how to think?" Mummy said and started to take the curlers out of her hair. As she took them out, her hair was beautiful and it shimmered. "And besides, last night they didn't have time to even think of food. They were screening Kokour."

"What is screening?" I asked once more. But neither Mummy nor Tentvůj would give me the information. Tentvůj was eating a carrot and Mummy was putting on her earrings in front of a concave mirror.

I noticed Brezhnev sitting outside the door to the garden, watching what was going on in the kitchen. When Mummy stood up, opened the fridge and took out ham for my sandwich. Brezhnev stuck out his tongue and licked his moustache.

Next morning there was no ham in the fridge. Mummy asked Tentvůj what was the point of watching his weight in the daytime if at night he secretly stuffed himself with ham. But Tentvůj denied it and I couldn't say, because I had been fast asleep all that night.

But from then on, something was missing from the fridge every morning. Mummy made a ruckus all the time, but Tentvůj each time denied stuffing himself, and he weighed smaller and smaller calories, watched attentively by Kokour. The ruckus got bigger every day, until at one point Tentvůj took Mummy to the washroom, stepped on the scale and said, "Look here. Last week I lost another nine pounds. How do you explain that if—as you claim—last week I secretly packed away a whole ham, half a cold roast, a dozen chicken drumsticks and two turkey legs, six Italian sausages, a whole Polish salami? Plus four pounds of mortadella, two half-eaten cans of sardines, and two frozen T-bone steaks, obviously raw? Topping it off each time with a whole loaf of Uncle Peter's Jewish bread? And doing it at night, when one puts on most weight?"

Mummy couldn't explain. Tentvůj looked at me and said to Mummy, "How about asking our very own Marx?" and he pointed at me. "Isn't he putting on a bit of weight? Derek! On the scale!"

He put me on the scale and I weighed three pounds more than last week.

"He's growing," said Mummy.

"He's getting wider," said Tentvůj.

"And taller as well!" said Mummy. She took me off the scale and stood me up against the giraffe measure taped to the wall.

I had grown an inch since last week.

So the suspicion still stuck to Tentvůj.

Next morning was my birthday. I got up early and went with Mummy in her see-through nightgown down to the kitchen where I knew my birthday cake was in the fridge.

It wasn't. There were only some leftovers scattered in front of the fridge and the floor was an awful mess.

"I'm going to divorce him!" Mummy first shouted and then she screamed, "Otto! Come down immediately!"

Sleepy Tentvůj came down in his pyjamas. Not saying a word, Mother pointed at the mess on the floor. "This was a cream cake with chocolate icing."

"OK," said Tentvůj, and without another word he went to the washroom and stepped on the scale.

"Two pounds less than yesterday morning. And I haven't had a movement in three days," said Tentvůj.

Mummy wanted to check the scale and stepped onto it. Tentvůj looked over her shoulder and Mummy suddenly blushed.

"Well! Look at this!" declared Tentvůj. "Five pounds more than yesterday!"

Mummy said, still blushing:

"Yesterday I weighed myself—just so!"

"Then it's going to be 'just so' again!" Tentvůj decided. "Derek! Out!"

A little while later they came down. Mummy was still wearing her see-through nightgown and I didn't understand why Tentvůj sent me outside. She was crying.

"Why don't you just say I'm responsible for the nightly orgies!" she sobbed.

"*Well*," said Tentvůj and put a carrot on the scale. Then he cut an inch off it. "Even in the just so you're up a couple of pounds."

Mummy blushed and said, "Yesterday afternoon Petra took me to Cakemaster. And I also haven't yet gone today."

"I see. You didn't mention anything!" said Tentvůj.

"Since when do I have to tell you everything?" said Mummy.

"Was it Petra? Or maybe someone called Peter?"

"Come on! Next you'll start suspecting me of cheating on you!"

"One never knows," said Tentvůj.

"Then how about your business trip to New York, the last time?" said Mummy. "I called the Algonquin and they told me you weren't registered!"

"They had no vacancy at the Algonquin. They moved my reservation to the Prince Edward."

"Who knows," said Mummy. "They all say that."

"Fine," said Tentvůj. "Yesterday I called Petra and her husband told me that she went at two by bus to Kitchener!"

"She only went at five."

"Who knows," said Tentvůj. "They all say that."

"By the way," said Mummy. "Why exactly did you call Petra?"

Tentvůj blushed and stayed quiet. Mummy threw herself on the table and her hair shook as she cried. Tentvůj bit into the carrot and screamed. He broke his tooth on the hard carrot.

I knew the situation was serious. It was heading towards divorce and all because of the mysterious robberies of ham, wursts, chicken drumsticks, salamis, and finally my birthday cake.

I decided that I must find out what was going on in this house.

At night that day I waited until both Mummy and Tentvůj had fallen asleep. Then I got up and went down to the living room, where I hid under the sofa. But nothing happened for a long time; only the cuckoo clock tick-tocked and the moonlight bathed the kitchen through the sliding door. I was sleepy and in the end I fell asleep before I was able to find anything out. In the morning Mummy found me under the sofa, but in the fridge she *didn't* find a whole stick of Hungarian salami, which Uncle Peter had given us.

"Godalmighty! You gobbled it up, skin and all! Aren't you sick?"

But I denied eating the stick of salami, which was taller than me, and after that Mummy didn't talk to Tentvůj all through breakfast. Tentvůj weighed calories—watched by Kokour—and ate one celery stick instead of the stick of salami, which he unsuccessfully searched for all through the fridge. Nobody said a single word and the atmosphere was definitely cold. I was afraid that Mummy and Tentvůj really meant to get a divorce.

I couldn't stand it because I love Tentvůj and I love Mummy even more. I went into the garden, sat under the maple tree and thought very hard. Suddenly I noticed a piece of salami skin sticking out of the bed planted with morning glory. I pulled it out and discovered that it was the skin from the Hungarian stick missing from our fridge. Someone had expertly peeled it off, eaten the salami and buried the skin, although carelessly.

I searched further at the spot where I pulled out the skin.

I found a hairball. The kind of hairball that Kokour vomits when he stuffs himself too full of pet food. The hairball contained remnants of Hungarian salami.

I thought very hard.

The salami was obviously eaten by Kokour. But how could Kokour so expertly peel the salami? Besides, Kokour always ate salami with the skin on.

And how could Kokour open the fridge? Kokour doesn't have fingers. And furthermore, animals don't know how to think.

The mystery was deeper than before the discovery of the carelessly buried skin. The mysterious events in the night were really bugging me.

That afternoon, Mummy dialled a number and when she got through, she said, "May I speak to Dr. Čermák, please?"

I knew that things were getting tough. Dr. Čermák is a Czech lawyer. He is also an actor who stars at the New Czech Theatre. Mummy doesn't star there. She doesn't even get bit parts. She's pretty, but on stage she is wooden, said Mr. Čulík, who is a comic actor and directs the productions. And so Mummy only gets to sell the tickets. I deduced that she isn't calling Dr. Čermák on account of theatre, but because of the divorce. I became sure when she saw I was listening and sent me out to play in the garden.

Buba was standing above a large earthworm that was trying to screw itself back into the flower bed. With her head inclined, she followed it with a surprised look. Then she turned around and started to bury the worm with her back legs, although she had not peed or pooed. I deduced that she must be stuffed with food already.

What food?

The Chef's Dinner in the cat's bowls had sat there since morning, practically untouched.

I went on deducing. But I wasn't puzzled.

In the evening I secretly swallowed three Wake Up! pills, which Tentvůj uses when he takes Dristan for a cold and then has to drive to his office. Again I waited until both Mummy and Tentvůj fell fast asleep, and I went down to the kitchen. In the fridge was half a stuffed turkey from this evening's dinner. I took it out and hid it under the davenport. Then I crawled in after it.

It was August and the harvest moon was shining like a silver dollar. The cuckoo clock tick-tocked, the cuckoo bird came out every half hour and announced the time, but because I had taken the three Wake Up! pills I wasn't sleepy. It was almost midnight when I suddenly heard strange noises. I didn't know where they were coming from. The moonlight was falling on the stovepipe of the Franklin stove, which we have in the living room instead of a fireplace, when out of it crawled Buba. She stood still and then turned. Another strange sound came and then the stovepipe moved. From inside the pipe came shuffling sounds and, suddenly, out of the Franklin stovepipe crawled the mother raccoon. I was dumbstruck and amazed.

Then in the light of the moon the raccoon kittens followed their mother, six altogether, and after them Kokour, Jůlinka, and many alley cats, led by Brezhnev, Daddy, and Cocktail. Then four squirrels. When they were all out of the stovepipe, the mother raccoon turned and the whole company followed her, with the squirrels bringing up the rear. The mother raccoon stopped in front of the fridge.

At that moment another sound came out of the stovepipe. I glanced over just in time to see Blbeta fall out of the Franklin stovepipe, landing on her back. She turned over, saw me and slunk away to hide under the liquor cabinet. She watched me from under there.

I watched the kitchen. The mother raccoon sat on her hind legs and with her front hands expertly opened the fridge. She took out Uncle Peter's bread, started to peel it and gave bits of the crumbs to the raccoon kittens. When the bread was peeled, she threw it to the squirrels who started to fight over it.

The mother raccoon looked again into the fridge and snorted. With her front paws she began taking out cans of tomatoes and salad dressing, still snorting. Cocktail bleated and pushed against the fridge with his front paws. Buba also stood and stared inside.

But I didn't wait any longer. I carefully wiggled out from under the davenport, took a cushion and quietly stuffed it into the stovepipe. Then I closed the iron door of the Franklin stove and ran up to the bedroom.

"*Mom!*" I whispered. "*Wake up!*"

Mummy was wearing pyjamas that weren't see-through, but her face was white with night cream and the curlers in her hair were pink. She turned and mumbled:

"Leave me alone! You aren't getting any, Otto!"

"*Mom!*" I whispered in her ear where she had the hole for her earring. "I found out who stuffs himself at night with the food from the fridge!"

Mummy woke up. Tentvůj also woke up.

"What's gotten into you?" asked Tentvůj.

"Nothing! But I've gotten the robbers!" I said. "Quiet! So we don't scare them away!"

We tiptoed to the staircase. The animals crowded around the Franklin stove and the mother raccoon was just opening the iron door with her front paws.

"*See?*" I said. Surprised, Mummy and Tentvůj who looked at each other. The mother raccoon opened the door and squeezed

herself into the stovepipe. But there she was stopped by the cushion. She was almost completely in the stovepipe, only her fat
ringed tail stuck out. We could hear her scratching the cushion.

Suddenly Tentvůj roared, "So that's how it is!"

And he ran down the stairs.

The animals panicked. They ran in all directions and the alley
cats jumped up against the window but they couldn't get out. The
squirrels climbed on the furniture. Kokour stretched out on the
floor and pretended to be asleep. Cocktail vomited a hairball and
Jůlinka stood in front of the Franklin stove and swore at the
mother raccoon.

Mummy ran to the kitchen and opened the sliding door. One
after another the panicky animals escaped into the garden, until
the only one left was the mother raccoon stuck in the stovepipe.
Tentvůj pulled her out by her tail, but before she too made her
escape, I noticed that she had a mask on her face. And I understood what was meant by screening. It has to do with robber bands
accepting new members. The mother raccoon also ran away
through the door into the garden. The disappointed animals forgot to close the fridge and the squirrels left behind the half-eaten
piece of bread. Brezhnev was so scared that he left a smelly mess
on the carpet in front of the Franklin stove.

We were sitting at the table and I explained how I deduced the
solution of the mysterious events of the night. How I had seen
Buba eating a dew worm inside a closed house with screens on all
the windows, and then a moment later she was out in the garden
attending the screening of Kokour and Jůlinka. How Brezhnev sat
and listened when Mummy scolded Tentvůj that first night, when
he really did eat Uncle Peter's bread, and then she took the ham
out of the fridge. How I found the skin from the stick of
Hungarian salami carelessly buried in the flower bed and next to
it a hairball full of salami, and how Buba buried the dew worm
and how I noticed that the bowls of Chef's Dinner were

untouched. How I saw the mother raccoon peel pieces of meat off the rib roast. And how I put it all together and I made up my mind to prevent the divorce.

"Our own little Sherlock Holmes," said Mummy and gave me a kiss. She smelled like sandalwood.

"More like Nero Wolfe," said Tentvůj and stuck his finger into my belly.

"He's still growing," said Mummy and got up. "And we have to get that pillow out of the chimney."

We went to the Franklin stove, Mummy bent down and pulled out the cushion. She held it up in the moonlight and foam spilled out of it.

"Animals know how to think," I said. "Like people."

"It only looks like they can," said Tentvůj. "It's all instinct."

Something ran out from under the liquor cabinet, flew between Tentvůj's legs and jumped up into the Franklin stove. The stovepipe heaved and furious squeezing was heard.

It was Blbeta. She was afraid of being spanked. When she saw that Mummy pulled the cushion out of the stovepipe, she made the best of the opportunity and made a beeline for the stove.

"You might be right, Derek," said Mummy, "although we were taught differently at school."

We went upstairs, they put me to bed in my room and I heard Mummy say at the bedroom door, "It's just like the tropics tonight. Really humid. Too warm for pyjamas. Bring me my nightgown, Otto. It's hanging in the washroom."

She meant her see-through nightgown. I knew that Dr. Čermák wasn't going to do any business with her. And I thought it would be nice to have a kid brother. Or even better, a sister.

Next morning it was Sunday and Mummy and Tentvůj slept in. I went down to the living room. Buba was asleep on the sofa. She was lying on her back, her paws sticking up, and every now and then she'd wave them. Probably she was dreaming.

I noticed something under the sofa. I looked there. On the floor was the skeleton of the turkey, neatly stripped of every bit of meat.

1985

VI

All's Well
That Ends Well

Wayne's Hero

(An English Story)

Wayne Hloupee denied any Czech ancestry. He pronounced his name "Hlupi" and was unaware of the word's unflattering etymology (for, in Czech, the word means Stupid). "I'd never thought about it, sir," he replied, as though I had offended him. My spy, Wendy, divulged to me that in the cafeteria after the seminar he had contended that I "see Czech even in James Fenimore Cooper—" which just went to show that my seeming compatriot had been following my lecture with only half an ear. I proposed a Czech origin—perhaps implausibly—not for the novelist himself, but for the heroine of his novel *The Spy*, whose maiden name was Phillipse.

But maybe Wayne had paid more attention to my conversation with the blonde beauty Linda Wessely, whom I did ask about her ethnic origins, for in Czech, her name means Gay. She had said, somewhat apologetically, that she was probably German, because her people had come to Canada from Mecklenburg.

"But that was back in the last century," she said emphatically, "so the family has nothing to do with Horst Wessely, the German president during the reign of Fuehrer Hitler."

"I'd never thought about that before, sir," Wayne Hloupee had answered and then added, "but my grandmother was Shawnee." Maybe that was supposed to explain the double *e*, or else to alert me to his deep North American roots.

When, shortly after that, Wayne appeared at the creative writing seminar with a metal ring in his left ear, I lacked the courage to inquire about his sexual orientation, even though at that time such a question was not considered impertinent. Gays distinguished themselves that way, and Wendy taught me that a ring in the left ear meant "she" and in the right meant "he"—or maybe the other way around; I've already forgotten. Then everyone started wearing earrings, sometimes even in both ears, and Jake Wasserman even showed up on campus with a ring in his nose (which, Wendy assured me, he always took out on the way home, because he was a nice Jewish boy). Even before Jake, Fatima Smythin started wearing a ring in her nose, but since she was half Afghan and clearly female, it didn't seem like such a big deal. At the time I thought that Wayne was just an early adherent to that fashion, rather than one of the brotherhood of queers.

Otherwise Wayne was a typical Canadian guy: his quivering belly flowed over the top of his jeans, his face was covered with stubble—he probably wanted to grow a beard, but his whiskers refused to grow any further, so the stubble had become permanent. On top of this he had shoulder-length, unwashed hair; in short, he looked like Harry the Horrible from the free-style American wrestling matches on TV. It seemed unlikely to me that he would hold much appeal for a sex noted for its refined sensibilities.

That Wayne was heterosexual, in spite of the ring, was confirmed by the first sentence of the story he composed for my seminar on the theme "Write a story about the beginning or the end of a relationship told from the point of view of the opposite sex: men from the woman's—it was no longer politically correct to call students 'boys' and 'girls'—and vice versa."

As a model, I recommended Hemingway's "The End of Something," but Wayne obviously hadn't taken it to heart, because he got right down to business: "When I first saw Romula, a new freshman, at Grace Greerson's party, I felt such a rush of desire that I ran right up and all but cuddled her." Then Romula dragged Wayne—or rather Wayne's nameless hero, who narrated the story in flawless first person—around all night like a dog on a leash, and he kept his eyes so firmly glued to her that, apart from Romula, he mentioned only some girl in a see-through blouse with no bra underneath, but even that entry was so vague that it didn't suffice to draw my attention away from the magic freshman. Otherwise, all the girls at the party blended into the background, and there might as well have been no boys there at all.

I considered myself too old for semiotics and believed that with undergraduates I could get by just as well with a traditional approach, grounded in literary-critical eclecticism. However, I really should have studied that postmodern science, if only superficially. Or at least remembered Stout's essay on the sexual orientation of Dr. Watson. Or at the very least thought of the ring in Wayne's ear. But I didn't recall it and I neglected the study of semiotics, so I didn't notice the signs that might have tipped me off. A young man in the clutches of Eros, who literally "runs up to" a girl and then "all but cuddles" her?

The story then dealt in considerable detail with Wayne's three further attempts at seducing Romula, a girl whose outstanding secondary characteristics (sexually, not semiotically, speaking) were much emphasized by the text. These signs certainly did not escape my notice, but one other detail did escape me: Wayne's hero was notably adhesive—"I pawed her all over" (a more dissolute youth would have said, "I felt her up"), "I snuggled close to her," etc.—all that during a religious studies lecture that they were listening to (evidently with one ear) from adjacent seats—and furthermore at a time when we already had a sexual harassment officer on campus and when men (boys, really) were afraid even to take a peek at the decorous Muslim Smythin's exceptionally promising bosom, for fear she would squeal to the officer. Such was reality on our campus. It's true that reality and literature are sometimes—as, for instance, in Wayne's story—two very different things. But still.

Yet instead of semiotics, Wayne's story about the beautiful Romula made me think of my own long-past and not much more successful attempts at making up to Irena. Only on very rare occasions did we pass the "touching" stage, as I confessed to Father Meloun, and the few kisses she did allow me were through the glass door of her father's house. Cuddling was not a part of my sexual repertoire: Irena was an energetic, athletic girl and she wouldn't have stood for it.

For that reason, it didn't strike me as strange that after the third attempt Wayne's hero had a nervous breakdown. Behind the bushes in the college's park, he ventured to embrace his beloved and Romula started gasping for breath as though she were having an asthma attack. Wayne's hero took fright and offered to run for a doctor, but Romula, still choking, refused his offer and took to her heels.

Wayne's nameless hero was, by his own admission, "somewhat obese" (clearly an autobiographical touch): he ran after Romula, but couldn't catch the fleeing girl. So he had a nervous breakdown. He went all to pieces and, hidden behind the bushes, literally howled in despair. This attracted the attention of three curious and good-hearted girls—Grace Greerson, Trudi Eisencracker, and Paola Fentolini. It took over half an hour for the spasms to subside and the hysterical hero to come to his senses sufficiently for the girls (who kept calling him all sorts of things: darling, sweetie, honey, etc.) to take him back to his dormitory.

Still—on account of my own experiences—nothing jumped out at me. I had never howled because of Irena or her sister or any of the other Kostelec girls, but one winter, in the depths of despair, I sneaked out of my sleeping parents' apartment around midnight and hiked several kilometres through the snowy woods to Černá Hora, then to Pekelský Valley and along the frozen Ledhuje River back to town, arriving quietly back home just before six. At seven I got up for school and by eight-thirty Bivoj had already given me an F in exponential equations. Those exponential equations stuck in my head, allowing me to date my nocturnal odyssey precisely: it must have been in sixth form.

I should instead have been reminded, but wasn't, of Dobroslava.

She howled one night in the girls' dorm and her friends phoned me, saying maybe I'd better come, or Dobra might do something to herself ... and I could hear those howls over the phone and got scared (the era of kisses through the glass door being long past). I jumped on a tram and went to Větrník. However, Dobra had calmed down by the time I got there and the girls' silhouettes at the window cheerfully told me to beat it, Dobra never wanted to see me again.

I should have thought of that, but I didn't. Wayne's hero also calmed down and shortly after the breakdown ran into Romula in the half-empty cafeteria. She was drinking amaretto-flavoured coffee, but when Wayne's hero asked if he might join her, she curtly refused.

"No! You can't sit with me!"

"Why, Romula?"

"I'm not that type!"

"But I only wanted—I only wanted to be near you—"

"Yeah—right," said Romula. "I know your kind. And I tell you, I'm *not* that kind. So leave me alone!"

How could I not think of Irena and her little sayings?—"I'll have none of that." "I didn't invite you here for that." "I know your kind." All that. Wayne's story instantly took me back more than a quarter of a century to that unobtainable girl. How could I not remember it? And also her "Leave me alone!" More than once.

One dismissal was enough for Wayne's hero. The end of the story was elegiac and truly beautiful, albeit strongly influenced by Hemingway:

> *I turned away. Some girls by the coffee pot were staring at me. I didn't care. I left the cafeteria and went back to the dorm in the rain.*
> *The next day I went home and never went back to Smith College.*

Only then it dawned on me! Only then at the very end of the story—just as Poe says—the unnoticed signs jumped out at me and arranged themselves into a meaningful pattern.

"Just like you wanted, sir," I heard Wayne Hloupee saying, "it's about the beginning and the end of an amorous infatuation and I told it from the viewpoint of the opposite sex—"

I looked at him. Naturally. From the viewpoint of the opposite sex. And it came to me that English, despite the hypereroticism of modern life, is a grammatically asexual language. In the first person the sex of the unnamed narrator could not be determined, because English doesn't have feminine forms.

"Sir," I heard Wayne trying to get my attention.

"Sorry, Mr. Hloupee, I was thinking."

"I combined that point of view with the 'twist in the tale technique you explained to us before—O. Henry and the denouement of Faulkner's 'Roses for Emily' and all that."

It worked well for you, Wayne, I thought, while my student kept silent. It's an A.

"Only I'm not sure, sir," Wayne continued, "I mean, *I* know, because my sister went there. But, sir, do you think most Canadians would know that Smith College in Massachusetts is a women's college? Because otherwise they'd probably miss the point."

1996

According to Poe

(A Freudian Story)

"He was kneading her breasts, licking her nipples, and Aimée could feel his penis exploring her pubic hair. A wave of passion engulfed her and she opened to him. With thumb and forefinger, she directed James' penis to her vagina. It was huge, erect, but, slathered with her juices, it slipped easily into her."

I stopped listening to the story that James Gordon Buchanan was—without the slightest trace of embarrassment—reading aloud, and looked out the window. As always at this time of day, an Edenvale raven was making its way along the snowy plain from the pub, the Lame Duck, to the frozen pond. What would have happened to me at James Gordon Buchanan's age if Vojta had discovered pornography like that in my composition book? Vojta was not only a Czech teacher (albeit without a degree, as the Germans had closed the university), he was also a pastor of the Czech Brethren. He was no prig—that human type had probably never set foot in his church—but he certainly didn't approve of immorality. Once during recess he looked through the open door of the sixth-form A classroom and saw a map of Greater Germany all set up for geography class. He went in and started scanning the map for Lešno. Irena didn't notice him standing at the map. As she was washing the board (a punishment from Latin) she dripped dirty water on her new dress and vented her displeasure with a phrase she'd picked up from the mountaineers. Vojta heard it, said nothing, but called her father. Irena no longer went climbing. Neither did I.

The raven turned around and headed back for the pub, leaving

tracks in the fresh snow. Now its footprints crossed over the previous track, marking a path over the frozen plain to the lake. Then
it changed its mind again, turned in a second semicircle, and made
once more for the pond. The symbol for infinity appeared in the
snow, printed by its three-toed feet.

Nothing much would have happened, probably. Vojta would
have called my father down to school; father would have confiscated my pornography, stopped my allowance for a while, and
then read the work *sotto voce* to the delight of his friends when they
all got together at the Sokol restaurant. It would have been worse
if Professor Hrubec had found such a thing. He once got hold of a
pornographic poem about Lord Screw, traditionally ascribed to
Jaroslav Vrchlický, and sometimes even to Svatopluk Čech, which
Josef Krátký, a poet from fourth A, kept under his desk for his own
private delectation. Hrubec denounced him and he was expelled
from our school and had to go to gymnasium in Mýto. This was
much to his advantage: Mýto wasn't quite the chamber of horrors
the Kostelec school was. But that was all before the war. During
the Protectorate even Professor Hrubec would only have called
Mr. Krátký, the bank executive, down to school. The Germans
were sticklers for morality and for Lord Screw they could easily
have transported Krátký to the Reich, if not straight to a concentration camp. Professor Hrubec may've been a monster, but he
wouldn't have wanted the life of a Czech student on his conscience. Or perhaps he didn't believe in the ultimate triumph of
the Reich, and feared that sort of morality wouldn't pay off for
him after the war.

I turned back to Buchanan. He was still reading his opus in a
steady drone—and those two were still at it. There was no hint of
any other action. Only the technique varied. Aimée was now performing fellatio, which she continued through to ejaculation;
Buchanan compared the taste of semen to coconut milk. Never
having tasted that particular fluid, myself, I was wondering if

Buchanan had that from personal experience, when Viviana Damiani weighed in with a critical comment:

"Not coconut milk. It's more bitter."

"Let Mr. Buchanan finish his reading, Miss Damiani." I squelched that debate before it could develop further. "Make notes and we'll discuss it later."

Buchanan's story was on the theme "Write a Love Story," the fourth of twelve topics I'd given to the department secretary to type out and photocopy for all my seminar students. Our famously sieve-headed secretary managed to make only five copies of their final products this time, so we had to read aloud. I had expected the theme to produce descriptions of the emotional confusions typical of puberty. But it seemed there was a generation gap. With my students, although some confusions did present themselves, they were mainly of a technical nature.

James Mitchell and Aimée had switched roles: now they were engaged in cunnilingus. The technical description took up half a page, after which Aimée got ready for coitus *cani modo* (from the context I understood that this was a question of intercourse from behind; Buchanan had really done his homework). Absolutely nothing else happened in the story. A half-page later, James turned to another style of gymnastics. But he could only keep this one up for a short paragraph. Buchanan was truly well pre-pared, though, and his repertoire was absolutely amazing. There simply was no other activity in the story, however, and I planned to reproach him for this in our final discussion. It ended abruptly: *James' penis became limp from amorous fatigue.* After that Buchanan had written The End. He got that from the movies, or more likely from television.

In the end I didn't criticize Buchanan for his lack of plot. The other stories of the day were notable for the same flaw. As I lis-tened to them, I was assailed by an inferiority complex over my lack of modernity—from which, as it later turned out, I was suf-fering needlessly.

I managed to head off discussion by simply taking over, and instead of listening to an exchange of views among my seminar participants—my usual method of instruction—I repeated my lecture on Henry Miller's concept of erotic prose and how it differs from pornography, which is not arousing aesthetically, but only sexually. The class listened in silence, with about as much comprehension as if I'd been talking about set theory. It lasted me the remaining twenty minutes of class and then I let them go without further discussion.

From the clutches of my complex, I reflected that these inhibitions were probably a result of my Catholic upbringing. Then I remembered how I had once lent Přema a marriage manual complete with a "Diagram of the Female Genitalia" (as the book described that multipurpose resource). Přema later told me off, saying that I could take the manual and stuff it, all he wanted was to get married and that picture made him sick. I think I really traumatized him. Even years later, ages after he'd moved to Australia, he still hadn't married. He died, and he wasn't even fifty. He was found in his bachelor flat, already in an advanced stage of decay, by a friend who'd begun to wonder why he wasn't coming to work any more. Good old Přema ...

The students trickled out into the corridor until only James Gordon Buchanan and Aimée Teopoulos still lingered in the classroom, and it flashed through my head that he really might have taken it all from personal experience: the first names were exactly the same. Maybe he'd enriched his repertoire a little with the help of a marriage manual. Or more likely a video.

Aimée asked, "Sir, I thought these stories were awfully monotonous, and we've only gotten through the first half—"

"You've read them all already? Even though there weren't enough copies?"

"We all trade off in the cafeteria. We have two hours free before your seminar."

They had evidently discussed the question of coconut milk, as well. Still, I somehow didn't want to believe that the college could be so blatant an illustration of the alleged hypereroticism of Western youth. Viviana Damiani, maybe. She could have been lifted straight from an Italian comedy and spoke English *prestissimo*, just like her mother tongue (which, in fact, she didn't know). That day she had not only ruled authoritatively on the flavour of semen, but also made a fool of Freddie Hamilton, when she proved that coitus from behind and standing—the woman standing in the shower, the man penetrating her from outside the tub—as Freddie had described it in a story we had covered the previous day, was impossible. Apparently she'd tried it with her boyfriend after the seminar, and it just didn't work. Again I headed off further debate by urging them to make notes, thus saving a blushing Freddie Hamilton, convicted fantasist, from further humiliation.

So yes, Viviana, maybe. But Wendy? That freckle-faced, self-confessed virgin, forward of the college field-hockey team? Or Kristina Tarkowski who, judging by her nationality and the crucifix around her neck, was a bigoted Catholic?

"So I was thinking, sir, if you have nothing against it. ..."

From my meditations on morality I returned to the probably authentic Greek.

"I was thinking ..."

"Yes?"

"Just for the sake of variety—so it isn't just more of the same ..."

"What do you want to write about?"

"Gays."

My Catholic inhibitions kicked in as I imagined a technical description of that form of sex.

"Write about lesbians," I said and left the room.

The next two seminars, as well, were filled with descriptions of all possible forms of intercourse. As Aimée had said, it was extremely monotonous. Only Prachna Dewitt relieved the tedium, at least linguistically. In her story, the girl gave orders couched in the language of the *Kama Sutra*, which both lovers obeyed (the girl's partner was African-American). Drifting between mental jaunts to idyllic Kostelec and abrupt returns to reality, I got the impression that the story described the lovemaking of acrobats. But it was just Indian sex.

And since Kristina Tarkowski skipped the two seminars following the demonstration of Freddie Hamilton's ignorance, I fell into a state of despair. None of the texts could be defined (in Henry Miller's terms) as anything but pornography. At the end of the seminar I weakly reminded them of Poe's cardinal rule about the necessity of a strong ending, because one after another the stories ended in amorous exhaustion, or at best with the lighting of a post-coital cigarette. "My story had a strong ending!" objected Jake Wasserman from Heidelberg (Ontario) and I was forced to admit it did, passing over in silence the fact that my rebuke had concerned literary technique. Wasserman's lovers (a Jew and a Japanese woman) contrived to reach orgasm simultaneously, so that *"their blissful sighs sounded a duet of some wild and barbaric love song."* "I can't imagine a stronger ending for this kind of story," the good student claimed defiantly. He was right: for that kind of story there probably is nothing better.

My Kostelec memories reminded me of Bedřich Böhnel's novel *Immorality*, which in the days of my youth passed for hardcore porn, even though Böhnel was also the author of a book of etiquette. I read the novel secretly and eagerly, waiting to see what the heroes characterized by the title would get up to; however, my eagerness soon gave way to boredom. The story recounted the sufferings of a gymnasium teacher who was joined in a sexually (not socially) unequal marriage with a comely nympho—it did not, however, contain any of what I was reading it for. The closest the author gets is a scene where the pregnant wife falls on her head from a diving board at the pool and her husband is terrified that she will lose the baby. It was a struggle to overcome the boredom, but hope did not completely desert me until page 324.

On that page the hero was tormented by fears not only that his wife was neglecting their two-month-old baby, which came into the world after the fall, but that the child was not even his. Goaded by suspicion, one day the teacher returned home unexpectedly before noon and heard suspicious noises coming from the bedroom, but when he went in no one was there, only his wife in bed (a migraine, she said) and the window onto the garden wide open. Urged on by a fairly amazing premonition, the hero went into the bathroom, which one entered from the bedroom, and in the toilet bowl he found, unflushed, the *corpus delicti.* Böhnel called it a "rubber article"; I figured out what he meant. And that was all. For the sake of a rubber article I had to read three hundred and twenty-four pages and I didn't even find out what exactly the rubber article proved about paternity. I cast the book aside, as the saying goes, in disgust.

Aimée read her opus. It differed slightly from the previous ones: it featured a new rubber article, which in Husák's Prague they would have called a double dildo. It was a battery-operated massage instrument in the form of two erect penises facing in opposite directions, which allowed the author's lesbian couple (a Canadian and an American) to enjoy simultaneous vaginal massage. It wasn't clear to me what the two Anglo-Saxons were getting out of this, considering that one was, so to speak, the man, and the other, the woman. My Catholic inhibitions didn't permit me to inquire.

Last in line came Wendy, and she didn't disappoint me. She offered a sweet ballad, set at Lake Tasso in northern Ontario, full of sparkling silver waves, canoes, parents' empty cottages (the lovers skipped school to go there on weekdays), and waterfowl called loons which—as Wendy explained—are remarkable for the fidelity of the mates and for carrying their two chicks around the lake on their backs. A charming tale, framed by the silence of the deep Canadian forest, but it clearly belonged to another century. Lorraine and Graham, students at Edenvale College, rather than engaging in detailed coitus in Lorraine's parents' empty cottage, paddle aimlessly around the smooth surface of the lake, sometimes in silence (most of the time, so Wendy padded the story out to the required length with the games of the loon parents and their lazy children) or else talk about the novel *The Serial* (and here the story changed into a literary analysis, in which Wendy polemicized with "her professor" about the book's quality). When dusk falls Lorraine and Graham lapse back into silence and the splashing of oars. The natural tendency of young people being, however, to draw closer, their lips (as they always write in this kind of romance) meet—but to accomplish this meeting, Graham had to turn around in the canoe, at which point he lost his balance, the canoe tipped, and the almost-lovers tumbled into the cold waves of Lake Tasso.

Wendy obviously considered this the requisite strong effect at the end—just what Poe ordered—for here the story ended. Handwritten at the end was added, "the drenched lovers reached the shore only with the greatest of effort," evidently so that no one would think they'd drowned. Wendy put down the printout, glanced at me with green eyes just like Lorraine's—"two emeralds in an Andromeda of freckles"—and said apologetically:

"Sir, I know that's not on the subject you gave us. But I must've read the topic sheet carelessly or something. I mean, I just didn't read it right and I thought we were supposed to write a love story."

"Well, wasn't that your topic?"

"No. Here it says *Write a lovemaking story*." Wendy pointed at the topic sheet. "But if you insist, I'll write about sex for next time."

I resolutely told her not to, to write for the next time on topic five—I looked down at the photocopied list of topics—"Tell a story about yourself, but as it would appear to your parents. In third person." And as I read the instructions, I stole a glance at number four. It was right there in black and white: "*Write a lovemaking story.*"

Since they were all well brought up (or something), every single one of them had done it. Only the Catholic, Tarkowski, had preferred truancy.

I racked my brain. How could I have led them into such depravity ...?

Then suddenly it dawned on me. I imagined secretary Tinhead, that dolled-up and perfumed blonde, reading my topic list out of one eye, while staring with the other at the snapshot of her stud of the week enshrined in a gilt frame on her desk. Her fingers with their green-painted nails mechanically typing out my list and inserting a hefty Freudian slip. Then later Wendy committed the same error, only in reverse, while everyone else read my instructions attentively.

It struck me that the whole seminar really had worked out according to Poe: we had saved the best for last.

1996

Jezebel from
Forest Hill

(A Love Story)

It's always the same in these situations: I know from the start that I won't refuse. Just one thing escapes me—to this day I haven't figured it out—do I do it out of the goodness of my heart, or out of stupidity? Not that it doesn't amount to the same thing.

But I did at least try to weasel out of it.

"I'm no playwright, Miss Steiner. I've never written a play in my life. I don't know how it's done." By way of examples (Henry James, Hemingway, Sinclair Lewis), I vainly attempted to demonstrate to the anorexic little brunette how few notable prose writers were also the authors of successful plays. The associations took me back to a day at the Reduta Theater when a world-renowned dramatist roundly condemned the play I'd submitted for his critical judgment. "This is interesting," he said, "—it's just that you ought to ..." I never found out what it was I ought to have done. Not that it was necessary. I already knew perfectly well: I ought to forget the whole thing. The world-renowned dramatist didn't have the chance to give me this advice himself, however, because just then the young actress Marcela Janu came running up to receive his criticism of her own little lyric drama. The world-renowned dramatist forgot my opus in an instant. With the words, "Listen, that last thing you showed me; it's not that bad ..." he swept off to the bar with the lovely poetess clad in that novelty of novelties (in those days at least)—a miniskirt.

"I asked Professor McMountain," said Lea Steiner, a note of despair creeping into her voice, "and Professor O'Sullivan, but each of them already has two students. I don't know where else to turn. You're the only one left in Edenvale, and Professor O'Sullivan said she thought you didn't have any independent project students yet ..." I already had three, but Lea Steiner's doe eyes were fixed on me imploringly, and I had already had three whiskies. "OK," I gave in to the poor student without a teacher, willingly agreed to help her with her play, and signed the form.

"Thanks, sir," she said with a warmth that might even have been genuine, "I'll bring you the synopsis in a week, OK?" Not waiting for my OK, she headed over to a table where Freddie Hamilton sat, immersed in a book titled *Nordic Sagas*. He had a guitar leaning against his chair, because for the next two hours the Edenvale Earwarmers intended to fill the Lame Duck with something that resembled music only in that it was audible. Very. I got up and left.

All the way back to Toronto I cursed myself, but of course it was too late.

The "independent project" bore some resemblance to those courses said to be taught all over North America by Mickey Mouse: The Aesthetics of Comics, Dramatic Strategies of TV Sitcoms, Queer Theory of Literature, Sexual and Racial Politics of African-American Women Novelists, etc. Not that anyone was expecting that level of scholarship, but the projects were certainly more personal than scientific in nature. A student would just dream something up—a collection of ecological poems, say, or a novel about the plight of women in American patriarchal society; find among the professors a supervisor willing to countenance such a thing; and drop by once in a while over the course of the school year to tell him or her how it was going. I don't know how my colleagues did it: apparently some of them demanded weekly meetings with their students (usually in the Lame Duck) and subjected their efforts to ruthlessly constructive criticism. So, at least, I was assured by Wendy, who failed her independent project with McMountain (she had chosen the theme, "Who Killed Edwin Drood?" and never did find out). I was more liberal: I expected only one meeting a month and always expressed myself in the most general terms. The students all turned in synopses, but no one ever finished a project. Not under my tutelage, at any rate.

I expected to receive no more than ten pages, double-spaced, at these monthly sessions—emphasizing quality over quantity, I called it—because that was the largest dose of their prose I felt I could tolerate. Independent project students were, as a rule, an exceptionally uninspired lot, but they were tremendously crafty, and word spread that I was an easy grader. There were no final exams, everything was decided face to face.

Before we entered the age of sexual harassment, it seems that some enterprising girls procured good grades by taking their projects to male instructors. Thanks to my stupidity (or the goodness of my heart), I had no personal experience of that. The golden age came to an end in Edenvale when a second-year student, Cricket Jason, complained to the sexual harassment officer that Professor Tyson from classical philology, who had failed her, had then offered her an A in return for non-academic services. Naturally, there was no proof. Seeming to take as its motto Tyson's own slogan *Condemnat mare parcit cunnis male iudex* (I don't understand this myself, but it's rumoured to be indecent), the sexual commission failed to recognize that at the end of the second semester Cricket's average grade was a D. Tyson resigned. He then opened a restaurant on Queen Street, Caupona Tysonis, right next door to the Czech pub the Heart of Europe, where he proved that in culinary matters he was a true disciple of Apicius. It was a success for a while, but then he tried to start a chain and wound up going broke. Cricket took up another independent project and married her adviser.

Lea Steiner promised me a synopsis of her play in a week; it took her three. But she did it in style, as even I couldn't fail to notice: she stood out against the college uniform of a T-shirt and jeans like a rose blooming in a muddy sidewalk. Wendy assured me the outfit came from Schiaparelli's, but I later discovered that Wendy (who herself wore the uniform, embellished with artistic holes at the knees) thought all clothes came either from Schiaparelli's or from Honest Ed's, that Toronto saviour of fashion-conscious but impoverished young women.

Lea just came in regular clothes: in a dress, that is, nothing unisex. The beery atmosphere of the Lame Duck was invaded by a pleasant perfume. "I've been looking for you in your office for a week, sir," she began boldly, so I couldn't chide her for tardiness, "You're never there," she added, with some justice. I did far prefer the pub, so long as there was no so-called music being perpetrated. "I brought you the synopsis."

Her synopsis consisted of three brief lines:

A drama about the complicated evolution of the emotional relationships between two men and one woman, in the course of which the woman abandons the first man and deepens her emotional attachment to the second.

"Well," I opined, "You certainly didn't write too much."

"I had ... problems," Lea said, worrying her lower lip with her perfect white teeth. She would have been a truly beautiful girl, if only she weren't built like Olive Oyl, Popeye the Sailor's girlfriend. Looking over her clothes, I concluded that they definitely hadn't come from Honest Ed's.

"You don't know where to go from here, right?" I pronounced, hoping all the while that she wouldn't ask for advice on playwriting, because when it comes to plays I really haven't got a clue. I bought myself the latest mail-order handbook from California, *Plots for All Occasions. A Resource for Generating a Virtually Limitless Number of Story Plots, for Writing Short Stories, Novels, Plays and Scripts.* However, I was too lazy to decipher the manual's complicated instructions:

/272/
(250) (259-1) (22b chs Jennifer, Lorraine)
Lorraine vows to remain celibate.
Andrew falls in love with Jennifer (55) (134 a,b)

/273/

(139) (24b)

Andrew falls in love with Jennifer, who gets involved with his friend,
Fred (122 chs Gary, Fred)

(157) (211) (294 a,b) etc.

The letters and numbers referred to a system of elaborate
plot schemes. I tried to unravel one and came up with: "Jennifer
falls in love with Andrew and her jealous friend Fred a) kills
Andrew, b) beats Andrew up, c) commits suicide, d) drops
Jennifer, e) reveals that he is gay, in which case he 1) takes up
with Gary, 2) seduces Andrew, 3) joins the army." A result like
that was just not worth the trouble of decoding, which required
constant flipping back and forth through the book. I glanced
over at the girl, who was seated on the bar stool next to me in
her short Schiaparelli dress, and said kindly, "Your problem is
that you don't know how to fill in this abstract synopsis with
concrete details, right?"

Lea turned to me, her face a mask of unhappiness, and said,
"No, that's not it ... in fact, my problem's just the opposite," and
here she burst into sobs, all the while furtively eyeing my whisky. I
was a Lame Duck regular: all I had to do was point to my glass and
raise two fingers. Lea didn't hesitate for an instant, but slurped
down whisky mixed with her own tears.

So the reality wasn't one woman caught between two men, but
the reverse. Poor girl.

"Well, I won't insist that you tell me about it," I said, hoping she
would do just that, "but you must elaborate on this synopsis. Who
are these two men, what are they like, what kind of temperaments
do they have—surely they're not both the same. And what about
this girl, what does she look like ... simply flesh out this skeleton
with living detail," I went on, wishing all along that the romantic
secrets of this charming anorexic would be revealed to me in living detail. However Lea said only, "Yes, sir," drank off her whisky,
leaving behind in the glass only tears, rose from the bar stool in

her pretty dress, and said, "I'll write it concretely for next week." I didn't see her for another month.

What stuck in my mind was the brooch that sparkled on her bosom as she rose from the bar stool. She didn't get that at Honest Ed's, either.

She came in again in a month, this time to my office. She was wearing another nice dress and another brooch on her bosom.

"That's a pretty brooch you have there."

"Thanks. My parents gave it to me for my birthday."

"It's different from the one you were wearing last time at the Lame Duck, isn't it?"

"They gave me that one last year, sir ..." She looked at me entreatingly. "Could I still change my project just a little bit? I know we're already halfway through the semester, but ..."

"But" plus silence apparently equalled a total lack of arguments.

"What do you want to write about now?" I asked gruffly, for it seemed that her interesting problem now belonged to the past, and there was no longer a chance of confession.

"My subject is the same, only I'd like—with your permission, sir—to change the genre."

From psychological drama to detective story, maybe? But I soon learned she had something else in mind.

"I thought instead of a play I could write a novella on the same subject."

Almost shyly she placed before me on the desk a paper with a few lines of writing. I read:

> *The action takes place in Krakow. Rebecca, a medical student, loves Peter, a lawyer from Lodz. However, Peter is romantically involved with Ester, the daughter of a rabbi from Katovice. In the course of the story, Peter leaves Rebecca and deepens his emotional attachment to Ester.*

I looked up at the shimmering brooch and then into the eyes of my apprentice, newly converted to fiction.

"Have you ever been to Poland?"

Lea shook her head.

"It can be treacherous to locate a story in a place you've never been," I said wisely. "Why did you choose Poland?"

"My parents are from Poland."

Her eyes shone moistly. Taken aback, I asked, "They left Poland before Hitler?"

She shook her head again. Even her ear lobes sparkled. Not even Margaret Dribble-Thomson, the daughter of the chief stockholder and director of the Grail brewery, came to class so gaudily decked. To tell the truth, the millionaire's daughter wore the college uniform: a T-shirt emblazoned with the words Drink Molson!, which was her way of rebelling against her parents. Molson was the other big brewery in Ontario, and her father didn't own a single share of it.

"No, they stayed in Poland. They were sent to Auschwitz. That's where they met."

She started sobbing.

I nearly put my hand on her shoulder to comfort her, but remembered the sexual harassment officer. Lea sadly asked, "May I write it as a novella, sir? Otherwise it's the same, only ... reversed."

"You may," I said soothingly. "Actually, I'm glad. You know I'm a novelist. I'll be better able to advise you."

Lea was clearly struggling with her emotional problem, but if it was that her parents had been at Auschwitz, I didn't quite follow.

"Were you born in Canada?"

She nodded and sniffled.

"So I really can, sir?"

"Yes. And—" I stopped. Prying into her emotional state didn't seem quite appropriate, under the circumstances.

"I'll be back in a week," she promised.

I guessed that to mean a month.

At the time, I was assisting at the birth of another novel. This one was the independent project of a certain Ewan Kennelly from Holy Trinity College, on the main campus in town. My fame as an easy marker and all-around good guy had spread even there, and grad students in search of easy credits gladly undertook the twenty-mile journey to Edenvale on the rickety university bus. Of course Kennelly had his own car, a '59 De Soto, but it was in such a state that the university bus seemed luxurious in comparison. Holy Trinity belonged to the Anglicans, and Kennelly's synopsis promised a mix of adventure and religious experiences set in the jungles of Brazil. These two themes were to be united in the person of Jim Doherty, a TV evangelist who delivered the word of God through a loudspeaker, dressed in a sequined suit and gold pants. He didn't much resemble an Anglican priest.

I glanced quickly through the synopsis and asked, "Have you ever been to Brazil?"

"No, but last year I took a course in Latin American film."

He brought me the first instalment in a week. He obviously wasn't suffering from Lea's problems.

Jim Doherty stood at the podium of the gigantic stadium in Rio, an imposing figure attired in (see above). One final time he looked down at the crowd gathered in the depths below him, eagerly awaiting his words. Then he nodded to the interpreter and, in a voice greatly amplified by loudspeakers, began to preach:

"God who at sundry times and in diverse manners spake in time past unto the fathers by the prophets, hath in these last days spoken unto us by his Son."

The text (he later identified it for me as St. Paul's Epistle to the Hebrews 1:1) continued for two pages, ending with the words *How shall we escape, if we neglect so great salvation?* which was chapter 2, verse 3.

Here ended the first instalment, as well. Looking like a man with a bellyache, Kennelly started in explaining to me how at that precise point he had been set upon by writer's block. He then proceeded to elaborate orally—and somewhat abstractly—the further development of the plot. Overcome with boredom, I understood only that Doherty's helicopter makes a forced landing in the rainforest and the preacher has a vision. A vision of what, the author had not yet decided.

He droned on about the problems of developing a plot he had yet to devise. My thoughts turned to Lea, because the image of that well-dressed young lady was far pleasanter. And then, God knows why, I thought of Hanka: another thin girl, barefoot even, when she limped into Kostelec among the first waves of refugees forced to march by the SS—the death march, people would later call it. The SS officers were already cornered but still, absurdly, tried to cover their tracks—or maybe they just didn't know what to do next—and so decided to drive the starving Jews to the West. Hanka wasn't thin from anorexia, of course, and she was dragging with her the still more emaciated Arpad. Her sister (married to an Aryan named Svatopluk Kebrle, and so spared from the transports) fed him up into a sturdy young man and Hanka married him. Another Auschwitz romance.

I heard Ewan Kennelly fall silent, and hastened to say, "Well, I hope you aren't expecting me to plot your story for you. You have to do it yourself. You may, however, use a handbook," and here I handed the blocked writer my useless copy of *Plots for All Occasions*.

He stopped looking as though his stomach pained him, thanked me warmly, and was gone.

As I had guessed, Lea made her appearance a month later. It was the end of November and had begun to snow. She brought me no writing, but instead: "Sir ... I know I've already wasted more than half the semester" (she'd wasted four-fifths, to be exact) "but I've been sick."

"Nothing serious, I hope?"

"Depression," she said, not turning a hair. Today's number really might have come from Schiaparelli's. A strand of teardrop pearls glistened at the neck of her black silk blouse.

"Have you recovered?" I asked rather coldly, so she wouldn't think I was that easily moved. She shook her head.

"But I wanted to ask you ... I know it's really asking too much, sir, but ..."

Lack of reasons brought her to a standstill.

"You want to change the genre again?"

Those doe eyes, beautiful and unmoving, met mine.

"Yes."

Her candour disarmed me. I was forced to take evasive action.

"Well?"

"I'd like to—that is, if you'll allow me ..."

There was such trust in her beautiful eyes that I was charmed in spite of myself.

"I'd like to write a short-story triptych. Each story will have"—she switched from conditional to an authoritative future—"a different narrator. First, Peter—"

"The lawyer from Lodz?"

"You remember?" She was astonished.

"It's not as though you'd written so much."

Her eyes shifted to the floor and a blush spread over her checks. That can't be faked.

"I know. I do apologize, sir. But—"

"I don't doubt you had reason."

Lea sat silent.

"So go on!"

She continued hesitantly, "The second story will be told by Ester, and the third would be told by Rebecca."

She looked up at me. She might even have had a clear conscience. Maybe the depression was for real.

"Rebecca would sort of draw these—these relationships—together and bring them to a climax."

I gave my blessing to her new plans, and Lea—as much as was possible in her post-depressive condition—brightened and disappeared from my office. From the window I saw her walk down the snowy path, considerately making way for a sacred Edenvale raven that was grappling with a half-empty bag of French fries, and run into Maggie Dribble-Thomson, who took

her arm while Lea rested her head on the brewer's daughter's
stately shoulder.

The next day I pulled up a bar stool next to Maggie Dribble-
Thomson in the Lame Duck. She was drinking Molson Pilsner
and was more than happy to talk. Among other things, she confirmed my suspicion that Lea had not lied.

"No, sir, she's not making it up. She really does have big prob-
lems," she exclaimed passionately. "She's such a Nice Jewish Girl
(I'd never heard the feminine form before), but Chaim is no Nice
Jewish Boy."

"He beats her?"

"Oh, no, nothing like that. He torments her mentally. He's an
awful Lothario."

Once she had filled me in on the lifestyle of that Not-So-Nice
Jewish Boy, currently enjoying great popularity on the main campus, I fully understood Lea's depression. It was a thoroughly banal
Forest Hill story: well-brought-up, monogamous girl meets boy
endowed with Portnoian potency, who sows his wild oats among
the coeds of the Catholic college of St. Michael's, the Anglican
Holy Trinity, and the progressive New College. Not so much
among the Jewish girls, because there was no Jewish college. And
each time, having sown them, he would return to Lea, refreshed,
and she would forgive him. The same old story.

"I like Lea a lot," said Maggie, "and I'm trying to get her to quit
that relationship, but no luck so far. Last weekend I took her to the
North Pole and she just burst into tears, right over the Pole."

I'd never heard of the North Pole: apart from the Lame Duck, I
wasn't too familiar with the student dives. But as it turned out,
Maggie hadn't taken Lea to a pub, but to the actual North Pole.
Maggie's father had gotten the Canadian licence for a certain
Bavarian lager, and celebrated the occasion by renting a
Concorde and flying the major stockholders of the Grail brew-
ery to the North Pole, where they toasted the Bavarian lager with
Canadian champagne. He took his rebellious daughter with him

on this outing, and when she brought Lea along he didn't object. Obviously you can pack lots more than thirty executives and their wives into a Concorde. To make the trip worthwhile, they flew around the pole for nearly two hours, till they were all completely stewed. Lea spent the time sobbing, and even tried to jump out the window, which is hard to do in a Concorde.

"Lea's a hopeless case," Maggie concluded. "I just hope Chaim gets her pregnant."

It seemed she was thinking of a shotgun wedding. I was amazed to hear such an old-fashioned sentiment. Edenvale feminism apparently didn't run too deep; at least not in the Jewish community. But that was hardly surprising. The Jews have always been cleverer than us, on average.

Ewan Kennelly returned in a week, exultant.

"That was an excellent book you loaned me! I entered the 'Superplot' chapter into my personal word processor, and it's a great help to me. See," and he pointed to a page of the borrowed book.

I read,

The Superplot of Plots for All Occasions *consists of three paragraphs: A, B. C. A is the protagonist paragraph, B establishes and sustains the action, C continues the action and resolves it. Any paragraph may be used in conjunction with any other. You will find instructions for developing the plot in the chapter titled "The Conflict Situation." Conflict situations appear under the headings "Story Type" and "Story Sub-Type" and are further subdivided in the full text of the model B-paragraph.*

Maybe Ewan Kennelly really did understand all this. He belonged to the computer generation, after all. But I was of a different age, and knew of no handbook for inspiration—let alone a hard disk.

Not that it had done him a heck of a lot of good. He offered me a new and improved first instalment. The first paragraph differed not a whit from the previous version—it described Jim Doherty and his dazzling get-up in exactly the same words as before.

However, when he set to preaching, this was what he preached:

"*Now, I beseech you, brethren, by the name of our Lord Jesus Christ ...*" for two pages, up to "*That, according as it is written, He that glorieth, let him glory in the Lord.*" Kennelly had simply replaced the Epistle to the Hebrews with the Epistle to the Corinthians, 1:10–31, and offered it up whole and unadulterated.

He watched fixedly as I read the apostle's words.

"Sir, I think that the Epistle to the Corinthians will fit in better with my plot than the Epistle to the Hebrews."

"Both are very powerful texts. But what about the plot? You need to be careful that your own text—in contrast with the epistles—isn't too—how shall I put it?—unremarkable."

"You're absolutely right. That won't be easy," Kennelly said thoughtfully.

"And how about that plot?"

Despite *Plots for All Occasions*, the personal word processor, and the hard disk, the plot had not advanced beyond a helicopter crash and a certain, still unspecific vision.

I thought of Lea Steiner, who perhaps was also blocked, and then—God knows why—I remembered Hanka pregnant, and how they had hanged her husband. Under socialism, that was. I ran into her a couple of days after the—as the official press invariably put it—harsh but just punishment. She was keeping a stiff upper lip, not crying; she was already in her eighth month, at least. And didn't miscarry. Adam was a posthumous child.

I shook my head to clear it of that very specific vision.

"Well, it should be easier now. Have a good look at that manual and come back in another fourteen days."

Kennelly got up, a thoughtful expression on his face and a portable word processor in his hand, and went off to wrestle with his block.

Christmas passed and Lea did not appear. Only Kennelly came to Edenvale in his gargling De Soto, bringing yet another rendition of the superplot. It began with the paragraph he had used twice before, still unchanged, followed by a new sermon—from St. Paul's Epistle to the Ephesians, 2:1–22—which now covered close to three pages. After that came a new sentence, genuine Kennelly: "The next day Jim Doherty sat in a helicopter, looking down at the rain forest deep below him." At that, the author found himself blocked again, so his opus still hadn't made it as far as the accident, much less the vision.

Frost set in at the start of the winter semester and I was a more and more frequent guest of the Lame Duck, where the bartender really could make honest-to-goodness Dickensian punches and hot toddies. And Lea appeared there one day, like a spectre. She was wearing a dark blue sweater seeded with glass diamonds, which maybe weren't glass at all, though surely she wouldn't wear such a thing to school. But where Lea was concerned I had already begun to believe the unbelievable. She sat down sadly next to me with a look that could only be interpreted as guilt. I made the necessary gesture and the bartender unerringly placed before my student a steaming drink, from which the scent of rum rose to mingle with her perfume. Lea didn't say a word.

"Well," I said, infusing the syllable with several choice words, from which my student chose precisely the one I had in mind.

"I'm really ashamed of this, but—"

"You've been sick?"

"I had to see my psychoanalyst every other day. Sometimes daily. It would have been unbearable otherwise."

"What?" I asked almost coldly. The flight around the Pole had somehow soured me on this spoiled missy from Forest Hill. I quickly controlled myself, however. Suffering is suffering, whether caused by puppy love at seventeen or the death of a beloved mother at fifty. I've known both, and both are unbearable.

"You know," Lea gasped, "my interpersonal relations have gotten horribly complicated and my emotional experience is underdeveloped," she said in the jargon of pop psychology, and my heart again hardened. Why can't she just say she's unhappy in love, for God's sake? Or that she has a broken heart, if she wants to be metaphoric? But Lea—just like Kennelly—was of a generation endowed with another lexicon entirely.

Nonetheless, I cynically pronounced, "You mean to say your boyfriend is cheating on you?"

I thought of it as a form of shock therapy, but Lea's gaze remained painfully fixed on me. I melted.

"You could put it that way," she admitted sadly.

"OK," I said soothingly, "So you probably haven't given a thought to that triptych."

Lea shook her head.

"Well ... so come back in fourteen days and show me at least a first draft of the first story. You have to give me something, you know, if you want a grade."

"I know, sir," those same beautiful and guileless eyes. "I hardly dare to say it, sir, but ..."

"But what?"

"I'd like to ..."

"Well?"

I waited to hear how she'd reply to that empty yet highly ambiguous word.

"I'd like to write a collection of verse."

"What?"

"Instead of the triptych. A collection of verse. In ... monologues."

I remembered a similar artefact. But surely Lea couldn't know of the poetic sins of Kundera's youth.

"You mean something in different voices? Voice of Rebecca, voice of Ester ..."

"Yes."

"I'm not a poet, you know. I certainly don't consider myself an expert—"

"But you understand poetry. Last year in English Lit 112 you explained Eliot's 'Ash Wednesday' beautifully."

Straight from the manual. But I didn't have to say that aloud.

The imploring eyes were fixed on me and all my resolution vanished.

"OK, but in fourteen days you have to show me at least one poem in each voice. Understand, you simply must bring me something if you want a grade."

"I know. I'll bring it, sir."

"In fourteen days," I repeated.

I figured even three weeks would be breakneck speed.

That was mid-January. Ewan Kennelly hadn't been seen since just after Christmas. Maybe he *had* managed to get a handle on the Superplot's complex instructions, but even having fed them into his computer—which did save him constantly flipping through the book—it looked as if he still couldn't unblock himself.

Indeed he couldn't. He caught up with me at the pub in early February, having reached Edenvale after five: the De Soto had breathed its last, three miles from campus, and he'd had to walk the rest of the way. When I inquired after the latest version of his masterpiece, he asked if he could read it aloud. That excellent but exacting guide, the Superplot, apparently recommended it. Stylistic blunders are more evident to the ear than to the eye.

He started reading. He usually spoke distinctly, I would say, but now he began to mumble almost incomprehensibly. Nonetheless, I recognized a paragraph beginning with the words *Jim Doherty stood at the podium of the gigantic stadium* and it struck me—I'd already had three bourbons—that I must be experiencing the aural equivalent of double vision, except that a mere three bourbons shouldn't do that to me. No. It was his fourth go at the novel, which now bore the title (as far as I could understand Kennelly's mumbling) *The Aircrash of Jesus Christ*; and it was identical to the previous version, except that it was now followed by yet another text (still, unfortunately, not original): *He that hath an ear, let him hear what the Spirit saith unto the churches ...* right up to, *And there went out another horse that was red: and power was given to him that sat thereon ...* Five pages in its entirety, uninterrupted by any intertext or commentary, straight from the Revelation of St. John the Divine (3:6–4).

I said, "A very nice quote. Especially when read aloud. And how have you developed the plot?"

Well, he hadn't.

"I'm following this excellent book you lent me. But somehow …. The thing is, you see, I need somehow to capture the intensity of the vision experience, but," he took a printout from his executive briefcase and read aloud: "On the page immediately following the Superplot is found a listing of Conflict Situations arranged under Paragraph B—Plot Type, or b) Plot Sub-Type." He set the printout aside and continued gloomily, "Except I haven't found the category 'Vision' under either paragraph B—plot type, or b) plot subtype. Maybe it isn't even a Conflict Situation. But if not—"

I interrupted him. "And is the helicopter in there?"

He shot me a look of suspicion—even, it seemed to me, of pain. I had gone too far.

I hastily continued, "You know, Mr. Kennelly, I've misled you. This handbook is designed for authors of formula stories. Your story is too original."

"You think so?" he asked almost inaudibly. "That would probably explain the block."

He sat there, as the Czechs so aptly put it, like a heap of misery.

"Give me back that book, Mr. Kennelly. And if you want a seasoned author's advice, this—" I raised my glass—"is much better for a block, though usually in those quantities," and I pointed to a bottle of Jack Daniel's among the sources of inspiration arrayed behind the bartender. The bartender interpreted the gesture in his usual fashion.

"I don't drink," said Kennelly, "I gave up alcohol for my New Year's resolution."

"You're drinking for the sake of your writing, not for immoral purposes."

Kennelly took a drink. For the sake of writing, to borrow

Faulkner's unforgettable phrase, he was clearly prepared to murder his own mother. Over the next hour he pounded away at the block with four more Jack Daniel's, which was perfectly fine because his car was dead and he'd have to take the bus anyway. Wayne Hloupee, who was in the Lame Duck playing poker, eventually led him away. I somehow doubted that my creative method would prove effective in Kennelly's case.

Winter drew to an end, and in mid-March my anorexic poetess put in an appearance. She came like Hamlet, all in black, with a tiny bundle of books in one hand and a white football helmet in the other. She put the helmet down on my desk.

"You have a brother?"

"No. My ... friend left it in the locker room when his team was here playing the Edenvale Idiots. So I promised him—"

Chaim's football helmet shone just like Yorick's skull. *Love's Labours Lost?*

I asked, "You don't have a sister either?"

I have no idea why I asked that. She shook her head. Probably because I didn't really want to ask about her collection of verse, knowing from experience that she hadn't written a single poem.

She picked up the helmet from my desk and put it in her lap.

"I'm afraid to ... it's impudent of me, I know, sir, and you have every right to refuse ..."

"You didn't write those poems, huh?"

"No."

I took a deep breath and reached into the drawer for a cigar. This was before the spread of moral insanity in North America, and I didn't yet have to take my cigar outside to freeze.

"Miss Steiner." I took a gulp of smoke. "I know that this school year you've been suffering from—to express it as you undoubtedly would yourself—interpersonal emotional problems. I understand. But you also need to understand me. As I've already explained, I must have something from you on paper. A play, a novel, a collection of poems—it's all the same, but I must have something."

She was gazing deep into my eyes, conscience completely untroubled.

"I thought, sir, if you would be so kind—"

"Have I ever been otherwise?"

"No, sir." Now she looked at the floor, apparently ashamed. "I thought if I could write one longer poem—"

"Certainly not!"

"Rhymed," she whispered ever so softly. "I have *The Modern Rhyming Dictionary* at home, and—"

Well, why not? After *Plot for All Occasions*, why not *The Modern Rhyming Dictionary*?

"You know, I write the lyrics for the Forest Hill Jezebels—"

"For the what?"

"We have this all-girl rock band in Forest Hill. But naturally," her pale face turned a healthy purple, "naturally I'd make this a serious poem. ..."

I sighed.

"Why don't you bring me a couple of those rock lyrics? Of course I couldn't give you an A for them, but ..."

"Oh, no, sir! That wouldn't do at all!"

The purple abruptly shifted to red. What in the world could they be singing? Forest Hill Jezebels, indeed! This delicate blossom, who recuperates from her boyfriend's infidelities on the psycho-analyst's couch rather than in someone else's bed ... Clearly a more complicated piece of work than she appears. Forest Hill Jezebels!

But she really was red as a beet.

In my usual genial way I offered her a graceful escape.

"You're trying to say that your lyrics aren't sufficiently academic?"

"That's just it." She paled a little.

"All right, Miss Steiner." I sighed again, exhaling smoke. "You may write one long poem. But make sure it really is long. And, if at all possible, rhymed. So I can have something in writing."

"I will, sir!" she sighed and stood up, holding the white helmet by the chinstrap and shoving her bundle of books inside it. "Thank you, sir! I'm so grateful to you. Really!"

She turned to go, and through my cloud of smoke I caught a delicious whiff of perfume. I remembered how Hanka's posthumous son was born, how in '68 they left for Israel, how in '73 on Yom Kippur little Adam was killed. God knows why. God knows why I should think of it now, I mean.

The first day of April arrived. Kennelly didn't appear—maybe because after the Apocalypse you run out of the Bible. It seemed my sage advice had not helped him penetrate his block.

But Jezebel did come.

A spring outfit: yellow blossoms on a blue ground, at her throat a gold Star of David studded with something, probably diamonds. And the face of a woman whose lover has drowned.

Now it all annoyed me slightly.

"You aren't bringing me anything?"

She shook her head; her well-brushed hair rippled; her eyes were trained on the floor. Then firmly, piercingly they met my own stern gaze: sincerity itself. But this time I didn't melt.

Not much.

"I thought ..."

"And what am I supposed to think?"

"I know ..."

"Hardly. I'm going to have to fail you."

"Please, sir, don't do it! Please!"

"This grade means so much to you?"

"I told my parents that ..."

My mind settled on that Czech idiom for unwilling confession—the one that involves dust slowly emerging as one beats a heavy blanket.

"So, tell me. What it is you told your parents!"

It was like pulling teeth, but finally I got out of her that she had dropped all her courses last term—"I had those emotional problems, sir! It was really awful!"—and explained it to her parents by claiming that she had to concentrate all her energies on the terribly difficult task of writing a novel under my supervision.

"But you didn't write a novel, did you?"

"I wanted to. Only I was too scared to tell you so, because I was afraid you'd say I was overestimating my abilities. So instead I told you I'd just write a play."

"But you didn't write it!"

"I had—"

"Emotional problems. But not only did you not write a play, Miss Steiner, you didn't write a short-story triptych, or a collection of poems, or one long poem, or even one short poem, rhymed or otherwise—in fact, Miss Steiner, you have written precisely nothing! Over practically an entire school year! What were you thinking?"

"I was thinking, sir ..." Her eyes rested on her shoes, then she raised them to mine. "Last fall you gave a noon lecture in the common room on Chandler's wisecracks—you quoted lots of them— I could tell you really liked them ..."

"So what?" I was almost angry. "Maybe now you want to write a wisecrack? And have that be your year-long independent project? A wisecrack?"

"Not a wisecrack, exactly. I thought maybe I could write an epigram ... Like Martial—"

Then I got mad. That really was the limit. I know I'm reputed to be an easy marker. I know Jezebel isn't the first to coax a good mark out of me for next to nothing. For nothing at all, to be precise. Gradually I calmed down. Jezebel was standing in front of me meekly, almost in tears. Is she really such a delicate blossom? Or is she sneaky? Or what is she?

Well, she's quite pretty.

"OK, Miss Steiner," I said. "But you only have a week. The deadline for independent projects is the fourteenth of April."

The earth seemed to have swallowed Kennelly. The morning of the fourteenth—a warm, almost-summer day—Jezebel appeared in white with a necklace of blue stones and a scent of violets, and, for a change, not empty-handed. She offered me a single page.

I read, *No woman ever falls in love with a man unless she has a better opinion of him than he deserves.*

It was—in the context of the past academic year and all its emotional complications—very nearly a tragic epigram. It could also have been a line from a Forest Hill Jezebel's song with ideas above its station. But it was a perfectly decent epigram. And since I'd gotten to know this anorexic girl over the year, it resonated with me strongly.

"OK," I said, "that's a good epigram, though it is rather short for an independent project—"

"You won't fail me, will you, sir?"

That transfixing gaze.

"I have to think about it."

"Well ... have a good vacation, sir."

"You too."

Jezebel turned. Something struck me.

"What are you going to tell your parents?"

"As long as you don't fail me—"

"That's not the point. But since you lied and said you were writing a novel ..."

She turned again to face me, looking me right in the eye. I had the impression that she was starting to fill out a little. The dress was tight across the bosom. Were her emotional problems at an end? Had she grasped the truth of her own epigram and drawn the appropriate conclusion?

Or had Maggie Dribble-Thomson's wish come true?

"You know, sir, my dad never reads. He's at work all day, and at night he just stares at the TV—"

"And your Mom?"

"She can't read. She got hit over the head during the war and years later, here in Canada, she started going blind. She can still see, but not to read."

"Hmm," I said. "Then have a good vacation. And say hello to your parents."

"I will, sir!"

She turned and ran down the path to the cafeteria. I had never seen her run before. Her white skirt fluttered after her, the banner of a new life.

Jezebel's epigram was stuck in my head. It seemed somehow familiar. I went to the bookshelf, took down *Bartlett's Quotations* and leafed through the Love entries. It didn't take long. It was about the fifth quote down on the third page: *No woman ever falls in love with a man unless she has a better opinion of him than he deserves.*

That disappointed me. And made me angry.

I headed for the Lame Duck to fill out my grade sheets. The pub was totally empty: they were all busy stuffing their heads for next week's exam period. Over in one corner sat Jacques Saint-Dupuis, who didn't care about credits and mostly audited the courses that interested him. He owned a bike shop on Bloor Street that had just begun to prosper since, with the high price of gas and all, bicycles had come into fashion.

O Jezebel! In my heart I called her a cheat. I drained my glass. She disappointed me. And I was furious. I hit bottom and waved to the bartender. Furious. And how! My heart turned to stone: I energetically wrote a sweeping F in the blank. In pencil. My subconscious was already at work.

So I erased it. I thought of Hanka, of her Auschwitz romance that ended on the Prague gallows. And of little Adam and Yom Kippur. A wave of the hand brought another Jack Daniel's my way and in place of the expunged F I wrote in a shadowy D. I hesitated. I erased the D. Mama went blind in Canada, but from a European blow. Damn it! I started a new glass.

Gradually, under the sympathetic gaze of Jacques Saint-Dupuis, who—clearly because of Pernille Gunnarsdottir—was also drowning his sorrows, I filled in the form with a double A. AA.

But that was the well-known optical illusion.

Ewan Kennelly had definitely disappeared, so I could fill in his form with a clear conscience—NC, not completed.

My grading methods are nothing to boast of. I know.

1996

A Magic Mountain

and a

Willowy Wench

I convinced my future wife of my extraordinary suitability as a husband by taking her to my hometown of Náchod. In my books I call it Kostelec.

It was a warm spring day in 1958. We drove a Felicia, the Czech-made convertible, and had a panoramic view of the countryside. My future wife was unhappy because she had had a perm done by one of my nieces in order to impress her potential in-laws, and even I could see that my niece was not a master hairdresser. But as we crossed the imaginary line near the village of Česká Skalice, which divides the magic country of my youth from the rest of the world, my future wife turned to me from the wheel (she had a strange hobby—car-racing—which impressed me since I don't drive) and she exclaimed in amazement, "It's a fact!"

"Didn't I tell you?" I replied and I knew that I had her where I wanted her.

"It actually works!" she said, flabbergasted.

She was referring to the power of the legendary mountain spirit, Krakonoš, which extends to my native town all the way from his domain in the Giant Mountains north of the Náchod region. When you look out from Dobrošov, the mountain ridges stretch out in all directions like huge stage sets, giant backdrops.

What's the show about?

Is it perhaps about the history that was mislaid here, far from the chroniclers? After all, this is where Slavic tribes entered the immense valley of Bohemia some centuries after the Celts. The names of the tribes blended into the single one that this westernmost Slavic mixture bears to this day: the Czechs. Phonetically identical with "cheques," in Canada it is sometimes the source of obvious puns.

After the Czechs had settled in the valley, perhaps mixing with the Celts, perhaps pushing them out—for in those very old days my ancestors were fearsome warriors, not Shweikian doves—caravans of merchants came, entering through the mountain pass where Náchod was founded in the thirteenth century. Its name is etymologically related to "entry"; in old history books the town was known as Porta Regionis, the gate to the region. Along this path of entry, in little hilltop castles, robber knights lay waiting to ambush the traders. In time, there arrived armies of interlopers.

Everyone left something behind: a ruin, a mountain chapel, a painting, a legend. The sandstone rocks, jutting out of the woods and meadows, provided material for Baroque masters who sculpted the likenesses of saints. They still stand in the forests and on the façades of churches in hamlets and villages. Centuries of rain and summer sun have changed their beauty but certainly not destroyed it. Villages twinkle in the mountain shadows, with graveyards telling tales of lives embraced in races of names carved on sandstone tombstones.

That's why, many years later, it did not come as a surprise to me when the same thing happened to Seth Thistlethorne that had happened to my future wife on our fatal journey in the Felicia convertible. Actually, it began happening to him when he read *The Swell Season*, a tale about my youthful shenanigans in Náchod, the beautiful town of Kostelec. Two inaccessible girls dominate the stories: Irena and Marie. Thistlethorne fell in love with the latter. Strange, but the book is soaked through with the frustrations that the teasing duo of witches had once filled me with, and Thistlethorne—in these days of easy sex—yearned, perhaps, for sweet frustrations. So he wrote to me, desiring a photograph: not an autographed likeness of me, the author, but a photo of the sorceress called Marie Dreslerová. I owned one she had sent me just a year before; but from it you can see she is no longer the willowy wench of my tales. Fortunately, I keep photos of all my old flames, and so I had a copy made of a portrait created in the photo salon of Mr. Kudelík in Náchod in 1943. It captures the looks of the beautiful sixth-former faithfully—that is, magically. I briefly hesitated whether I should not send another photo of Marie from the same period in her bathing suit, but decided against it. For sweet frustration, Marie's face would do.

Thistlethorne didn't even thank me. Nothing happened for a year, until one Friday he appeared in Toronto and called me to come to a disco where his rock band played a gig. He turned out to be a bearded youngster, indiscernible—at least to my eyes—from all other bearded youngsters. "This is not what I normally do," he apologized, and shortly afterwards, when his band started the ruckus, I truly hoped that this indeed was not what he normally did. Fortunately, I have a safety valve in my mind, a fuse, for which my late father is responsible. Whenever I put one of my Jimmie Luncefords on my wind-up gramophone, my father would exclaim: "That noise again! Annie [my mother], fetch me a piece of cotton wool!" And when Mother fetched him what he requested, he demonstratively stuffed it into his ears. Whenever, listening to rock, I am tempted to show similar resentment, the safety valve goes into action, I keep silent and do not impress the company as a biased old man—even though my father's unjust criticism of the gentle saxophone music of my youth would have been quite in place in the disco where bearded youngsters and girls in miniskirts did what they, I suppose, called dancing.

I autographed his well-thumbed copy of *The Swell Season* and wrote in a heartfelt dedication. His interest in my book was sweet music to my soul, although it focused on just one character. Whether he appreciated its other, more literary aspects, I didn't ask. I also feared he would inquire about the *real* Marie. But he didn't. The photograph was obviously all he needed.

Another year went by, and I did not hear from him. Then, like a penny from heaven, the postman brought me a CD. On it was what the young man from Saskatchewan normally did. A fusion of jazz and rock, unsuitable for the speakeasies now called discos. However, he did not send me the CD to familiarize me with his normal production. Among nice musical evocations of his father's farm and the Saskatchewan landscape, there was also a "Blues for Marie Dreslerová," a song about my old Marie from Náchod.

The song warmed my heart, and the warmth increased as I tried to remember various pieces of pop music inspired not by pop music. Les Brown's "Everybody's Making Money But Tchaikovsky"; that song about "Mr. Paganini"; Dvořák's "Humoresque," so beautifully transformed into swing by a whole bunch of jazzmen, from Emilio Caceres to John Kirby to Charlie Mingus to Oscar Peterson. I remembered the swing number made from Bizet's "L'Arlésienne" and the several versions of "Song of India," sometimes performed on instruments Rimsky-Korsakov probably didn't even know. But the only work of *literature* I could think of that would inspire pop song writers was *Oliver Twist*. Dickens was not responsible for it, though; it was just that the name of his character became the title of a hit during the twist craze in Czechoslovakia.

So I copied the "Blues for Marie" and mailed it to her in Náchod, with an explanation of what had happened in distant Saskatchewan. "He must be nutty as a fruitcake, don't you think?" she opined, in a note for me enclosed with a letter to Thistlethorne. The letter was written on pink paper, the kind I used to pen love letters to her on, aeons back. I translated the letter for Thistlethorne. Marie generously praised his "Blues"; I think she really liked it. But then I, too, was flattered by the song, and I am not the former most beautiful girl of the entire universe.

I thought that, gradually, the emotions would fade away: a couple more letters perhaps—because what can a youngster from Saskatchewan have to write to an old lady from Náchod about?

Well, I was wrong. Thistlethorne called again, this time from Pearson Airport.

"I'm on my way!" he said. There was unmistakable excitement in his voice.

"Where to?" I asked, and the young man with a name difficult to pronounce even in Saskatchewan, not to speak of in Kostelec, said: "To Kostelec!"

Then he hung up.

Fortunately, Marie owns a telephone. I invested fifty-seven dollars in my old flame because she, even at her no longer tender age, is fond of talking long-distance.

"So he really is nutty!" she said.

"What are you going to do?" I suddenly felt afraid that Thistlethorne might lose his literary illusions since beauties do not age in books.

"You *really* think he is so crazy for me?" Marie asked.

"Well ..."

"I mean," she interrupted quickly, "for that old photo from Mr. Kudelík's?"

"Well," I said again. "I think he is crazy for his music, which is rather nice, isn't it?"

"Very nice!" said Marie. "Even our Molly likes it," she said, referring to her granddaughter. "And she no longer likes even that— what do they call it? Ascorbic rock or what?"

"Acid rock," I informed her, although I had no idea what this kind of noise was. "I suspect he only used you, Marie. Every composer is after inspiration at any price, and for Saskatchewan ears you probably have an exotic name. Or maybe he was reminded of the film star—" I stopped abruptly.

"Which one?"

I immediately regretted my slip of the tongue because Marie Dressler from Hollywood had never been a beauty, not even in her tender age.

"You don't know her," I hastened to assure Marie. "Her films were not shown during the Russian occupation. But I think that he just misused you for the production of a piece of music."

"Hardly, Dannykins. There is a big chunk of heart in that little ditty," said Marie.

This shamed me. "You're right, of course," I said. Marie always had a much better ear for music than I. "And now he'll spend lots of money on a costly transatlantic trip to Kostelec—he must be crazy for you."

After fifty-seven dollars, I managed to hang up and I shuddered a little. I did not want Thistlethorne to lose his illusion the way many of my female readers lost them when they saw me in person. In her present shape, the former most beautiful girl of the entire universe looked like her Hollywood namesake rather than the photograph from Photo Salon Kudelík.

There was, of course, no reason for fear. Thistlethorne would be affected by two things which I, of little faith, did not take into account. But fear held me fast.

In the meantime, in celebration of my seventieth birthday the entire jazz band from my books—except the dear departed— assembled in Náchod, and jammed in the nightclub of Hotel Beránek, which must be one of the most beautiful fin de siècle hotels in Europe. The post–Velvet Revolution mayor of Náchod, Mr. Čermák, thoroughly modernized its facilities while retaining the decor. He joined in with the band on tenor sax, on which he is much better than the celebrated tenor man from Washington.

Various girls, too, made their appearance. My wife is usually not kind to girls because she is jealous of my past, mostly with no good reason. However, they were only *former* girls, and so she was kind to them. Except Irena. The first thing the silly woman told her was "You should quit smoking!"—and that day my wife had just opened only her second pack of Marlboros. So she wasn't kind to Irena; the bitch, she told me, was a "jogging cow," which in the vocabulary of my car-racing wife is an absolute pejorative. Unlike her—as soon as the queen of sandstone appeared, after almost half a century—I fell victim to an olfactory illusion: I smelled the sweet odour of moss on the sandstone towers, and I heard the music of the wind blowing through the pine trees.

Irena's bodily shape has not changed, although if she wanted to pass for a teenager, she would have to be seen from the rear only. She came to the party in tennis shoes, nowadays called Adidas loafers or whatever, and a tartan skirt like the kind she used to wear back then. She was accompanied by her dog, who was still called Sweet. It must have been at least Sweet IV, provided all ancestors of the legendary black-and-tan terrier lived to ripe old dog age. Perhaps she and her dog, too, were part of the strange thing that, on her first trip to Náchod, made my wife exclaim, "It actually works!"

To Marie, my wife was kind. I saw her—due to the myopia of rustproof love—as she had looked in that swimsuit in Photo Salon Kudelík, but my wife knew immediately that Marie, unlike Irena, was no "jogging cow." And so she was kind to her.

When I returned to Toronto, Thistlethorne called me again. He was in Prague and had just spoken over the phone with Marie. He admired her youthful voice, which sounded exactly as he had imagined it. He was also pleasantly surprised by her English— why didn't she write the pink letter in that language, he wondered. Accented, of course, he said. But sweet. "See you tomorrow!" he told Marie, and in the morning he rushed to Hertz to rent a car. Equipped with an old rickety Volkswagen, he set out after his holy grail.

As soon as he crossed the imaginary line, he later told me, a strange feeling filled his soul.

"What feeling?" I inquired.

"Hard to tell," he said. "Like something out of Tolkien. Like a fairy tale."

"It's Krakonoš's country," I said, but he had never heard about Krakonoš. So we agreed on Tolkien.

He arrived in Kostelec at dusk, but he had a town map. Who knows where he managed to get hold of it? The magic worked. He drove up the steep slope of the Black Mountain, although the rented Volkswagen had a gearshift and he wasn't used to it, stopped in front of the villa at 865 Maple Street and rang the bell.

Marie opened the door.

When he set out on his transatlantic journey he had been crazy for her. At that moment he became even crazier—if that was at all possible. But of course it was possible. This Marie was made of flesh and blood and satin skin, the kind the girls of Kostelec used to have then, and still have now. She wasn't just an image conjured of words. *Verba caro facta sunt.* The words were made flesh.

What happened?

I underestimated the power of the imaginary line, and I grossly underestimated Marie. She always liked practical jokes. In my native country—not in my adopted one—they are called "Canadian jokes." Thistlethorne may be the only Canadian who knows why.

Just like Irena's identical doggie—at least the fourth of that name—the satin-skin-covered Marie whom Thistlethorne saw at the door was the third of her lineage. That was the joke the two girls, the grandmother and the granddaughter, played on him.

I am thrilled that, thanks to my mental creation, I helped a nice Czech girl to marry into the beautiful province of Saskatchewan.

One always wakes up from a story like this. Dreams, I am told, are of very short duration. Perhaps only a few seconds. This dream happened when we crossed the imaginary line in the Mercedes-Benz, rented in Germany to impress folks in my home town, and I fell asleep.

Then I woke up, saw the portly castle above the town, the colourful façade of Hotel Beránek, the mountain ridges stretching all the way to the bluish horizon; and heard the sound of Gabriel and Michael, the bells of the Old Gothic St. Lawrence Church on the town square, tolling, probably for me. And, suddenly, I heard my wife say, "It is *still* working."

Whoever wants to test this magic, let him or her confidently try. Náchod, the beautiful town of Kostelec, is only 140 kilometres east of Prague. A matter of two hours of comfortable driving on perfect, post-Communist highways.

1996

Credits

The stories in the collection have previously appeared as follows:

The translation of "Why I Learnt How to Reed" appears by permission of Michal Schonberg. It was originally published as "Proč jsem se naučil číst" in *Nový domov*, No. 26, Vol.48, 1997, Toronto.

The translation of "Eve Was Naked" appears by permission of Julie Hansen. It was originally published as "Eva byla nahá" in *Horkej svet*, Odeon Publishers, Prague, 1969.

"Why Do People Have Soft Noses" was originally published as "Proč mají lidé měkké nosy" in *Ze života lepší společnosti*, Mladá fronta, Prague, 1965.

"A Remarkable Chemical Phenomenon" was originally published as "Pozuru hodný jen chemický" in *Ze života lepší společnosti*, Mladá fronta, Prague, 1965.

The translation of "The Onset of My Literary Career" appears by permission of Káča Poláčková-Henley. It was originally published in *Antheus*, Spring-Autumn 1990.

The translation of "My Uncle Kohn" appears by permission of Julie Hansen. It was originally published as "Můj strýček Kohn" in *Sedmiramenný svícen*, Naše vojsko, Prague, 1964.

The translation of "My Teacher, Mr. Katz" appears by permission of Julie Hansen. It was originally published in *The Troubadour*, Vol. I, Issue I, 1995, San Francisco.

The translation of "Dr. Strass" appears by permission of Julie Hansen. It was originally published in *Trafika*, Prague, 1994

The translation of "The Cuckoo" appears by permission of Paul Wilson. It was originally published in *The Phoenix Revue*, No. I, Summer 1986/7, Australia.

The translation of "Fragments About Rebecca" appears by permission of Paul Wilson. It was originally published in *WRIT*, No. 14, 1982, Toronto.

The translation of "Feminine Mystique" appears by permission of Paul Wilson. It was originally published in *GRANTA*, No. 29.

The translation of "An Insoluable Problem of Genetics" appears by permission of Michal Schonberg. It was originally published as "Neřešitlený problém genetický" in *Prism International*, July 1983, Vancouver.

The translation of "Three Bachelors in a Fiery Furnace" appears by permission of Káča Polóčková-Henley. It was originally published as "Tři mládenci v peci ohnivé" in *Plamen*, No. 6, 1963, Prague.

The translation of "The End of Bull Mácha" appears by permission of Paul Wilson. It was originally published in the *San Francisco State University Review*, Fall 1994.

"Spectator on a February Night" was originally published as "Divák v únorocé noci" in *Neuilly a jiné příběhy*, Ivo Železný, Prague, 1996.

"Laws of the Jungle" " was originally published as "Zákony džungle" in *Příběhy o Líze a mladém Wertherovi a jiné povídky*, Ivo Železný, Prague, 1994.

"Filthy Cruel World" was originally published as "Špinavý, krutý svět" in *Příběhy o Líze a mladém Wertherovi a jiné povídky*, Ivo Železný, Prague, 1994.

The translation of "Song of Forgotten Years" was originally published in *Writing Today in Czechoslovakia*, Penguin Books, 1968.

The translation of "Pink Champagne" appears by permission of Peter Kussi. It was originally published in *Evergreen Review*, March 1969.

"The Mysterious Events at Night" was originally published as "Mysteriózní eventy v noci" in *Ze života české společnosti*, Sixty-Eight Publishers, Toronto, 1985.

The translation of "Wayne's Hero" appears by permission of Rachel Harrell. It was originally published as "Waynův hrdina" in *Povídky z Rajského údolí*, Ivo Železný, Prague, 1966.

The translation of "According to Poe" appears by permission of Rachel Harrell. It was originally published as "Podle Poea" in *Povídky z Rajského údolí*, Ivo Železný, Prague, 1996.

The translation of "Jezebel from Forest Hill" appears by permission of Rachel Harrell. It was originally published in *Descant* 100, Spring 1998, Vol. 20, No. 1.

"A Magic Mountain and a Willowy Wench" was originally published in *Toronto Life*, March 1966.